Euripides' *Hippolytus*

OKLAHOMA SERIES IN CLASSICAL CULTURE

Oklahoma Series in Classical Culture

Euripides' *Hippolytus*

A Commentary for Students

Hanna M. Roisman

University of Oklahoma Press : Norman

Publication of this book is made possible in part by a grant from the University Press Language Tutorial Fund.

Library of Congress Cataloging-in-Publication Data

Names: Roisman, Hanna, author. | Euripides. Hippolytus.
Title: Euripides' Hippolytus : a commentary for students / Hanna M. Roisman.
Description: Norman : University of Oklahoma Press, 2024. | Series: Oklahoma
    series in classical culture ; volume 64 | Includes bibliographical references
    and index. | Commentary in English, play in Greek. | Summary: "Euripides'
    Hippolytus is a Greek drama about passion, innocence, rejection, betrayal, and
    the tragic breakdown of a family. This commentary, designed for intermediate and
    advanced students of ancient Greek, helps readers understand and fully appreciate
    this classic tragedy in all its rich complexity"—Provided by publisher.
Identifiers: LCCN 2023050470 | ISBN 978-0-8061-9365-6 (paperback)
Subjects: LCSH: Euripides. Hippolytus. | BISAC: FOREIGN LANGUAGE
    STUDY / Ancient Languages (see also Latin) | FICTION / Classics |
    LCGFT: Literary criticism. | Drama.
Classification: LCC PA3973.H7 R64 2024 | DDC 882/.01—dc23/eng/20231204
LC record available at https://lccn.loc.gov/2023050470

Euripides' Hippolytus*: A Commentary for Students* is Volume 64 in the Oklahoma
Series in Classical Culture.

For

Yossi
Elad and Helaina
and my granddaughters Talia and Yael
～•～

and for Shalev and Diana
and my granddaughters Noa and Esti
～•～

And in memory of
Cecelia Anne Eaton Luschnig

CONTENTS

Preface and Acknowledgments

Euripides' *Hippolytus* usually finds its way into the curriculum as part of a general literature course, a course on Greek tragedy in translation, or a course in Greek language. The latter's audience is the one toward which this commentary is geared. *Hippolytus* is a fascinating play about passion, rejection, innocence, betrayal, deception, and the breaking down of a family. It is my hope that this commentary will help students—whether undergraduate or graduate—to delve into the Greek text and read through it fluently, not only overcoming the hurdles of vocabulary and the various syntactical structures, but also appreciating the literary and rhetorical devices Euripides used to enrich the characterization of the characters, from Phaedra to her nurse, and from Hippolytus to his father, Theseus, each one with their own set of moral, ethical, and religious beliefs.

The Greek text in this commentary is offered in brief chunks of various lengths focused on their syntactical coherence and plot progression, followed by notes and comments organized by line numbers related to these short segments; when needed, metrical analysis is also included. This is done in order to help students follow the text more closely, with no need to repeatedly flip back from the notes and comments to the very beginning of the commentary, where usually the running Greek text is included. These brief segments of Greek are dissected not only by giving the meanings of the vocabulary, but also by offering a meticulous grammatical and syntactical breakdown of the words. For the most part, translations are offered as well, especially in the first part of the play. In order to enable students to see the entire picture, a running Greek text of the play is also offered toward the end of the book.

Finally, in addition to the introduction, which includes the hypotheses (brief ancient summaries of the play) and information about the play, the notes and comments are followed by a glossary, an index of grammatical, syntactical, literary, and rhetorical figures, a list of irregular Greek verbs, the Greek play text, a bibliography, and an index. The purpose is to help students as much as possible with the Greek text, which is not particularly daunting but requires clarification, elucidation, and explanation of the various Greek forms. It is vital that before students delve into the commentary, they familiarize themselves with the guidelines for its use and the list of abbreviations, where all the markings and symbols used in the notes and comments are explained.

I owe thanks to Alessandra Tamulevich of the University of Oklahoma Press for her encouragement and patience when I needed more time to complete the manuscript, and to the publishers' referees, who not only proved to have an open mind, but also provided instructive and helpful comments. I am especially thankful to Jane Lyle and Marta Steele, who, with their professional copyediting expertise, keen eye, general knowledge, and willingness to understand what it was that I wanted to say and help me to express it in the right way, not only saved me from many errors but made the experience of revieweing the edited manuscript so much more bearable than it usually is for me. It is very important at this stage of making final changes to trust someone. I am very grateful to a wonderful and supportive group of friends who were there for me during a particularly rough time in my life, always willing to help: to Karen Gillum of Colby College for making the translations more readable, for her meticulous proofing (the remaining errors are all mine), and for her helpful insights and comments; and to my dear friends Drs. Jill Yonassi and Julie Brown, who not only made the entire manuscript more readable but whose questions and insights rendered it more accessible to students.

As always, I dedicate this book to my beloved family, who are the essence of my life: to Yossi, Elad, Shalev, Helaina, Diana, Talia, Noa, Yael, and Esti.

During the final stages of writing this commentary, my dear friend Cecelia Anne Eaton Luschnig passed away. We collaborated on two earlier commentaries published by the University of Oklahoma Press. She loved the *Hippolytus* very much and died shortly after finishing its translation. I dedicate this book to her memory as well.

Euripides' *Hippolytus*

INTRODUCTION

1. UNCERTAINTY

In writing a commentary on Euripides' *Hippolytus*, it seems wise to point out that although we have the text of the tragedy and know that it was awarded first prize when it was first performed in 428 BCE in the Great City Dionysia of Athens, we remain sadly uninformed about much of the context of that performance, and about fifth-century drama in general, which might have impacted the audience's reaction to the play. In the case of the extant *Hippolytus*, known also as *Hippolytus the Wreathbearer*, the problem is compounded by Euripides' having also written a play entitled *Hippolytus Veiled*, of which we have only fragments, and which met with great disapproval from the audience. It has usually been assumed that this latter play was presented prior to *The Wreathbearer*, although no clear evidence supports that assumption.[1]

If we possessed more than scant details of Euripides' life, we might have more hints about his views and preferences on which to base our interpretations of his plays. We cannot judge the veracity of Aristophanes' portrayals of him, which might have biased our perceptions. It is thought that Euripides was born in Phyla in Attica ca. 480 BCE and died in Macedonia in 406. Nineteen out of a possible ninety-two of his plays have survived. However, all of these uncertainties prompt close critical examination of the text, which, beyond providing the intense enjoyment inherent to gaining a better appreciation of a master craftsman's work, could also yield tantalizing glimpses of deeper hidden messages.[2]

2. The Hypotheses

Hypothesis (Latin *argumentum*) is the ancient introductory note, sometimes including the plot outline, that usually precedes the dramatic text in the manuscripts.[3] For *Hippolytus* we have two such ancient summaries.

ΥΠΟΘΕΣΙΣ ΙΠΠΟΛΥΤΟΥ

Θησεὺς υἱὸς μὲν ἦν Ποσειδῶνος, βασιλεὺς δὲ Ἀθηναίων· γήμας δὲ μίαν τῶν Ἀμαζονίδων Ἱππολύτην Ἱππόλυτον ἐγέννησε, κάλλει τε καὶ σωφροσύνῃ διαφέροντα. ἐπεὶ δὲ ἡ συνοικοῦσα τὸν βίον μετήλλαξεν, ἐπεισηγάγετο γυναῖκα, τὴν Μίνω τοῦ Κρητῶν βασιλέως θυγατέρα Φαίδραν. ὁ δὲ Θησεὺς Πάλλαντα ἕνα τῶν συγγενῶν φονεύσας φεύγει εἰς Τροιζῆνα μετὰ τῆς γυναικός, οὗ συνέβαινε τὸν Ἱππόλυτον παρὰ Πιτθεῖ τρέφεσθαι. θεασαμένη δὲ τόν νεανίσκον ἡ Φαίδρα εἰς ἐπιθυμίαν ὤλισθεν, οὐκ ἀκόλαστος οὖσα, πληροῦσα δὲ Ἀφροδίτης μῆνιν, ἣ τὸν Ἱππόλυτον διὰ σωφροσύνην ἀνελεῖν κρίνασα τὴν Φαίδραν εἰς ἔρωτα παρώρμησεν, τέλος δὲ τοῖς προθετεῖσιν ἔθηκεν. στέγουσα δὲ τὴν νόσον χρόνῳ

---

1. Gibert (1997) claims convincingly that there is no clear evidence for the order of the two plays' performances.

2. For the implicit messages behind the explicit statements in this play, see Roisman 1999. For latent meanings and symbolism, see Fitzgerald 1973.

3. See Easterling 2014.

πρὸς τὴν τρόφον δηλῶσαι ἠναγκάσθη κατεπαγγειλαμένην αὐτῇ
βοηθήσειν, ἥτις παρὰ τὴν προαίρεσιν αὐτῆς λόγους προσήνεγκε
τῷ νεανίσκῳ. τραχυνόμενον δὲ αὐτὸν ἡ Φαίδρα καταμαθοῦσα
τῇ μὲν τρόφῳ ἐπέπληξεν, ἑαυτὴν δὲ ἀνήρτησεν. καθ᾽ ὃν καιρὸν
ἐπιφανεὶς Θησεὺς καὶ καθελεῖν σπεύδων τὴν ἀπηγχονισμένην,
εὗρεν αὐτῇ προσηρτημένην δέλτον δι᾽ ἧς Ἱππολύτου φθορὰν
κατηγόρει καὶ ἐπιβουλήν. πιστεύσας δὲ τοῖς γεγραμμένοις τὸν μὲν
Ἱππόλυτον ἐπέταξε φεύγειν, αὐτὸς δὲ τῷ Ποσειδῶνι ἀρὰς ἔθετο,
ὧν ἐπακούσας ὁ θεὸς τὸν Ἱππόλυτον διέφθειρεν. Ἄρτεμις δὲ τῶν
γεγενημένων ἕκαστα διασαφήσασα Θησεῖ, τὴν μὲν Φαίδραν
οὐ κατεμέμψατο, τοῦτον δὲ παρεμυθήσατο υἱοῦ καὶ γυναικὸς
στερηθέντα· τῷ δὲ Ἱππολύτῳ τιμὰς ἔφη γῇ ἐγκαταστήσεσθαι.

Hypothesis to the *Hippolytus*

Theseus was the son of Poseidon and king of the Athenians. After mar-
rying Hippolytē, one of the Amazons, he fathered Hippolytus, who was
outstanding in both beauty and virtue. After his wife passed away, he
married a woman, daughter of Minos, king of the Cretans, Phaedra. After
Theseus killed Pallas, one of his relatives, he went into exile to Troezen
with his wife, where, it so happened, Hippolytus was being brought up by
Pittheus. Once Phaedra saw the young man, she fell in love [with him],
not on account of being unchaste, but because she was fulfilling the anger
of Aphrodite, who, having decided to kill Hippolytus because of his virtue, had stirred Phaedra into passion and achieved the end she intended.
Keeping the disease secret, in time Phaedra was forced to reveal it to the
Nurse, who, after promising to help her, brought the story forward to the
young man, contrary to Phaedra's plan. After Phaedra learned of his harsh
reaction, she rebuked the Nurse and hanged herself. At this very moment
Theseus appeared, and, hastening to lower the hanged woman, he found
that she had attached a tablet to herself on which she accused Hippolytus
of moral corruption and treachery. Believing what was written, Theseus
commanded Hippolytus to go into exile, and himself invoked upon Hippolytus curses in the name of Poseidon, which the god heard, and [he]
destroyed Hippolytus. But Artemis, after making everything that had happened clear to Theseus, did not blame Phaedra but comforted him because
he was bereft of a son and a wife; and she said she would establish rites for
Hippolytus in the land.

⟨ΑΡΙΣΤΟΦΑΝΟΥΣ ΓΡΑΜΜΑΤΙΚΟΥ ΥΠΟΘΕΣΙΣ⟩

ἡ σκηνὴ τοῦ δράματος ὑπόκειται ἐν †θήβαις†. ἐδιδάχθη ἐπὶ Ἐπαμείνονος ἄρχοντος ὀλυμπιάδι πζ' ἔτει δ'. πρῶτος Εὐριπίδης, δεύτερος Ἰοφῶν, τρίτος Ἴων. ἔστι δὲ οὗτος Ἱππόλυτος δεύτερος, ⟨ὁ⟩ καὶ στεφανίας προσαγορευόμενος. ἐμφαίνεται δὲ ὕστερος γεγραμμένος· τὸ γὰρ ἀπρεπὲς καὶ κατηγορίας ἄξιον ἐν τούτῳ διώρθωται τῷ δράματι. τὸ δὲ δρᾶμα τῶν πρώτων.

τὰ τοῦ δράματος πρόσωπα· Ἀφροδίτη, Ἱππόλυτος, οἰκέτης, τροφός, Φαίδρα, θεράπαινα, Θησεύς, ἄγγελος, Ἄρτεμις, χορός.

<Hypothesis of Aristophanes of Byzantium>

The scene of the drama is set in †Thebes†. It was produced in the archonship of Epameinon in the fourth year of the 87th Olympiad. Euripides was first, Iophon second, Ion third. This is the second *Hippolytus*, the one called also *The Wreathbearer*. It appears that it was written later, for whatever was untoward and worthy of condemnation was corrected in this drama. This drama is among the best.

The characters in the play: Aphrodite, Hippolytus, Household Slave, Nurse, Phaedra, Female Servant, Theseus, Messenger, Artemis, Chorus.

The Hypothesis of Aristophanes of Byzantium conveys the message that the characterizations in *Hippolytus* amend the characterizations in *Hippolytus Veiled* that led to that play's unpopular reception. It is believed that Phaedra was portrayed there as a brazen woman who made sexual advances toward her stepson, Hippolytus, who subsequently covered his head in shame; hence the title *Kalyptomenos (Veiled) Hippolytus*. According to Tierney (1937/1938), Wilamowitz-Moellendorff postulated that *Hippolytus Veiled* was the third play in a trilogy, with *Aegeus* and *Theseus* being the missing first two plays, the content of which would have influenced the audience's understanding of *Hippolytus Veiled*. Tierney describes Phaedra in *Hippolytus Veiled* as a demonic character who was prepared to go to any lengths, even using magic, to gain her stepson's love.[4]

The goddesses Artemis and Aphrodite may have been an innovation in *Hippolytus*, with Hippolytus' own character now being associated with

4. Tierney 1937/1938, 60.

an ideological celibacy represented by Artemis. This obsession with celibacy, however, infuriates Aphrodite, the goddess of sexual love, who interprets it as an insult to her and has decided to manipulate events in order to punish Hippolytus. Therefore, the plot of the other play probably centered on Phaedra's intense passions rather than on any subplots, including Hippolytus' own motivations. Furthermore, Sophocles at some uncertain date wrote a play, *Phaedra*, based on the same mythic material, with extant fragments indicating that Phaedra was under some kind of external influence, thus pardoning any untoward behavior. The question remains as to how our play, *Hippolytus*, fits between these two interpretations of the myth.

3. THE MYTH

Although we are familiar with the general mythic background of the play, many versions exist. We cannot know what other versions Euripides might have been familiar with, and whether he was influenced by other, no longer extant, plays on the same theme. In all known mythic versions, Hippolytus is presented as a celibate young man dedicated to the worship of Artemis, who despised sexual relations. In this way he contrasts with his father, Theseus, a philanderer who had abandoned Phaedra's sister Ariadne under dubious circumstances after she helped him escape from the Minotaur.[5] The perception that Phaedra's mother, Pasiphaë, was so sexually voracious that she had relations with the Cretan Bull, subsequently giving birth to the Minotaur, may also have tainted the image of Phaedra. Ariadne's own passion for Theseus was the reason she had betrayed her family. The myth of both plays follows a well-known pattern, sometimes associated with the biblical tale of Potiphar's wife: a married woman desires a young man who rebuffs her sexual overtures; in revenge, she accuses the young man of rape, telling this to her husband. In our play the story features Phaedra, who during the exile of Theseus and his close family in Troezen becomes infatuated with

5. For a full discussion of Theseus, see Roisman 1999, 123–65 and passim with bibliography. For a more positive view of Theseus, see Mills 2002, 74–7, who points out that in our play Theseus' philandering adventures are not mentioned, only his "more virtuous journey to an oracle" (74). One should note, however, that the spectators are aware of the mythic lore in the background to Theseus' persona, and are unlikely to limit themselves only to what is told in the play. Hippolytus' presence alone brings to mind Theseus' former love affairs, to which the Chorus allude even before Phaedra's entrance in lines 151–60. Theseus himself hints at his former escapades in lines 976–80.

her stepson Hippolytus. The action of the play is set in motion by Aphrodite and brought to an end by Artemis.

Theseus, like many other heroes, had both a mortal and an immortal father. He was known as the son of Poseidon, but also of Aegeus, the king of Athens, and of Aethra, daughter of Pittheus, the king of Troezen. After Aegeus' death, Theseus became the king of the Athenians. Hippolytus' illegitimate birth resulted from Theseus' liaison with the queen of the Amazons. Hippolytus was raised by Pittheus in Troezen. Theseus then married Phaedra, the daughter of Minos and Pasiphaë.

4. THE PLOT

In our play, as Aphrodite herself tells the audience, when Hippolytus came from Troezen to Athens to participate in the holy mysteries, Aphrodite made Phaedra fall in love with the young man, knowing that he would rebuff her. Aphrodite did this to punish Hippolytus for willfully neglecting her and fervently worshiping Artemis instead. Later, Theseus is exiled from Athens after killing his cousins and comes to reside in Troezen with Phaedra in tow. The play opens at a time when Theseus is absent. We later learn that he is on a mission to the oracle, and Phaedra at least appears to be fighting her overpowering desire for Hippolytus.

At this point in time, she is refusing to eat. Pressed by her nurse, she describes the various ways she has tried to overcome her passion. Because she has failed to do so, she has decided to starve herself. Unwilling to let her mistress die, the Nurse approaches Hippolytus, who, as a virgin and honor-bound to remain so, is shocked at the offer to have a sexual encounter with his stepmother and leaves the stage, promising to keep the Nurse's proposition a secret. Phaedra, however, fearing that he will disclose what happened to Pittheus and damage her reputation, thereby also harming her sons, writes a letter accusing Hippolytus of rape. This she attaches to her hand, and she then hangs herself.

Upon his return, Theseus finds the letter and exiles Hippolytus from the land, after praying to Poseidon to grant his wish and kill Hippolytus. As Hippolytus drives his chariot into exile along the seashore, Poseidon sends a monstrous bull from the sea, which scares Hippolytus' horses. Entangled in the reins, Hippolytus falls out of the chariot and is fatally injured. He is brought back to Theseus' court, where Artemis tells Theseus that Phaedra had deceived him. She orders Theseus to take his dying son in his arms and

embrace him, and urges Hippolytus not to hate his father. She also promises to bring death upon the next mortal whom Aphrodite cares for, as well
as to establish a cult for Hippolytus.

5. THE CHARACTERS

Theseus

Background Myth

Theseus was born in Troezen and raised there by his mother, Aethra. Upon
moving a rock under which Aegeus had hidden his sword and sandals, Theseus discovered his identity and set off to Athens. His journey took him
around the Saronic Gulf. Along this route he encountered and killed various bandits who had terrorized travelers. After reaching Athens and prov-
ing his identity to Aegeus, Theseus sailed to Crete, the kingdom of Minos
and Pasiphaë, to destroy the man-eating Minotaur. Ariadne, the daughter of
Minos and Pasiphaë, helped him to defeat the Minotaur and escape from
the labyrinth, after which he abandoned her on a deserted island. Myths
also recount that Theseus abducted Helen in his youth with his friend Pir-
ithous, leaving her in Troezen while the two unsuccessfully attempted to
take Persephone from Hades. While they were in the Netherworld, Helen's
brothers, the Dioscuri, rescued her. As king of Athens, Theseus is attributed
with having united Attica under Athens: the *synoikismos*. Theseus' adven-
ture with the Amazons is rather confusing, but it is clear about his liaison with one of these warrior women, Antiope/Hippolytē, whom in early
treatments he abducts and with whom he fathers Hippolytus. It is also not
entirely clear how the relationship ends. She is killed in battle either against
or at Theseus' side, after which he marries Phaedra, Ariadne's sister. Exiled
from Athens for a year for having killed his cousins the Pallantidae, the renowned hero has taken Phaedra with him to Troezen, where Hippolytus is
living with Pittheus, Theseus' grandfather. Theseus is absent from Troezen
at the start of the play.

In Hippolytus

Theseus enters in line 790, garlanded, as he is returning in triumph from an
embassy to the oracle, only to discover that Phaedra has hanged herself. He
grieves deeply for Phaedra, though when compared to the depth of the grief
that Briseis shows in her lament for Hector, one may suspect that Theseus

cares more about his own loss than for what she might have suffered.[6] In his boundless rage, he attacks Hippolytus for his apparently deceitful boasts of virtue, and banishes him from the kingdom while calling for his own divine father, Poseidon, to fulfill a promised curse on the younger man. Theseus' indifference toward his mortally wounded son does not cease until Artemis tells him that Phaedra had deceived him. Even then, his words to Hippolytus reveal not sympathy and compassion for the young man's suffering, but rather his worry that his son won't absolve him from the miasma of kindred bloodshed that would bring the Erinyes upon him.

Phaedra

Background Myth

Daughter of Minos and Pasiphaë, sister of Ariadne, Phaedra married Theseus after he had killed the Minotaur, run away from Crete with Ariadne and abandoned her on the island of Naxos, and fathered Hippolytus with the Amazon queen or her sister.[7]

In Hippolytus

We are told in the prologue that Phaedra had already been seized in her heart with a terrible passion for Hippolytus when she saw him in Athens at the holy mysteries. As a result of her passion, she has built a temple to Aphrodite that looks toward Troezen, where Hippolytus lives. In the play she too lives in Troezen, in the same court as Hippolytus, since Theseus is in exile from Athens. Trying to withstand her impulses, she has decided to die rather than submit to temptation, and thus she has refused food for several days before the plot action begins. The prologue reveals that Phaedra is in fact a victim of the machinations of Aphrodite, and it is the goddess who has caused her to feel an overpowering desire for her stepson, which eventually leads to her own death and that of Hippolytus. From the start of the play Phaedra is restless, changing her mind about where she wants to be and how to act. While many have assumed that she genuinely tries to keep her infatuation secret, Euripides' text seems

---

6. *Iliad* 19.287–300. For a detailed discussion, see Roisman 1999, 127–33.

7. For the importance of Phaedra's Cretan background, see Reckford 1974, 322–8, as well as the note on νόθος in line 309.

to point in a different direction. From her earliest lines she drops barely concealed hints about her obsession. She begins by asking for her hair to be unbound and spread over her shoulders, which was usually interpreted as an attempt to attract a man's attention.[8] She then talks of the meadows and mountains favored by Hippolytus, as well as of hounds hunting deer, Hippolytus' favorite pastime, and of his beloved horses, before reacting to his name with sighs of pain. When Phaedra tells the women of Troezen that she has decided to die, with this being the noblest course of action in her predicament, it is possible that she is being sincere, but she may also be waiting for an intervention, which is not long in coming. In her words Phaedra depicts herself as a mirror image of Hippolytus, praising chastity, but her actions seem more akin to those of Theseus, Hippolytus' father. She depicts herself as helpless and determined to die to avoid succumbing to temptation, yet she succeeds in implanting the idea in the Nurse's head that she should tell Hippolytus of Phaedra's infatuation (520).[9]

Despite periods of frenzied restlessness, Phaedra is largely passive for the first part of the play, until she overhears Hippolytus' reaction to the Nurse's words (565) and decides to take immediate action (599–600). She is clear about having fallen victim to *erōs*, a hateful or bitter passion, as she calls it (727). Throughout the play, Phaedra distinguishes between the genuine love and care she feels for her children and the overwhelming passion she has experienced toward Hippolytus, which has quickly turned into a deadly hatred. The path she chooses is to kill herself after berating the Nurse for her "treachery"' and writing a letter in which she accuses Hippolytus of having assaulted her.[10] Her final act, intended to save her own children at the expense of Hippolytus' life, allows for the completion of Aphrodite's plan. Her deceitful letter will cause Theseus to use one of the wishes Poseidon has granted him to invoke a curse on Hippolytus and cause his own son's death.

---

8. The veil, as Llewellyn-Jones (2003, 18; cf. 264) claims, "acts as a barrier to contain female miasma, especially the pollution inherent in female sexuality."

9. My interpretation of Phaedra's conduct as intentionally trying to bring the Nurse to interfere on her behalf with Hippolytus follows the view of Wilamowitz-Moellendorff (1963 [1875], 209–19; 1891, 48–50), whose view was already anticipated by a scholiast in some allusive comments. See Roisman 1999, 17, 25n55.

10. For a full discussion of Phaedra, see Roisman 1999, 46–107 and passim with bibliography; 2021, 247–66 with bibliography.

Hippolytus

Background Myth

Hippolytus was the bastard son (*nothos*) of Theseus, born either to Hippolytē, the queen of the Amazons, or to her sister, Antiope. The exact circumstances of his birth differ in various mythic versions. Whether Hippolytus' mother was kidnapped by Theseus and later murdered by him, or whether she fell in love with him and was later killed in a war between the Athenians and the Amazon women, it is clear that she was not an Athenian, and he was therefore considered a *nothos* (see note on line 309). After Hippolytus died, a cult was established in his name.

In Hippolytus

From his entrance, Hippolytus emphasizes his association with Artemis, openly proclaiming his disdain for Aphrodite and his pride in remaining celibate. The text also emphasizes his connection with his Amazon mother. Aphrodite (10), the Nurse (307), and Phaedra (581) all call him the son of the Amazon (10), further highlighting his traits of chastity, a proclivity for horsemanship, and a proud nature. Indeed, he is depicted as spending his time either in meadows with Artemis or with his male associates on horseback, hunting and participating in athletics. At the same time, until his final words, Hippolytus remains humiliated by the circumstances of his birth as a *nothos*, the bastard son of Theseus, the king of Athens.

Hippolytus is obsessed with his own virtue, perhaps in part to compensate for his origins, but also in a desperate yet futile attempt to gain favor with his father. His self-obsession, coupled with his disdain for the feelings of others, borders on narcissism. He speaks some of the most misogynous lines in extant tragedy (617–69), asserting that men should have been able to reproduce without women, who, loathsome creatures that they are, only bring trouble to their husbands. Hippolytus initially appears to be completely unlike his father. However, as the play progresses, similarities emerge both in their backgrounds and in their behavior. Both men were born to foreign women, wives or mistresses of Athenian kings, and thus are bastards. In the play, both are self-obsessed and both display a volatile temper, reacting to others with extreme anger: Hippolytus to the Nurse after hearing her suggestion that he become intimate with Phaedra, and Theseus to Hippolytus when he believes that his son did indeed violate his wife. While Theseus could also have been considered a *nothos*, born to Aethra, daughter of Pittheus, the king of Troezen, and Aegeus, the king of Athens, he ultimately became the most iconic hero king of Athens.[11] He rose to the throne after Aegeus jumped to his death when Theseus forgot to change his boat's sails to white upon his return from Crete, the agreed signal that he had successfully vanquished the Minotaur. Hippolytus, it seems, has no possibility of becoming king after Theseus, as the legitimate sons of Phaedra will inherit this title, although the Nurse thinks differently (304–10). He is a "spare" member of the royal family, with no official role. This, however, does not seem to affect his ego, which remains intact throughout the play. Like his father, Hippolytus expresses no self-doubt or concern for others, whatever he has done to them. His boastful pride goads him into tactless criticism of Phaedra in defense of himself when he is accused by his father of having sexually assaulted her. He continues to call himself the "best of men" when approaching his death.[12]

The Goddesses

Aphrodite explains what she has set in motion in the play's prologue. Her plan is for Hippolytus to be punished for favoring Artemis instead of seeking "the bed of love" and thus worshiping Aphrodite. She has already caused Phaedra to have an overwhelming desire for Hippolytus, and will ensure that Theseus discovers what has happened. He then, with the help of Poseidon, will bring about his son's death. She is wrong, however, in promising that Phaedra will die with a good name (cf. Knox 1986 [1952], 217), even though Artemis does somewhat absolve Phaedra at the end, placing the blame on the gods' machinations. In Aphrodite's characterization, we see a complete divide between *erōs* or sensual desire and the sexual acts that take place in the "marriage bed" that Aphrodite states that Hippolytus shuns (14), and a kind of platonic love or love for one's children that may be referred to as *philia* or *agapē*. While promoting sexual love and eroticism, Aphrodite shows such complete disdain for human beings that she is prepared to cause the death not only of Hippolytus, who shuns her, but also of Phaedra, who has married, given birth, and experienced passionate love, and is her ardent worshiper to boot.

---

11. For discussion of bastards in Greek society, see Patterson 1990; Kamen 2013, 62–70.
12. See Roisman 1999, 27–45, as well as 123–65 and passim with bibliography; 2021, 262–3 and bibliography; and forthcoming (c).

As with other characters in the play who come to mirror those from whom they had previously appeared to be poles apart, Artemis, the goddess of hunting, but also of chastity and childbirth, comes to mirror Aphrodite by the end of the play.[13] Although the Chorus rightly name Aphrodite as holding sway over the fate of mortals, or at least Phaedra and Hippolytus, it is Artemis who appears in the end to explain to Theseus what took place. She does not intervene in the mortals' fates, as planned by Aphrodite, but lets them suffer and die. Hippolytus was Artemis' most ardent admirer, but when he is dying, not only does the goddess refrain from saving him, but when she appears in the final scene, she fails to even approach him to offer him comfort. She has become almost as heartless and cruel as Aphrodite. She does not cry, excusing this by claiming that divine law forbids her to shed tears (1396). She also claims that she loves Hippolytus (1398), using the word προσφιλής, making it clear that this is a platonic love and not the passion that Aphrodite represents; but nevertheless, instead of easing his pain, she promises revenge by killing the mortal whom Aphrodite loves most (1420–2). The only comfort that Artemis offers Hippolytus is that he will have a cult after his death and that "Phaedra's lust for you will not fall nameless and be kept silent" (1429–30). To what extent he could appreciate this promise is a matter of interpretation. In a way, Artemis offers him the kind of immortal fame that many Greek heroes were prepared to die for.

The Nurse

During the plot development, various characters mirror each other in their uncompromising adherence to self-centered goals accompanied by a hard-hearted lack of concern for the well-being of others, with their actions leading to the deaths of Phaedra and Hippolytus. In displaying compassion for another human being, the Nurse alone does not mirror any of the other characters and vice versa. While she delivers endless aphorisms that by their very number lose their meaning, her intentions are good, and she is mainly concerned with saving Phaedra's life. Despite being attentive to her ailing mistress, the Nurse sounds hopelessly confused, managing to miss all of the clues Phaedra gives her as to the cause of her malady. However, the Nurse has sufficient understanding of Phaedra to try to dissuade her from committing suicide by explaining that if she takes her own life,

---

13. The mirroring of the characters is discussed in Roisman, forthcoming (c).

Hippolytus will become master of her children, who will lose their rights as free citizens to inherit Theseus' throne (304–10). Her initial reaction to Phaedra's eventual admission of her secret passion for Hippolytus is one of excessive horror (lines 353–61), which is turned on its head a mere eighty lines later (433–81) when she reacts to Phaedra's love as being something quite natural, claiming that humans are imperfect and should accept their own faults. Simpleminded enough to act on Phaedra's words that she may tell Hippolytus of Phaedra's desire for him, she later pleads with Hippolytus not to reveal her mistress's secret. The Nurse does not seem to have an agenda of her own, yet she advances the plot by revealing Phaedra's forbidden love to Hippolytus. Being the object of his explosive rage, she also forms an integral part of the play's symmetry, with this scene, which causes Phaedra's death, being reflected later in Theseus' explosive rage against Hippolytus. The father's curse triggers events that result in the son's death, just as Hippolytus' outrage at the Nurse's words triggers the death of Phaedra.

6. Theater and Performance

While we are confident that *Hippolytus* was first performed at a festival in the City Dionysia in 428 BCE and was awarded first prize, many other details are uncertain. There is still some controversy about the size of the audience, which has been estimated at between 3,700 and 15,000 spectators.[14] The first few rows of the theater were occupied by the elite: the priest of Dionysus, Athenian magistrates, and visiting ambassadors from various states.[15] Most of the audience, however, consisted of ordinary Athenian citizens—by definition male. Women, who some claim were not permitted to watch the comedies, were allowed to attend the tragic performances;[16] and boys attended with their *paedagogoi*, slaves who brought them up when they were young and accompanied them to their tutors when they were older. The plays were part of the formal competitions that were held at the festival. They were judged by a panel formed by a combination of selection

---

14. For the vast difference in audience estimation, see Bosher 2014; Bers 2014; Meineck 2014.

15. See also Csapo and Slater 1995, 289–90.

16. On the question of women's presence in the audience, see Csapo and Slater 1995, 286–7, 290–3; Taplin 1996, 193–4.

and lot.[17] The purpose of choosing by lots was to diminish the risk of bribery and corruption. Given the important role of the City Dionysia in the life of fifth-century Athens, it is likely that the judges would have been chosen on the basis of some criteria of education and discernment, meaning that they would have come from the elite. Yet the documentation that has come down to us contains telltale grumbling that the judges were often swayed, or even intimidated, by the reactions of the audiences.[18] Put differently, this tells us that the winning playwrights were likely to have been appreciated by the ordinary folk as well. From the public records of the plays, we can calculate that Euripides (and his *chorēgoi*) won only five prizes in the course of his career, two of which were postmortem.[19]

Thus, even though classical Greek drama was state supported, we can surmise that it was popular drama in the best sense of the term: drama written not for the elite, but for the entire *polis*—drama that moved the ordinary Athenians of the time, addressed their concerns, and was fairly congruent with their thinking and worldview.

The plays must have provided breathtaking spectacles, mounted as they were in the open air at the Theater of Dionysus, on the southeast slopes of the Acropolis. The audiences might well have been spellbound not only by the tragic plots and visual elements of performance, but also by the dancing and music. The successive performances began in the early morning and continued, with breaks, throughout the day. The performing area, located on a leveled space at the bottom of the hillside, consisted of a large *orchēstra*,[20] or dancing place, for the chorus, and probably a narrow, elevated platform that served as a stage for the actors and was connected to the *orchēstra* by several steps in the center.

At the back of the *orchēstra* stood a flat-roofed building, probably with double doors, about twelve meters long and four meters high, where actors changed their costumes and masks. It was termed the *skēnē* (tent), after its

---

17. For the problematics of the lottery and the decision procedure, see Csapo and Slater 1995, 158–60.

18. Pickard-Cambridge 1973, 38.

19. See Torrance 2019, 13. Three first prizes: in 441 (the plays are not known), in 428 with *Hippolytus* (the other plays are not known), and posthumously in 405 with *Iphigenia at Aulis*, *Alcmaeon in Corinth*, and *Bacchae* (fourth play unknown). One second prize: in 438 with *Cretan Women*, *Alcmaeon in Psophis*, *Telephus*, *Alcestis*. And one third prize: in 431 with *Philoctetes*, *Dictys*, *Medea*, *Harvesters*.

20. Wiles (1997, 44–52) maintains that the *orchēstra* was circular; others assert that it was rectangular or trapezoidal. On the interpretations of the various archeological remains of theaters, see Moretti 1999–2000.

origins as a tent or hut, with actors making their entrances to the stage from the *skēnē* and returning to it when exiting the stage.[21] When *Hippolytus* was produced, the *skēnē* was probably still a temporary wooden structure that could be removed after the festival. Most of the action of the Greek tragedies took place in the outdoor space in front of the stage building, with offstage actions occurring within the building. On either side of the *orchēstra*, running up to the stage building, were two broad aisles, usually referred to as *eisodoi* or *parodoi* (side paths), which served as entrances for the chorus and characters arriving from the outside. The pathways could also be used by the spectators. The top of the *skēnē* furnished another level of action: it was called the *theologeion* ("god platform"). It was on the *theologeion* that both Aphrodite and Artemis appeared at the beginning and the end of *Hippolytus*. In other plays the *theologeion* serves human characters as well, such as the Watchman in Aeschylus' *Agamemnon*.

Stage furniture was minimal. According to Aristotle (*Poetics* 1449a18), Sophocles introduced scene painting (*skēnographia*).[22] Whether the painting was done on cloth draped over the stage building or on wooden panels placed or hung in front of it is not known. In either case, most of the audience sat very far from the stage and would not have been able to see details. Therefore, it is reasonable to assume that the painting probably depicted little more than the type of location (e.g., urban, rural, seashore) and the type of edifice the stage building represented. In *Hippolytus* the *skēnē* represents the palace in Troezen, in the northern Peloponnesus, where Theseus, Phaedra, and Hippolytus live. We should assume that in front of the center doorway the audience saw two statues, one of Aphrodite, the other of Artemis, symbolizing the two powerful forces with which the play is concerned. Having them in clear view would have reminded the spectators of their power. We know that a statue of Aphrodite was close to the door: characters speak to it as they enter the house (101, 113, 114–20, 522–4, 1461). It is unclear where Artemis' statue stood.[23]

The possibilities of production were expanded by the use of mechanical devices, of which two, the *mēchanē* and the *ekkyklēma*, have a bearing on *Hippolytus*. The *ekkyklēma* was a wooden platform on wheels, approximately 2.5 by 1.5 meters, positioned in the central doorway of the stage

---

21. See Bosher 2014.

22. Beer (2004, 25–9) argues that by *skēnographia* Aristotle meant a verbal scene setting rather than "scene painting"—that he referred to the topographical, spatial, and temporal scene setting typically found in the prologues of the plays.

23. See discussion in Barrett 1964, 154.

building, but it obviously could have been moved about. It was this device that would have been used to wheel Phaedra's body out from the palace for Theseus to see. The *mēchanē*, or crane, consisted of a wheel hanging on a hook fixed to the left side of the stage building. By turning the wheel, the dramatist could bring an actor or a large statue of a god to the roof or lower it down in front of the stage building, or he could facilitate any other winged entrance. The main function of the *mēchanē* gave rise to the well-known Latin phrase *deus ex machina*: "god from the machine."[24]

Props are used sparingly by Greek tragedians, and therefore their employment has thematic significance. They add an element of reality to a plot usually based on a mythic story. In Euripides' *Hippolytus*, the young man enters carrying a wreath that he dedicates to Artemis at her statue. Phaedra's headdress becomes a prop once she insists on having it removed (201–2). Theseus enters wearing a wreath in celebration of his successful embassy to the oracle (792–3), but he throws it off when he is notified of Phaedra's death (806–7). As Luschnig (2014, 1020) notes: "The three gestures with wreath or head-covering connect the three main characters emotionally." In addition, when Phaedra's body is rolled out, there is the calumnious tablet attached to her hand. Some think that the injured Hippolytus is carried in on a litter, on which he dies (see comment following lines 1341–2).

The Greek tragedies have come down to us without stage directions.[25] Since the poets directed—and often acted in—their own plays (tradition has it that Sophocles had to stop performing because of a weak voice) and were on the spot to give instructions, written stage directions would have served no purpose. Thus, for us, the plays' staging is a matter of surmise, based on deduction from information that the protagonists provide about themselves and other characters so that the audience will know who they are, where they are, and what they are doing. Therefore, one has to fill in some stage directions from the text itself, and of course not everyone agrees about how the play was first staged. For example, some scholars assume that Aphrodite delivers her speech on the *theologeion* above the *skēnē*,[26] others that she enters via one of the *eisodoi*.[27] Another staging issue concerns the question of what happens after line 600. From line 565 to 600, Phaedra is in great distress, asking the Chorus to listen to noises coming from within the

---

24. See Levett 2014.
25. For further discussion, see Taplin 1985, 16–19, 179.
26. E.g., Ferguson 1984, 45; Lawall and Lawall 1986, 29; Kovacs 1995, 125.
27. E.g., Halleran 1995, 65.

palace, on the other side of the closed palace door by which she is standing. Scholars who believe that Phaedra exits here, before Hippolytus comes out and makes his misogynistic speech,[28] point to Hippolytus' reference to her in the third person (662) and to Phaedra's apparent unawareness that he has sworn not to disclose her secret (690–1). Those who believe that she remained on stage adduce textual and dramatic reasons.[29] Indeed, the text provides no rationale for Phaedra to leave the stage at line 601 and then return after Hippolytus' misogynistic tirade. Only after his tirade does she declare her intention to avenge his rejection of her (682–92). His misogynistic denunciation and talking at her rather than to her would make it a deeply personal and painful insult, thereby reinforcing, and providing justification for, both her resolve to die and her determination to harm Hippolytus. Moreover, upon seeing Phaedra's corpse, Hippolytus says that he has just left her "looking at this light of day" (907–8); he could not have just left Phaedra had she exited before he entered.

Early Greek tragedies were performed with two speaking actors and one or two mute characters. Aristotle credits Sophocles with adding a third speaking actor (*Poetics* 1449a18). All parts of a tragedy are divided among the protagonist (first actor), the deuteragonist (second actor), and the tritagonist (third actor). All roles of characters or chorus were played by males, who wore bewigged masks. The actors wore the same masks for the characters they played, with the same fixed expression, throughout either the whole or most of the play; as a result, facial expression could not be used to show emotion at all. To compensate for the masks hiding their faces, actors were trained to use meaningful gestures of head and body to project emotions, with skillful dynamic poses to bring the characters to life. Indeed, it has been suggested that by moving the mask in certain ways, skilled actors may have created an impression of differing emotions, thereby contributing to characterization.[30] In the absence of these vehicles of emotional expression, the ability to convey feeling through variations in vocal tone and cadence became essential. Of all the qualities required of an actor, the most important was therefore a strong and versatile voice.[31]

---

28. E.g., Kovacs 1995 on lines.

29. E.g., Walton 1987, 113; Taplin 1985, 155; Knox 1986 (1952); Barrett 1964 on lines. See also Parker 2001.

30. See Meineck 2011 for a detailed explanation; Roisman, forthcoming (a), passim.

31. Cf. Hall 2002 on the function of the voice. Also Pavlovskis 1977, 113; Owen 1936, 148–54; Damen 1989, 318, who offers a para-dramatic treatment of the actors and the roles they play.

The use of masks remedied the issue that there were more characters than actors and that the actors were male. The masks worn by the actors and the members of the chorus completely covered their heads in front and back, with openings only for the eyes and mouth. The tragic costume consisted of a tunic and two mantles, one long and one short, and was worn by nearly all the characters, although they were not necessarily uniform. These costumes were reminiscent of everyday costumes but more elaborate. Both male and female characters of the upper classes wore a floor-length costume consisting of a long *peplos* or *chitōn* (which was no longer in fashion for men in Euripides' day). They might have had a *himation*, a traveler's cloak, over it. Hippolytus must have appeared in hunting gear, whatever that entailed. Phaedra must have been elaborately dressed.[32]

Casting must be deduced from the text. The most likely casting would have been to have the same actor, whether the protagonist or deuteragonist, play Phaedra and Theseus, and a different actor play Hippolytus. Since all three characters have singing lines, both actors would have needed strong and versatile voices. If the actor who played Phaedra and Theseus also played Aphrodite, then a single voice would have connected the destructive goddess with her victims. Alternatively, Aphrodite could have been left for the deuteragonist (presupposing that the protagonist played Phaedra and Theseus) or tritagonist, who would also have played the Nurse (who has more lines than Phaedra or Theseus), Artemis, and the non-singing minor characters. In this case Aphrodite and Artemis would have been connected by a single voice.

Greek tragedies can be described as verse musicals. Song and dance were essential components, along with speech and recitative (declamatory song or chanting). The entire script was in verse, and the dance, song, and recitative were all accompanied by the music of double reed flutes. Every Greek tragedy featured a chorus, initially of twelve members, later fifteen, who danced and sang, whether alone or in dialogues (termed *kommoi*) with the main characters. Scenes were generally divided from one another by antiphonal choral odes termed *stasimons/stasima*. The choral songs and monodies (lyric solos), both accompanied by a double reed flute, were written in a great variety of meters and rhythms. The characters spoke mostly in iambic trimeter, which according to Aristotle is the metrical rhythm closest to spoken cadence (*Poetics* 1449a18–19, Demetrius *On Style* 43). The

---

32. See Llewellyn-Jones 2014.

recitatives were in other meters. Song or recitative punctuated the spoken dialogue and monologues throughout a tragedy.

Classical Greek tragedy was formal, stylized, nonrealistic, and consciously removed from everyday life. The masks and costumes identified the plays as tragedies and as dramas, as opposed to depictions of "real life," and along with the minimalist scenery and props, the formal structure, and the mythic background, they announced that the events portrayed took place in another realm, beyond the mundane.

7. Parts of Greek Tragedies

Greek tragedies are not divided into scenes or acts; the division is into spoken parts and songs accompanied by dance:

PROLOGUE: the part before the entrance of the chorus

PARODOS: the entrance song of the chorus as they file in along the *parodoi*

EPISODES: dialogues between choral songs

STASIMA (sg. *stasimon*): choral songs and dances

EXODOS: everything after the last stasimon

Hippolytus is divided as follows:

PROLOGUE (1–120): Aphrodite reveals her plans to avenge Hippolytus' rejection of the erotic love she represents and his devotion to the virgin goddess Artemis. She tells the spectators that Phaedra, in whom she has instilled passion for the young man, will die the victim of her machinations, but with a good reputation.[33] Hippolytus comes on stage with a wreath for Artemis, declares his devotion to her, and boasts of his *sōphrosynē*, which denotes chastity, temperance, moderation, and restraint.

PARODOS (121–69): The Chorus sing of Phaedra's weakness, apathy, and loss of appetite, and speculate about the cause.

FIRST EPISODE (170–524): Phaedra is brought out of the palace. She is so weak that she has to be supported by her old nurse. In response to the Nurse's worried prodding, she finally reveals her illicit passion for Hippolytus. She recounts her unsuccessful efforts to master her passion and announces her decision to commit suicide. The Nurse dissuades her with the promise of a love medicine that will alleviate her suffering.

---

33. As Barrett (1964, 47) puts it: "And, the other, Phaidra, she shall die with her honor safe, but die she shall."

FIRST STASIMON (525–64): The Chorus reflect on the destructive power of passionate love.

SECOND EPISODE (565–731): Having overheard the Nurse tell Hippolytus of her passion, Phaedra again concludes that she has no choice but to kill herself. Hippolytus, shocked and repelled by the Nurse's revelation, delivers a misogynistic tirade. Phaedra reproaches the Nurse and determines to die in a way that will both preserve her good name and harm Hippolytus.

SECOND STASIMON (732–75): In the first half of the ode, the Chorus sing an escapist song imbued with utopian and mythological imaginings, including the union of Zeus and Hera. The second half relates to Phaedra's transport from Crete, the mortal union between her and Theseus, and the Chorus's prediction of her suicide as a consequence of this union.

THIRD EPISODE (776–1101): The Nurse discovers that Phaedra has hanged herself and seeks help to take her body down. Theseus, having returned from abroad, finds the tablet on which Phaedra accuses Hippolytus of rape and asks his father Poseidon to kill his son. Deaf to Hippolytus' claims of innocence, he exiles him.

THIRD STASIMON (1102–50): The Chorus sing of their dismay at the deeds of humans and the instability of fortune, and of their sorrow at Hippolytus' exile.

FOURTH EPISODE (1151–1267): The Messenger (one of Hippolytus' attendants) describes Hippolytus' chariot wreck in gruesome detail. A bull emerging from the sea chased the chariot and scared the horses. Trying to control his panicked horses, Hippolytus was thrown out and became entangled in the reins, suffering grievous injuries. Barely alive, he was taken by his attendants back to the palace.

FOURTH STASIMON (1268–1281): A brief song on Aphrodite's power.

EXODOS (1283–1466): Artemis rebukes Theseus for murdering his son, revealing Aphrodite's machinations and Phaedra's deception. Hippolytus enters, supported by his attendants, and is reconciled with his father before he dies. Artemis promises to reward him for his devotion by founding a cult in his name.

8. OTHER COMMON ELEMENTS OF GREEK TRAGEDY

KOMMOS: a lyric lament shared by chorus and actors. In *Hippolytus* a short lament (362–72) is sung by the Chorus, or just the leader of the Chorus, which corresponds to the lament sung by Phaedra in lines 669–79, rendering these two sections strophe and antistrophe of a *kommos*. This textual separation between a strophe and antistrophe by 300 lines is, according to Barrett 1964, "remarkable in tragedy."

STICHOMYTHIA: a rapid exchange of one- or two-line utterances, a common rhetorical device in Greek tragedy to convey emotional agitation. The expression is concise, and at times grammatical constructions are extended from line to line for the sake of speed and brevity, as, for example, in the heated discussion between Phaedra and the Nurse (315–50).

AGŌN: a formal debate with matched speeches used as a rhetorical device, perhaps more natural to the Athenians than to us, inclined as they were toward speechifying in the assembly and the courtroom. Euripides is particularly fond of these, which are often brilliant rhetorical displays, but the perfect balance of the speeches makes them unrealistic at times. The *agōn* between Hippolytus and Theseus (902–1101) is an excellent example of arguments in which neither side convinces the other, with the result of the *agōn* having in actuality been decided before the formal debate started.[34]

ANGELOS: a messenger from the outside or from the house. Almost every tragic play has a messenger scene. Messenger speeches are a wonderful display, allowing the poet scope for a different kind of writing. Violence is usually avoided on stage and transferred to verbal descriptions, often in reports by a messenger. However, that some deaths are enacted on stage (for example, Hippolytus', Alcestis', Ajax's) casts doubt on speculation that there was a taboo against showing death in theater.[35] In the case of *Hippolytus*, the Messenger, who must have been one of Hippolytus' attendants, also gives his own view of the nobility and honesty of Hippolytus and counters and criticizes Theseus' treatment of his son (1153–264).

9. METER AND PROSODY

Classical drama is written in verse. The dialogue is spoken, mostly in iambs. The choral odes and some other parts (e.g., *kommoi*) are sung.

Scanning Greek iambs: Greek meters are described as alterations of long and short syllables in regular patterns. In Greek meter, the metron is the smallest unit of long and short syllables forming a repeating pattern typical of the particular metrical sequence. Several named types of metra are listed below.

---

34. See also Roisman, forthcoming (b).
35. For further discussion, see Sommerstein 2010, 30–46.

The iambic metron is closest to the rhythm of ordinary conversation (Aristotle *Poetics* 1449a19, Demetrius *On Style* 43). A syllable is long if it contains a long vowel or diphthong, or a short vowel followed by two or more consonants or a double consonant (ψ, ξ, ζ). The two consonants need not be in the same word. A mute (labial π, β, φ; guttural κ, γ, χ; dental τ, ζ, θ) followed by a liquid (λ or ρ) does not always cause the preceding vowel to count as long. A syllable is short when its vowel is short (and is followed by only one consonant or mute + liquid). A vowel or diphthong at the end of a word, followed by a word beginning with a vowel, usually counts as short.

iamb ˘ – (short/long)

In dramatic verse these appear in groups of two, that is to say, in dipodic units. The most common line of dialogue consists of six iambs, or three such groups:

˘ – ˘ –| ˘ – ˘ – | ˘ – ˘ –

The following substitutions are permitted:

spondee – – (two longs) may substitute for the first iamb of each unit—that is, the first, third, and fifth iamb

tribrach ˘ ˘ ˘ (three shorts) may be used for the first five iambs

anapest ˘ ˘ – (short short long) may be used anywhere a spondee can occur, i.e., in place of the first iamb of each unit—that is, the first, third, and fifth iamb

dactyl – ˘ ˘ (long short short) may be used anywhere a spondee can occur, i.e., in the first iamb of each unit—that is, the first, third, and fifth iamb

A final short in any line is counted as long (syllaba anceps X).

Resolution

Resolution is the substitution of two shorts for either a long or a short in iambic trimeter. The most common place for resolution is in position 6, otherwise termed the third longum (Devine and Stephens 1980, 66–7).

Anaclasis

Anaclasis is the inversion of a short and a long syllable, so that in the case of iambic meter, for example, a trochaic foot would be inserted in the line (Maas 1962, 33.4; Raven 1962, 84–5).

Choral Songs

In tragedy, lyric meters—that is to say, meters that are sung rather than chanted or recited—are organized according to strophic structure. This is a structure of pairs of stanzas, strophe and antistrophe, that differ in words but have the same metrical structure line by line (resolutions are often allowed). The metrical structure of each strophe/antistrophe unit is unique. Occasionally, after the last antistrophe in a song there follows a stanza with no metrical responsion, called an epode. An epode ends the song.

The choral odes and lyric dialogues between a character and the chorus (*kommoi*) are composed in lyric meters, analysis of which appears in the commentary below the relevant text as well as in Stockert 1994a, 110–18; there is in some places analytical variation between the two.

Examples of Iambic Trimeter (*Hippolytus* lines 10–13)

ὁ γάρ με Θησέως παῖς, Ἀμαζόνος τόκος,

˘ — ˘ — — — ˘ —| ˘ — ˘ X

(synizesis: -εως in Θησέως is pronounced as one syllable)

Ἱππόλυτος, ἁγνοῦ Πιτθέως παιδεύματα,

— ˘ ˘ ˘ —| — — ˘ —| — — ˘ X

(resolution in 2nd position)

μόνος πολιτῶν τῆσδε γῆς Τροζηνίας

˘ — ˘ —| — — ˘ —| ˘ — ˘ X

λέγει κακίστην δαιμόνων πεφυκέναι·

˘ — ˘ —| — — ˘ —| ˘ — ˘ X

10. LEXICALITY

One aspect of this commentary is that the occurrence of each word (except prepositions, conjunctions, etc.) is marked, documenting whether this is the word's sole occurrence in the play, in the Euripidean extant corpus, or in extant tragedy. Analysis based solely on occurrences of words is not typically undertaken in classical scholarship; however, as I have already pointed out (Roisman 2020, 219), we know from Aristotle that usage of common (*kyrioi*) and uncommon (rarely used, *xenikoi*) words was a critical consideration in ancient times for assessment of the style's register, as it is today. As the register of a speech transmits valuable information such as the background, sophistication, and intentions of the speaker, modern playwrights may deliberately use altered ratios of common to uncommon words as a characterization tool when differentiating between their characters' speech styles. Aristotle claims that a composition overburdened with uncommon words (loanwords, metaphors, etc.) would suffer from a lack of clarity, while being limited to ordinary or common words would result in a banal, platitudinous, or dull style. He therefore suggests a moderate mix of common and uncommon words to render the style pleasant and to maintain clarity (*Poetics* 1458a–b).[36] Furthermore, Aristotle recommends stricter regulation of the use of unfamiliar and uncommon words in iambic poetry, because the iambic meter is largely an imitation of ordinary speech, which calls for immediate intelligibility. A character's adherence to these directives may indicate a high level of eloquence, indicating rhetorical skill and intelligence.

The scholarship of Greek tragedy has sporadically engaged with word usage, notably hapax words, which appear only once in extant Greek literature. It has been used, for example, in the case of *Rhesus,* mostly with the aim to dispute Euripides' authorship of that play on the basis that *Rhesus* contains a high percentage of words that are not used elsewhere in tragedy or in classical literature.[37] However, it might be more fruitful to ask whether the hapax words can be used by a playwright as a literary tool. That Euripides might have used lexicality as a characterization tool could be gleaned from *Trojan Women,* for example, where in Hecuba's *agōn* with Helen, he gives Hecuba eleven rare words that appear only there and in

---

36. See also discussion in Larkin 1971, 56–71.
37. For discussion, see Liapis 2012, liii–lviii.

a few other places in extant tragedy, while only one such word is allotted to Helen.[38] Without further study of word occurrences, it is impossible to know whether this application of noncommon words makes Hecuba more old-fashioned and thus in some way more authoritative, or whether it merely underscores her non-Greekness in contrast to Helen.

These observations suggest that students could gain useful insights into characterization by undertaking exercises comparing word usage. This may lead them to discover that certain characters, for example, use hapax words more frequently than others, thus adding an additional tool for their appreciation of these characters. Were they depicted as foreigners or as people seeking to distinguish themselves from the other characters for some reason? It is interesting to contemplate whether Hippolytus, who is accused by his father of excessive intellectuality, tends to use more words that occur only once than his father, to point to his aloofness.[39] Also, students could ascertain whether the Nurse, in her 220 words, uses fewer rarely occurring words than Hippolytus in his 271 words or than Phaedra and Theseus, who speak 187 words each. As the Nurse would be expected to be less educated than the other characters, it would be interesting for students to discover whether Euripides gave her a lower percentage of hapax words to help emphasize this.[40] Taking stock and renegotiating our relationship with the text is always a good idea, and the significance of this kind of approach, however technical it is, can be assessed only by testing it.

11. Survival of the Text and Its Reception

While over 1,000 tragedies were probably composed in fifth-century Athens, only around 30 have survived: 7 out of around 90 by Aeschylus, 7 out of around 125 by Sophocles, and 18/19 out of around 92 by Euripides. All of the full tragedies by other fifth-century playwrights have been lost. It is known that some of Euripides' plays were re-performed in the fourth century in Athens, and various copies were made of some of his manuscripts,

---

38. Euripides, *Trojan Women*, Hecuba: ξεμαργώθης (992), κατακλύζω (995), ἐγκαθυβρίζειν (997), ἀνολολύζω (1000), δοριπετής (1002), ἀγωνία (1003), ἀνταγωνιστής (1006), ἀκουσίως (1011), συνεκκλέπτω (1018), κατάπτυστος (1024), ἀποσκυθίζω (1026). *Helen* contains one word that is attested only once more in Euripides, but not in any other extant tragedy: θεοπόνητος (953).

39. A cursory lexical study of the play shows that out of its 8,269 words, 710 (8.6%) appear only once in the play, and 77 (0.9%) appear only once in Euripidean tragedy.

40. Cf. Knox 1986 (1952), 205.

until Lycurgus decided in the 330s that official state copies of the tragedies should be made. These may have ended up in Alexandria in the third century, with copies being sent back to Athens in their place.[41]

A process of selection occurred, so that some of Euripides' tragedies were preserved in ancient collections, whereas others seem to have been lost, having been either discarded or destroyed. Eventually, during the second or third century CE, a definitive selection of ten plays was made, to which *Hippolytus* belongs.[42] Seven of these plays also retained their scholia (annotations). It is not entirely clear how the ten plays were chosen, to the exclusion of the other extant nine plays.[43] The assumption is that the choice was influenced either by school requirements or by the dramatic opportunities that these particular plays offered popular actors. By whatever means they were selected, ten of Euripides' plays were performed several hundred years after they were written, in a revival of Greek tragedies during the third century CE, and *Hippolytus* was selected as one of those ten.

Throughout the ages, Euripides' *Hippolytus* has been both admired and found deeply troubling. The tragic story of Phaedra, Hippolytus, and Theseus enchanted not only the Greek playwrights Sophocles and Euripides, but also the Latin writer Seneca and the French playwright Racine. We do not know what the first treatment of the story by Euripides was, nor the treatment in Sophocles' play. However, *Hippolytus* and the plays of Seneca and Racine, which differ from each other not only in the tastes of the period but in their dramatic strategies and techniques, have survived.

As mentioned above, *Hippolytus* was one of two treatments by Euripides of the Phaedra-Hippolytus myth, and our understanding of it must take into consideration the other version, *Hippolytus Veiled*, which according to the Hypothesis of Aristophanes of Byzantium included "unseemly" material that was "corrected" in the second version. As Gibert (1997) pointed out, however, it is uncertain which play came first. Either way, it was

---

41. Finglass 2020, 33–4.

42. The ten are *Hecuba, Orestes, Phoenician Women, Medea, Hippolytus, Andromache, Alcestis, Rhesus, Trojan Women*, and *Bacchae*.

43. The remaining nine extant plays by Euripides came to light purely by chance when a codex containing *Hecuba* (which belongs to the selected ten) and eight other plays came into the possession of a Byzantine scholar around 250 CE. The plays in this codex were arranged alphabetically and probably formed part of a complete edition. The scholar copied these nine plays, together with the selected ten, all of which have reached us. The nine are known as the "Alphabetical Plays" because their titles begin with the Greek letters *epsilon, eta, iota*, and *kappa*: *Helen, Electra, Heraclidae, Heracles, Suppliants* (*Hiketides*), *Ion, Iphigenia among the Taurians, Iphigenia at Aulis*, and the satyr play *Cyclops* (*Kyklops*).

unusual for a Greek tragedian to produce a second play on a myth he had already handled. In fact, there is no indication that any other Greek tragedian composed two tragedies on the same mythic episode. Why Euripides did this remains a mystery.[44]

I have already suggested elsewhere that what was "unseemly" in the other treatment was not necessarily that Phaedra approached Hippolytus herself and thus presented herself as a brazen woman.[45] Euripides faced an intricate dramatic problem. In the mythic tradition, Hippolytus was dedicated to the worship of Artemis and despised the sexuality of women, while Phaedra, with familial ties to Pasiphaë and Ariadne, would have been perceived by the audience as prone to an excess of sexual desire. Setting Phaedra opposite Hippolytus would have created utterly unrealistic expectations. The heroine could have expected nothing but humiliating, contemptuous pity or harsh rejection from her stepson, and she would have been left with no recourse but vengeance. An experienced playwright, as Euripides was, would have shunned a plot so lacking in complexity and ambiguity. I suggested, therefore, that the proposition to Hippolytus in *Hippolytus Veiled*, whether by Phaedra or by her nurse as an intermediary, could have contained not only the expression of Phaedra's obvious interest in the young man, but the offer of the throne as well, which would also have made it necessary to kill Theseus.[46] Such incitement against the legendary king of Athens would hardly have pleased the Athenian spectators and would account much more plausibly than Phaedra's explicit sexual immorality for the disfavor met with by the first play.[47]

Seneca's *Phaedra* presents a woman-hating, virginal Hippolytus, obsessively desired by his scheming, lustful stepmother, who has been abandoned by her husband, Theseus, who has gone in search of Persephone in

---

44. It should be noted, however, that he wrote three other plays on the topos of "Potiphar's Wife," which have not survived: *Phoenix*, *Stheneboea*, and *Peleus*.

45. While writing my 1999 book on *Hippolytus*, I followed the hypothesis by Aristophanes of Byzantium that *Hippolytus Veiled* preceded *Hippolytus*. The suggestion by Gibert (1997) that the plays might have not followed the traditionally held sequence was not available to me then, but greatly supports my view that *Hippolytus* was not a correction or answer to *Hippolytus Veiled* (see Roisman 1999, 1–26); nor had it to do solely with a sexual offer, but rather with a political proposition.

46. Cf. Reckford 1974, 312.

47. The Athenian horror of patricide is attested to in the context of Athenian law that surrounds so much of Athenian tragedy. The word πατραλοίας (*patraloias*) 'patricide' had great power to injure a person to whom it was applied. It was one of the four "unspoken" words of the Athenian law against verbal abuse. See Clay 1982.

the Netherworld.[48] Phaedra appears to have some kind of political motivation in Seneca's play, suggesting that Hippolytus might take his father's place as king, in addition to becoming her bedfellow (617). Phaedra's depiction here might have more in common with that postulated to have been presented in Euripides' *Hippolytus Veiled*. As I have discussed, it may also represent Phaedra's implicit character in *Hippolytus*. In Ovid's *Heroides*, Phaedra's letter to Hippolytus declares her love for her stepson rather than condemning him for assaulting her and so causing her suicide. Her opening lines, "What harm can there be in reading a letter," are heavy with tragic irony for everyone familiar with Euripides' letter from Phaedra that causes the innocent Hippolytus' death. Phaedra's opening (11) refers to her love, "*Amor*," which drives the action, in place of Aphrodite/Venus' machinations. In calling Hippolytus "the Amazon's son" (2), she is imitating the Euripidean Phaedra, who identifies her beloved to the Nurse in that way, incidentally emphasizing both his virility and his lack of familial relationship with the Cretan Phaedra. In Ovid's letter, Phaedra's attempts to convey her passion to Hippolytus may be related to the past depictions by Euripides and Sophocles in which she either speaks brazenly or attempts to keep silent.[49]

In Racine's *Phèdre* (1677), Theseus has been gone from the palace for six months, in which time Phaedra has developed an illicit passion for her stepson Hippolytus. The young man is in love with Aricia, who against her will is forbidden to marry. By the end of the play, only Theseus and Aricia are alive, although Hippolytus has been cleared of guilt and Phaedra's schemes have been revealed; the youth has died by Theseus' curse. Without the presence of the goddesses, there are no tangible external influences to blame for Phaedra's actions. Sarah Bernhardt portrayed Racine's Phèdre in the 1870s with a heartbreaking realism that made her a sympathetic figure overwhelmed by her own intense passions.[50] Since then, Phaedra's character has been depicted in modernity in various genres, including drama, dance, opera, and film. The operatic *Fedra* by Ildebrando Pizzetti (1915) was composed using a libretto by Gabriele D'Annunzio. Fedra dominates the opera, with her closing aria declaring "*io vinco . . . ancora vinco*" as she triumphs, doing so by dying on her own terms. Martha Graham was the first to choreograph Greek tragedies in modern dance, creating a unique

---

48. For comparison between Seneca's depiction of Phaedra and Euripides' in *Hippolytus*, see Roisman 2000b.

49. See Casali 1995, 2.

50. Mckee 2017, 167–9.

form of tragic dance theater.[51] Her overtly sexual interpretation of "Phaedra," first performed in 1962—in which Phaedra's depiction of the rape was visualized—scandalized audiences with Phaedra's lust, and has been regularly re-created since its original performance. Graham retained Euripides' device of making Aphrodite possibly responsible for at least some of Phaedra's passion.

In 1996, *Phaedra's Love*, an erotically explicit modern adaptation of the myth by Sarah Kane, was staged at the Gate Theatre in London. Although many attributes of Hippolytus himself have been changed (he is not chaste here, but rather obese, depressed, and prone to having sex with random women), many elements of the play follow the plot of Euripides' *Hippolytus* rather than of Seneca's *Phaedra*.[52] Notably, Phaedra hangs herself off stage after being rejected by Hippolytus and writes a letter accusing him of rape. Crucially for our interpretation of the play, however, Phaedra's character is clearly, and perhaps strangely, obsessed with Hippolytus. Her compulsion in seducing him is as destructive in Kane's version as in any of its predecessors. As in *Hippolytus*, Phaedra dies before her stepson, rather than killing herself after his death as in Seneca's play. During the twenty-first century, several productions in Greece have followed on from Kane's play, including *Hippolytus Kalyptomenos* (*Hippolytus Veiled*, 2005) by Vasilis Papageorgiou and *Phaedra or Alcestis—Love Stories* by Elena Penga (2007).[53]

12. Grammatical, Rhetorical, and Literary Figures

adynaton: a hyperbole that insinuates complete impossibility.
anacoluthon: a grammatical or syntactical inconsistency. A deliberate or inadvertent deviation in the structure of a sentence in which a construction started at the beginning is not followed out consistently. It usually cannot be reproduced in a translation into English (S #3004–8).
anaphora: the repetition of a word, a group of words, a phrase, or cognate words at the beginning of successive verses, clauses, phrases, or lines (S #3010).

---

51. Foley 2012, 78–9.
52. See Valtadorou 2018 for an extensive discussion of plot differences and similarities between Kane's play and those of Euripides and Seneca treating the same myth.
53. See Alexiou 2020.

anastrophe: shifting the accent on a dissyllabic preposition from the ultima to the penult when the preposition follows its noun or pronoun (S #175).

aphaeresis: the elision of ε at the beginning of a word after a word ending in a long vowel or diphthong (S #76).

apokoinou: (ἀπὸ κοινοῦ 'in common') a word fulfilling two syntactical functions.

assonance: repetition of the sound of a vowel or diphthong in enough proximity to be discernible.

asyndeton: a lack of connectives in a series of grammatically or semantically coordinated words, phrases, or sentences (S #3016).

consonance: repetition of identical or similar consonants in neighboring words. As opposed to alliteration, in consonance the repeated sounds may occur at any place in the words.

correption: the shortening of a long vowel before another vowel.

crasis: a blending of syllables, the contraction of a vowel or diphthong at the end of a word with a vowel or diphthong at the beginning of the next word. S #62: "over the syllable resulting from contraction is placed a *corōnis* (κορωνίς hook)." For example, κοὐκ from καὶ οὐκ, τἀμά from τὰ ἐμά.

enjambment: the carrying over of a word or phrase to the next line; the breaking of a syntactical unit between two verses.

figura etymologica: the use of two or more words from the same root in close proximity for rhetorical effect. For example, ἐρῶσ(α) ἔρωτα.

hypallage: a figure of speech in which a modifier is syntactically linked to a word other than the one that it modifies semantically.

hyperbaton: separation of words that naturally belong together; used for emphasis (S #3028).

hypophora: a rhetorical device in which the same speaker both proposes and rejects a series of suggestions (S #3029; GP 10–11, iv).

litotes: an understatement in which a positive statement is expressed by negating its opposite, giving emphasis to the positive idea.

majestic plural (*pluralis maiestatis*): the "royal we." The use of plural to refer to a single person, often to lend dignity (S #1006).

oxymoron: a juxtaposition of words explicitly contradictory to each other (S #3035).

periphrasis: the use of more words than are needed to express an idea; a roundabout explanation (S #3041).

prolepsis: anticipation; in particular, adjectives or nouns whose placement early in a sentence anticipates the result of the action of the verb (S #3045). The classic example is "Consider the lilies of the field how they grow."

syncope: the disappearance of a short vowel between consonants (S #44b).

synecdoche: the use of a part for the whole, or conversely the whole for a part (S #3047).

synizesis: the uniting of two vowels, or a vowel and a diphthong, in successive syllables to form a single syllable when pronounced, although with no change in writing (S #60, 61).

tmesis: the separation of a preposition from the verb with which it normally forms a compound (S #1650–3.)

GUIDELINES FOR USING
THE COMMENTARY

1. The commentary is based on *Euripides: Hippolytus,* edited by W. Stockert, Bibliotheca scriptorum Graecorum et Romanorum Teubneriana (Stutgardiae et Lipsiae: in aedibus B. G. Teubneri, 1994), with some small adjustments. It also relies on and refers to the commentary by W. S. Barrett, *Euripides: Hippolytos* (Oxford, 1964).

2. In addition to a running vocabulary, the commentary offers grammatical and syntactical explanations as well as translations. For the first part of the play, the commentary offers full translations for most of the text. However, as students progress through the text and will gradually have acquired more grammatical and syntactical knowledge, as well as vocabulary, the number of translations offered is gradually reduced.

   To enable further study, specific references to relevant grammar and syntax books are included (see the list of abbreviations). After an explanation of a particular syntactical or grammatical phenomenon with a reference to one or more grammar/syntax books, the reference usually won't be repeated in additional cases where the same phenomenon is repeated. However, the reader can find the first mention with the references and other occurrences in the index of grammatical, syntactical, literary, and rhetorical figures. In approximately the last third of the play, less categorizing of cases or participle uses will be offered, unless one is uncommon, has not been mentioned recently, or has not been mentioned at all. The same applies to literary devices. However, all categorizations are mentioned in the index of grammatical, syntactical, literary, and rhetorical figures.

3. Running vocabulary is included in the notes and comments, as well as in the glossary, according to the following guidelines:
   - Words are given as often as possible in their dictionary form, to reinforce the experience of using dictionaries.

- Words that appear only twice in the play are listed both times in the notes and comments, unless the occurrences are less than fifty lines apart. These words are not listed in the glossary, but the line in which the word appears again is indicated in parentheses at the end of the note.
- Words that appear more than twice are marked by a raised plus sign (e.g., +οὐρανός). These are usually mentioned only once in the notes and comments, but they are included in the glossary. *Students are expected to memorize these words.* (See the list of abbreviations for further instructions.)

4. Irregular verbs are marked by an asterisk (e.g., *καλέω). Their forms (unless the verb occurs only once) are to be found in the list of irregular verbs.

5. Translations are enclosed in single quotation marks, while double quotation marks indicate translations or direct comments from a cited work. Grammatical and syntactical pointers appear usually before the translations, which use denotative and connotative meanings of the words. *It is important for students to note that translations do not always match the lexical meanings.* This should help them understand the concept that literal translations are not always possible or preferable.

6. Resolutions are noted in the spoken parts only (see "Meter and Prosody" in the introduction).

7. After line 100 or so, *crasis* is not pointed out as a category, even if the words are spelled out in full.

8. Words that appear only once in Greek tragedy, in Euripides' plays, or in *Hippolytus* are noted in square brackets.

9. From time to time, notes include some questions that are intended to pique students' curiosity and help them to further explore the ideas presented to them by the text while they are thinking of the play as a whole and as a dramatic text.

10. Definitions of grammatical, rhetorical, and literary figures used in the commentary are found on pp. 31–33. References to these figures are italicized in the commentary for extra emphasis.

11. The number of adjectival endings is indicated by parenthetical numbers: (3) for three endings, (2) for two endings, and (3/2) when both three and two endings are found.

12. Simple conditional clauses are usually not noted.

13. For the Greek metrical display of the odes, consult also the running Greek text at the end of the book.

Main Abbreviations and Bibliographical References

Reference Works

B.   W. S. Barrett. 1964. *Euripides: Hippolytos*. Oxford: Oxford University Press.

Ferguson   J. Ferguson. 1984. *Euripides: Hippolytus*. Bristol: Bristol Classical Press.

G   W. W. Goodwin. 2004 (1894). *Greek Grammar*. Bristol: Bristol Classical Press.

GMT   W. W. Goodwin. 2001 (1875). *Syntax of the Moods and Tenses of the Greek Verb*. Bristol: Bristol Classical Press.

GP   J. D. Denniston. 1991 (1950). *The Greek Particles*. 2nd ed. Revised by K. J. Dover. London: Duckworth.

Halleran   M. R. Halleran. 1995. *Euripides: Hippolytus*. Warminster: Aris & Phillips.

Hamilton   R. Hamilton. 1982. *Euripides' Hippolytus*. Bryn Mawr, PA: Bryn Mawr Commentaries.

Lawall   G. and S. Lawall. 1986. *Euripides, Hippolytus: A Companion with Translation*. Bristol: Bristol Classical Press.

LSJ   H. G. Liddell, R. Scott, and H. S. Jones (rev.). 1996. *A Greek-English Lexicon*. 9th ed. with rev. supplement. Oxford: Clarendon.

S   H. W. Smyth. 1984 (1956). *Greek Grammar*. Revised by G. M. Messing. Cambridge, MA: Harvard University Press.

SS   A. C. Moorhouse. 1982. *The Syntax of Sophocles*. Leiden: Brill.

Symbols

⁺	Words marked by a raised plus sign should be learned as they come up in the text; their meaning won't usually be repeated, but the words appear in the glossary at the end of the commentary
*	Asterisks are used to mark irregular verbs; their forms are found in the list of irregular Greek verbs
‡	A double dagger marks a hypothetical reconstruction, i.e., unattested form
†	A dagger or obelus marks an insoluble textual problem
×	A times sign preceded by a numeral indicates the number of times that something occurs (i.e., $8\times$ = eight times)
<	comes from, is derived from
( )	Parentheses contain (1) grammatical explanations, (2) cross-references, or (3) the line number in which the word appears again in the play
[ ]	Square brackets (1) contain words that do not occur in the text but need to be inserted in translation or (2) mark a single occurrence of a word in the play or in the extant plays of Euripides or extant tragedy
⟨ ⟩	Angle brackets indicate an editorial insertion of something considered missing from the transmitted text
Λ	syncopation

Abbreviations

acc.	accusative
act.	active (voice)
adj.	adjective, adjectively
adv.	adverb, adverbial
aor.	aorist
aor.¹	first aorist
aor.²	second aorist
artic.	article, articular
attr.	attributive
compar.	comparative

conj.	conjunction
correl.	correlative
dat.	dative
demon.	demonstrative
dep.	deponent (voice)
enclit.	enclitic
fem.	feminine
fut.	future
gen.	genitive
impf.	imperfect
impv.	imperative
indecl.	indeclinable
indef.	indefinite
indic.	indicative (mood)
indir. disc.	indirect discourse
inf.	infinitive
interrog.	interrogative
intrans.	intransitive
irreg.	irregular
lit.	literally
masc.	masculine
metaph.	metaphor, metaphorically
mid.	middle (voice)
neut.	neuter
nom.	nominative
obj.	object, objective
opt.	optative (mood)
partit. gen.	partitive genitive
pass.	passive (voice)
pcl.	particle
pers.	person(s), personal, personally
pf.	perfect (tense)
pf.[2]	second perfect (tense)
pl.	plural
plupf.	pluperfect (tense)
possess.	possession, possessive
postpos.	postpositive
prep.	preposition
pres.	present (tense)

privat.	privative
pron.	pronoun
ptc.	participle
relat.	relative, related
sg.	singular
subj.	subject, subjective
subjv.	subjunctive (mood)
subst.	substantive, substantival, substantivizing
superl.	superlative
supplem.	supplementary
trans.	transitive
voc.	vocative

Notes and Commentary

Prologue: Lines 1–120

Setting: The play is set in front of the royal palace of Theseus at Troezen, some thirty miles across the Saronic Gulf from Athens. In view of the spectators are two statues, one of Aphrodite, close to the door (101), the other of Artemis, the exact location of which is unclear. It is likely that Aphrodite appears on the *theologeion* rather than entering at stage level, as does Artemis in her later appearance.

The prologue consists of three scenes: (a) In lines 1–57, Aphrodite gives the audience the essentials they need to follow the play: the scene, the characters, their relationship, and the state of affairs as the play begins. Euripides also uses this opportunity to portray the goddess as powerful, proud, intolerant, and without scruples or pity, which would arouse sympathy for her victim from the start. (b) Lines 58–87 are a hymn to Artemis sung in lyrical meters by Hippolytus and his attendants, followed by Hippolytus presenting a wreath to Artemis with devotional words to the goddess. (c) Lines 88–120 present a stichomythic exchange between Hippolytus and a servant who remonstrates with him for neglecting Aphrodite altogether.

Scene A: Lines 1–57

Aphrodite appears on the *theologeion* above the *skēnē*.

ΑΦΡΟΔΙΤΗ

> Πολλὴ μὲν ἐν βροτοῖσι κοὐκ ἀνώνυμος
> θεὰ κέκλημαι Κύπρις οὐρανοῦ τ᾽ ἔσω·
> ὅσοι τε Πόντου τερμόνων τ᾽ Ἀτλαντικῶν

ναίουσιν εἴσω, φῶς ὁρῶντες ἡλίου,
τοὺς μὲν σέβοντας τἀμὰ πρεσβεύω κράτη,   5
σφάλλω δ᾽ ὅσοι φρονοῦσιν εἰς ἡμᾶς μέγα.

1   ⁺**πολύς, πολλή, πολύ**   great and large, mighty, powerful

μέν   surely, indeed, really (μέν *solitarium*, i.e.,
with no corresponding δέ clause, is emphatic but not always translatable; here stressing and affirming the idea of the verb: S #2896–98;
GP 359–60)

⁺**ἐν** (prep.)   + dat. (locative); in, at, near, by, on, among
(S #1687)

⁺**βροτός, ὁ**   mortal (οισι[v] appears often in poetry for metrical convenience: S #234)

κοὐκ   = καὶ οὐκ; *crasis*, a blending of syllables, the
contraction of a vowel or diphthong at the end of a word with a vowel
or diphthong at the beginning of the next word (S #62, 68c)

⁺**ἀνώνῠμος** (2)   without name, anonymous (ἀ privat., ὄνυμα,
Aeolic for ὄνομα; οὐκ ἀνώνῠμος 'not without name,' 'famous'; an
example of *litotes*, an understatement in which a positive statement
is expressed by negating its opposite, giving emphasis to the positive
idea. Note that Artemis will be using the same adj. in line 1429.)

2   ⁺**θεά, ἡ**   goddess

*⁺**καλέω**   call (κέκλημαι, pf. pass. indic.) [1x *Hipp.*]

⁺**Κύπρις, ῐδος**   Cypris: from the island of Cyprus, a common
epithet of Aphrodite, who was born there

⁺**οὐρανός, ὁ**   heaven/sky, as the seat of the gods

⁺**ἔσω/εἴσω**   + gen.: within, into, in (improper prep., i.e., an
adv. used as a prep. but incapable of forming compounds: S #1647,
1700) – 'Powerful and not without name among mortals and in heaven
alike, I am called the goddess Cypris' [1x *Hipp.*]

3   ⁺**ὅσος, η, ον**   (relat. correl. pron.) how much, as great as, as
much as; in pl.: all that, as many as (S #340)

⁺**Πόντος, ὁ**   sea (gen. because of εἴσω). As a proper name,
ὁ Πόντος signifies in vernacular Attic the Black Sea. In tragedy it is

usually 'sea' in general or 'Black Sea.' Here the idea of the Black Sea makes more sense and agrees with line 1053, where Theseus banishes Hippolytus from Troezen and Attica to beyond the Black Sea and the Pillars of Atlas. Aphrodite refers to all humankind between the eastern and western limits of the world.

⁺τέρμων, ονος, ὁ   = τέρμα; a boundary, an end, a goal

Ἀτλαντικός (3)   of Atlas; the boundaries of Atlas are located by the Straits of Gibraltar, the traditional western limit of the known world (1053)

4   ⁺ναίω   dwell, inhabit (ὅσοι . . . ναίουσιν, *hyperbaton*, separation of words belonging together for emphasis: S #3028; here it stresses the intervening clause describing the geographical expanse over which Aphrodite rules)

⁺φῶς, ωτός, τό   (contraction of ⁺φάος) light

*⁺ὁράω   see (ὁρῶντες, pres. act. ptc. of attendant circumstance/descriptive, coincidental with the finite verb ναίουσιν: S #2068, 1872; GMT #843)

⁺ἥλιος, ὁ   sun; – 'as many as live between the Black Sea and the Pillars of Atlas, looking on the light of the sun'

5   ⁺σέβω   worship, honor

τἀμὰ   = τὰ ἐμά (κράτη), *crasis*

πρεσβεύω   put first in rank, honor [1x *Hipp.*]

κράτος, εος, τό   strength, might, prowess [1x *Hipp.*]

6   *⁺σφάλλω   make fall, trip up (τοὺς μὲν σέβοντας . . . πρεσβεύω . . . σφάλλω [τοὺς] δ' ὅσοι; the glossed over [τοὺς] is the antecedent of ὅσοι) – 'those on the one hand who revere my powers, I honor, on the other hand, I trip up all [those] who . . .'

⁺φρονέω   think; φρονέω μέγα, think proudly, think big, be arrogant

⁺μέγας, μεγάλη [ᾰ],   great; μέγα (adv.) very much, exceedingly
μέγα

⁺εἰς/ἐς (prep.)   + acc. only; toward, into; up to, until, toward, to, for

ἡμεῖς, ἡμῶν, ἡμῖν, ἡμᾶς   we (1st pl. pers. pron.: S #325; *majestic plural* emphasizing Aphrodite's importance: S #1006) – 'those who think proudly toward me'

ἔνεστι γὰρ δὴ κἀν θεῶν γένει τόδε·
τιμώμενοι χαίρουσιν ἀνθρώπων ὕπο.
δείξω δὲ μύθων τῶνδ' ἀλήθειαν τάχα·
ὁ γάρ με Θησέως παῖς, Ἀμαζόνος τόκος,   10
Ἱππόλυτος, ἁγνοῦ Πιτθέως παιδεύματα,
μόνος πολιτῶν τῆσδε γῆς Τροζηνίας
λέγει κακίστην δαιμόνων πεφυκέναι·

7   ⁺ἔν-*⁺ειμι   be within, be in or among (S #768)

γὰρ δή   an idiomatic use for "arresting attention at the opening of a narrative": GP 243 (1)

⁺καί (adv.)   also; even; κἀν = καὶ ἐν, *crasis*

⁺γένος, ους, τό   race, stock, kin

⁺ὅ-δε, ἥ-δε, τό-δε   this (demon. pron.: S #333; ὅ-δε has a fixed point of reference; it points out what is present or before one; hence it is called *deictic*: S #1241; the following line explains τόδε) – 'For this exists also among the race of the gods'

8   ⁺τῑμάω   hold worthy, honor, respect (τιμώμενοι, pres. pass. ptc. of attendant circumstance, coincidental with the finite verb χαίρουσιν; see ὁράω in line 4)

*⁺χαίρω   rejoice; welcome, farewell

⁺ἄνθρωπος, ὁ   man/woman (ἀνθρώπων, gen. of agent with ὑπό: S #1678) – 'they enjoy being honored by mortals'

⁺ὑπό (prep.)   + gen.: by, under, through, from (+ὑπό with gen. of pers. agent: S #1493; ὕπο: the accent is thrown back when a disyllabic prep. follows its case, called *anastrophe*: S #175a)

9   *⁺δείκνῡμι   show, reveal

⁺δέ (postpos. pcl.)   and (connective continuative pcl. at the beginning of a sentence: GP 162–3A; S #2836)

⁺μῦθος, ὁ   word, speech

ἀλήθειᾰ, ἡ   truth [1x *Hipp.*]

τάχα (adv.)   quickly, soon; – 'And I will soon show the truth of these words' (182)

10 με   (acc. of ἐγώ: S #325; με . . . κακίστην . . . πεφυκέναι, acc. and inf.; *hyperbaton* in which Aphrodite emphasizes herself. B.: "The position of με here is the effect of a very ancient tendency in the Greek language . . . for enclitics . . . to occupy the second place in their sentence or clause.")

⁺παῖς, παιδός, ὁ   child

⁺Θησεύς, έως, ὁ   Theseus (-εω in Θησέως is pronounced as one syllable by *synizesis*: S #60, 61)

⁺Ἀμαζών, όνος, ἡ   Amazon. Why isn't she mentioned by name (Hippolytē or Antiope)?

⁺τόκος, ὁ   (τίκτω, bring forth, bear) offspring, child, son

11 ⁺Ἱππόλυτος, ὁ   Hippolytos (Ἱππόλυτος, resolution in 2nd position)

⁺ἁγνός (3)   + gen.: pure, chaste, unsullied (by)

⁺Πιτθεύς, έως, ὁ   Pittheus, Hippolytus' great-grandfather, father of Theseus' mother Aethra, a former king of Troezen. B. suggests that since Theseus is considered the king of Troezen, one should assume that Pittheus must have retired in Theseus' favor.

παίδευμα, ατος, τό   (παιδεύω, teach, bring up a child) that which is reared or educated, pupil; that which is taught. (Abstract for concrete is often used in Greek; cf. line 407 for -μα noun used for person. According to B., the pl. renders stylistic elevation.) [1x *Hipp.*]

12 ⁺μόνος (3)   only, alone

⁺πολίτης, [ῐ] ου, ὁ   citizen (partit. gen.: S #1306)

⁺γῆ, ἡ   earth, land (possess. gen.: S #1297)

⁺Τροζήνιος (3)   (Τροιζ- codd.) of Troezen, a place in the northeastern Peloponnese, on the Argolid Peninsula

13 *⁺λέγω   say, state (as a verb of saying, λέγω here takes the acc. and inf. as indirect statement: S #2016, 2017b)

⁺κακός (3)   bad, evil in its kind, worthless

⁺δαίμων ονος, ὁ, ἡ   deity (superl. with partit. gen.: S #1306, 1315)

**⁺φύω   [ῠ/ῡ] bring forth, produce; aor.²: grew, was; pf.:
be by nature = εἶναι (πεφῦκέναι, pf. act. inf.) – 'Hippolytus . . . alone
of the citizens of this land of Troezen, says that by nature I am the most
vile of deities'

ἀναίνεται δὲ λέκτρα κοὺ ψαύει γάμων,
Φοίβου δ᾽ ἀδελφὴν Ἄρτεμιν, Διὸς κόρην,   15
τιμᾷ, μεγίστην δαιμόνων ἡγούμενος,
χλωρὰν δ᾽ ἀν᾽ ὕλην παρθένῳ ξυνὼν ἀεὶ
κυσὶν ταχείαις θῆρας ἐξαιρεῖ χθονός,
μείζω βροτείας προσπεσὼν ὁμιλίας.

14 ἀναίνομαι   reject, refuse, spurn [1x *Hipp.*]

⁺λέκτρον, τό   couch, bed; in pl. mostly: marriage bed

κοὺ   = καὶ οὐ, *crasis*

ψαύω   + gen.: touch [1x *Hipp.*]

⁺γάμος, ὁ [ᾰ]   marriage, wedding (some think the pl. comes
from repeated intercourse; others note the use of pl. for festivals and
festivities: SS 6 §3) – 'he rejects the bed and does not touch marriage'

15 Φοῖβος, ὁ   (φοῖβος, pure, bright, radiant) Phoebus, the
Bright or Pure, an old epithet of Apollo (536)

ἀδελφή, ἡ [ᾰ]   daughter of the same mother, sister [1x *Hipp.*]

⁺Ἄρτεμις, ιδος, ἡ   Artemis, daughter of Zeus and Leto (acc. Ἄρτεμιν or Ἀρτέμιδα)

⁺Ζεύς, ὁ   Zeus (Διός, Διί, Διά, Ζεῦ; Ionic and poetic: Ζη-
νός, Ζηνί, Ζῆνα: S #285.12)

⁺κόρη, ἡ   girl; daughter. What does Aphrodite emphasize
in the rather extensive background she gives for both Hippolytus and
Artemis, and why?

16 ⁺μεγίστην   superl. of ⁺μέγας, μεγάλη [ᾰ] μέγα (acc. in
indir. disc. following ἡγούμενος; με is included in μεγίστην, subj. of the
omitted εἶναι) – 'considering her the greatest of deities'

ἡγέομαι   + acc.: hold as, regard as, suppose, believe,
consider (185)

17 χλωρός (3)   bright green, the color of young grass
[1x *Hipp.*]

⁺ἀνά (prep.)   + acc.: through, throughout

ὕλη [ῠ], ἡ   wood, forest (215)

⁺παρθένος, ἡ   virgin, maiden (Artemis is also called
Παρθένος)

⁺σύν-*⁺ειμι   associate, live with, consort (ξυνών, pres. act.
ptc.; ξυν- = συν-; σύν-ειμι + dat. often implies sexual liaison. Does
Aphrodite intend to undermine Hippolytus' claim to celibacy in his
worship of Artemis, even though there is no explicit reference to sexuality here? The ptc.'s conjunction with παρθένῳ renders a contemptuous *oxymoron* [S #3035] suggesting Hippolytus' unnatural and artificial restraint.) – 'throughout the green wood always consorting with
the virgin goddess'

ἀεί (adv.)   (ᾰ/ᾱ) ever, always

18 ⁺κύων, κυνός, ὁ, ἡ   a dog, a hound (as a hound it is usually fem.,
hence ταχείαις; declension: S #285; dat. of means: S #1507)

⁺ταχύς, εῖα, ύ   quick, swift, fast

⁺θήρ, θηρός, ὁ   wild beast of prey, wild animals (declension: S
#259)

ἐξ-αιρέω   take out, take out of, remove (ἐξ- in composition implies thoroughness: S #1688.2. Aphrodite exaggerates the results of Hippolytus' hunting by stating that he rids the land of all wild
animals in order to portray him as negatively as she can.) [1x *Hipp.*]

⁺χθών, χθονός, ἡ   the earth, ground (gen. of separation: S #1392).
– 'with his swift hounds he clears the land of wild beasts [lit.: removes
the wild beasts from the land]'

19 ⁺μείζων, μεῖζον   μείζω = μείζονα, bigger (here acc. sg. with
omitted ὁμιλίαν; compar. of ⁺μέγας with gen.: βροτείας ὁμιλίας: S #1066,
1431)

⁺βρότειος (3/2)   human, mortal

προσ-*πίπτω   (-πίτνω) + acc.: fall down to, fall before, supplicate (aor.² act. ptc. of attendant circumstance, coincidental with the finite verb ἐξαιρεῖ; see ὁράω in line 4) [1x *Hipp.*]

⁺ὁμῑλία, ἡ   companionship, intercourse; another word packed with sexual innuendo (see σύν-ειμι in line 17) – 'falling in with a companionship more than mortal'

τούτοισι μέν νυν οὐ φθονῶ· τί γάρ με δεῖ;   20
ἃ δ᾽ εἰς ἔμ᾽ ἡμάρτηκε τιμωρήσομαι
Ἱππόλυτον ἐν τῇδ᾽ ἡμέρᾳ· τὰ πολλὰ δὲ
πάλαι προκόψασ᾽, οὐ πόνου πολλοῦ με δεῖ.

20 ⁺οὗτος, αὕτη, τοῦτο (demon. pron.)   this, that (designates the nearer of two things, places, times, thoughts; declension: S #333; opposed to +ἐκεῖνος; τούτοισι = τούτοις, dat. pl. masc. or neut., but most probably refers to Hippolytus and Artemis)

φθονέω   bear a grudge, be envious, be jealous [1x
***Hipp.*]**

τί (adv.)   why? [1x *Hipp.*]

⁺γάρ (postpos. conj.)   for (introduces a reason for the preceding statement: S #2803, 2810)

⁺νυν (enclit. pcl., postpos.)   S #2926: "rarely temporal, usually inferential, as now is used for *then, therefore*" (often best not translated)

⁺δεῖ   it is necessary (quasi-impersonal verb: S #933b; usually takes the dat.; the following acc. με is rare and only in poetry, on the analogy of δεῖ with the inf.: S #1400) – 'I do not envy them [i.e., their companionship], for why should I?' Do we believe her assertion that she is going to punish Hippolytus not out of envy for his affection for Artemis, but only because of anger at his neglect of her, i.e., Aphrodite?

21 ⁺ὅς, ἥ, ὅ (relat. pron.)   which, that (acc. neut. pl.; declension: S #338. The antecedent of ἅ is omitted. Such omission occurs when the antecedent expresses the general idea included or effected by the verb, which renders the ἅ an internal object of ἡμάρτηκε: S #1554a.)

⁺ἐγώ (pers. pron.)   ἐμέ, acc. sg. (declension: S #325) [εἰς ἐμέ:
1x *Hipp.*]

*⁺ἁμαρτάνω, ἡμάρτηκε   miss the mark; err; – 'But on the other hand, for his errors against me . . .' Lit.: he committed 'mistakes' or 'errors,' but since Aphrodite sees them as moral transgressions, they are usually translated as 'sins.' Lawall: "A vocabulary of mistakes or errors (*hamartia* and related terms) recurs throughout the play as the characters become entangled in situations which they do not fully understand and so make mistakes of judgment and action" (cf. lines 320, 323, 507, 615, 690, 1334, 1409, 1434).

τῑμωρέω   (τῑμωρός) mid. + acc.: exact vengeance upon . . . for, punish X for Y (takes double acc.) (1422)

22   **⁺ἡμέρα, ἡ**   day; ἐν τῇδε ἡμέρᾳ 'on this day,' 'before this day is out'

⁺Ἱππόλυτος, ὁ   Ἱππόλυτον, resolution in 2nd position

τὰ πολλά   adv.: for the most part

23   **⁺πάλαι (adv.)**   long ago, formerly, before

προ-κόπτω   intrans. in act.: make one's way forward, make progress (πάλαι προκόψασα, circumstantial ptc.; the action of the aor. ptc. is usually antecedent to that of the leading verb: S #1872c; note the emphatic *enjambment*). It is noteworthy that this unusual metaphor is repeated by Artemis in line 1297: – 'for his errors toward me, I will exact vengeance on Hippolytus before this day is out, having long ago made progress with most of my plans, I do not need much effort.' (1297)

⁺πόνος, ὁ   hard work (οὐ πόνου πολλοῦ με δεῖ; – 'I do not need much effort'; acc. with δεῖ, instead of the usual δεῖ μοι in prose, on the analogy of δεῖ with the inf.: 'it is necessary that I . . .': S #1400, 1985. Here there is also an *anacoluthon*, a break in sentence construction, which often reflects natural speech. Aphrodite starts the sentence thinking of herself as the subj., hence the nom. προκόψασα, but she then moves to a syntactical construction in which she becomes grammatically acc.: με. Since Euripides is not inclined to use *consonance* as frequently as Aeschylus and Sophocles, the repetitive π sound in lines 22–3 may possibly be used to convey Aphrodite's scorn.)

ἐλθόντα γάρ νιν Πιτθέως ποτ' ἐκ δόμων
σεμνῶν ἐς ὄψιν καὶ τέλη μυστηρίων   25

Πανδίονος γῆν πατρὸς εὐγενὴς δάμαρ
ἰδοῦσα Φαίδρα καρδίαν κατέσχετο
ἔρωτι δεινῷ τοῖς ἐμοῖς βουλεύμασιν.

24 **⁺ἔρχομαι, ἦλθον**   come, go (ἐλθόντα, aor.² act. circumstantial ptc. denoting time: S #2061; the action of the aor. ptc. is usually antecedent to that of the leading verb: S #1872c)

⁺νιν   = αὐτόν (enclit. poetic acc. of 3rd pers. pron.)

⁺ποτέ (indef. adv. enclit.)   at some time, once (especially in telling a story: LSJ III.1a)

⁺ἐκ, ἐξ (prep.)   + gen. (ἐξ before a vowel, movable σ: S #136): out of, from; after; as a result of; by

⁺δόμος, ὁ   house, chamber (pl. because the house contains multiple rooms: SS 4 §3)

25 ⁺σεμνός (3)   august, holy, solemn; haughty, grand

ὄψις, εως, ἡ   viewing, vision, apparition [1x *Hipp.*]

τέλος, εος, τό   initiation, completion (87)

μυστήριον, τό   a mystery, secret, rite; pl.: the mysteries, religious celebrations (σεμνῶ . . . μυστηρίων, *hyperbaton*) [1x *Hipp.*]

26 Πανδίων, ονος, ὁ   Pandion, a legendary king of Athens/Attica, father of Philomela and Procne, in whose reign Demeter came to Athens. Πανδίονος γῆ = Athens (Πανδίονος, resolution in 2nd position). – 'One day when he came from the house of Pittheus for the viewing and rites of the holy mysteries of the land of Pandion . . .' [1x *Hipp.*]

⁺πατήρ, τρός, ὁ   father (syncopated noun: S #44, 262)

⁺εὐ-γενής, ές   (εὖ, γένος) noble, of high descent

⁺δάμαρ, αρτος, ἡ   [ᾰ] (δαμάω, subdue, yoke) wife, spouse

27 **⁺ἰδοῦσα**   see (ὁράω, aor.² ptc.; circumstantial ptc. denoting time; see ἐλθόντα in line 24) – 'having seen'

⁺Φαίδρα, ἡ   Phaedra

⁺καρδία, ἡ   heart (acc. of respect, frequent with parts of the body: S #1600, 1601a) – 'was seized in respect to her heart, i.e., in her heart'

⁺κατ-⁺ἔχω   seize (κατέσχετο, aor.² mid. for pass. indic.)

28 ⁺ἔρως, ωτος, ὁ   love, desire (ἔρωτι, dat. of means)

⁺δεινός (3)   fearful, terrible, powerful

⁺βούλευμα, ατος, τό   (βουλεύω, take counsel, give counsel) resolution, plan, design; – 'his father's highborn wife, Phaedra, [having seen him she was seized in her heart by . . .] saw him, and her heart was seized with terrible desire according to my designs'

καὶ πρὶν μὲν ἐλθεῖν τήνδε γῆν Τροζηνίαν,
πέτραν παρ' αὐτὴν Παλλάδος κατόψιον   30
γῆς τῆσδε, ναὸν Κύπριδος ἐγκαθείσατο,
ἐρῶσ' ἔρωτ' ἔκδημον· Ἱππολύτῳ δ' ἔπι
τὸ λοιπὸν ὀνομάσουσιν ἱδρῦσθαι θεάν.
ἐπεὶ δὲ Θησεὺς Κέκροπίαν λείπει χθόνα
μίασμα φεύγων αἵματος Παλλαντιδῶν   35
καὶ τήνδε σὺν δάμαρτι ναυστολεῖ χθόνα
ἐνιαυσίαν ἔκδημον αἰνέσας φυγήν,
ἐνταῦθα δὴ στένουσα κἀκπεπληγμένη
κέντροις ἔρωτος ἡ τάλαιν' ἀπόλλυται
σιγῇ· ξύνοιδεν οὔτις οἰκετῶν νόσον.   40

29 ⁺πρίν (conj.)   [ῐ] before, formerly (when subordinated to an affirmative clause, usually takes inf.: S #2431, 2454)

30 ⁺πέτρα, ἡ   rock, crag

⁺παρά (prep.)   + acc.: running along, beside, next to

⁺αὐτός, αὐτή, αὐτό (intensive pron.)   -self (in oblique cases, pers. pron. of 3rd pers.)

Παλλάς, Παλλάδος, ἡ   Pallas, one of Athena's cult titles (πέτρα Παλλάδος = the Acropolis at Athens, sacred to Pallas Athena) (1459)

κατ-όψιος (2)   (κατά, ὄψις) full in sight, opposite, overlooking [1x Eur.]

31 γῆς τῆσδε   'from this land' (*enjambment* underscoring that Phaedra can see the temple from Troezen)

ναός, ὁ   temple (Doric form is metrically easier than Attic νεώς: S #238c) (620)

ἐγ-καθίζω   seat upon, establish in, set up, place (i.e., in Athens) [1x *Hipp.*]

32 *⁺ἐράω/ἔραμαι   love (ἐρῶσα, aor.¹ act. ptc.; circumstantial
causal ptc.: S #2064; ἐρῶσα ἔρωτα 'loving a love,' *figura etymologica*, the
use of two or more words from the same root in close proximity for rhetorical emphasis; note the *assonance* of the -ε- sound)

⁺ἔκ-δημος (2)   (ἐκ, δῆμος) abroad, away from home, foreign – 'Before she came to this Troezenian land, she set up next to the
very rock of Pallas (the Acropolis) a temple to Cypris overlooking this
land, since she was in love with one who was abroad/outside of the
house'

⁺ἐπί (prep.)   + dat.: over, for, near (ἔπι, *anastrophe*; Ἱππολύτῳ, resolution in 8th position)

33 λοιπός (3)   (*⁺λείπω, leave) remaining (τὸ λοιπόν = the
remainder, the future) [1x *Hipp.*]

ὀνομάζω   (ὄνομα, name) name, call by name (treated
here as a verb of saying, requiring indir. disc. in the form of acc. and
inf.: ἱδρῦσθαι θεάν) [1x *Hipp.*]

ἱδρύω   set up, establish, found (ἱδρῦσθαι, pf. mid. inf.;
θεάν: Aphrodite speaks of herself in the 3rd pers.; cf. line 31) – 'and in
the future men will name the goddess [goddess's shrine] as set up for
Hippolytus.' In Troezen, in a precinct devoted to Hippolytus, there was
a temple of Aphrodite *Kataskopia*, i.e., the "Spy" (cf. κατόψιον in line
30), built above a racecourse named in Hippolytus' honor. According
to Pausanias (2.32.3), the name of the temple comes from Phaedra's
"spying" on Hippolytus whenever he practiced his exercises below.
Euripides is fond of etiology. (639)

34 ⁺ἐπεί (**conj.**)   of time: after, when, from time when; of cause:
since, seeing that, for that

Κεκρόπιος (3)   Cecropian = Athenian. Cecrops was a legendary king of Athens/Attica. (Κεκροπίαν, resolution in 6th position) [1x
Hipp.]

*⁺λείπω   leave (tragedy prefers historical pres. for vivid
portrayal of a past action; usually translated by a past tense: S #1883;
GMT #33)

35 ⁺μίασμα, ατος, τό   [ῐ] stain, defilement, pollution

*⁺φεύγω   flee, run away (φεύγων, pres. act. ptc. of attendant circumstance, coincidental with the finite verb λείπει; see ὁράω in
line 4)

⁺αἷμα, ατος, τό   blood (αἵματος, gen. of explanation/apposi-
tion, explains the meaning of a more general word: S #1322)

Παλλαντιδής, οῦ, ὁ   son of Pallas (Παλλαντιδῶν, gen. of explana-
tion/apposition). The Pallantidai were cousins of Theseus, who dis-
puted his right to inherit Aegeus' rule over Athens. Theseus killed
them, incurring thereby pollution for kindred bloodshed, which he ex-
piated by a year's exile from Athens. [1x *Hipp.*]

36 **⁺σύν** (prep.)   + dat.: with; adv.: together, at once, jointly; besides, moreover

ναυστολέω   intrans.: go by sea, sail (historical pres.;
τήνδε . . . χθόνα, *hyperbaton*, emphasizes Troezen) [1x *Hipp.*]

37 **ἐνιαύσιος** (3/2)   for a year, lasting a year (ἐνιαυσίαν, resolution
of 1st anceps in 1st position) [1x *Hipp.*]

*⁺αἰνέω   praise, speak in praise of, consent to (αἰνέσας,
aor.¹ act. ptc.; αἰνέω keeps a short vowel in the aor. and fut.: S #488b;
circumstantial ptc. denoting time; see ἐλθόντα in line 24)

⁺φὕγή, ἡ   exile, banishment; – 'And after Theseus left
the land of Cecrops, fleeing the pollution of Pallantid bloodshed, and
having consented to a yearlong exile from his home, he sailed with his
wife to this land'

38 **ἐνταῦθα** (adv.)   of place: here, there; of time: then, now, ever
since [1x *Hipp.*]

⁺δή (pcl.)   of course, indeed, quite, naturally (postpos., i.e.,
it cannot come first in a sentence or phrase and is usually put second,
but can come first in translation; adds explicitness, i.e., marks something as immediately present and clear to the mind: S #2840, 2841)

⁺στένω   sigh; trans.: bemoan, lament, deplore, com-
plain (pres. act. ptc.; only in pres. and impf.; ptc. of manner describing
ἀπόλλυται: S #2062; GMT #836)

⁺ἐκ-*πλήττω   strike out of one's senses, drive from one's
senses (generally of any overpowering passion), scare, astound

(κἀκπεπληγμένη = καὶ ἐκπεπληγμένη, *crasis*; pf.² pass. ptc. of manner describing ἀπόλλυται: S #2062)

39 ⁺**κέντρον, τό**   (κεντέω, goad) point, spike, sting; metaph.: spur, goad (κέντροις, dat. of means; ἔρωτος, gen. of explanation/apposition)

⁺**τάλᾱς, τάλαινᾰ,**   (‡τλάω, suffer) suffering, wretched, enduring
τάλᾰν

⁺**ἀπ-*⁺όλλῡμι**   act.: destroy utterly; mid.: ἀπ-όλλῡμαι perish,
die, cease to exist

40 ⁺**σῑγή, ἡ**   silence (σιγῇ, dat. of manner: S #1516; emphatic *enjambment* underscores that in spite of Phaedra's insistence on not saying a word about her infatuation, Aphrodite will reveal her love to everyone)

⁺**συν-*⁺είδω**   share in the knowledge (σύν-*οιδα, pf.² indic. with pres. sense: S #794; the pres. of this stem does not exist; the *anacoluthon* underscores the secrecy) (425)

οὔ-τις, οὔ-τι (pron.)   nobody; neut. οὔτι as adv.: by no means, not at all, not in any way (41)

οἰκέτης, οῦ, ὁ   (οἰκέω, dwell) an inhabitant, dweller (partit. gen.) [1x *Hipp.*]

⁺**νόσος, ἡ**   sickness, disease, malady, illness; – 'ever since, the poor woman, groaning and struck out of her wits by the goads of desire, is dying in silence, and no one in the household understands her sickness'

ἀλλ' οὔτι ταύτῃ τόνδ' ἔρωτα χρὴ πεσεῖν,
δείξω δὲ Θησεῖ πρᾶγμα κἀκφανήσεται.
καὶ τὸν μὲν ἡμῖν πολέμιον νεανίαν
κτενεῖ πατὴρ ἀραῖσιν ἃς ὁ πόντιος
ἄναξ Ποσειδῶν ὤπασεν Θησεῖ γέρας,   45
μηδὲν μάταιον ἐς τρὶς εὔξασθαι θεῷ.
ἡ δ' εὐκλεὴς μὲν ἀλλ' ὅμως ἀπόλλυται
Φαίδρα· τὸ γὰρ τῆσδ' οὐ προτιμήσω κακὸν
τὸ μὴ οὐ παρασχεῖν τοὺς ἐμοὺς ἐχθροὺς ἐμοὶ
δίκην τοσαύτην ὥστε μοι καλῶς ἔχειν.   50
ἀλλ' εἰσορῶ γὰρ τόνδε παῖδα Θησέως

στείχοντα, θήρας μόχθον ἐκλελοιπότα,
Ἱππόλυτον, ἔξω τῶνδε βήσομαι τόπων.

41 ⁺ταύτῃ (adv.)   in this way or manner (refers to what precedes, i.e., that Phaedra should die in silence)

*⁺χρή   it is necessary (indecl. noun, 'necessity,' with ἐστί supplied; with acc. and inf.: τόνδ' ἔρωτα πεσεῖν: S #1562, 1985b) – 'But that is not the way that this love/desire must turn out'

*⁺πίπτω   fall, turn out, happen (πεσεῖν, aor.² act. inf.). Note that in lines 1429–30, Artemis will be using the same verb when speaking of Phaedra's love falling namelessly away.

42 ⁺πρᾶγμα, ατος, τό   deed, matter

⁺ἐκ-*⁺φαίνω   bring to light, reveal (κἀκφανήσεται = καὶ ἐκφανήσεται, fut. pass. ind.; *crasis*; tautological, for emphasis?) – 'I will reveal the matter to Theseus, and [it] will be brought to light.' Does this claim coincide with the argument of the play? Why does Euripides make Aphrodite mislead the audience? Does this half-truth have an impact on Aphrodite's characterization?

43 τὸν μὲν ... ἡ δ'   'him on the one hand ... she on the other hand' (47)

ἡμῖν   for our sake (ethical dat. or dat. of feeling to denote the speaker's interest: S #1486; *majestic plural* emphasizing her importance)

πολέμιος (3/2)   (πόλεμος, war) hostile, ill-disposed, adversarial (indicates a public enemy or a political or military foe, while ἐχθρός points to a private enemy; πολέμιον, resolution in 6th position). How does this classification serve Aphrodite? (963)

νεανίας, ου, ὁ   a young man, youth (Hippolytus' youth comes up also in lines 114 and 118) (784)

44 *⁺κτείνω   kill, slay (κτενεῖ, fut. act. indic.)

⁺ἀρά, ἡ   prayer for evil, a curse (ἀραῖσιν, dat. of means: S #1507)

⁺πόντιος (3/2)   of/from/in the sea, ruling the sea

45 ⁺ἄναξ, ἄνακτος, ὁ   lord, king, master (applied to all gods)

⁺Ποσειδῶν, ῶνος, ὁ   Poseidon (similarly to Heracles, Theseus had a twofold parentage, a divine one, Poseidon, and a human one, Aegeus)

ὀπάζω   give, grant, bestow (890)

γέρας, αος, τό   gift, privilege (a predicative noun has no artic.: S #910, 1150) – 'as a gift' (84)

46 ⁺μηδείς, μηδέν   not even one, no one; μηδέν, adv. acc.: not at all (S #1606, 1609)

⁺μάταιος (3/2)   [ᾰ] unmeaning, trifling, in vain, thoughtless

τρίς (adv.)   three times; cf. lines 887–90 (εἰς τρίς, three times in all) [1x *Hipp.*]

⁺εὔχομαι   pray, boast (εὔξασθαι, aor.¹ mid. inf.; appositive inf. standing in apposition to γέρας: S #1987)

⁺θεός, ὁ   god; – 'And his own father will kill the youngster hostile to me with the curses that Poseidon, lord of the sea, granted to Theseus as a gift—up to three times to pray to the god, not in vain.' According to the scholiast, Theseus used up two prayers while escaping from Hades and the Labyrinth, although that is not mentioned in this play.

47 ⁺εὐκλεής, ές   of good fame, glorious, noble (care for her good name and reputation is Phaedra's main concern in this play; cf. lines 329, 423, 489, 687, 1299)

⁺μέν   surely, indeed, really (on μέν *solitarium*, see line 1; stresses the idea of the verb ἀπόλλυται)

⁺ὅμως (adv.)   nevertheless, still; ἀλλ' ὅμως = but still, all the same, nonetheless (note the *hyperbaton* of ἡ δ'... Φαίδρα and the emphatic *enjambment* of Φαίδρα)

ἀπόλλυται   B.: "'prophetic' pres. for fut., as often in oracles . . . to the prescient the future event is already actual" (oracular pres.: S #1882) – 'She, on the other hand, Phaedra, [will die] with her name intact, but die she will.'

48 προ-τῑμάω   honor something/someone above/before another [1x *Hipp.*]

49 ⁺παρ-*⁺ἔχω   hold beside, grant, supply (παρασχεῖν, aor.²
act. inf., with τὸ μή is used after many verbs that denote or imply some
sort of denial or omission. The μή underscores the negated leading verb
οὐ προτιμήσω. When the leading verb itself is negated, as in this case, the
double negative τὸ μὴ οὐ is generally used instead of τὸ μή. The οὐ is ple-
onastic and not translated. The artic. inf. might sometimes denote merely
the result of the omission mentioned in the leading verb: GMT #811; for
negation: S #2745, 2749; G #1616, cf. line 658; μὴ οὐ, *synizesis*.) – 'I will
not consider her misfortune of greater importance *so as not to inflict* on my
enemies . . .'

⁺ἐχθρός (3)   hated, hateful; as subst. ἐχθρός, ὁ, one's enemy (a type of generalizing pl. to deemphasize one's uniqueness by
avoiding specificity: SS 6 §4b, 8–10 §5. Hippolytus is no more than a
representative of her enemies.)

50 ⁺δίκη, ἡ   order, custom, right; atonement, satisfaction,
penalty, retribution

⁺τοσοῦτος, -αύτη, -οῦτο   (demon. pron.) so great, so large

⁺ὥστε (conj.)   so as, so that (with the inf. implies a possible or intended result or tendency rather than actual fact: GMT #587;
S #2011)

μοι   = ἐμοί; enclit. dat. of ἐγώ (S #181a)

⁺καλῶς (adv.)   well

*⁺ἔχω   have, hold; be able to; καλῶς ἔχειν, be well off,
fare well; – 'such a punishment as will satisfy me [as I will fare well
with].'

51 ⁺ἀλλά (conj.)   (neut. pl. of ἄλλος with changed accent) but;
with commands and exhortations: well (here ἀλλά indicates that she breaks
off her former narrative, while the following γάρ introduces "a parenthe-
sis . . . giving a reason for the main sentence, βήσομαι" [B.])

⁺εἰσ-*⁺οράω   look at, look upon (τόνδε is deictic: 'here'; B.:
"equivalent of a pointed finger")

52 ⁺στείχω   walk, go, come, approach (pres. act. ptc. of
attendant circumstance, coincidental with the leading verb, εἰσορῶ; see
ὁράω in line 4; *enjambment*)

θήρα, ἡ   hunting, hunt, eager pursuit of anything (gen. of explanation specifying the meaning of the more general word μό-χθος: S #1322) (233)

⁺μόχθος, ὁ   toil

⁺ἐκ-*⁺λείπω   leave out, forsake, abandon (ἐκλελοιπότα, pf. act. ptc.; in compound verbs, ἐκ can signify 'utterly, completely': S #1688.2; circumstantial ptc. of time; the pf. expresses a present state resulting from a past act: S #1852b1, 2061; GMT #42, 44)

53 Ἱππόλυτον   (emphatic *enjambment* following Hippolytus' description as the son of Theseus, with two ptcs. referring to him; for resolution, see line 11)

⁺ἔξω   + gen.: away, out of (improper prep.; see ἔσω in line 2)

*⁺βαίνω   go (fut. mid. indic.)

⁺τόπος, ὁ   place (the pl. of τόπος is common in Greek and goes back to Homer; this happens when there is an underlying idea of plurality: SS 4 §3) – 'But now that I see Theseus' son approaching, all done with the toil of the hunt, Hippolytus, I will depart from this place.'

πολὺς δ' ἅμ' αὐτῷ προσπόλων ὀπισθόπους
κῶμος λέλακεν, Ἄρτεμιν τιμῶν θεὰν   55
ὕμνοισιν· οὐ γὰρ οἶδ' ἀνεῳγμένας πύλας
Ἅιδου, φάος δὲ λοίσθιον βλέπων τόδε.

54 ⁺ἅμα   + dat.: together with, at the same time with (improper prep., see ἔσω in line 2)

⁺πρόσ-πολος, ὁ/ἡ   (προσ-πολέω, attend, wait upon) servant, attendant (partit. gen.)

ὀπισθό-πους, ὁ/ἡ -πουν, τό; gen. -ποδος   (ὄπισθε, πούς, behind, foot) walking behind, following, attendant (1179)

55 κῶμος, ὁ   a revel; band of revelers; metaph.: any riotous band or company (πολὺς . . . ὀπισθόπους/κῶμος: *hyperbaton* and *enjambment* emphasizing the large band following Hippolytus) [1x *Hipp.*]

*λάσκω   speak loudly, shout, howl (λέλᾱκε, pf.² act. indic.; intensive pf., denoting here an action rather than a present state

resulting from an action, equivalent to a strengthened pres.: S #1947)
[1x *Hipp.*]

56 ὕμνος, ὁ   song, hymn (dat. of means: S #1507; *hyperbaton*) – 'A great riotous throng of attendants follows him closely and shouts along with him, honoring the goddess Artemis with hymns' [1x *Hipp.*]

**οἶδα   see with the mind's eye; know (old pf. used as pres.)

ἀν-*οίγνῦμι   open; metaph.: lay open (ἀνεῳγμένας, pf. pass. supplem. ptc. in indir. disc. after verb of knowing οἶδ': S #2106; *synizesis* of εῳ) (793)

⁺πύλη, ἡ   [ῠ] gate

57 ⁺ Ἅιδης, ου, ὁ   Hades, the god of the Netherworld

⁺φάος, εος, τό   light, daylight (in poetry often signifies life versus the darkness of the Netherworld)

λοίσθιος (3/2)   last (in predicative function 'as his last')
[1x *Hipp.*]

*⁺βλέπω   see, look (pres. act. ptc.; cf. line 56: ἀνεῳγμένας) – 'for he does not know that the gates of Hades lie open, and that he is looking at this day's light as his last.'

Scene B: Lines 58–87

Hippolytus enters straight from the hunt, followed by a band of servants. All of them gather next to Artemis' statue and sing a brief hymn of praise to her. This secondary chorus of servants, brought in for this song, is an addition to the regular Chorus, who enter afterward, and is a rare device in tragedy termed a παραχορήγμα. The song is followed by Hippolytus addressing Artemis, standing in front of her statue, presenting her with a wreath.

    Choral passages admit some Doric forms: ᾱ for η (S introduction C, D, #30, 32, 214.D1): e.g., τὰν = τὴν, ᾷ = ᾗ, σεμνοτάτα = σεμνοτάτη, Λατοῦς = Λητοῦς, καλλίστα = καλλίστη.

ΙΠΠΟΛΥΤΟΣ

ἕπεσθ' ἄδοντες ἕπεσθε	Follow me, follow me singing
τὰν Διὸς οὐρανίαν	of Zeus' heavenly daughter
Ἄρτεμιν, ᾷ μελόμεσθα. 60	Artemis, who takes care of us!

⌣ – – – ⌣ ⌣ – ⌣   enoplian

– ⌣ ⌣ – ⌣ ⌣ –   hemiepes

– ⌣ ⌣ – ⌣ ⌣ – ⌣   hemiepes pendant

58 *⁺ἕπομαι   follow

*ᾄδω   (contracted for ἀείδω) + acc.: praise (pres. act.
ptc. of attendant circumstance/descriptive) [1x *Hipp.*]

59–60 τὰν Διὸς ... Ἄρτεμιν   Names of deities usually omit the artic.,
except when emphatic (S #1137).

οὐράνιος (3/2)   heavenly (166)

*⁺μέλω   be an object of care or concern (ᾆ = ῇ, Doric al-
pha; μελόμεσθα = μελόμεθα, pres. mid. indic.; -μεσθα appears often in
poetry for metrical convenience: S #465d; – 'to whom we are a care')

ΧΟΡΟΣ ΚΥΝΗΓΩΝ

πότνια πότνια σεμνοτάτα,		Lady, Lady, most revered,
Ζηνὸς γένεθλον,		offspring of Zeus,
χαῖρε χαῖρέ μοι, ὦ κόρα		greetings, my greetings, oh
Λατοῦς Ἄρτεμι καὶ Διός,	65	Artemis, daughter of Leto and
καλλίστα πολὺ παρθένων,		Zeus, most beautiful by far of
ἃ μέγαν κατ'οὐρανὸν		maidens, you who dwell in great
ναίεις εὐπατέρειαν αὐ-		heaven, in the court of your noble
λάν, Ζηνὸς πολύχρυσον οἶκον.		father, the house of Zeus adorned in gold.
χαῖρέ μοι, ὦ καλλίστα	70	My greetings, you're the most beautiful, the
καλλίστα τῶν κατ' Ὄλυμπον.		most beautiful of all who dwell in Olympus.

⌣⌣ ⌣ ⌣⌣ ⌣ – ⌣ ⌣ –   glyconic

– – ⌣ ⌣ –   dactylo-epitrite

– ⌣ – ⌣ ⌣ – ⌣ –   glyconic

– – – ⌣ ⌣ – ⌣ –   glyconic

– – – ⌣ ⌣ – ⌣ –   glyconic

– ⌣ – ⌣ – ⌣ –   lecythion

– – – ᴜ ᴜ – – –	glyconic
– – – ᴜ ᴜ – – ᴜ –	hipponactean
– ᴜ ᴜ – – – – –	anapestic dimeter catalectic
– – – – ᴜ ᴜ – –	anapestic dimeter catalectic

62 πότνιᾰ, ἡ lady, mistress, queen (only in nom. and voc.)
[1x *Hipp.*]

63 γένεθλον, τό descent, offspring [1x *Hipp.*]

64 *⁺χαῖρε Greetings! (μοι, ethical dat. or dat. of feeling:
S #1486)

65 ⁺Λητώ, οῦς, ἡ (Doric: Λᾱτώ) Leto, mother of Artemis and
Apollo

66 ⁺πολὺ by far, much, very, many times, often (adv. acc.
here increases the force of the superl. καλλίστα: S #1091, 1609)

⁺παρθένων (partit. gen. following a superl. καλλίστα: S
#1306, 1315)

67 ἃ = ἥ, fem. relat. pron., Doric alpha (antecedent:
ὦ κόρα . . . Ἄρτεμι) – 'you who . . .'

68 εὐ-πᾰτέρεια, ἡ (εὖ, πατήρ) belonging to a noble sire [1x *Hipp.*]
αὐλή, ἡ court, hall [1x *Hipp.*]

69 πολύ-χρῡσος, ον rich in gold, adorned with gold [1x *Hipp.*]
⁺οἶκος, ὁ house, abode, dwelling; home

71 Ὄλυμπος, ὁ Olympus, abode of the gods (τῶν κατ᾽ Ὄλυμπον, noun-making power of the artic. with advs.: S #1153e) [1x *Hipp.*]

Ιπ. σοὶ τόνδε πλεκτὸν στέφανον ἐξ ἀκηράτου
λειμῶνος, ὦ δέσποινα, κοσμήσας φέρω,
ἔνθ᾽ οὔτε ποιμὴν ἀξιοῖ φέρβειν βοτὰ 75
οὔτ᾽ ἦλθέ πω σίδηρος, ἀλλ᾽ ἀκήρατον
μέλισσα λειμῶν᾽ ἠρινὴ διέρχεται,

Αἰδὼς δὲ ποταμίαισι κηπεύει δρόσοις,
ὅσοις διδακτὸν μηδὲν ἀλλ᾽ ἐν τῇ φύσει
τὸ σωφρονεῖν εἴληχεν ἐς τὰ πάντ᾽ ἀεί,   80
τούτοις δρέπεσθαι, τοῖς κακοῖσι δ᾽ οὐ θέμις.
ἀλλ᾽, ὦ φίλη δέσποινα, χρυσέας κόμης
ἀνάδημα δέξαι χειρὸς εὐσεβοῦς ἄπο.
μόνῳ γάρ ἐστι τοῦτ᾽ ἐμοὶ γέρας βροτῶν·
σοὶ καὶ ξύνειμι καὶ λόγοις ἀμείβομαι,   85
κλύων μὲν αὐδῆς, ὄμμα δ᾽ οὐχ ὁρῶν τὸ σόν.
τέλος δὲ κάμψαιμ᾽ ὥσπερ ἠρξάμην βίου.

73 ⁺**πλεκτός** (3)   plaited, twisted, twined

στέφᾰνος, ὁ   wreath, crown (στέφᾰνον, resolution in 6th position) [1x *Hipp.*]

⁺**ἀ-κήρᾱτος** (2)   (ἀ privat., κεράννυμι, mix) unmixed, untouched, pure

74 ⁺**δέσποινα, ἡ**   mistress, lady

⁺**λειμών, ῶνος, ὁ**   (λείβω, pour) any moist grassy place, meadow

κοσμέω   arrange, prepare (κοσμήσας, aor.[1] act. ptc., circumstantial ptc.; see προκόψασα in line 23) [1x *Hipp.*]

*⁺**φέρω**   bring, carry, bear; endure

75 **ἔνθᾰ**   where (correl. relat. adv. taking the place of
οὗ), when (738)

οὔτε ... οὔτε   (⁺οὔτε, and not) neither ... nor

ποιμήν, ένος, ὁ   (ποία, ἡ, grass) herdsman, shepherd [1x *Hipp.*]

ἀξιόω   + inf.: deem right to (1044)

φέρβω   feed [1x *Hipp.*]

βοτόν, τό   (βόσκω, feed, drive to pasture) anything that is
fed, beast [1x *Hipp.*]

76 **πω** (enclit. pcl.)   to this time, yet, ever (mostly with negatives)
(919)

⁺**σίδηρος, ὁ**   iron; anything made of iron, tool, implement,
scythe

77 μέλισσα, ἡ (μέλι, honey) bee (The audience would know that the name "Melissa" was given to the priestesses of Aphrodite. Euripides seems to underscore the conduct of the two goddesses toward humans by this transference of the symbol of virginity from one goddess to her counterpart.) (563)

ἠρῐνός (3) (ἦρ, τό, spring) of spring [1x *Hipp.*]

δι-*⁺ἔρχομαι go through, go across, pass through; – 'For you, lady, I bring this woven garland that I fashioned from an untouched meadow, where neither a shepherd thinks it right to pasture his flocks, nor iron has ever come, but only the spring bee passes through the untouched meadow.' [1x *Hipp.*]

78 ⁺αἰδώς, οὖς, ἡ sense of shame, modesty, reverence

ποτάμιος (3/2) [ᾰ] (ποτᾰμός, ὁ, river) of a river (ποταμίαισι, resolution in 4th position) (127)

κηπεύω tend (a garden) [1x *Hipp.*]

δρόσος, ἡ dewfall, pure water; – 'Reverence/Modesty tends it with streams of river water' (127)

79 διδακτός (3) (διδάσκω, teach) that ought to be taught, taught, instructed (verbal adj.; μηδέν, acc. is rarely found after verbal adjs.: S #1598) [1x *Hipp.*]

⁺φύσις, εως, ἡ [ῠ] (φύω, bring forth) nature, inborn quality; natural origin

80 ⁺σωφρονέω be of sound mind, practice self-control (τὸ σωφρονεῖν, subj. The artic. makes the inf. more prominent as a noun in the sentence: S #2025–6, 2031; GMT #789, 790. The artic. inf. was especially developed in tragedy and favored by Sophocles: SS 245–6 §10. B. on 79–81 comments: "*Sophrosyne* has become in Attic control over one's natural desires and appetites.") Hippolytus and Theseus mirror each other in their views on acquired versus innate *sōphrosynē*, variably translated as 'moderation, virtue, chastity.' In Hippolytus' view, it can be only innate, not taught, as he claims that only the ones who owe nothing to teaching but in whose nature chastity (*to sōphronein*) in all things is inborn can pluck from the untouched meadow (79–80). Theseus likewise berates all humankind who never sought how to teach sense (*phronein*) to those in whom there is no sense (916–20). For both of them, *sōphrosynē* can be only natural. Phaedra, on her part, desires life marked by *sōphrosynē*. Phaedra states that to be right in judgment is agony (247). She hates those who are 'chaste' (*sōphrones*, 413) in word, but in secret engage in a base daring. The Nurse tells Phaedra explicitly that she is not a 'chaste woman' because of her inner thoughts, and therefore no lofty speech would help her, but the only remedy would be the attainment of the man she wants (494–6). In short, all the mortal characters claim to respect a life marked by *sōphrosynē*, but fail to attain it due to their exaggerated conduct. Cf. lines 384–6, σχολή, and Roisman, forthcoming (c).

    *λαγχάνω   obtain by lot; here: 'is allotted, has its place assigned' (εἴληχα, pf.² act. indic.) [1x *Hipp.*]

81   δρέπω   cull, pluck [1x *Hipp.*]

    ⁺θέμις, θέμιστος, ἡ   law, right (agreed upon by common consent or prescription); θέμις [ἐστί], is right; – 'for those who owe nothing to teaching, but sound mind has its place assigned in their inborn nature in all things alike, to these it is allowed to pluck; to the wicked ones it is not allowed.'

82   χρύσεος (3/2)   golden [1x *Hipp.*]

    κόμη, ἡ   hair (1426)

83   ἀνάδημα, ατος, τό   (ἀναδέω, bind up) a headband (ἀνάδημα, resolution of 1st anceps) [1x *Hipp.*]

    *⁺δέχομαι   receive, accept (δέξαι, aor.¹ mid. impv. 2 sg.)

    ⁺χείρ, χειρός, ἡ   hand (declension: S #285, 28)

    ⁺εὐσεβής, ές   pious, reverent

    ⁺ἀπό (prep.)   + gen.: from, off, away from (ἄπο = ἀπό, *anastrophe*) – 'But, dear mistress, accept a headband for your golden hair from a reverent hand.'

85   ἀμείβομαι   answer, reply; converse with (1108)

86   ⁺αὐδή, ἡ   voice

    ⁺ὄμμα, ατος, τό   eye (face by *synecdoche*, the use of a part for the whole)

⁺κλύω   + gen.: hear, give ear, listen to; – 'For I alone
of mortals have this privilege: I consort with you and speak with you,
keep hearing your voice but never seeing your face.'

87 τέλος, εος, τό   an end accomplished, fulfillment of anything
(25)

κάμπτω   bend, bow; turn (κάμψαιμι, aor.[1] act. opt.; opt.
of wish: S #1814; GMT #721.I, 722) [1x *Hipp.*]

⁺ὥσπερ (**conj.**)   just as, as (introduces compar. clause of quality)

*⁺ἄρχω   + gen. or inf.: begin, rule

⁺βίος, ὁ   life, the course of life, lifetime; – 'May I
round the goal of my life as I have begun it.' Hippolytus' wish was
granted: his life 'started,' according to one version, with the abduc-
tion of his mother by Theseus and ended violently because of Theseus
as well.

Scene C: Lines 88–120

The scene consists of stichomythic exchanges between Hippolytus and his
servant. The servant attempts gradually, tactfully, and politely to convince
Hippolytus that mortals ought to honor all the gods, but Hippolytus remains intransigent in his attitude toward Aphrodite.

ΘΕΡΑΠΩΝ

	ἄναξ, θεοὺς γὰρ δεσπότας καλεῖν χρεών,	
	ἆρ' ἄν τί μου δέξαιο βουλεύσαντος εὖ;	
Ἱπ.	καὶ κάρτα γ'· ἦ γὰρ οὐ σοφοὶ φαινοίμεθ' ἄν.	90
Θε.	οἶσθ' οὖν βροτοῖσιν ὃς καθέστηκεν νόμος;	
Ἱπ.	οὐκ οἶδα· τοῦ δὲ καί μ' ἀνιστορεῖς πέρι;	
Θε.	μισεῖν τὸ σεμνὸν καὶ τὸ μὴ πᾶσιν φίλον.	
Ἱπ.	ὀρθῶς γε, τίς δ' οὐ σεμνὸς ἀχθεινὸς βροτῶν;	
Θε.	ἐν δ' εὐπροσηγόροισίν ἐστί τις χάρις;	95
Ἱπ.	πλείστη γε, καὶ κέρδος γε σὺν μόχθῳ βραχεῖ.	
Θε.	ἦ κἂν θεοῖσι ταὐτὸν ἐλπίζεις τόδε;	
Ἱπ.	εἴπερ γε θνητοί θεῶν νόμοισι χρώμεθα.	
Θε.	πῶς οὖν σὺ σεμνὴν δαίμον' οὐ προσεννέπεις;	
Ἱπ.	τίν'; εὐλαβοῦ δὲ μή τί σου σφαλῇ στόμα.	100
Θε.	τήνδ' ἣ πύλαισι σαῖς ἐφέστηκεν πέλας.	

Ιπ.   πρόσωθεν αὐτὴν ἁγνὸς ὢν ἀσπάζομαι.
Θε.   σεμνή γε μέντοι κἀπίσημος ἐν βροτοῖς.   103
Ιπ.   οὐδείς μ' ἀρέσκει νυκτὶ θαυμαστὸς θεῶν.   106
Θε.   τιμαῖσιν, ὦ παῖ, δαιμόνων χρῆσθαι χρεών.   107

88 ⁺δεσπότης, ου, ὁ   master

⁺χρεών   (indecl.) that which must be (ἐστί omitted after
expression of necessity: S #944b) – 'Master, for only gods should be
called lords'

89 ⁺ἆρα (interrog. pcl.)   S #2650: "introduces questions asking merely
for information," with no expectation as to the answer implied (neither *yes*
nor *no*)

ἄν . . . δέξαιο   (aor.¹ mid. opt.; potential opt. with ἄν here is-
sued for a request; pres. and aor. opts. are used for fut. time: S #1824,
1828, 1830)

⁺βουλεύω   take   counsel;   give   counsel;   consider
(μου . . . βουλεύσαντος, possess. gen. or gen. of origin: S #1297, 1298,
following indef. τι, which receives its accent from enclit. μου)

⁺εὖ (adv.)   well; – 'would you take some well-meant advice from me?'

90 ⁺κάρτα (adv.)   very,   very   much   (καί   emphasizes   κάρτα;
when καὶ κάρτα replies to a question, καί is adv.: GP 317.I) – 'most
certainly'

⁺ἦ (affirmative pcl.)   in truth, truly, verily (here strengthened further
by γάρ, whose clause supports the truth of the assertion: 'for otherwise': GP 62–3)

⁺σοφός (3)   clever, wise, learned (subst. adj. without artic.:
G #932.1; S #1021; SS 163 §1; pl. of modesty: S: #1008)

**⁺φαίνω   bring to light; pass.: appear, seem (φαινοίμεθα,
pres. pass. opt.; potential opt. with ἄν: S #1824) – 'Most certainly, for
otherwise I would not appear wise.'

91 *⁺οἶδα   know (οἶσθα, pf. act. indic. 2 sg.: S #794)

⁺οὖν (conj.)   so now, therefore, then, in fact, at all events
(inferential: marks transition to a new thought: S #2964; GP 426)

καθ-*⁺ἵστημι   set down, establish (καθέστηκε, pf. act. indic. 3 sg.; intrans.: 'established') [1x *Hipp.*]

⁺νόμος, ὁ   (νέμω, assign) custom, convention, law (inverse attraction in which an antecedent is attracted to the case of the relat.: νόμος has been attracted to the case of the relat. pron.; properly: οἶσθα νόμον ὅς . . .: S #2533) – 'Now, you know the rule that is established among mortals?'

92 τοῦ   = τίνος (interrog. pron.: S #334, in *hyperbaton* with περί)

ἀν-ιστορέω   make an inquiry, ask (καί stresses the verb, 'exactly') [1x *Hipp.*]

⁺περί (prep.)   + gen.: about, in regard to (πέρι, *anastrophe*) – 'No, I don't. What are you asking me about exactly?'

93 ⁺μῖσέω   hate

⁺πᾶς, πᾶσα, πᾶν   all, every, everything

⁺φίλος (3)   loved, dear, friendly, friend (the answer explains the above νόμος ἐστὶ) – 'to hate what is haughty and not friendly to all'

94 ὀρθῶς (adv.)   rightly, justly, truly, really (1170)

⁺γε   at least, at any rate, indeed, certainly (postpos. intensive pcl., usually untranslatable, but often rendered by intonation; in conversation to be translated 'yes'; cf. line 96: GP 115; S #221; here it emphasizes ὀρθῶς)

ἀχθεινός (3)   (ἄχθος, grief) burdensome, oppressive (οὐ goes with ἀχθεινός; βροτῶν, partit. gen.) – 'Yes, right, for what mortal who is haughty does not give pain?' [1x *Hipp.*]

95 εὐ-προσήγορος (2)   of easy address, affable, courteous [1x *Hipp.*]

⁺χάρις, ἡ   [ᾰ] grace, favor; delight (gen. χάριτος, dat. χάριτι, acc. χάριν; declension: S #257) – 'And is there delight in being affable?'

96 ⁺πλεῖστος (3)   very much, very great, most (superl. of πολύς; see on γε in line 94) (397) κέρδος, εος, τό   gain, profit [1x *Hipp.*]

μόχθος, ὁ   toil, hardship [1x *Hipp.*]

⁺βραχύς, εῖα, ύ   short, brief; – 'Very much so, and profit too,
with little effort'

97 ἦ   untranslatable interrog. pcl. asking for information without implying anything about the answer expected (*yes* or *no*):
S #2650

κἄν   = καὶ ἐν, *crasis*; ταὐτὸν = τὸ αὐτὸν, *crasis*

ἐλπίζω   hope, expect (takes the inf., which here needs
to be supplied: S #2580, 1868a: ταὐτὸν εἶναι) – 'Do you think/expect
this thing holds among the gods too?' [1x *Hipp.*]

98 εἴπερ γε   if indeed, if really (501)

⁺θνητός (3/2)   mortal (θεῶν, *synizesis*)

*⁺χράομαι   + dat.: use, experience; engage in, practice; –
'Yes, if we mortals use the laws of the gods.'

99 ⁺πῶς (interrog. adv.)   how? in what way/manner? (S #346)

προσ-εννέπω   address; – 'Why then don't you address a high/
solemn goddess?' (793)

100 ⁺τίς, τί (interrog. pron.)   who, which, what (declension: S #334)

εὐλαβέομαι   be cautious; beware of (here takes the structure
of verbs of fearing, μή with subjv. in 1st sequence, +σφαλῇ, aor.¹ pass.
subjv.: S #2210b, 225; GMT #365) [1x *Hipp.*]

⁺τὶς, τὶ (indef. pron.)   anyone, someone; anything, something (declension: S #334; τι is adv., 'in some way')

⁺στόμα, ατος, τό   mouth, tongue; – 'Whom? Be careful lest your
tongue slip in some way.'

101 ⁺ἐφ-*⁺ίστημι   intrans. in pf.: stand (ἐφέστηκε, pf. act. indic.) – 'This one here, who stands near your gates.'

⁺πέλας   near, close (improper prep., mostly + gen. but
also + dat.; see +ἔσω in line 2)

102 ⁺πρόσωθεν (adv.) from afar, from long ago

ἀσπάζομαι greet (emphatic *hyperbaton* προσώθεν . . . ἀσπάζομαι; ὤν, causal ptc.: S #2064) – 'This one I greet from afar because I am pure.' [1x *Hipp.*]

103 ⁺μέντοι (μέν +τοι) as an asseverative pcl.: certainly, surely, of course; as an adversative pcl.: however, yet

ἐπί-σημος, ον distinguished, famous, renowned (κἀπίσημος = καὶ ἐπίσημος) – 'Yet she is revered and renowned among mortals.' [1x *Hipp.*]

106 ἀρέσκω + acc.: conciliate, propitiate, appease (μ'= με; in tragedy only short vowels are elided: S #70, 74) (184)

θαυμαστός (3) wondered at, wonderful, admirable (supply ἐστί) (278)

⁺νύξ, νυκτός, ἡ night; – 'none of the gods that are worshiped at night pleases me.'

107 ⁺τῑμή, ἡ honor, esteem (δαιμόνων, obj. gen.: S #1328, 1331) – 'Oh child, it is necessary to engage with the honors [for the gods] due to gods.'

Ιπ.	ἄλλοισιν ἄλλος θεῶν κἀνθρώπων μέλει.	104
Θε.	εὐδαιμονοίης, νοῦν ἔχων ὅσον σε δεῖ.	105
Ιπ.	χωρεῖτ', ὀπαδοί, καὶ παρελθόντες δόμους	108
	σίτων μέλεσθε· τερπνὸν ἐκ κυναγίας	
	τράπεζα πλήρης· καὶ καταψήχειν χρεὼν	110
	ἵππους, ὅπως ἂν ἅρμασι ζεύξας ὕπο	
	βορᾶς κορεσθεὶς γυμνάσω τὰ πρόσφορα.	
	τὴν σὴν δὲ Κύπριν πόλλ' ἐγὼ χαίρειν λέγω.	

Hippolytus and his attendants exit into the palace.

Θε.	ἡμεῖς δέ, τοὺς νέους γὰρ οὐ μιμητέον	
	φρονοῦντας οὕτως, ὡς πρέπει δούλοις λέγειν	115
	προσευχόμεσθα τοῖσι σοῖς ἀγάλμασιν,	
	δέσποινα Κύπρι· χρὴ δὲ συγγνώμην ἔχειν.	
	εἴ τίς σ' ὑφ' ἥβης σπλάγχνον ἔντονον φέρων	

μάταια βάζει, μὴ δόκει τούτου κλυεῖν·
σοφωτέρους γὰρ χρὴ βροτῶν εἶναι θεούς.   120

104 ⁺μέλει   impersonal use with dat.: it is a care (to me)

⁺ἄλλος (3)   another, other (ἄλλοισιν ἄλλος, *figura etymologica*)

θεῶν   *synizesis* (κἀνθρώπων = καὶ ἀνθρώπων) – '[A different god pleases different people] Different men like different gods.'

105 εὐδαιμονέω   be prosperous, well off, happy (opt. of wish, no introductory pcl.: S #1814; GMT #721.1, 722) [1x *Hipp.*]

⁺νοῦς, νοῦ, ὁ   mind, thought; – 'May you have good fortune and the good sense you need!'

108 ⁺χωρέω   make room for another, give way, go forward, advance, go, come

ὀπᾱδός, ὁ   (Doric for Attic ὀπηδός) an attendant (1151)

παρ-*⁺έρχομαι   arrive at, come to (παρελθόντες, aor.² act. ptc. usually antecedent to the leading verb, μέλεσθε: S #1872c; see line 23) [1x *Hipp.*]

109 σῖτος, ὁ   (irreg. pl. σῖτα, τά) food, meal; – 'Go, attendants, enter the house and take care of the meal' (953)

⁺τερπνός (3)   delightful, pleasant, agreeable, pleasurable, cheering (supply ἐστί)

κῡνᾱγία, ἡ   (Doric for Attic κῡνηγία, ἡ) hunt [1x *Hipp.*]

110 τράπεζα, ἡ   [ᾰ] table [1x *Hipp.*]

πλήρης, ες   full, complete; full of + gen.; – 'after a hunt, a full table is pleasurable' [1x *Hipp.*]

κατα-ψήχω   rub down, grate down [1x *Eur.*]

111 ⁺ἵππος, ὁ, ἡ   horse (ἵππους is governed by both ζεύξας and γυμνάσω; emphatic *enjambment* underscoring Hippolytus' obsession with horses and hunting)

⁺ὅπως (conj.)   so that (opens final clause here with aor.¹
subjv., γυμνάσω; ἄν may or may not be added to a purpose clause
without affecting meaning: S #2193, 2196; GMT #325, 328)

⁺ἅρμα, ατος, τό   chariot

ζεύγνῡμι   yoke (ζεύξας, aor.¹ act. ptc. of time) (549)

⁺ὑπό   + dat.: under (ὕπο, *anastrophe*)

112 βορά, ἡ   food, meat (952)

κορέννυμι   satisfy, have one's fill (κορεσθείς, aor.¹ pass.
ptc. of time) [1x Eur.]

γυμνάζω   train, exercise [1x *Hipp.*]

πρόσ-φορος, ον   convenient, suited to; τὰ πρόσφορα as adv.:
fitly; – 'and it is necessary to rub the horses down, so that once I have
eaten my fill I may yoke them to my chariot and give them their proper
exercise.' (1362)

113 *⁺χαίρειν   with adv. acc. πολλ(ά); see μηδέν in line 46
(note the antithesis between the contemptuous τὴν σὴν and ἐγώ; a similarly
dismissive tone is found in Theseus' words in line 1059) – 'And as for your
Cypris, I bid her long farewell.'

114 ⁺νέος (3/2)   young; unexpected, untoward (subst. use of artic. with adj.: S #1153a) – 'the young'

μιμητέος (3)   to be imitated (μιμέομαι, imitate; verbal adj.:
S #358.2b; neut. sg.: 'one must imitate'; supply ἐστί) [1x *Hipp.*]

115 ⁺οὕτως (adv.)   in this way, in this manner, thus

πρέπει   it is fitting (with inf. *⁺λέγειν, as subj.:
S #1984, 1985) [1x *Hipp.*]

δοῦλος, ὁ   slave (1249)

116 προσεύχομαι   offer prayers; worship (προσευχόμεσθα = προ-
σευχόμεθα) [1x *Hipp.*]

⁺ἄγαλμα, ατος, τό   image of a god as an object of worship; – 'But
we/I—for young people thinking in this way should not be imitated—
offer prayers to your statue, in words that befit slaves, Lady Cypris'

117 συγγνώμη, ἡ   forgiveness; – 'for [it is necessary to have for-
giveness] one should forgive' (1326)

118 ἥβη, ἡ   youth [1x *Hipp.*]

σπλάγχνον, τό   internal parts; heart, seat of feelings, one's
inward nature (*⁺φέρων, ptc. of attendant circumstance, coincidental
with βάζει; see ὁράω in line 4) [1x *Hipp.*]

ἔντονος, ον   strained; intense, vehement [1x *Hipp.*]

119 ⁺μάταια   acc. neut. pl. as adv. acc. of manner or internal
obj. (S #1554a, 1606, 1608)

βάζω   speak (with double acc.: σε . . . μάταια) – 'tells
nonsense about you' (Stockert, followed by Kovacs, prefers κλυεῖν,
aor.² inf. act., instead of the pres. inf. here and in lines 270, 344, 485,
904, 912, 1202, 1238, most probably to emphasize the momentary aspect of the verb 'to hear.' Murray, B., Diggle, and Halleran print κλύ-
ειν.) [1x *Hipp.*]

⁺δοκέω   form an opinion, think, imagine; intrans.:
seem, appear (pres. act. impv. 2 sg.; personal construction: S #1983)
– 'If someone having an intense spirit due to his youth tells nonsense
about you, pretend not to hear him.'

120 βροτῶν   gen. of comparison (S #1431) – 'For it is necessary that gods be wiser than mortals.'

The servant leaves the stage.

Parodos 121–69

The Chorus enter: fifteen highborn young married women of Troezen enter the
stage. Although not explicitly stated, they have come in hope of hearing the
latest news of Phaedra's illness. No one knows what this illness is, but we learn
that Phaedra has been in bed for three days and has eaten nothing. The cause
for this conduct is unknown to the women but well known to the audience
from the prologue, which produces tragic irony in the second half of the song.

The ode consists of two strophic stanzas and an epode. Often the Chorus come in to anapests, a marching rhythm. Here they dance in complex
lyric meters.

ΧΟΡΟΣ

Ὠκεανοῦ τις ὕδωρ στάζουσα πέτρα λέγεται, [στρ. α There is said to be a rock
                                                        dripping water
βαπτὰν κάλπισι πα-   from Oceanus, pouring forth
                                                        over its steep bank
    γὰν ῥυτὰν προιεῖσα κρημνῶν.   a running stream where
                                                        pitchers are dipped.

τόθι μοί τις ἦν φίλα   125   My friend was there
πορφύρεα φάρεα   soaking her crimson clothes
ποταμίᾳ δρόσῳ   in the river water
τέγγουσα, θερμᾶς δ᾽ ἐπὶ νῶτα πέτρας   and laying them down
                                                        on the back of

εὐαλίου κατέβαλλ᾽· ὅθεν μοι   a hot, well-sunned rock;
                                                        [it was] from there that

πρῶτα φάτις ἦλθε δεσποίνας,   130   a word about my mistress
                                                        first came to me.

121–30 = 131–40

1	– ◡ ◡ – ◡ ◡ – – – ◡ ◡ – ◡ –	choerilean (= B.)
2	– – – ◡ ◡ –	hemiepes with substitution for the first double short
3	– – – ◡ ◡ – ◡ – –	hipponactean
4	◡ ◡ – ◡ – ◡ –	telesillean?
5	– ◡ – ◡ –	hypodochmiac
6	◡ ◡ ◡ – ◡ –	hypodochmiac
7	– – ◡ – – ◡ ◡ – ◡ – –	iamb & aristophanean
8	– – ◡ – ◡ ◡ – ◡ – –	trochee & pherecratean
9	– – ◡ ◡ – ◡ – – –	telesillean + spondee

122 Ὠκεανός, ὁ   Oceanus. In Greek geography going back to
Homer, Oceanus was a river that went around the entire known world (gen.
of source/origin: S #1298). [1x *Hipp.*]

⁺ὕδωρ, ατος, τό   water

στάζω   fall drop by drop, drip (στάζουσα, ptc. of attendant circumstance, coincidental with the leading verb, λέγεται; see
ὁράω in line 4) (526)

τις ... ⁺πέτρα   'a rock' (a nom. in a personal construction
with λέγεται, supply εἶναι: S #1982a) [– 'A rock dripping water of
Oceanus is talked about']

123 βαπτός (3)   (= βαπτήν, Doric alpha) dipped [1x *Hipp.*]

κάλπις, ιδος, ἡ   pitcher [1x *Hipp.*]

124 πηγή, ἡ   (= πηγήν) spring, well [1x *Hipp.*]

ῥῦτός (3/2)   (= ῥυτήν, ῥέω, flow) flowing, running, fluid
(653)

προ-*ίημι   + gen.: send forth from, pour forth (προ-ιεῖσα,
pres. act. ptc.; see στάζουσα) [1x *Hipp.*]

κρημνός, ὁ   beetling crag, steep bank or edge [1x *Hipp.*]

125 τόθι (adv.)   there, at that place (μοί, dat. of possess.:
S #1476) [B.: 1x extant tragedy]

127 ⁺πορφύρεος (3)   purple, dark, crimson (πορφύρεα, *synizesis*)

φᾶρος/φάρος, εος, τό   cloth (B.: choral lyric spells φάρεα uncontracted even when it scans -εα contracted in *synizesis*) (133)

ποτάμιος (3/2)   [ᾰ] (ποτᾰμός, ὁ, river) of a river (78)

δρόσος, ἡ   dewfall, pure water (78)

128 ⁺τέγγω   wet, soak; soften, melt (τέγγουσα, ptc. of attendant circumstance; see στάζουσα in line 121) (68)

θερμός (3/2)   warm, hot [1x *Hipp.*]

νῶτον, τό   back [1x *Hipp.*]

129 εὐήλιος, ον   well-sunned, sunny, warm [1x *Hipp.*]

κατα-*βάλλω   lay down, put down [1x *Hipp.*]

⁺ὅθεν (adv.)   from where, whence

130 ⁺πρῶτος (3)   (πρῶτα = πρώτη, Doric alpha) first

φάτις, ἡ   (φημί) speech, report (only in nom., voc., and
acc.; δεσποίνας, obj. gen.) (579)

τειρομέναν νοσερᾷ κοίτᾳ δέμας   [ἀντ. α   that wasting away on a bed
    ἐντὸς ἔχειν   of sickness,
οἴκων, λεπτὰ δὲ φά-   she keeps her body within
                                              the house,

ρη ξανθὰν κεφαλὰν σκιάζειν·   and fine cloths shade her
                                                blond head;
τριτάταν δέ νιν κλύω   135   and I hear that for three
                                                days now,
τάνδ᾽ ἀβρωσίᾳ   she keeps her body pure
στόματος ἀμέραν   of Demeter's grain by
Δάματρος ἀκτᾶς δέμας ἁγνὸν ἴσχειν,   starving herself, wishing on
κρυπτῷ πάθει θανάτου θέλουσαν   account of a secret grief to
                                                run ashore
κέλσαι ποτὶ τέρμα δύστανον.   140   toward the wretched end
                                                that is death.

131 **τείρω**   wear out; pass.: worn out (τειρομέναν =
τειρομένην, Doric alpha; ptc. of attendant circumstance, coincidental with
ἦλθε, see ὁράω in line 4; indir. disc. after φάτις in acc. and inf. construction: [αὐτὴν] τειρομέναν . . . ἔχειν) [1x *Hipp.*]

   νοσερός (3)   (νόσος, ὁ, illness) sickly, ill (179)

   ⁺κοιτή, ἡ   bed

   ⁺δέμας, τό   body (only in nom. and acc.)

   ἐντός   + gen.: inside with, at the same time with (improper prep.; see ἔσω in line 2) [1x *Hipp.*]

132 **⁺οἶκος, ὁ**   house, abode, dwelling (pl. often stands for a
single house)

   λεπτός (3)   delicate, fine (indir. disc. in acc. and inf. construction: λεπτά . . . φάρη . . . σκιάζειν) [1x *Hipp.*]

134 **ξανθός** (3)   yellow, golden, blond (220)

   ⁺κεφαλή, ἡ   head

   σκιάζω   shade, overshadow [1x *Hipp.*]

135 **τρίτᾰτος** (3)   the third (poetically lengthened form of τρίτος; τριτάταν [= τριτάτην] . . . τάνδ᾽ . . . ἀμέραν, acc. of extent of time:
S #1582–3; νιν . . . ἴσχειν, acc. and inf.; *hyperbaton* x2) [1x *Hipp.*]

136 **ἀ-βρωσία, ἡ**   (ἀ privat. + βρῶσις, εως, eating) want of food,
fasting, starving, not eating (dat. of means: S #1507; στόματος, subj. gen.:
S #1330) – 'by means of starving of her mouth'

138   Δημήτηρ, τερος/τρος, ἡ   (= Δήμητρος) Demeter, goddess of ag-
riculture, in particular of grain (gen. of explanation/apposition: S #1322)
[1x *Hipp.*]

ἀκτή, ἡ   meal and bread made of it, grain (ἀκτᾶς =
ἀκτῆς; gen. of separation: S #1427) [1x *Hipp.*]

ἴσχω   hold, check, restrain; stop (a form of *+ἔχω,
found only in pres. and impf.) [1x *Hipp.*]

139   κρυπτός (3)   hidden, secret (154)

⁺πάθος, εος, τό   (παθεῖν, suffer) suffering, misfortune, calamity
(dat. of cause: S #1517)

⁺θάνᾰτος, ὁ   (θανεῖν, die) death (gen. of explanation:
S #1322)

⁺θέλω   = *+ἐθέλω, poetic; will, desire, wish (θέλουσαν, ptc. of attendant circumstance, coincidental with the leading verb,
see ὁράω in line 4; θέλουσαν . . . κέλσαι, continuation of the indir.
disc. in acc. and inf.)

140   *κέλλω, ἔκελσα   push ashore, reach a haven (κέλσαι, aor.¹ act.
inf.) [1x *Hipp.*]

ποτί   (Doric for ⁺πρός + acc. expresses motion: toward, to, upon) [1x *Hipp.*]

⁺τέρμα, ατος, τό   end, goal, finish line

⁺δύστηνος (2)   (δύστανον = δύστηνον, Doric alpha) wretched,
unhappy, unfortunate

†σὺ γὰρ† ἔνθεος, ὦ κούρα,   [στρ. β   Are you wandering, girl,
εἴτ' ἐκ Πανὸς εἴθ' Ἑκάτας   possessed by Pan, or Hecate,
ἢ σεμνῶν Κορυβάντων φοι-   or by holy Corybantes,
   τᾷς ἢ ματρὸς ὀρείας;   or the mountain mother?
†σὺ δ'† ἀμφὶ τὰν πολύθη-   145   [Or] are you wasting away be-
                                                 cause of
ρον Δίκτυνναν ἀμπλακίαις   offenses against Diktynna of
                                                 many animals,
ἀνίερος ἀθύτων πελάνων τρύχῃ;   being unholy due to unoffered
                                                 cereal?

φοιτᾷ γὰρ καὶ διὰ Λίμ-	For she also roams through the lagoon
νας χέρσον θ᾽ ὕπερ πελάγους	and across the dry land of the sea
δίναις ἐν νοτίαις ἅλμας. 150	and among the wet eddies of the brine.

141 †σὺ γὰρ†   (the words σὺ γὰρ are unmetrical; they scan as ⌣ ⌣, but – ⌣ is needed)

     ἔν-θεος (2)   inspired, frenzied (Ionic κούρη = κόρη)
     [1x *Hipp.*]

142 εἴτε . . . εἴτε   either . . . or [1x *Hipp.*]

     Πάν, Πανός, ὁ   Pan, Arcadian god of the wildwood [1x *Hipp.*]

     Ἑκάτη, ἡ   Hecate, goddess of the Netherworld (= Ἑκά-
     της) [1x *Hipp.*]

143 Κορύβᾱς, αντος, ὁ [ῠ]   Corybant priest of Kybele in Phrygia.
[1x *Hipp.*]

144 ⁺φοιτάω   go to and fro, roam wildly about, wander. Yet again Euripides connects the two goddesses by using the same verb in lines 447–8 for Aphrodite's 'roaming' through the air. Cf. lines 2, 41, 77.

     ⁺μήτηρ, μητρός, ἡ   mother (syncopated noun: S #262)

     ὄρειος (3/2)   (ὄρος, τό, mountain) of the mountain (1127)

145 ⁺ἀμφί (prep.)   + acc.: around, in attendance on, against

     πολύ-θηρος (2)   accompanied by many animals [1x *Hipp.*]

     Δίκτῡνα/Δίκτυννα, ἡ   Diktynna, Cretan divinity of wildwood, identified with Artemis (1130)

146 ⁺ἀμπλακία, ἡ   error, offense (dat. of cause: S #1517)

147 ἀν-ίερος (2)   (ἀ privat., ἱερός, holy) unholy, impious (with gen. of accountability ἀθύτων πελανῶν: S #1425) – 'unholy because of the unsacrificed holy batter/porridge' (B.: "a kind of batter or porridge poured on the altar in sacrifice and burnt") [1x *Hipp.*]

ἄ-θῦτος (2) (ἀ privat., θύω, sacrifice) not offered in sacrifice [1x Eur.]

πέλᾰνος, ὁ libation of honey, meal, and oil [1x *Hipp.*]

τρύχω pass.: be worn out (τρύχῃ, pres. pass. indic.
2 sg.) [1x *Hipp.*]

148 Λίμνη, ἡ the Lagoon (= Λίμνης, a lagoon just north of
Troezen, where Artemis was worshiped. Artemis had a temple on the lagoon's shore with the cult title Artemis Saronia.) (744)

⁺διά (prep.) + gen. or acc.: through, throughout

149 ⁺τε (enclit. pcl.) and

χέρσος, ἡ dry land [1x *Hipp.*]

⁺ὑπέρ (prep.) + gen.: beyond, on behalf of

πέλαγος, εος, τό sea, high sea, open sea (822)

150 δίνη, ἡ eddy [1x *Hipp.*]

νότιος (3/2) wet, damp, watery [1x *Hipp.*]

⁺ἅλμη, ἡ water of the sea, brine

ἢ πόσιν, τὸν Ἐρεχθειδᾶν	[ἀντ. β	Or your husband, the leader of the sons of
ἀρχαγόν, τὸν εὐπατρίδαν		Erechtheus, the nobly born,
ποιμαίνει τις ἐν οἴκοις κρυπ-		does someone in the house shepherd [him]
τᾷ κοίτᾳ λεχέων σῶν;		in a bedding secret from your marriage?
ἢ ναυβάτας τις ἔπλευ-	155	Or has some mariner that set forth from
σεν Κρήτας ἔξορμος ἀνὴρ		Crete sailed into the harbor most
λιμένα τὸν εὐξεινότατον ναύταις		welcoming to sailors
φήμαν πέμπων βασιλεί-		bearing news to the queen,
ᾳ, λύπᾳ δ' ὑπὲρ παθέων		and by grief over her troubles
εὐναία δέδεται ψυχά;	160	her spirit is bound bedfast?

141–50 = 151–60

– ∪ – ∪ ∪ – – –	glyconic [with *anaclasis*]
– – – ∪ – ∪ ∪ –	wilamowitzian/glyconic [with *anaclasis*]
– – – ∪ ∪ – – –	glyconic – – +
– – – ∪ ∪ – –	pherecratean
– – ∪ – ∪ ∪ –	Λ wilamowitzian +
– – – <u>∪</u> – ∪ ∪ –	wilamowitzian
∪ ∪∪ ∪ <u>∪∪</u> – ∪ ∪ – – –	wilamowitzian + spondee
– – – – ∪ ∪ –	Λ wilamowitzian +
– – – ∪ – ∪ ∪ –	wilamowitzian
– – – ∪ ∪ – – –	glyconic – –

151 ⁺ἤ (conj.)   disjunctive: or; interrog.: ἤ . . . ἤ, either . . . or, whether . . . or; compar.: than

πόσῐς, ιος, ὁ   husband [1x *Hipp.*]

Ἐρεχθεῖδαι, οἱ   Erechtheidae are Athenians, descendants of Erechtheus, legendary early king of Athens [1x *Hipp.*]

152 ἀρχηγός, ον   (ἄρχω, begin; ἡγέομαι, lead) beginning, originating, leading; as a subst.: leader (subst. artic.: see νέος in line 114) (881)

εὐ-πατρίδης, ου, ὁ   of a noble father (1283)

153 ποιμαίνω   shepherd, guide (κρυπτᾷ κοίτᾳ, dat. of means: S #1507) – 'by means of a secret bed [i.e., affair].' Theseus was known for his philandering, but what image of him is conveyed here? Does the text assign him agency in the affair? [1x *Hipp.*]

154 ⁺λέχος, εος, τό   marriage bed, a marriage

155 ⁺ναυ-βάτης, ου, ὁ   [ᾰ] (ναῦς, βαίνω) seaman, mariner, sailor

*πλέω   sail (aor.¹ act. indic.) [1x *Hipp.*]

156 Κρήτη, ἡ   Crete (= Κρήτης) [1x *Hipp.*]

ἔξ-ορμος (2)   sailing from a harbor, embarking for [1x *Hipp.*]

157 λῐμήν, ένος, ὁ   harbor, haven [1x *Hipp.*]

εὔ-ξεινος (2)   (εὖ, ξένος) hospitable (λιμένα τὸν εὐξεινότατον, attr. position of the artic.: S #1159) [1x *Hipp.*]

ναύτης, ου, ὁ   (ναῦς, ship) seaman, sailor (745)

158 ⁺φήμη, ἡ   rumor, news, voice, story

*⁺πέμπω   send (πέμπων, ptc. of attendant circumstance,
coincidental with ἔπλευσε; see ὁράω in line 4) – 'sending/bearing
news'

βασίλεια, ἡ   queen (175)

159 λύπη, ἡ   pain, sorrow (dat. of cause)

160 εὐναῖος (3)   in one's bed, on one's couch [1x *Hipp.*]

*δέω   bind, tie, fasten (1237)

⁺ψῡχή, ἡ   spirit, soul, life

φιλεῖ δὲ τᾷ δυστρόπῳ γυναικῶν   [ἐπῳδ Wretched helplessness
stemming

ἁρμονίᾳ κακὰ   from birth pangs and
irrationality

δύστανος ἀμηχανία συνοικεῖν   tends to dwell together
ὠδίνων τε καὶ ἀφροσύνας.   with women's awkward
disposition.

δι' ἐμᾶς ᾖξέν ποτε νηδύος ἅδ'   165 Through my womb this chill
breeze

αὔρα· τὰν δ' εὔλοχον οὐρανίαν   once darted; I kept calling on
the heavenly

τόξων μεδέουσαν ἄϋτευν   easer of childbirth, the mistress of the arrows,

Ἄρτεμιν, καί μοι πολυζήλωτος αἰεὶ   Artemis, and causing me to
be envied, with

σὺν θεοῖσι φοιτᾷ.   gods' help, she always comes
to me.

161–9

⌣ – ⌣ – – ⌣ – ⌣ – –   iambs + ithyphallic
– ⌣ ⌣ – ⌣ –   dodrans

− − ◡ ◡ − ◡ ◡ − ◡ − −	wilamowitzian & bacchiac
− − − ◡ ◡ − ◡ ◡ −	3½ dactyls
◡ ◡ − − − ◡ ◡ − ◡ ◡ −	2 anapests
− − − − ◡ ◡ − ◡ ◡ −	2 anapests
− − ◡ ◡ − ◡ ◡ − −	2 anapests catalectic
− ◡ − − − − ◡ − − − ◡ − −	3 trochees
− ◡ − ◡ − −	ithyphallic

161 φιλέω love, treat affectionately; 3 sg.: be wont to, tend to, be accustomed to (315)

δύσ-τροπος (2) (δυσ-, τρέπω) hard to turn or direct; stubborn, wayward [1x *Hipp.*]

⁺γῠνή, ἡ woman (gen. γυναικός, acc. γυναῖκα, voc. γύναι; pl. γυναῖκες, γυναικῶν, etc.)

162 ἁρμονία, ἡ (ἁρμόζω, fit together) fitting together, composition; harmony, agreement [1x *Hipp.*]

163 ἀ-μηχᾰνία, ἡ want of means, helplessness, incapacity [1x *Hipp.*]

συν-⁺οικέω + dat.: dwell together, live together with (1220)

164 ὠδίς, ῖνος, ἡ pain of childbirth (the gens. ὠδίνων τε καὶ ἀφροσύνας are the source of ἀμηχανία) – 'wretched helplessness originating in birth pangs and irrationality' [1x *Hipp.*]

ἀφροσύνη, ἡ (= ἀφροσύνης) folly, thoughtlessness [1x *Hipp.*]

165 ᾁσσω shoot, dart, leap, rush (ᾖξέν, aor.[1] act. indic.) (1351)

νηδύς, ύος, ἡ womb [1x *Hipp.*]

166 αὔρα, ἡ wind, chill, breeze (ἤδ' αὔρα) [1x *Hipp.*]

εὔ-λοχος (2) helping in childbirth [1x Eur.]

οὐράνιος (3/2) heavenly (59)

167 τόξον, τό in pl.: bow and arrows, arrows (1422)

μεδέουσα   (fem. of μέδων) ruler (τὴν ... μεδέουσαν ...
Ἄρτεμιν) [1x *Hipp.*]

ἀϋτέω   [ῡ] cry, shout, call aloud, call to (ἀϋτευν, epic
impf.; verb used only in pres. and impf.) [1x *Hipp.*]

168 πολυ-ζήλωτος (2)   much envied/revered, much desired [1x Eur.]
σὺν θεοῖσι   with gods' help

The double doors of the palace open and the Nurse emerges, followed by serving-women who carry Phaedra lying on a bed.

First Episode Lines 170–524

Phaedra dominates this lengthy episode, first by her silence, then by her delirious expressions, and finally with her admission to being infatuated with Hippolytus.

Structurally, the episode is divided into two main scenes by a choral stanza (362–72), which is answered by Phaedra much later in the play (669–79). This unusual belated strophic response reflects the tension of this part of the play, which focuses not only on Phaedra's admission of her passion for her stepson, but also on Hippolytus' reaction to this revelation. The two scenes are not of equal length: Scene A has 192 lines (170–361), and Scene B has 152 lines (373–524).

The episode consists of different rhythms and meters. In lines 170–266, the Chorus, Phaedra, and the Nurse chant in anapests, marking a higher emotional register. It is mostly anapestic dimeter (⌣ ⌣ − − ⌣ ⌣ − ‖ ⌣ ⌣ − − ⌣ −). A long − can substitute for two shorts, ⌣ ⌣, but ⌣ ⌣ ⌣ ⌣ is avoided. Monometer lines (⌣ ⌣ − − ⌣ ⌣ −) occur at times (174, 180, 185, 204, 212, 217, 221, 242, 251, 260, 265). Speeches often end with a shortened form of the dimeter, called "paroemiac": ⌣ ⌣ − − ⌣ ⌣ − ‖ ⌣ ⌣ − − (175, 190, 197, 207, 238, 249, 266). The rest of the episode returns to spoken iambic trimeters, whether in speeches or *stichomythia*, with the exception of the choral ode.

The episode starts with the Nurse's reflections, followed by Phaedra's 'delirium' (198–266), in which she expresses wishes incomprehensible to the Nurse. The following *stichomythia* between the Chorus leader and the Nurse focuses on the nature and cause of Phaedra's sickness (267–83). Next, the Nurse addresses Phaedra in a speech in which she points out that in the event of Phaedra's death, Hippolytus will rule over her sons (284–310). In the *stichomythia* that ensues between Phaedra and the Nurse, Phaedra finally reveals her passion for Hippolytus (311–61). The Chorus react in a lyric stanza expressing their shock at the revelation (362–72), and Phaedra follows with a longish reasoned speech on how she has responded to her passion and about her resolve to die (373–430). After a brief choral comment, the Nurse presents her counterarguments, attempting to convince Phaedra to treat her love as a natural phenomenon (433–81). In the dialogue that follows another brief choral comment, and in the *stichomythia* that develops between the two women, the Nurse convinces Phaedra to allow her to try to remedy her infatuation (486–524).

Scene A: Lines 170–361

The Chorus leader announces in anapests the entrance of the Nurse and Phaedra from the palace.

– – – ἀλλ᾽ ἥδε τροφὸς γεραιὰ πρὸ θυρῶν	170
τήνδε κομίζουσ᾽ ἔξω μελάθρων.	
[στυγνὸν δ᾽ ὀφρύων νέφος αὐξάνεται.]	
τί ποτ᾽ ἐστὶ μαθεῖν ἔραται ψυχή,	
τί δεδήληται	
δέμας ἀλλόχροον βασιλείας.	175

170 – – –   The dashes mark what the editor thinks is a change of speaker. Lines 170–5 were probably spoken by the leader of the Chorus.

⁺**ἥδε** (demon. pron.)   in deictic function: 'here' (cf. line 51; supply 'is')

⁺**τροφός, ὁ/ἡ**   (τρέφω, nourish) rearer, nurse

⁺**γεραιός** (3)   old (*correption* of -αι-, the shortening of a long vowel before another vowel)

πρό (prep.)   + gen.: before, in front of (the omicron does not elide: S #72c) [1x *Hipp.*]

θύρα, ἡ   door [1x *Hipp.*]

171 ⁺**κομίζω**   bring, carry, welcome (κομίζουσα, ptc. of attendant circumstance, coincidental with supplied ἐστί; see ὁράω in line 4)

⁺μέλαθρον, τό   crossbeam, rafter, roof; in pl.: house; – 'But
here before the door is her old Nurse, bringing her outside the palace'

172 ⁺στυγνός (3)   hateful; sullen, sad, gloomy

ὀφρύς, ύος, ἡ   brow (290)

νέφος, εος, τό   cloud [1x *Hipp.*]

αὐξάνω   increase, make grow; – 'And a gloomy cloud
on her brow is growing.' Line 172 is bracketed by Murray and Stockert; B. (following Wilamowitz-Moellendorff) transposes it after line
180. The claim is that the Chorus cannot know that the cloud "is growing" without having seen her beforehand. The Chorus can, however,
describe what they see as happening. There seems to be no reason to
excise or transpose the line. (750)

173 τί ποτ(ε) ἐστί   'what in the world the matter is' (indirect
question)

*⁺μανθάνω, ἔμαθον   learn by inquiry

174 δηλέομαι   harm, destroy (δεδήληται, pf. mid.) [1x Eur.]

175 ἀλλό-χροος (2)   of another color, changeful of hue, discol-
ored (proleptic/anticipatory adj., i.e., it anticipates the result of the action of the verb: S #3045; lit.: 'why is the-changed-in-color body of the
Queen ravaged') – 'my heart [spirit] desires to learn what in the world it
is, why is the body of the Queen ravaged, *so as to be changed in color*.'
[1x Eur.]

ΤΡΟΦΟΣ
ὦ κακὰ θνητῶν στυγεραί τε νόσοι·
τί σ' ἐγὼ δράσω, τί δὲ μὴ δράσω;
τόδε σοι φέγγος, λαμπρὸς ὅδ' αἰθήρ·
ἔξω δὲ δόμων ἤδη νοσερᾶς
δέμνια κοίτης.   180
δεῦρο γὰρ ἐλθεῖν πᾶν ἔπος ἦν σοι,
τάχα δ' ἐς θαλάμους σπεύσεις τὸ πάλιν.
ταχὺ γὰρ σφάλλῃ κοὐδενὶ χαίρεις,
οὐδέ σ' ἀρέσκει τὸ παρόν, τὸ δ' ἀπὸν
φίλτερον ἡγῇ.   185

176 στὕγερός (3)   (στὕγέω, hate) hated, loathsome [1x *Hipp.*]

177 σ'   = σε, not σοι (in tragedy only short vowels are
elided: S #70, 74)

*⁺δράω   do, accomplish (δράσω, aor.¹ subjv.; the μή indicates that it is aor. subjv. rather than fut. indic.; deliberative subjv.: S
#2639; GMT #287) – 'Oh the troubles of mortals, the hateful illnesses!
What am I to do for you? What am I not to do?'

178–80 ***⁺φέγγος, εος, τό** light, sunlight (σοι, dat. of possess.: S #1476)

λαμπρός (3)   bright, brilliant, radiant [1x *Hipp.*]

αἰθήρ, έρος, ὁ   open air, upper air (447)

⁺ἤδη (adv.)   already, by this time, now, immediately, in the
past

δέμνιον, τό   (δέμω, build) a bed, bedding (mostly in pl.) –
'Here is your light, here is your open air, and the bed [of sick lying]
where you lie sick is outside.' [1x *Hipp.*]

181–82 ⁺δεῦρο (adv.)   to this place, hither, over here

⁺ἔπος, εος, τό   word (σοι, dat. of possess.)

τάχα (adv.)   (τᾰχύς, quick) quickly, soon, immediately (9)

γάρ (pcl.)   'you see' (B.: "seems to introduce an explanation not of any particular words that the Nurse has just uttered, but of
the underlying idea 'it's impossible to please you.'" GP 61–2, 2)

θάλαμος, ὁ   an inner room, chamber, bedroom (540)

σπεύδω   hasten, hurry (780)

⁺πάλιν (adv.)   back, again (τὸ πάλιν = πάλιν) – 'You see, your
every word was to come here, but soon you will rush back into your
chamber.'

183 ⁺ταχύ   soon, immediately (adv. acc.: S #1606, 1608;
τάχα, ταχύ: *anaphora*; σφάλλῃ < **⁺σφάλλω, pres. pass. indic. 2 sg.: 'get upset')

⁺οὐδείς, οὐδεμία, οὐδέν   no one, nothing (declension: S #349b; =
καὶ οὐδενί, dat. of means: S #1507) – 'for you are quickly [tripped up]
upset and do not enjoy anything.'

184 ἀρέσκω   + acc.: conciliate, propitiate, appease (σ'= σε;
in tragedy only short vowels are elided: S #70) (106)

⁺πάρ-*⁺ειμι   be present (παρ-όν, pres. ptc. neut., subst. use
of artic. with ptc.: S #1153b, 2050–2; GMT #825) – 'what is present'

⁺ἄπ-*⁺ειμι   be absent (ἀπ-όν, pres. ptc. neut., subst. use of
artic. with ptc.: S #1153b) – 'what is absent'

185 ἡγέομαι   consider, think, reckon; – 'what is at hand does
not please you, but you deem dearer what is absent.' (16)

> κρεῖσσον δὲ νοσεῖν ἢ θεραπεύειν·
> τὸ μέν ἐστιν ἁπλοῦν, τῷ δὲ συνάπτει
> λύπη τε φρενῶν χερσίν τε πόνος.
> πᾶς δ' ὀδυνηρὸς βίος ἀνθρώπων
> κοὐκ ἔστι πόνων ἀνάπαυσις.   190
> ἀλλ' ὅτι τοῦ ζῆν φίλτερον ἄλλο
> σκότος ἀμπίσχων κρύπτει νεφέλαις.
> δυσέρωτες δὴ φαινόμεθ' ὄντες
> τοῦδ' ὅτι τοῦτο στίλβει κατὰ γῆν
> δι' ἀπειροσύνην ἄλλου βιότου   195
> κοὐκ ἀπόδειξιν τῶν ὑπὸ γαίας,
> μύθοις δ' ἄλλως φερόμεσθα.

186 ⁺κρείσσων, ον   better, stronger, mightier (irreg. compar. of
ἀγαθός: S #319). It may well be that at this point the Nurse turns to the
spectators and addresses the rest of her philosophical musings to them.

⁺νοσέω   be ill

θεραπεύω   wait on, tend to [1x *Hipp.*]

187 ἁπλοῦς, ῆ, οῦν   simple, onefold (note the τὸ μέν . . . τῷ δέ construction) [1x *Hipp.*]

συν-άπτω   tie together, join together, bring together, attach (515)

188 ⁺φρήν, φρενός, ἡ   heart, mind, sense; – 'the one is simple, but to
the other attaches both grief of heart and toil for one's hands.'

189 ὀδυνηρός (3)   painful, grievous, distressing [1x *Hipp.*]

190 ⁺ἀνάπαυσις, εως, ἡ   rest, cessation, relief (note the existential meaning of ἔστι; cf. line 378) – 'But all life of mortals is painful, and there is no rest from toils.'

191 *⁺ζάω   live (ζῆν, pres. inf. act.; verb in -άω that contracts to η: S #394, 395; τοῦ ζῆν, the artic. makes the infinitive more prominent as a noun in the sentence: GMT #789; τοῦ ζῆν, gen. of comparison: S #1431)

ὅτι . . . ἄλλο   'whatever other thing is dearer than life.'

192 ⁺σκότος, ὁ   darkness, gloom

ἀμπ-ίσχω   (= ἀμπ-έχω) surround, enwrap, cover (ἀμπί-σχων, ptc. of attendant circumstance, coincidental with κρύπτει; see ὁράω in line 4) [1x Hipp.]

*⁺κρύπτω   hide

νεφέλη, ἡ   cloud (dat. of means: S #1507) – 'But whatever other thing is dearer than life, darkness hides it, enwrapping it with clouds' [1x Hipp.]

193 δύσ-ερως, ωτος, ὁ, ἡ passionately loving, sick in love with, madly in love with. (There is an *asyndeton* between this sentence and the previous one. The δή, according to B., here lacks the meaning "'therefore' which . . . seems unknown in tragedy" and emphasizes δυσέρωτες. τοῦδ(ε) completes δυσέρωτες as obj. gen.: S #1328, 1331: 'madly in love with this.') [1x Eur.]

*⁺φαινόμεθα *⁺ὄντες   'we are revealed as being' (*⁺φαίνω is one of the verbs that can take either a ptc. or an inf., with slight distinction between the two. With ptc. it means: 'I am plainly'; with inf.: 'I appear to be': S #2143.)

⁺ὅστις, ἥτις, ὅ τι (indef./general relat. pron.) whoever, anyone who, anything which (S #339); ὅτι = 'which [ὅ] whatever it is [τι]'

στίλβω   shine, glitter [1x Hipp.]

⁺κατά (prep.)   + acc.: over, throughout

195 ἀπειροσύνη, ἡ   (ἀ privat.) inexperience [1x Hipp.]

⁺βίοτος, ὁ   life, way of life

196 ἀπόδειξις, εως, ἡ   (ἀποδείκνυμι, show) showing forth, revelation (τῶν = τῶνδε; the artic. was originally a demon. pron. and occasionally retains that force: S #1099; obj. gen.: S #1328, 1331) [1x Eur.]

   ⁺γαῖα, ἡ   poetic for γῆ: earth, ground, soil

197 ⁺ἄλλως (adv.)   in vain, without purpose; – 'We are revealed as being obsessively in love with this thing [τοῦδ'] that [ὅ], whatever it is [τι], glitters here on earth, because of inexperience of another life and through non-revelation of things beneath the earth; we are carried along by tales with no purpose.'

ΦΑΙΔΡΑ

αἴρετέ μου δέμας, ὀρθοῦτε κάρα·
λέλυμαι μελέων σύνδεσμα φίλων.
λάβετ'εὐπήχεις χεῖρας, πρόπολοι.   200
βαρύ μοι κεφαλῆς ἐπίκρανον ἔχειν·
ἄφελ', ἀμπέτασον βόστρυχον ὤμοις.

Τρ.   θάρσει, τέκνον, καὶ μὴ χαλεπῶς
μετάβαλλε δέμας·
ῥᾷον δὲ νόσον μετά θ' ἡσυχίας   205
καὶ γενναίου λήματος οἴσεις.
μοχθεῖν δὲ βροτοῖσιν ἀνάγκη.

Φα.   αἰαῖ·
πῶς ἂν δροσερᾶς ἀπὸ κρηνῖδος
καθαρῶν ὑδάτων πῶμ' ἀρυσαίμαν
ὑπό τ' αἰγείροις ἔν τε κομήτῃ   210
λειμῶνι κλιθεῖσ' ἀναπαυσαίμαν;

For the meter, see the introduction to the First Episode.

198 *⁺αἴρω   raise, lift up

   ⁺ὀρθόω   set straight, put right (The pres. impv. means 'hold upright.' Phaedra implies that she has no strength to hold her head upright by herself.)

   ⁺κάρα, τό   [ᾰ] head

199 ⁺λύω   [ῠ] loose, unfasten, release, relax, lay aside, be profitable (λέλῡμαι, pf. pass. indic.)

μέλος, εος, τό   limb (φίλος with parts of the body retains its Homeric meaning of possess.: 'of my limbs') [1x *Hipp.*]

σύν-δεσμος, ὁ   that which binds together (irreg. pl.: τὰ σύνδεσμα; acc. of respect, frequent with parts of the body: S #1600, 1601a; the common lyric epithet of Eros is λῡσιμελής 'limb-loosening') – 'Lift my body, keep my head erect, (I am loosened in respect of the joints of my limbs =) my limbs are loosened.' [1x *Hipp.*]

200 *⁺λαμβάνω   take, seize (λάβετε, aor.² act. impv.)

εὔ-πηχυς, υ   with beautiful arms (calls to mind the epithet used for Penelope's arm, παχεῖα χεῖρ, 'stout 'or 'firm' arm, *Od.* 21.6) – 'Take my beautiful arms, servants!' [1x *Eur.*]

201 ⁺βᾰρύς, εῖα, ὁ   heavy, burdensome (supply ἐστι)

ἐπί-κρᾱνον, τό   a covering for the head, a headdress; – 'It is a burden to have a headdress on my head' [1x *Hipp.*]

202 ⁺ἀφ-*αιρέω   take away (ἄφ-ελε, aor.² impv. act. 2 sg.; Phaedra addresses the Nurse here, not the attendants)

ἀνα-πετάννῡμι, -επέτασα   (poetic ἀμπέτασον = ἀναπέτασον, aor.¹ impv. act. 2 sg.) unfold, spread [1x *Hipp.*]

βόστρυχος, ὁ   lock of hair [1x *Hipp.*]

ὦμος, ὁ   shoulder; – 'Take it off, [Nurse]! Spread my locks on my shoulders!' A married woman's hair was usually veiled and covered, as spread-out tresses are sexually alluring. The veil, as Llewellyn-Jones (2003, 18; cf. 264) claims, "acts as a barrier to contain female *miasma*, especially the pollution inherent in female sexuality." Women with uncontrolled free-flowing hair pose the greatest sexual threat to men. Phaedra wishes to attract and seduce Hippolytus and therefore asks for her hair to be unbound. That she is aware of the impropriety of her wish and its purpose is proven when she asks to have her hair covered as soon as she appears to come out of her alleged delirium (243, 245; cf. Roisman 2021, 76). [1x *Hipp.*]

203 θαρσέω   be of good courage, be of good cheer (pres. impv. act.) (860)

⁺τέκνον, τό   (τίκτω, give birth; bear) child

χαλεπῶς   harshly, violently [1x *Hipp.*]

204 μετα-*βάλλω   toss, turn around (pres. impv. act.) – 'Courage, my child! Do not toss your body so violently!' (1116)

205 ῥᾴων, ον   easier (irreg. compar. of ⁺ῥᾴδιος; ῥᾷον, adv. acc.: S #1606, 1608)

⁺μετά (prep.)   + gen.: with, by means of

ἡσῦχία, ἡ   quiet, stillness; rest [1x *Hipp.*]

206 ⁺γενναῖος (3)   suitable to one's birth or descent, noble

λῆμα, τό   will, spirit, courage; – 'You will bear your sickness more easily with calm and noble spirit.' [1x *Hipp.*]

207 μοχθέω   be weary with toil, suffer greatly, bear trouble (301)

⁺ἀνάγκη, ἡ   constraint, necessity; – 'It is necessary for mortals to endure trouble.'

208 δροσερός (3)   dewy, watery (226)

κρηνίς, ῖδος, ἡ   [ῑ] (diminutive of κρήνη) spring, well (diminutives may sometimes express affection or familiarity: S #856) [1x Eur.]

209 κᾰθᾰρός (3)   clear, pure (1120)

πῶμα, ατος, τό   drink, draught, potion (227)

ἀρύω   draw water; mid.: draw water for oneself (ἀρυσαίμαν = ἀρυσαίμην, aor.¹ opt. mid.; opt. of wish following πῶς ἄν in line 208. B.: "πῶς ἄν [with opt.] 'how could I' often in tragedy has the force of a wish, 'would that I might'; usually, as here, a wish of whose fulfilment the speaker has little or no hope"; cf. 345. Phaedra's excitement comes through in her use of Doric α in place of Attic η. This is usually a mark of lyric, i.e., song with music, but Phaedra continues to use ordinary nonlyric anapests. It is unclear if this usage suggests a somewhat different delivery or is intended to differentiate Phaedra's state from that of the Nurse, who sticks to η. Phaedra uses Doric forms of nouns and adjs. all through her 'delirium.') [1x Eur.]

210 αἴγειρος, ἡ   black poplar [1x Eur.]

κομήτης, ου, ὁ   grassy, leafy [1x *Hipp.*]

211 *κλίνω   cause to recline; pass.: lean, rest, lie down (κλι-θεῖσα, aor.[1] pass. ptc.; circumstantial ptc.: the action of the aor. ptc. is usually antecedent to that of the leading verb: S #1872c) [1x *Hipp.*]

ἀνα-παύω   come to stop; mid.: rest (ἀνα-παυσαίμαν = ἀνα-παυσαίμην, aor.[1] opt. mid.; see ἀρυσαίμαν, 209) – 'If only I might draw a drink of pure water from a dewy spring, and having reclined beneath black poplar trees in a grassy meadow take my rest!' (1354)

Τρ.	ὦ παῖ, τί θροεῖς;
	οὐ μὴ παρ᾽ ὄχλῳ τάδε γηρύσῃ,
	μανίας ἔποχον ῥίπτουσα λόγον;
Φα.	πέμπετέ μ᾽ εἰς ὄρος· εἶμι πρὸς ὕλαν 215
	καὶ παρὰ πεύκας, ἵνα θηροφόνοι
	στείβουσι κύνες
	βαλιαῖς ἐλάφοις ἐγχριμπτόμεναι.
	πρὸς θεῶν· ἔραμαι κυσὶ θωΰξαι
	καὶ παρὰ χαίταν ξανθὰν ῥῖψαι 220
	Θεσσαλὸν ὅρπακ᾽,
	ἐπίλογχον ἔχουσ᾽ ἐν χειρὶ βέλος.
Τρ.	τί ποτ᾽, ὦ τέκνον, τάδε κηραίνεις;
	τί κυνηγεσίων καί σοι μελέτη;
	τί δὲ κρηναίων νασμῶν ἔρασαι; 225
	πάρα γὰρ δροσερὰ πύργοις συνεχὴς
	κλειτύς, ὅθεν σοι πῶμα γένοιτ᾽ ἄν.
Φα.	δέσποιν᾽ ἁλίας Ἄρτεμι Λίμνας
	καὶ γυμνασίων τῶν ἱπποκρότων,
	εἴθε γενοίμαν ἐν σοῖς δαπέδοις 230
	πώλους Ἐνετὰς δαμαλιζομένα.

212 θροέω   shriek, cry aloud, cry out (stage direction: we learn that Phaedra must be shrieking her alleged delirious wishes) (571)

213 ⁺παρά (prep.)   + dat.: by the side of, beside, by

⁺ὄχλος, ὁ   throng of people, crowd

γηρύω   utter, speak, say (γηρύσῃ, fut. mid. indic.; 2 sg.
with οὐ μὴ + fut. indic. indicates strong prohibition in dramatic poets:
S #1919, 2756a; GMT #297; it is usually translated 'don't . . .') (1074)

214 μανία, ἡ   madness [1x *Hipp.*]

⁺ῥίπτω   hurl, throw, cast (ῥίπτουσα, ptc. of attendant
circumstance, coincidental with γηρύσῃ; see ὁράω in line 4)

ἔπ-οχος, ον   (ἐπ-έχω, hold upon) mounted upon, borne on,
riding on ('Riding on madness' is a striking metaphor, which Phaedra
will borrow in her next utterance, expressing the wish to go to the
mountains and hunt, which can be done only by riding a horse. The
pattern that will emerge is that while Phaedra capitalizes immediately
on the implications of the Nurse's language, the Nurse responds to the
explicit only. Cf. Roisman 1999, 49–63.) [1x Eur.]

⁺λόγος, ὁ   (λέγω, speak) word, report, rumor (λόγος is
used here as a collective sg. denoting more than one word: S #996)
– 'Oh child, why are you crying out? You must not say these things
before a crowd, hurling words borne on madness!'

215 ⁺ὄρος, τό   mountain, hill (233)

⁺εἶμι   I shall go (the verb has only the present sys-
tem; for conjugation, see S #773; serves as the fut. of ἔρχομαι: S #774)

ὕλη, ἡ   (ὕλαν = ὕλην) wood, forest, woodland (17)

216 πεύκη, ἡ   fir, pine (1254)

⁺ἵνα (relat. adv.)   + indic.: where

θηρο-φόνος (3/2)   slaying wild beasts [1x *Hipp.*]

217 στείβω   go, tread [1x *Hipp.*]

218 βᾱλιός (3)   spotted, dappled [1x *Hipp.*]

ἔλαφος, ὁ/ἡ   deer [1x *Hipp.*]

ἐγ-χρίμπτω   bring near to; mid. and pass.: attack, fall upon,
pursue + dat. ('hound' is usually fem. in hunting; ἐγχριμπτόμεναι, ptc.
of attendant circumstance, coincidental with εἶμι; see ὁράω in line 4)
– 'Take me to the mountain! I shall go to the forest and to the pine

trees, where hounds that kill wild beasts tread, running close after the dappled deer.' [1x Eur.]

219 ⁺πρὸς θεῶν   please, in the name of the gods (B.: "an emphatic 'please!'; used always in entreaty, either in asking another to act [with impves., etc.] or in urgent questions [when one entreats the other to reply]")

θωΰσσω   cry out, shout (ἔραμαι ... θωῦξαι, note the inappropriate use of a verb with sexual innuendo, ἔραμαι, in this context. The proper vocabulary would be the neutral verb ποθεῖν 'I long for,' which is used in an adaptation of this same passage by Plutarch *Moralia* 959B. See discussion in Roisman 1999, 52–3.) [1x *Hipp.*]

220 χαίτη, ἡ   flowing hair (the movement is of holding the javelin beside the ear in order to poise it, which Phaedra must have seen being done) [1x *Hipp.*]

⁺ξανθός (3)   golden, auburn

221 Θεσσᾱλός (3)   (Attic: Θεττᾱλός) Thessalian [1x *Hipp.*]

ὄρπηξ, ηκος, ὁ   lance, spear, javelin [1x *Hipp.*]

222 ἐπί-λογχος (2)   barbed [1x Eur.]

βέλος, εος, τό   (βάλλω, throw) spear, weapon, bolt, arrow (ἔχουσα, ptc. of attendant circumstance, coincidental with ἔραμαι; see ὁράω in line 4) – 'Please, by the gods, [how] I desire (have a passion for [*eramai*]) to cry out to the dogs, to throw past my golden mane the Thessalian javelin, while holding in my hand the pointed spear.' [1x *Hipp.*]

223 τί ποτ(ε)   'why in the world?' 'why ever?' (τί ... τί, *anaphora*)

κηραίνω   be alarmed, be disquieted, be anxious, fret (τάδε, internal acc.; a pron. or a noun can reinforce the action of the verb: S #1554a, 1557) – Lit.: 'Why in the world are you alarmed by these thoughts? Why in the world are you alarmed in this way?' Or: 'Why in the world are you distressed in this way?' [1x *Hipp.*]

224 κὕνηγέσιον, τό   hunting establishment; hunt, pack of hounds
[1x Eur.]

καί (pcl.)   'at all,' 'to start with' (GP 313b: "καί, following an interrogative, denotes that the question cuts at the foundations of the problem under consideration. A question is put which, it is implied, cannot be answered, or cannot be satisfactorily answered: so that the discussion of any further, consequential question does not arise." Here καί emphasizes σοι.)

μελέτη, ἡ   care (B.: "Why do you concern yourself with hunting?") [1x *Hipp.*]

225 κρηναῖος (3)   (κρήνη, spring) of/from a spring [1x *Hipp.*]

νασμός, ὁ   a flowing current, stream, spring (gen. with verb of desire: S #1349) (653)

⁺ἔρασαι   Note that the Nurse repeats Phaedra's vocabulary (219: ἔραμαι) without really understanding that it is sexual desire that prompts it. She is also one utterance behind. – 'Why are you in love with/Why are you desiring flowing streams?'

226 ⁺πάρ-*⁺ειμι   be present, be at hand, be near + dat. (πάρα = πάρεστι)

πύργος, ὁ   tower; in pl.: walls and tower [1x *Hipp.*]

συνεχής, ές   + dat.: near, next to, adjacent [1x Eur.]

227 κλειτύς, ύος, ἡ   slope, hillside (δροσερά . . . κλειτύς, *hyperbaton*) [1x *Hipp.*]

**⁺γίγνομαι   be, become (aor.² opt. dep.; γένοιτ[ο] ἄν, potential opt. with ἄν: GMT #286; S #1824) – 'Besides, there is a dewy slope next to the city walls from which you could have a drink.'

228 ἅλιος (3/2)   of the sea (ἁλίας Λίμνας = ἁλίης Λίμης).
[1x *Hipp.*]

229 γυμνάσιον, τό   (γυμνάζω, train naked) exercise, place of exercise [1x *Hipp.*]

ἱππό-κροτος (2)   (ἵππος, horse; κροτέω, rattle) echoing with horses' hooves [1x *Hipp.*]

230 ἔιθε *⁺γενοίμαν = εἴθε γενοίμην (εἴθε + opt.: 'if only I might'; opt. of wish for the fut.: GMT #721; S #1815)

δάπεδον, τό   land, plain [1x *Hipp.*]

231 ⁺πῶλος ὁ/ἡ   a foal, whether a colt or a filly; in poetry often: a young girl

Ἐνετός (3)   Venetian (the Venetians dwelled near the Adriatic Sea and were famed for their horses) (1131)

δᾰμᾰλίζω   poetic form of δᾰμάω, subdue (Doric δαμαλιζομένα = δαμαλιζομένη; ptc. of attendant circumstance, coincidental with γενοίμαν; see ὁράω in line 4) – 'Oh mistress of the salty Lagoon and of the racetracks resounding with horses' hooves, if only I could be on your plains breaking in Venetian colts!' [1x Eur.]

Τρ.	τί τόδ᾽ αὖ παράφρων ἔρριψας ἔπος;
	νῦν δὴ μὲν ὄρος βᾶσ᾽ ἐπὶ θήρας
	πόθον ἐστέλλου, νῦν δ᾽ αὖ ψαμάθοις
	ἐπ᾽ ἀκυμάντοις πώλων ἔρασαι. 235
	τάδε μαντείας ἄξια πολλῆς,
	ὅστις σε θεῶν ἀνασειράζει
	καὶ παρακόπτει φρένας, ὦ παῖ.
Φα.	δύστηνος ἐγώ, τί ποτ᾽εἰργασάμην;
	ποῖ παρεπλάγχθην γνώμης ἀγαθῆς; 240
	ἐμάνην, ἔπεσον δαίμονος ἄτῃ.
	φεῦ φεῦ, τλήμων.
	μαῖα, πάλιν μου κρύψον κεφαλήν,
	αἰδούμεθα γὰρ τὰ λελεγμένα μοι.
	κρύπτε· κατ᾽ ὄσσων δάκρυ μοι βαίνει 245
	καὶ ἐπ᾽αἰσχύνην ὄμμα τέτραπται.
	τὸ γὰρ ὀρθοῦσθαι γνώμην ὀδυνᾷ,
	τὸ δὲ μαινόμενον κακόν· ἀλλὰ κρατεῖ
	μὴ γιγνώσκοντ᾽ ἀπολέσθαι.

232–3 παράφρων, ον,   gen. ονος out of one's wits [1x *Hipp.*]

⁺αὖ (adv.)   again, now; – 'And now what is this word you have hurled forth in frenzy?'

233 θήρα, ἡ   hunting, hunt, eager pursuit of anything (βᾶσα < *⁺βαίνω, aor.² act. ptc. of attendant circumstance; aor. ptc. is usually antecedent to that of the leading verb, ἐστέλλου; cf. προκόπτω in line 23; θήρας πόθον, obj. gen.: S #1328, 1331) – 'longing for the hunt' (52)

234 πόθος, ὁ   longing, desire (526)

στέλλω   set in order, arrange; mid.: set out on an expedition (ἐστέλλου, impf. indic. mid.) [1x *Hipp.*]

ψάμᾰθος, ἡ   sandy shore, the sands (1126)

235 ἀ-κύμαντος (2)   (ἀ privat.) waveless, not washed by the waves
[1x Eur.]

**ἔρασαι   Note the repeated use of a verb with sexual connotation by the Nurse, instead of the more neutral ποθεῖς, which could have gone nicely with πόθος (the verb governs the gen. πώλων: S #1349). – 'You were just going to the mountains, setting out (for [ἐπί] your longing of the hunt) for the hunt you long for, but now again you desire colts/horses on waveless sands.'

236 μαντεία, ἡ   prophesying, prophecy, divination [1x *Hipp.*]

⁺ἄξιος (3)   worthy

237 ὅστις θεῶν   which/who of the gods = which god (θεῶν,
partit. gen.)

ἀνα-σειράζω   pull back with a rein, control by reins, draw
aside [1x Eur.]

238 παρα-κόπτω   derange, distract, drive mad; – 'These things are worthy of much prophecy [to say] which god (who of the gods) makes you swerve from the course and strikes your wits awry, child.' [1x Eur.]

239 **ἐργάζομαι   do (to), work

240 ⁺ποῖ (correl. adv.)   whither? to what end? (sometimes + gen.)

παρα-πλάζω   cause to wander, lead astray (παρεπλάγχθην,
aor.¹ pass. indic.) [1x Eur.]

⁺γνώμη, ἡ   judgment, thought, mind

⁺ἀγαθός (3)   good, noble; – 'Wretched me! What have I done? Where did I wander from good thinking?'

241 *⁺μαίνομαι   be mad (ἐμάνην, aor.¹ pass. indic.)

⁺ἄτη, ἡ   destruction, ruin, folly, delusion, temporary clouding of the mind (δαίμονος, subj. gen.: S #1328, 1330; note the *asyndeton* between the verbs emphasizing her emotional state) – 'I was mad, I fell into a delusion orchestrated by some divinity.'

242 ⁺τλήμων, ονος, ὁ/ἡ   suffering, wretched

243 μαῖα, ἡ   nurse (311)

244 ⁺αἰδέομαι   respect, be ashamed of (+ acc.: S #1595a; αἰδούμεθα, *majestic plural* emphasizing her importance: S #1006. Would it remind the audience of Hippolytus' use of *majestic plural* in line 90? So far only Aphrodite, at 6, 43, and Hippolytus have used this literary device; cf. line 331.)

τὰ λελεγμένα   'what has been said by me' (⁺λέγω, pf. pass. ptc. acc. pl. neut.; artic. subst. ptc.; see πάρειμι in line 184; μοι, dat. of agent: S #1488) – 'Alas! Alas, miserable me! Nurse, cover my head again, for I am ashamed of what has been said by me.'

245 *⁺κρύπτε   The pres. impv. reiterates the aor.¹ impv., κρύψον, and marks a difference in aspect of the action. While the aor. indicated simply what had to be done, the pres. describes the process of covering: 'go on, cover [it].' For a similar play on a grammatical aspect, see lines 1034–5. Does the emphasis on covering her hair imply that Phaedra is not ashamed here of everything she has said before, but rather only of asking to have her hair let loose, which implied sexual misconduct?

ὄσσε, τώ   (neut. dual) eyes (1396)

⁺δάκρυ, υος, τό   (poetic for δάκρυον) a tear (collective sg., as is ὄμμα in the following line: S #996)

246 καὶ ἐπ'   *correption*, the shortening of a long vowel before another vowel. The -αι- here is short.

⁺αἰσχύνη, ἡ   shame

τρέπω   turn (τέτρεπται, pf. pass. indic.) – 'Go on, cover [it]. Tears stream down from my eyes and my eye/gaze has turned into shame.' This is probably a stage direction comment for the sake of the spectators rather than an indication that she has realized her disgrace. (1066)

247 τὸ ⁺ὀρθοῦσθαι   (the artic. can make the inf. more prominent as a noun in the structure of the sentence: GMT #789; see also 80: τὸ σωφρονεῖν)

ὀδϋνάω   cause pain to, pain, distress [1x Eur.]

248 ⁺κρατέω   prevail (over), win out, be best, hold sway (+ inf. *⁺ἀπολέσθαι, which in turn takes the acc. γιγνώσκοντα as its subj.)

249 *⁺γιγνώσκω   know (γιγνώσκοντα is masc., because Phaedra is generalizing: S #1015, ptc. of attendant circumstance, coincidental with κρατεῖ; see ὁράω in line 4) – 'For keeping the mind straight is painful, while madness [is] evil; it is best to perish without awareness.'

Τρ.	κρύπτω· τὸ δ' ἐμὸν πότε δὴ θάνατος	250
	σῶμα καλύψει;	
	πολλὰ διδάσκει μ' ὁ πολὺς βίοτος·	
	χρῆν γὰρ μετρίας εἰς ἀλλήλους	
	φιλίας θνητοὺς ἀνακίρνασθαι	
	καὶ μὴ πρὸς ἄκρον μυελὸν ψυχῆς,	255
	εὔλυτα δ' εἶναι στέργηθρα φρενῶν	
	ἀπό τ' ὤσασθαι καὶ ξυντεῖναι·	
	τὸ δ' ὑπὲρ δισσῶν μίαν ὠδίνειν	
	ψυχὴν χαλεπὸν βάρος, ὡς κἀγὼ	
	τῆσδ' ὑπεραλγῶ.	260
	βιότου δ' ἀτρεκεῖς ἐπιτηδεύσεις	
	φασὶ σφάλλειν πλέον ἢ τέρπειν	
	τῇ θ' ὑγιείᾳ μᾶλλον πολεμεῖν.	
	οὕτω τὸ λίαν ἧσσον ἐπαινῶ	
	τοῦ μηδὲν ἄγαν·	265
	καὶ ξυμφήσουσι σοφοί μοι.	

250 πότε   when? (interrog.; note the accent: S #181b, 346) [1x *Hipp.*]

251 καλύπτω   cover, hide (712)

⁺σῶμα, ατος, τό   body (ἐμὸν . . . σῶμα, the *hyperbaton*, may indicate the Nurse's distress) – 'I'm covering; but when will death conceal my body?'

252   *⁺διδάσκω   teach (+ double acc.: μέ, πολλά) – 'My long life has taught me many things'

253   *⁺χρή   (quasi-impersonal) it is necessary (χρῆν = χρὴ ἦν, impf.: it was necessary; indicates an unfulfilled present obligation: 'should'; with acc. and inf.: θνητούς ἀνακρίνασθαι: S #793, 1562, 1985b)

μέτριος (3/2)   within measure, moderate [1x *Hipp.*]

ἀλλήλων   one another, each other (reciprocal pron.; gen. pl. with no nom.; dat. ἀλλήλοις, αις, οις; acc. ἀλλήλους, ας, α: S #331, 1277) [1x *Hipp.*]

254   φιλία, ἡ   love, friendship (note the emphatic *hyperbaton* of μετρίας . . . φιλίας) (364)

ἀνα-κίρναμαι   mix, engage in (acc. and inf.: θνητούς is the subj. of ἀνακίρνασθαι) [1x *Hipp.*]

255   ἄκρος (3)   highest, peak; metaph.: extreme [1x *Hipp.*]

μυελός, ὁ   marrow; inmost part; – 'for mortals should mix with one another in moderate friendship, not to the extreme marrow of the soul' [1x Eur.]

256   εὔ-λῦτος (2)   (εὔ, λύω) easy to untie; metaph.: easy to dissolve or break [1x Eur.]

στέργηθρον, τό   (στέργω, love) love, affection, regard [1x Eur.]

257   ἀπ-ωθέω   drive away, shove away, thrust off (aor.¹ mid. inf.; *tmesis*) [1x *Hipp.*]

συν-τείνω   draw tight (both infs. explain εὔλυτα) – 'and affections of the mind should be easy to loosen—[easy] to shove away or draw tight' [1x *Hipp.*]

258   ⁺δισσός (3)   twofold, double

⁺εἷς, μία, ἕν   one (S #347, 349)

ὠδίνω   have the pains of childbirth, be in travail in any great pain [1x *Hipp.*]

259 ⁺βάρος, εος, τό   weight, burden; metaph.: misery (greatly emphatic *hyperbaton*: τὸ . . . βάρος)

χαλεπός (3)   hard to bear, grievous, difficult, sore (767)

260 ὑπερ-αλγέω   grieve exceedingly, feel afflicted, feel pain for; – 'it is a difficult burden for one soul to labor over two as I grieve for this one.' [1x *Hipp.*]

261 ἀτρεκής, ές   real, true, exact, rigid (1115)

ἐπιτήδευσις, εως, ἡ   attention, practice, behavior (ἀτρεκεῖς ἐπιτηδεύσει, subj. of the three infs.)

262 *⁺φημί   say (φημί, φῄς, φησί, φαμέν, φατέ, φᾶσί, φάναι; usually followed by inf.: S #2017a; here: σφάλλειν, τέρπειν, and πολεμεῖν)

⁺πλέον ἤ   more than

τέρπω   please, delight (727)

263 ὑγίειᾰ, ἡ   health [1x *Hipp.*]

⁺μᾶλλον   more

πολεμέω   be at war; – 'They say that strict practices in life bring about more falls than delight, and are at war with health.' [1x *Hipp.*]

264 ⁺λίαν (adv.)   too much (Hamilton: "The definite articles serve to put λίαν and μηδὲν ἄγαν in quotes, as it were.")

ἥσσων, ἧσσον   less (as irreg. compar. of positive κακός). [1x *Hipp.*]

ἐπ-*αινέω   approve [1x *Hipp.*]

265 ἄγαν (adv.)   too much (μηδὲν ἄγαν is an old proverb: 'nothing in excess,' i.e., 'moderation'; τοῦ, gen. of comparison: S #1431) – 'so I praise excess less than moderation.' [1x *Hipp.*]

266 σύμ-*⁺φημι + dat.: agree with; – 'And the wise will agree with me.' [1x Eur.]

Xo.	γύναι γεραιά, βασιλίδος πιστὴ τροφέ,
	Φαίδρας ὁρῶμεν τάσδε δυστήνους τύχας,
	ἄσημα δ᾽ ἡμῖν ἥτις ἐστὶν ἡ νόσος·
	σοῦ δ᾽ ἂν πυθέσθαι καὶ κλυεῖν βουλοίμεθ᾽ ἄν. 270
Τρ.	οὐκ οἶδ᾽, ἐλέγχουσ᾽· οὐ γὰρ ἐννέπειν θέλει.
Xo.	οὐδ᾽ ἥτις ἀρχὴ τῶνδε πημάτων ἔφυ;
Τρ.	ἐς ταὐτὸν ἥκεις· πάντα γὰρ σιγᾷ τάδε.
Xo.	ὡς ἀσθενεῖ τε καὶ κατέξανται δέμας.
Τρ.	πῶς δ᾽ οὔ, τριταίαν γ᾽ οὖσ᾽ ἄσιτος ἡμέραν; 275
Xo.	πότερον ὑπ᾽ ἄτης ἢ θανεῖν πειρωμένη;
Τρ.	†θανεῖν† ἀσιτεῖ δ᾽ εἰς ἀπόστασιν βίου.
Xo.	θαυμαστὸν εἶπας, εἰ τάδ᾽ ἐξαρκεῖ πόσει.
Τρ.	κρύπτει γὰρ ἥδε πῆμα κοὔ φησιν νοσεῖν.
Xo.	ὁ δ᾽ ἐς πρόσωπον οὐ τεκμαίρεται βλέπων; 280
Τρ.	ἔκδημος ὢν γὰρ τῆσδε τυγχάνει χθονός.
Xo.	σὺ δ᾽ οὐκ ἀνάγκην προσφέρεις πειρωμένη
	νόσον πυθέσθαι τῆσδε καὶ πλάνον φρενῶν;

267 βᾰσῐλίς, ίδος, ἡ queen (resolution in 6th position, βᾰσῐλίδος)
(778)

⁺πιστός (3) reliable, loyal, trustworthy

268 ⁺τύχη, ἡ fortune (τάσδε, deictic: 'here'; see line 7)

269 ἄ-σημος (3) (ἀ privat., σῆμα, sign) without sign or mark, obscure, unclear (371)

270 ἄν . . . ἄν The duplication does not affect the meaning. The first ἄν anticipates the second one. (κλυεῖν, aor.² inf. act.; see line 119)

*⁺πυνθάνομαι + gen.: ask, inquire, learn

⁺κλύω + gen.: listen

*⁺βούλομαι wish (pres. mid. opt.; potential opt. used to indicate a polite request: S #1824, 1827; cf. lines 336, 904) – 'Old

woman, trusted Nurse of the Queen, we see here Phaedra's wretched fortunes, but it is unclear to us what her illness is; we would like to learn and hear [about it] from you.'

271 ⁺ἐλέγχω   examine, question, disagree, refute (ἐλέγ-χουσα, aor.¹ act. ptc.; concessive ptc.: S #2066)

⁺ἐννέπω   tell (poetic lengthening of νέπω) – 'I don't know, although I have questioned [her]; for she refuses to tell.'

272 ἀρχή, ἡ   beginning (762)

⁺πῆμα, ατος, τό   suffering, misery, woe, trouble; – 'Not even what was the beginning/source of this trouble?'

273 ταὐτὸν   = τὸ αὐτό, the same; Hamilton: "You have come into the same," i.e., "you are where you were before."

ἥκω   have come, have arrived (like οἴχομαι, a pres. with pf. sense) [1x *Hipp.*]

⁺σῑγάω   be silent or still, keep silence; – 'You have reached the same point: she keeps silent about all these things.'

274 ⁺ὡς (adv.)   exclamatory: how (S #2682, 2998); just as (S #2992)

ἀσθενέω   be weak, feeble, sickly [1x *Hipp.*]

κατα-ξαίνω   tear in pieces, reduce to nothing (κατέξανται, pf. pass. 3 sg.; δέμας, acc. of respect) – 'How both weak and wasted her body is.' [1x *Hipp.*]

275 τρῑταῖος (3)   on the third day (poetic lengthening of τρίτος) [1x *Hipp.*]

**⁺εἰμί   be (ὤν, οὖσα, ὄν, pres. act. ptc. of attendant circumstance, see ὁράω in line 4)

ἄ-σῑτος (2)   (ἀ privat., σῖτος, food) without food, fasting; – 'And how not? She has been three days without food.' [1x *Hipp.*]

276 πότερον/πότερα . . . ἤ   whether . . . or (introduces direct alternative questions πότερον/πότερα, frequently left untranslated in English; πότερον, resolution in 2nd position) (516)

*⁺θνῄσκω   die (θανεῖν, aor.² inf. act.)

*⁺πειράομαι   attempt, try (πειρωμένη, pres. dep. ptc. of attendant circumstance, see ὁράω in line 4, parallel to οὖσα in line 275) – 'Due to madness, or is she trying to die?'

277 †θανεῖν†   This reading of the manuscripts is not that implausible. The Nurse answers the query of the Chorus by saying: 'to die. She fasts in order to [εἰς indicating purpose]/with the aim to depart from life.' Some editors follow θανεῖν with a question mark, i.e., 'to die [you ask]?' but the second half of the line is not structured as a reply.

ἀ-σιτέω   go without food, fast [1x Eur.]

ἀπό-στᾰσις, εως, ἡ   (ἀφίσταμαι, withdraw) departure, removal from [1x Eur.]

278 θαυμαστός (3)   to be wondered at, wonderful, remarkable (106)

*⁺εἶπον   say, proclaim (aor.² act. indic.; translated by pres. in English)

ἐξ-αρκέω   + dat.: satisfy (702)

πόσις, ιος, ὁ   husband (πόσει, dat. sg.) – 'What you are saying is remarkable, if this satisfies her husband.' [1x *Hipp.*]

279 οὐ *⁺φημί   deny

280 ⁺πρόσωπον, τό   (πρός, toward; ὤψ, eye) face

τεκμαίρομαι   perceive from certain signs, infer [1x *Hipp.*]

*⁺βλέπων   (circumstantial ptc. denoting time: S #2061; the action of the pres. ptc. is usually coincidental with that of the leading verb, τεκμαίρεται·: S #1872.1) – 'and he does not infer it when looking at her face?'

281 *⁺τυγχάνω   (τύχη, coincidence, chance) happen, hit the mark, obtain (often with supplem. ptc. in direct discourse, which tells what the main action is, while the finite verb tells something about how the action is occurring: S: #2096a; here with ὤν) – 'As it happens, he is out of the country right now.'

282 προσ-*⁺φέρω   apply in, lay to/upon (606)

283 πλάνος, ὁ   roaming, wandering about, straying; – 'But ar-
en't you applying force trying to learn about her sickness and the wandering of her wits?' [1x *Hipp.*]

Τρ.   ἐς πάντ' ἀφῖγμαι κοὐδὲν εἴργασμαι πλέον.
           οὐ μὴν ἀνήσω γ' οὐδὲ νῦν προθυμίας,   285
           ὡς ἂν παροῦσα καὶ σύ μοι ξυμμαρτυρῇς
           οἷα πέφυκα δυστυχοῦσι δεσπόταις.
           ἄγ', ὦ φίλη παῖ, τῶν πάροιθε μὲν λόγων
           λαθώμεθ' ἄμφω, καὶ σύ θ' ἡδίων γενοῦ
           στυγνὴν ὀφρῦν λύσασα καὶ γνώμης ὁδόν,   290
           ἐγώ θ' ὅπῃ σοι μὴ καλῶς τόθ' εἰπόμην
           μεθεῖσ' ἐπ' ἄλλον εἶμι βελτίω λόγον.
           κεἰ μὲν νοσεῖς τι τῶν ἀπορρήτων κακῶν,
           γυναῖκες αἵδε συγκαθιστάναι νόσον·
           εἰ δ' ἔκφορός σοι συμφορὰ πρὸς ἄρσενας,   295
           λέγ', ὡς ἰατροῖς πρᾶγμα μηνυθῇ τόδε.

284 *⁺ἀφ-ικνέομαι   arrive

285 ⁺μήν   however, yet, but (adversative pcl., especially
after a negative οὐ μήν: S #2920; GP 334.II[1]) – 'I have gone everywhere,
and yet have accomplished nothing.'

    ἀν-*ίημι   + gen.: let go, relax from (fut. act. indic. 1 sg.)
    [1x *Hipp.*]

    ⁺προθῡμία, ἡ   readiness, willingness, zeal; goodwill; – 'Even
    so, I certainly will not let go now of my zeal.'

286 ⁺ὡς (conj.)   so that, how (opens final clause with pres.
subjv., ξυμμαρτυρῇς in 1st sequence, ἀνήσω. ἄν may or may not be added to
a ἵνα clause without affecting meaning: S #2193, 2196; GMT #325, 326)

    συμ-μαρτύρέω   bear witness (pres. act. subjv. 2 sg.) [1x *Hipp.*]

287 ⁺οἷος, οἵα, οἷον (pron.)   such as, of such sort

    δυστυχέω   (δυσ-, τύχη, fate) be unlucky, unfortunate (δυ-
    στυχοῦσι δεσπόταις, generalizing or allusive pl. in which one person is
    alluded to in the pl.; it is always in masc., even when used in reference
    to women: S #1007; descriptive ptc., see ὁράω in line 4) – 'so that you
    being here may bear witness to the sort of person I am (by nature) to a
    mistress in misfortune.' (1264)

288 ἄγε (adv.)   well, come; come on (properly impv. sg. of
ἄγω, used as adv. Preferred reading to that of ἀλλά, because ἀλλά is used
when one is addressing a person and then breaks off in an appeal to that
person: GP 14. Here, however, until this point the Nurse has been talking
to the Chorus as if Phaedra is not present; now she turns from the Chorus to
Phaedra, whom she addresses directly. The exhortative ἄγε is therefore the
proper address. It is noteworthy that Phaedra is being talked at rather than
addressed up to this point by the Nurse. The Nurse obviously knows that
Phaedra is listening while she speaks to the Chorus. This dramatic tableau
will repeat itself later on in lines 601–67, when Hippolytus will be addressing the Nurse and scolding her about Phaedra's passion, knowing perfectly
well that Phaedra is listening.) [1x *Hipp.*]

⁺πάροιθε   before (τῶν πάροιθε λογῶν: an adv. may serve
as an adj. when it stands in an attr. position: S #1096)

289 *⁺λανθάνω   mid. and pass. + gen.: forget (λαθώμεθα, aor.²
subjv.; hortatory subjv.: 'let us forget': S #1797; GMT #256)

ἄμφω, τώ, τά, τώ   both of two (dual nom.) [1x *Hipp.*]

⁺ἡδύς, ἡδεῖα, ἡδύ   sweet, pleasant, welcome (ἡδίων, ἥδιον, compar.; γενοῦ, aor.² impv. dep. 2 sg.)

290 ὀφρύς, ύος, ἡ   brow (172)

λύσασα   When an aor. ptc. refers to the same action as
the aor. leading verb (here γενοῦ) or a fut. finite verb, it need not indicate prior action; in this case it is a ptc. coincidental with a leading
verb (of whatever mood): S #1872c2; cf. line 357. Here, according to
B., "Phaedra is to become more gracious not as a result of loosening
her brow but in loosening it." That is to say: 'become more gracious
in *loosening* [not: *having loosened*] your brow.' For further discussion,
see Roisman 1985.

⁺ὁδός, ἡ   path, way; – 'Come, dear child, let us both
forget our former words, and you, be more gracious, loosening your
gloomy brow and the path of your thinking'

291 ⁺ὅπη (indef. interrog. adv.) in which way, where

τότε (adv.)   at that time, formerly (τόθ' = τότε) [1x *Hipp.*]

μή ... εἱπόμην   Hamilton: "μή marks the generality of the
clause." (εἱπόμην, impf. of *⁺ἕπομαι + dat.)

292 ⁺μεθ-*ἵημι   let go, give up, let loose, release, abandon (μεθεῖσα, aor.² act. ptc.; ptc. antecedent to εἶμι: 'having given up . . . I will
go.' There is slight *anacoluthon*, a break in the grammatical structure, after
μεθεῖσα. It is not entirely clear what it is that she is giving up on. Is it her
'unsympathetic attitude' that she has just mentioned?)

βελτίων, ον   better (compar. of ἀγαθός; βελτίω = βελτίονα) –
'and where I failed to follow you sympathetically before, giving [it] up/
abandoning [this behavior] I will move on to better words.' [1x *Hipp.*]

293 ἀπόρρητος (2)   (ἀπ-ερῶ, renounce) that should not be spoken
(κεἰ = καὶ εἰ) [1x *Hipp.*]

τι   internal obj. of νοσεῖς: 'if you are sick with one
of the unspoken evils'

294 συγ-καθ-*⁺ίστημι   help in treating, cure (pf. inf. act.; final-consecutive inf.: GMT #770) – 'If you are sick with one of the unspoken evils,
there are women here to help treat the disease' [1x *Hipp.*]

295 ἔκ-φορος (2)   to be made known [1x *Hipp.*]

⁺συμφορά, ἡ   an event, in either a good or a bad sense; mis-
hap, misfortune (σοι, dat. of possess.: 'your')

ἀρσήν, ενος, ὁ   male, masculinity (970)

296 ἰατρός, ὁ   physician [1x *Hipp.*]

*μηνύω   inform, reveal, make known, disclose (μηνυθῇ,
aor.¹ subjv. pass.; ὡς . . . μηνυθῇ, final clause in 1st sequence, λέγε:
S #2196) – 'if, on the other hand, your misfortune can be told to men,
speak, so that this matter can be divulged to doctors' (1077)

εἶέν· τί σιγᾷς; οὐκ ἐχρῆν σιγᾶν, τέκνον,
ἀλλ᾿ ἤ μ᾿ἐλέγχειν, εἴ τι μὴ καλῶς λέγω,
ἢ τοῖσιν εὖ λεχθεῖσι συγχωρεῖν λόγοις.
φθέγξαι τι, δεῦρ᾿ ἄθρησον. ὦ τάλαιν᾿ἐγώ,   300
γυναῖκες, ἄλλως τούσδε μοχθοῦμεν πόνους,
ἴσον δ᾿ ἄπεσμεν τῷ πρίν· οὔτε γὰρ τότε
λόγοις ἐτέγγεθ᾿ ἥδε νῦν τ᾿ οὐ πείθεται.
ἀλλ᾿ ἴσθι μέντοι—πρὸς τάδ᾿ αὐθαδεστέρα
γίγνου θαλάσσης—εἰ θανῇ, προδοῦσα σοὺς   305

παῖδας, πατρῴων μὴ μεθέξοντας δόμων,
μὰ τὴν ἄνασσαν ἱππίαν Ἀμαζόνα,
ἣ σοῖς τέκνοισι δεσπότην ἐγείνατο,
νόθον φρονοῦντα γνήσι᾽, οἶσθα νιν καλῶς,
Ἱππόλυτον . . .   310
        Φα. οἴμοι.
                Τρ. θιγγάνει σέθεν τόδε;

297 εἰέν (pcl.)   well

τί   why?

ἐχρῆν   = +χρῆν, see line 253; – 'Well, why are you
silent? You shouldn't be silent, child'

299 λεχθεῖσι   (*+λέγω, aor.¹ ptc. pass. dat. pl. neut.; attr. to
λόγοις: S #912, 2049; GMT #824)

συγχωρέω   agree, compromise, come to terms (inf. required by ἐχρῆν) – 'but you should either refute me, if I say something
wrong, or else agree with what has been said right.' (703)

300 φθέγγομαι   utter a sound (φθέγξαι, aor.¹ impv. mid.) (880)

ἀθρέω   look closely at (ἄθρησον, aor.¹ impv. act.) –
'Talk to me, look over here, oh poor me!' [1x *Hipp.*]

301 μοχθέω   be weary with toil, suffer greatly, bear trouble; – 'Oh women, in vain we labor at these toils' (207)

302 τότε (adv.)   then, at that time (1072)

ἴσος (3)   equal to, the same as [1x *Hipp.*]

πρίν (adv. of time)   before, formerly (τῷ πρίν, in the past; subst.
use of artic. with an adv.: S #1153e; cf. line 706) [1x *Hipp.*]

ἄπ-*+ειμι   be away from, be absent; – 'we are as far off as
before' (184)

οὔτε γὰρ τότε   *enjambment* (οὔτε is answered by τ(έ) οὐ, not
by another οὔτε)

303 *+πείθω   persuade; mid.: obey; – 'for she was not soft-
ened by words then, and she is not being persuaded now.'

304 ἴσθι   (*⁺οἶδα, pf. impv. act. 2 sg.; with supplem. ptc.,
which represents a dependent statement when following verbs of knowing
and showing: S #2106, here προδοῦσα, 'know that you have betrayed . . .';
the tense of the ptc. has the same force as the corresponding tense of any of
the moods with ὅτι or ὡς) (519, 656)

   αὐθ-άδης, ες   [ᾱ] (αὐτός, self; ἥδομαι, enjoy oneself) self-
willed, willful, stubborn, headstrong [1x *Hipp.*]

305 θάλασσα, ἡ   the sea (gen. of comparison after the compar.
αὐθαδεστέρα: S #1069, 1431) (979)

   ⁺προ-*⁺δίδωμι   betray, fail one (προδοῦσα, aor.² ptc. act.
nom. sg. fem.; εἰ θανῇ [fut. indic. mid. 2 sg.] . . . ἴσθι προδοῦσα, fut.
emotional condition; in direct speech it would have been προύδω-
κας [B.]: S #229, 3b, 2297) – 'but know this—and then go on being
more stubborn than the sea—that if you die, you have betrayed your
children'

306 παῖδας   emphatic *enjambment* underscoring Phaedra's
sons; cf. line 310

   πατρῷος (3/2)   of a father, inherited from a father (1065)

   μετ-*⁺έχω   + gen.: have a share of (μεθέξοντας, fut. act.
ptc., ptc. of attendant circumstance, see ὁράω in line 4; μή depends on
the impv. ἴσθι; note the *consonance* μή μεθέξοντας followed by μά in
line 307) – 'who will have no share of their father's house' (731)

307 μά (pcl.)   + acc.: by, in (used in strong protestations and
oaths, usually confirming a negative statement) [1x *Hipp.*]

   ⁺ἄνασσα, ἡ   queen, lady, mistress

   ἵππιος (3)   of a horse, horses; – 'by the name of the Amazon, mistress of horses' [1x *Hipp.*]

308 γείνομαι   (trans.) bear, bring forth, beget (note the *hyperbaton* between ἥ and ἐγείνατο, which underscores the role of the Amazon,
former lover of Theseus) [1x *Hipp.*]

309 ⁺νόθος (3/2)   *nothos*, bastard. The Nurse must be com-
menting according to the myth in which the Amazon Hippolytē/Antiope,

Hippolytus' mother, was carried off by Theseus as a prize of war, and had she lived she would have been his concubine, not a wife. Legally, therefore, Hippolytus was born out of wedlock and is a bastard without the right of succession against Phaedra's children. The spectators, however, might also have understood the term νόθος in the context of their own time. After the Periclean law of 451/0 BCE, persons were eligible for Athenian citizenship only if both their parents were citizens of Athens. Those who had a non-Athenian mother or father were defined as bastards. According to this law, Hippolytus would not have had citizen rights and could not have inherited the throne. However, in this historical context, Theseus' and Phaedra's children would also have been considered bastards, as Phaedra was Cretan, not to mention that Theseus himself was a νόθος, having been born to a Troezenian mother. But as B. states: "The heroic world has of course no such nationalistic restrictions on legitimacy; nor did Athens before 451— Kleisthenes and Kimon, for instance, had foreign mothers." For the status of *nothoi*, see Patterson 1990; Kamen 2013, 62–70.

†γνήσιος (3) legitimate, highborn; – 'who bore a master for your children, a bastard, with thoughts of legitimacy, you know him well'

310 Ἱππόλυτον (emphatic *enjambment* that parallels that of παῖδας in line 306. Line 310 is a double *antilabe*; that is to say, it has two changes of speaker, indicating high excitement. Ἱππόλυτον, resolution in 2nd position.)

†οἴμοι woe's me! (exclamation of pain, fright, pity, anger, surprise)

†θιγγάνω + gen.: touch (σέθεν = σοῦ). Phaedra: – 'Oh no!' Nurse: – 'Does this touch you?'

Φα.	ἀπώλεσάς με, μαῖα, καί σε πρὸς θεῶν
	τοῦδ' ἀνδρὸς αὖθις λίσσομαι σιγᾶν πέρι.
Τρ.	ὁρᾷς; φρονεῖς μὲν εὖ, φρονοῦσα δ' οὐ θέλεις
	παῖδάς τ' ὀνῆσαι καὶ σὸν ἐκσῶσαι βίον.
Φα.	φιλῶ τέκν'· ἄλλῃ δ' ἐν τύχῃ χειμάζομαι.
Τρ.	ἁγνὰς μέν, ὦ παῖ, χεῖρας αἵματος φορεῖς;
Φα.	χεῖρες μὲν ἁγναί, φρὴν δ' ἔχει μίασμά τι.
Τρ.	μῶν ἐξ ἐπακτοῦ πημονῆς ἐχθρῶν τινος;
Φα.	φίλος μ' ἀπόλλυσ' οὐχ ἑκοῦσαν οὐχ ἑκών.

315

Τρ.	Θησεύς τιν' ἡμάρτηκεν ἐς σ' ἁμαρτίαν;	320
Φα.	μὴ δρῶσ' ἔγωγ' ἐκεῖνον ὀφθείην κακῶς.	
Τρ.	τί γὰρ τὸ δεινὸν τοῦθ' ὅ σ' ἐξαίρει θανεῖν;	
Φα.	ἔα μ' ἁμαρτεῖν· οὐ γὰρ ἐς σ' ἁμαρτάνω.	
Τρ.	οὐ δῆθ' ἑκοῦσά γ', ἐν δὲ σοὶ λελείψομαι.	
Φα.	τί δρᾷς; βιάζῃ, χειρὸς ἐξαρτωμένη;	325
Τρ.	καὶ σῶν γε γονάτων, κοὐ μεθήσομαί ποτε.	
Φα.	κάκ', ὦ τάλαινα, σοὶ τάδ', εἰ πεύσῃ, κακά.	
Τρ.	μεῖζον γὰρ ἤ σου μὴ τυχεῖν τί μοι κακόν;	

311 μαῖα, ἡ   nurse

     πρὸς θεῶν   by the gods!

312 ⁺ἀνήρ, ἀνδρός, ὁ   man (syncopated noun: S #44, 262)

     ⁺αὖθις (adv.)   hereafter, from now on

     λίσσομαι   beg, pray, entreat, beseech [1x *Hipp.*]

     ⁺πέρι   *anastrophe.* Phaedra's cry of distress at hear-
ing Hippolytus' name is misunderstood by the Nurse, who assumes
that Phaedra's anguish results from her fear for her children's sake and
thinks that by bringing up the future of Phaedra's sons, she has man-
aged to rattle her mistress. – 'You are killing me, Nurse, and I beg you
by the gods to be silent about this man from now on.'

313 φρονοῦσα   (concessive pres. act. ptc., coincidental with
θέλεις: S #2066; GMT #842)

314 *⁺ὀνίνημι   profit, benefit (ὀνῆσαι, aor.¹ inf. act.)

     ⁺ἐκ-*⁺σώζω   preserve, keep safe (ἐκσῶσαι, aor.¹ inf. act.) –
'You see? You are of the right mind, but even though you are, you don't
wish to benefit your children and save your life.'

315 χειμάζω   pass.: be driven or tossed by a storm, be distressed; – 'I love my children; in another fate I am tossed by a storm.' [1x
Hipp.]

316 μέν   B. quotes A. W. Verrall on *Medea* 676: "μέν
in an interrogative sentence . . . marks the prep. as preliminary"; that is to

say, she will continue with other possibilities that toss Phaedra like a storm: "Your hands, child, are clean of blood, I suppose."

φορέω   bear or carry constantly; possess [1x *Hipp.*]

317 ⁺**μίασμα**   B.: "The notion of an inner impurity resulting not from one's acts but from one's thoughts or intentions is still an unfamiliar one; and the Nurse quite fails to see what Phaedra means." Phaedra's use of μίασμα in this sense indicates how subtle and versed in current philosophical thinking she is, which in turn manifests itself in her formidable rhetorical skill. – 'My hands are clean, but my mind is somewhat stained.'

318 ⁺**μῶν** (interrog. pcl.)   = μὴ οὖν, can/could it be that (used in questions when a negative answer is expected)

ἐπ-ακτός (2)   (ἐπ-άγω, bring to) brought on/in from abroad; foreign, alien [1x *Hipp.*]

πημονή, ἡ   (poetic for πῆμα) suffering, harm; – 'It is not from harm brought from abroad by one of your enemies?' [1x *Hipp.*]

319 ⁺**ἑκών, ἑκοῦσα, ἑκόν** willing (Phaedra discards the Nurse's idea that her suffering is brought from abroad by using the φίλος 'near and dear') – 'No, one who is dear to me destroys me against my will and against his.'

320 **Θησεύς**   When Phaedra says that 'one who is dear' to her destroys her, the Nurse naturally assumes she means her husband, Theseus. When Phaedra vehemently rejects the idea, she might rightly expect that the Nurse will go to the second in line, Hippolytus, but the Nurse is at a loss.

⁺**ἁμαρτία, ἡ**   failure, error, sin (ἡμάρτηκεν ἁμαρτίαν, *figura etymologica*; the rhetorical device emphasizes the Nurse's suspicion) – 'Has Theseus committed some wrong against you?'

321 **μὴ ... ὀφθείην**   opt. of wish (ὀφθείην < *⁺ὁράω, aor. pass. opt.: S #1814) – 'May I not be seen doing him harm!'

322 **τί γάρ**   well, what (is) it? (GP 81)

ἐξ-αίρω   urge, incite; – 'Well, what is this terrible thing that incites you to die?' [1x *Hipp.*]

323 *⁺ἐάω   [ᾱ] let, suffer, allow, permit (ἔα, pres. act. impv. 2 sg.) – 'Let me err; for I am not erring against you!'

324 ⁺δῆτα (adv.)   (emphatic) assuredly, really, in truth; οὐ δῆτα, indeed/certainly not (in emphatic negative answers; 'refusing to obey': GP 275 [v])

λείπομαι   fall short (λελείψομαι, fut. pf. mid. indic.) – 'No! Not willingly! But if I fail, it will be because of you!'

325 βιάζω   force, constrain [1x *Hipp*.]

ἐξ-αρτάω   hang from/upon (ἐξαρτωμένη, pres. pass. ptc. of attendant circumstance, coincidental with the leading verb, see ὁράω in line 4. While Phaedra speaks, the Nurse kneels before her and clasps her mistress's hand and her knees in ritual supplication.) – 'What are you doing? Are you using force, hanging upon my hand?' [1x *Hipp*.]

326 καὶ ... γε   yes . . . and

γόνυ, τό   knee (gen. sg. γόνατος, dat. pl. γόνασι, resolution in the 5th position: γονάτον) – 'Yes, and [seizing] your knees too, and I will never let go.' (607)

327 πεύσῃ   (*⁺πυνθάνομαι, fut. indic. 2 sg.; σοί, dat. of disadvantage or incommodi: S #1481) – 'Bad, oh poor woman, will these things be for you, bad if you learn them.'

328 τυχεῖν   (*⁺τυγχάνω, aor.² inf. act.) + gen.: σοῦ

μοι   dat. of disadvantage (S #1481) – 'For what greater evil [could there be] *for me* than not to win you?'

Φα.	ὀλῇ· τὸ μέντοι πρᾶγμ' ἐμοὶ τιμὴν φέρει.	
Τρ.	κἄπειτα κρύπτεις, χρήσθ' ἱκνουμένης ἐμοῦ;	330
Φα.	ἐκ τῶν γὰρ αἰσχρῶν ἐσθλὰ μηχανώμεθα.	
Τρ.	οὔκουν λέγουσα τιμιωτέρα φανῇ;	
Φα.	ἄπελθε πρὸς θεῶν δεξιάν τ' ἐμὴν μέθες.	
Τρ.	οὐ δῆτ', ἐπεί μοι δῶρον οὐ δίδως ὃ χρῆν.	
Φα.	δώσω· σέβας γὰρ χειρὸς αἰδοῦμαι τὸ σόν.	335
Τρ.	σιγῷμ' ἂν ἤδη· σὸς γὰρ οὑντεῦθεν λόγος.	
Φα.	ὦ τλῆμον, οἷον, μῆτερ, ἠράσθης ἔρον.	

Τρ.	ὃν ἔσχε ταύρου, τέκνον; ἢ τί φῇς τόδε;	
Φα.	σύ τ', ὦ τάλαιν' ὅμαιμε, Διονύσου δάμαρ.	
Τρ.	τέκνον, τί πάσχεις; συγγόνους κακορροθεῖς;	340
Φα.	τρίτη δ' ἐγὼ δύστηνος ὡς ἀπόλλυμαι.	
Τρ.	ἔκ τοι πέπληγμαι· ποῖ προβήσεται λόγος;	
Φα.	ἐκεῖθεν ἡμεῖς, οὐ νεωστί, δυστυχεῖς.	
Τρ.	οὐδέν τι μᾶλλον οἶδ'ἃ βούλομαι κλυεῖν.	
Φα.	φεῦ·	
	πῶς ἂν σύ μοι λέξειας ἁμὲ χρὴ λέγειν;	345

329 **+ὄλλυμι**   act.: destroy; mid.: perish, die (ὀλῇ, fut. indic. mid. This is the worst-case scenario for the Nurse. B.: "It will be the death of you if I tell you." Phaedra's exaggeration of the Nurse's lot is underscored by her use of the pres. φέρει—as if she is already dying.) – 'You will die. But to me the deed *brings* honor.'

330 **+ἔπειτα** (adv.)   (ἐπί, εἶτα) thereupon, thereafter, then (κἄπειτα = καὶ ἔπειτα, marks the sequence of one thing upon another)

+χρηστός (3)   (χράομαι, use) useful; adj. used substantively: good services, benefits (χρῆσθ' = χρηστά, subst. adj. without artic.; for subst. adjs. without an artic., see, for example, σοφός in line 90)

*ἱκνέομαι   arrive, come to; come as a suppliant, beseech, entreat, implore (ἱκνουμένης ἐμοῦ, temporal/concessive gen. abs.: S #2070a, c) – 'when/although I implore you for your own good' [1x *Hipp.*]

331 **+αἰσχρός** (3/2)   shameful,   disgracing;   ugly,   ill-favored (τῶν . . . αἰσχρῶν, artic. subst. adj.; see νέος in line 114)

+ἐσθλός (3)   good (αἰσχρῶν ἐσθλά, *oxymoron*: S #3035)

+μηχανάομαι   contrive, devise, scheme (μηχανώμεθα, *majestic plural* emphasizing her agency: S #1006)

332 **οὔκουν** (adv.)   (= οὐκ οὖν) and so not? not therefore? not then? (often with 2nd pers. fut. indic., or opt. with ἄν, at the opening of a speech; φανῇ, 2 sg. fut. pass. < *+φαίνω; οὔκουν . . . φανῇ, *hyperbaton*; +λέγουσα, circumstantial ptc. denoting condition: S #2067; GMT #841) [1x *Hipp.*]

τίμιος (3/2)   (+τίμη, honor) 'valued, held in honor.' According to B., while Phaedra meant that she is contriving good by the

concealment of her behavior, the Nurse understands that she is con-
cealing her conduct because it is good and thus replies accordingly.
– 'Won't you then appear more honorable if you speak?' [1x *Hipp.*]

333 ἀπ-‡⁺ἔρχομαι   go away, depart from (ἄπελθε, 2 sg. aor.² act.
impv.) (708)

⁺δέξιος (3)   on the right-hand side (= δεξιάν τ' ἐμὴν
[χεῖρα]; μέθες < ⁺μεθίημι, 2 sg. aor.² impv. act.) (1360)

334 δῶρον, τό   gift

*⁺δίδωμι   give

*⁺χρῆν   'which you should have [given, but did not]'
(see χρῆν in line 253; supply διδόναι: GMT #415, 417; S #1774)

335 σέβας, τό   reverence, obligation, respect (σέβας χειρὸς τὸ
σόν = τὸ σῆς χειρὸς σέβας, *hypallage*; the possess. adj. should agree with
χείρ: S #3027; σέβας . . . τὸ σόν, when the noun takes no artic. before it,
but the artic. appears before its adj., the attr. adj. is added by way of explanation: S #1159) – 'for I respect the reverence of your [supplicating] hand'
[1x *Hipp.*]

336 ⁺σιγῷμι   pres. opt. act. 1 sg. (potential opt. is often used
for polite fut. in tragedy; see βούλομαι in line 270) – 'I will be silent now'

⁺σός (3)   your

ἐντεῦθεν (adv.)   hence, henceforth, afterward (οὑντεῦθεν λόγος
= ὁ ἐντεῦθεν λόγος, 'the from-here-on speech') [1x *Hipp.*]

337 ἔρον   = ἔρωτα (poetic acc. sg.: S #285.11; ἡράσθης
ἔρον, *figura etymologica*. Phaedra's mother was Pasiphaë, whom Poseidon made unnaturally lust for a beautiful white bull he gave her husband,
Minos. Eventually she gave birth to the Minotaur, part man and part bull.)
– 'Oh wretched mother! What a love you loved!' (449)

338 ⁺ταῦρος, ὁ   bull (ταύρου, obj. gen.: S #1328, 1331) –
'which she had for the bull, child? Or what is this you are saying?'

339 ὅμαιμος, ὁ/ἡ   (ὁμός, one and the same + αἷμα, blood) of the
same blood, kinswoman [1x *Hipp.*]

Διόνῡσος, ὁ   Dionysus (resolution in 8th position, Διονύ-σου; Ariadne, who at some point becomes Dionysus' wife, which ends unhappily in some accounts) [1x *Hipp.*]

340 ***⁺πάσχω**   suffer, experience; – 'what's the matter with you, child?'

σύγ-γονος (2)   born with, connected by blood, akin, brother, sister (1379)

κᾰκορροθέω   speak evil of, revile, abuse, slander [1x *Hipp.*]

341 **⁺τρίτος** (3)   (τρίς, three times; τρεῖς, three) third

342 **⁺τοί** (pcl. postpos. and enclit.)   in truth, surely, you (must) know (used often to express personal conviction: S #2984, 2985; GP 539, 541 [6]: "revealing the speaker's emotional or intellectual state")

ἐκ . . .*πέπληγμαι   = *⁺ἐκπέπληγμαι, *tmesis*; – 'I am utterly stunned!'

⁺προ-*⁺βαίνω   go toward, go forward, advance; – 'Where does this story lead to?'

343 **ἐκεῖθεν** (adv.)   thence, from that place [1x *Hipp.*]

νεωστί (adv.)   lately, just now, recently (ἡμεῖς . . . δυστυχεῖς, *majestic plural*: S #1006) – 'From there, not of late, comes our woe.' [1x *Hipp.*]

⁺δυστῠχής, ές   unlucky, unfortunate

345 **ἄν . . . λέξειας**   (*⁺λέγω, aor.¹ act. opt. 2 sg.; πῶς ἄν with opt. with the force of a wish, the fulfillment of which the speaker has little hope of attaining; cf. line 209; μοι, ethical dat. or dat. of feeling to denote the speaker's interest: S #1486; ἀμέ = ἃ ἐμέ) – 'Would that you might say for me what I must say?'

Τρ.	οὐ μάντις εἰμὶ τἀφανῆ γνῶναι σαφῶς.
Φα.	τί τοῦθ' ὃ δὴ λέγουσιν ἀνθρώπους ἐρᾶν;
Τρ.	ἥδιστον, ὦ παῖ, ταὐτὸν ἀλγεινόν θ' ἅμα.
Φα.	ἡμεῖς ἂν εἶμεν θατέρῳ κεχρημένοι.
Τρ.	τί φής; ἐρᾷς, ὦ τέκνον; ἀνθρώπων τίνος;
Φα.	ὅστις ποθ' οὗτός ἐσθ', ὁ τῆς Ἀμαζόνος . . .

350

Τρ.   Ἱππόλυτον αὐδᾷς;

            Φα. σοῦ τάδ᾽, οὐκ ἐμοῦ κλύεις.

Τρ.   οἴμοι, τί λέξεις, τέκνον; ὥς μ᾽ ἀπώλεσας.
            γυναῖκες, οὐκ ἀνασχέτ᾽· οὐκ ἀνέξομαι
            ζῶσ᾽, ἐχθρὸν ἦμαρ, ἐχθρὸν εἰσορῶ φάος.   355
            ῥίψω μεθήσω σῶμ᾽, ἀπαλλαχθήσομαι
            βίου θανοῦσα· χαίρετ᾽, οὐκέτ᾽ εἴμ᾽ ἐγώ.
            οἱ σώφρονες γάρ, οὐχ ἑκόντες ἀλλ᾽ ὅμως,
            κακῶν ἐρῶσι. Κύπρις οὐκ ἄρ᾽ ἦν θεός,
            ἀλλ᾽ εἴ τι μεῖζον ἄλλο γίγνεται θεοῦ,   360
            ἢ τήνδε κἀμὲ καὶ δόμους ἀπώλεσεν.

346   ⁺**μάντῐς, εως, ὁ**   diviner, seer, prophet, prophetess

            ἀφᾰνής, ές   (ἀ privat., φανῆναι, appear) unseen, invisible;
            hidden, unknown (τἀφανῆ = τὰ ἀφανῆ) (1289)

            γνῶναι   (*⁺γιγνώσκω, aor.² act. inf.; final-consecutive
            inf.: S #2008, 2011)

            σαφῶς (adv.)   clearly, plainly, for sure; – 'I am not a prophet
            so as to know clearly the things invisible.' (589)

347   B.: "The rel. clause begins with λέγουσιν = 'call,' as though it were
to be ὃ ἐρᾶν λέγουσιν ('which they call "being in love"'); ἐρᾶν then develops into the acc. and inf. ἀνθρώπους ἐρᾶν as though following λέγουσιν =
'say' ('they say that people "are in love"')." – 'What is it they mean when
they say that people are in love?'

348   **ἀλγεινός** (3)   giving pain, painful (ταὐτόν = τὸ αὐτόν, the
same) (775)

            ⁺**ἅμα** (adv.)   at the same time, at once; – 'The same thing is
            at the same time most pleasant and painful, child.'

349   ⁺**ἕτερος** (3)   one of two (θατέρῳ = τῷ ἑτέρῳ) (894)

            ἡμεῖς . . . *⁺**κεχρημένοι** (*majestic plural*: S #1006; masc. pl. serves as a
            generalizing gender: S #1015) – 'I have experienced the second of the
            two.'

350   ⁺**τίνος** (interrog. pron.)   (S #334; gen. required by ἐρᾷς: verbs of
desire take the gen.)

351 ⁺ὅστις (indef./general relat. pron.) (S #339; Phaedra pretends not to know his name). – 'Whoever this man is, the son of the Amazon . . .'

352 ⁺αὐδάω (αὐδή, human voice) + double acc.: speak, talk, say (Ἱππόλυτος, resolution in 2nd position)

353 *⁺λέξεις According to B., in seven other places in Euripides (*Hecuba* 712, 511, 1124; *Ion* 1113; *Helen* 779; *Phoenissai* 1274; *Medea* 1310), the fut. is used for pres. or aor. when the speaker "is violently disturbed by something he has just heard. The fut. is perhaps best explained by saying that she feels that the words just heard require elaboration" (ὡς, exclamatory 'how'). – 'Oh no! What are you saying, child? How have you destroyed me?!'

354 ἀνασχετός (2) to be suffered (οὐκ ἀνασχετ[ά] '[these are] things that cannot be borne/suffered'; *litotes*) [1x *Hipp.*]

ⁿ⁺ἀν-*⁺ἔχω continue to + ptc. (B. on 354–7: "Her distress is admirably brought out by her language: short sentences, *asyndeton*, repetitions." One could add *figura etymologica, enjambment,* and *anaphora*; ἀνασχετά, ἀνέξομαι, *figura etymologica*.)

355 ζῶσα (*⁺ζάω; supplem. ptc.: S #2088; emphatic *enjambment*) – 'I won't live any longer.'

ἦμαρ, ατος, τό (poetic for ⁺ἡμέρα) day (ἐχθρόν . . . ἐχθρόν, *anaphora*; *asyndeton* between ἐχθρὸν ἦμαρ and ἐχθρὸν εἰσορῶ φάος) [1x *Hipp.*]

356 ⁺ἀπ-αλλάττω set free, release, get rid of (ἀπαλλαχθήσομαι, fut. pass.; *asyndeton* between ῥίψω and μεθήσω)

357 βίου θανοῦσα (*enjambment*; βίου, gen. of separation: S #1392; when an aor. ptc. [θανοῦσα] refers to the same action as the fut. [here ἀπαλλαχθήσομαι] leading verb or an aor. finite verb, it is coincidental with the action of the leading verb (of whatever mood); see on λύσασα in line 290) – 'Dying I will free myself of life.'

⁺οὐκέτι (adv.) no more, no longer, no further (εἴμ' ἐγώ: note the accent that renders existential meaning to the usually enclit. verb; cf. S #187b) – 'I am no more.'

358 †σώφρων, ὁ, ἡ; σῶφρον, τό (gen. ονος) of sound mind, prudent, chaste; – 'For those who are chaste are in love with what's bad against their will, but yet they still do.'

359 ἄρ(α) (pcl.)   'after all'; expresses "the surprise attendant upon disillusionment" with a verb in the present or in the past (GP 35–6) (here with the imperfect ἦν describes a fact just realized)

360 εἴ τι   effectively = ὅ τι, whatever; – 'Cypris, after all, is not a god, but [if there is something else] whatever else is greater than a god.'

Dividing Choral Stanza Lines 362–72

This short lament sung by the Chorus, or just the leader of the Chorus according to B., with the actors on stage, corresponds to the lament sung by Phaedra in lines 669–79, which renders this strophe and antistrophe a *kommos*. This kind of a correspondence separated by three hundred lines is "remarkable in tragedy" (B.).

Χο.	[στρ.	
ἄιες ὤ, ἔκλυες ὤ,	362a	Ah! Did you note, ah! Did you hear
ἀνήκουστα τᾶς	362b	the unbearable
τυράννου πάθεα μέλεα θρεομένας;		sufferings that the queen cried aloud?
ὀλοίμαν ἔγωγε πρὶν σᾶν, φίλα,		I would rather die, my friend, before
κατανύσαι φρενῶν. ἰώ μοι, φεῦ φεῦ·	365	I arrive at your state of mind! Ah me! Alas!
ὤ τάλαινα τῶνδ᾽ ἀλγέων·		Oh how miserable you are because of these griefs!
ὤ πόνοι τρέφοντες βροτούς.		Oh the toils that rear mortals!
ὄλωλας, ἐξέφηνας ἐς φάος κακά.		You're undone, you've revealed bad things to the
τίς σε παναμέριος ὅδε χρόνος μένει;		daylight! What awaits you during this long day?
τελευτάσεταί τι καινὸν δόμοις·	370	Something unlucky to this house will be brought

ἄσημα δ' οὐκέτ' ἐστὶν οἷ φθίνει τύχα

Κύπριδος, ὦ τάλαινα παῖ Κρησία.

to pass. It is no longer unclear where the fortune

sent by Cypris ends, oh wretched child of Crete.

362a	⏑⏑ ⏑ – ⏑⏑ ⏑ –	creticus + creticus
362b	⏑ – – ⏑ –	dochmiac
363	⏑ – – ⏑ ⏑⏑ ⏑ ⏑⏑ ⏑⏑ ⏑ –	2 dochmiacs
364	⏑ – – ⏑ – ⏑ – – ⏑ –	2 dochmiacs
365	⏑ ⏑⏑ – ⏑ – ⏑ – – ⏑ –	2 dochmiacs
366	– ⏑ – ⏑ – – ⏑ –	creticus + dochmiac
367	– ⏑ – ⏑ – – ⏑ –	creticus + dochmiac
368	⏑ – – ⏑ – – ⏑ – ⏑ – ⏑ x	3 iambs
369	– ⏑⏑ – ⏑ ⏑⏑ ⏑ ⏑⏑ – ⏑ –	2 dochmiacs
370	⏑ – – ⏑ – ⏑ – – ⏑ –	2 dochmiacs
371	⏑ – ⏑ – ⏑ – ⏑ – ⏑ – ⏑ –	3 iambs
372	⏑ ⏑⏑ – ⏑ – ⏑ – – ⏑ –	2 dochmiacs

362 ἀΐω perceive, become aware of, note (ἄιες, impf.; used only in pres. and impf.)

ἀνήκουστος, ον (ἀ privat., ἀκούω) unheard of, unbearable (obj. of θρεομένας) [1x *Hipp.*]

363 ⁺τύραννος, ὁ, ἡ [ῠ] master, mistress

⁺μέλεος (3/2) wretched, unhappy

θρέομαι (used only in pres., mostly in mid.) cry aloud, shriek out, wail, lament (= θρεομένης, pres. mid. ptc.; gen. required by a verb of hearing, ἔκλυες: S #1361a) [1x *Hipp.*]

364 ὀλοίμαν = ὀλοίμην (*⁺ὄλλυμι, aor.² opt. mid.; opt. of wish: S #1814; GMT #721, 722; σᾶν = σῶν)

365 κατ-ᾰνύω + gen.: arrive at (aor.¹ inf. act.; ⁺πρίν + inf., see line 29) [1x *Hipp.*]

366 ⁺ἄλγος, τό pain, sorrow, grief, distress (ἀλγέων, gen. of cause in exclamation: S #1407, here explaining τάλαινα)

367 *+τρέφω   nourish, rear

368 +ἐξ-έφηνας   (+ἐκ-*+φαίνω) (ἐξ-έφηνας . . . φάος, *figura etymologica*)

369 πᾰν-ημέριος (3)   lasting all day (Doric: πᾱν-άμεριος) [1x *Hipp.*]
*μένω   remain, await (1322)

370 τελευτάω   pass.: come to pass, happen [1x *Hipp.*]
καινός (3)   new, strange (688)

371 ᾰ-σημος (3)   without sign or mark, obscure, unclear (ἄσημα . . . οὐκέτι, *litotes*; ἄσημα . . . τύχα, emphatic *hyperbaton* underscoring the certainty of the upcoming disaster) (269)

οἷ (relat. adv.)   to which place, whither (cf. correl. advs. ποῖ, ποι, ὅποι: S: #346) [1x *Hipp.*]

φθίνω   decline, decay, wane [1x *Hipp.*]

372 +Κρήσιος (3)   Cretan (Phaedra is the daughter of Minos and Pasiphaë, the rulers of Crete; the adj. is used of Phaedra only here. Phaedra's Cretan origin is not hugely emphasized, but it is mentioned, e.g., in 151–60, 337–43, 372, 719–20, 752–62.) Note how the proper name Cypris in an emphatic *enjambment* and the adj. 'Cretan' frame the last line of the Chorus.

Scene B: Lines 373–524

Φα.   Τροζήνιαι γυναῖκες, αἳ τόδ' ἔσχατον
         οἰκεῖτε χώρας Πελοπίας προνώπιον,
         ἤδη ποτ' ἄλλως νυκτὸς ἐν μακρῷ χρόνῳ   375
         θνητῶν ἐφρόντισ' ᾗ διέφθαρται βίος.
         καί μοι δοκοῦσιν οὐ κατὰ γνώμης φύσιν
         πράσσειν κάκιον· ἔστι γὰρ τό γ' εὖ φρονεῖν
         πολλοῖσιν· ἀλλὰ τῇδ' ἀθρητέον τόδε·
         τὰ χρήστ' ἐπιστάμεσθα καὶ γιγνώσκομεν,   380
         οὐκ ἐκπονοῦμεν δ', οἱ μὲν ἀργίας ὕπο,
         οἱ δ' ἡδονὴν προθέντες ἀντὶ τοῦ καλοῦ
         ἄλλην τιν'. εἰσὶ δ' ἡδοναὶ πολλαὶ βίου,

μακραί τε λέσχαι καὶ σχολή, τερπνὸν κακόν,
αἰδώς τε· δισσαὶ δ' εἰσίν, ἡ μὲν οὐ κακή,   385
ἡ δ' ἄχθος οἴκων· εἰ δ' ὁ καιρὸς ἦν σαφής,
οὐκ ἂν δύ' ἤστην ταῦτ' ἔχοντε γράμματα.
ταῦτ' οὖν ἐπειδὴ τυγχάνω φρονοῦσ' ἐγώ,
οὐκ ἔσθ' ὁποίῳ φαρμάκῳ διαφθερεῖν
ἔμελλον, ὥστε τοὔμπαλιν πεσεῖν φρενῶν.   390

373 ἔσχᾰτος (3)   the farthest

374 χώρα, ἡ   land, place (897)

Πελόπιος (3)   of Pelops [1x *Hipp.*]

προνώπιον, τό (often pl.)   space in front of, threshold, entrance
hall (τόδε . . . προνώπιον, *hyperbaton*; this geographic snapshot is
given from the point of view of an Athenian, in spite of the fact that
Phaedra has just been identified by the Chorus as Cretan. προνώπιος
"is the open space in front of a house, and Troezen when seen across
the Saronic Gulf from Athens lies in front of the main mass of the
Peloponnese" [B.]. Πελοπίας, resolution in 5th position.) – 'Women
of Troezen, you who live in this furthest outcourt of Pelops' land' [1x
Hipp.]

375 ⁺μακρός (3)   long (whether in space or time)

⁺χρόνος, ὁ   time, span of time

376 ⁺φροντίζω   think, consider, reflect, give heed

⁺ᾗ (adv.)   how, in what way; which way, where

*⁺δια-φθείρω   corrupt, destroy utterly (διέφθαρται, pf. pass. in-
dic. The verb is ambiguously used. It could mean the downfall of men's
lives, but could also refer to the corruption of their ways: "it is the latter
that Phaedra intends, but her use of the ambiguous word is the more
natural in that in her own case at least the two are inseparably linked"
[B.].) – 'Already in other circumstances during night's long hours, I have
pondered how the lives of mortals have been ruined/corrupted.'

378–9 *⁺πράσσω   fare, do, work, achieve (πράσσειν κακίον = do
worse; ἔστι, existential use [cf. line 190]; τὸ ⁺φρονεῖν, artic. inf.; see τὸ

σωφρονεῖν in line 80; ⁺πόλλοισιν, dat. of possess.: S #1476, *enjambment*) – 'And they seem to me to do worse, not because of the nature of their judgment; since many people possess good sense.'

⁺τῇδε (adv.)   in this way, in this direction

ἀθρέω   look closely at, observe (ἀθρητέον, verbal adj. expressing necessity: S #471, 473) – 'but it must be looked at in this way' (300)

380   τὰ ⁺χρήστ'   'good' (subst. use of artic. with adj.; see νέος in line 114; the accent is thrown back when the accented ultima is elided: S #174, hence χρήστ')

⁺ἐπίσταμαι   know (ἐπιστάμεσθα = ἐπιστάμεθα, for metrical convenience: S #465d; B.: "The combination of two near synonyms serves to emphasize how fully we are conscious of these moral values.")

381   ⁺ἐκ-πονέω   execute, carry out, accomplish by toil (B.: "bring to completion [ἐκ] by means of πόνος"; *enjambment*) – 'We understand and recognize what is good, but we fail to carry it out'

ἀργία, ἡ   idleness, laziness [1x *Hipp.*]

ὕπο   (*anastrophe*; οἱ μέν . . . οἱ δέ, some . . . others) – 'some out of laziness'

382   ⁺ἡδονή, ἡ   pleasure

⁺προ-*⁺τίθημι   put/set before, prefer (προθέντες, aor.² act. ptc.; artic. subst. ptc.; see πάρειμι in line 184)

383   ἄλλην τινα [ἡδονήν] *enjambment*; = 'others because of setting/preferring some pleasure in front of virtue'

384–6   λέσχη, ἡ   talking, gossip [1x *Hipp.*]

σχολή, ἡ   leisure (⁺αἰδώς τε, *enjambment*) – 'And there are many pleasures in life—both long hours of gossiping and leisure, a delightful evil, and also the sense of shame/modesty.' [1x *Hipp.*]

The claim of twofold αἰδώς is a notorious interpretative crux. Could she be referring to the inherent ambiguity of the word, in which it stands out from the other forms of pleasure and therefore is mentioned last? That is to say, while one and the same conduct or act can be considered by some a mark of high morality, which can be a source of delight, others may consider it disgraceful, the result of a faulty sense of shame (see Roisman 1999, 79–81). For an example of another of the many interpretations, see Ferguson 385: "Probably dream-escape of fantasizing, which is harmless, and an honest facing of her psychological problem in such a way as to overcome it, which she has found too hard." See also B. on 385–6; Halleran on 385–6a; Furley 1996. Dodds (1925, 103–4) has an interesting comment about the use of the terms αἰδώς and σωφροσύνη by the main three characters: "As Phaedra does violence to αἰδώς, in the name of αἰδώς, so does Hippolytus to σωφροσύνη in the name of σωφροσύνη: each is the victim of his own and the other's submerged desires masquerading as morality." While they use similar words, they may not actually agree on their meanings. For example, Theseus, Phaedra, and Hippolytus use the term αἰδώς. Hippolytus uses it to mean the shamefast awe with which the pure meadow is tended (78) and as reverence for the gods (998). Phaedra uses the negative when she is ashamed of her behavior (244) and in talking about her awe or reverence and as pleasure and shame here (cf. 335). Theseus uses it in terms of respect for the gods and religious customs (1258). Hippolytus uses the words fifteen times, almost always in praise of himself. Hippolytus lays claim also to piety. Phaedra mimics Hippolytus' sense of αἰδώς. In return, Hippolytus becomes increasingly concerned with his own reputation in the play's second half, as Phaedra is in the first half. Cf. σωφρονέω in line 80.

ἄχθος, εος, τό	weight, burden, load (οἴκων, obj. gen.) – 'the other a burden on the house' [1x *Hipp.*]
καιρός, ὁ	right measure, appropriate; right time (899)
⁺σαφής, ές	clear

387 ⁺γράμμα, ατος, τό (γράφω) letter (ἤστην < *⁺εἰμί, impf. indic. 3 dual; ταῦτ' = τὰ αὐτά; 'ἔχοντε, pres. act. ptc. nom. of attendant circumstance, coincidental with ἦν, see ὁράω in line 4; contrary-to-fact condition for the pres. time: impf. in both protasis, ἦν, and apodosis, ἤστην with ἄν: GMT #410; S #2304) – 'if what is proper were clear, there would not have been two of them spelled with the same letters.'

388–90 ⁺ἐπει-δή (conj.) since (τυγχάνω with supplem. ptc. φρονοῦσα, which tells what the main idea is, while the finite verb tells something about how the action is occurring: S: #2096a)

ὁποῖος (3) of whatever sort (S #340). [1x *Hipp.*]

⁺φάρμακον, τό drug, medicine, remedy, charm (φαρμάκῳ has been attracted to its relat. clause)

⁺μέλλω be about to, be on the point of doing, intend to (with pres./fut. inf. forms, the periphrastic fut. pres. inf. usually expresses will: S #1959a; ἔμελλον, *enjambment*) – 'Since I happen to hold to these views, there is no sort of drug by which I was about to destroy (my thought) . . .'

ἔμ-πᾰλιν (adv.) contrary to + gen. φρενῶν (τοὔμπαλιν = τὸ ἔμπαλιν) [1x *Hipp.*]

⁺ὥστε so as, so that (with the inf. πεσεῖν, implies a possible or intended result or tendency rather than actual fact: GMT #587; S #2011) – 'so as to fall into the opposite mindset.'

λέξω δὲ καί σοι τῆς ἐμῆς γνώμης ὁδόν,
ἐπεί μ' ἔρως ἔτρωσεν, ἐσκόπουν ὅπως
κάλλιστ' ἐνέγκαιμ' αὐτόν. ἠρξάμην μὲν οὖν
ἐκ τοῦδε, σιγᾶν τήνδε καὶ κρύπτειν νόσον·
γλώσσῃ γὰρ οὐδὲν πιστόν, ἣ θυραῖα μὲν   395
φρονήματ' ἀνδρῶν νουθετεῖν ἐπίσταται,
αὐτὴ δ' ὑφ'αὑτῆς πλεῖστα κέκτηται κακά.
τὸ δεύτερον δὲ τὴν ἄνοιαν εὖ φέρειν
τῷ σωφρονεῖν νικῶσα προυνοησάμην.
τρίτον δ', ἐπειδὴ τοισίδ' οὐκ ἀξήνυτον   400
Κύπριν κρατῆσαι, κατθανεῖν ἔδοξέ μοι,
κράτιστον (οὐδεὶς ἀντερεῖ) βουλευμάτων.
ἐμοὶ γὰρ εἴη μήτε λανθάνειν καλὰ
μήτ' αἰσχρὰ δρώσῃ μάρτυρας πολλοὺς ἔχειν.
τὸ δ' ἔργον ἤδη τὴν νόσον τε δυσκλεᾶ,   405
γυνή τε πρὸς τοῖσδ' οὖσ' ἐγίγνωσκον καλῶς,
μίσημα πᾶσιν· ὡς ὄλοιτο παγκάκως
ἥτις πρὸς ἄνδρας ἤρξατ' αἰσχύνειν λέχη
πρώτη θυραίους. ἐκ δὲ γενναίων δόμων
τόδ' ἦρξε θηλείαισι γίγνεσθαι κακόν·   410

ὅταν γὰρ αἰσχρὰ τοῖσιν ἐσθλοῖσιν δοκῇ,
ἢ κάρτα δόξει τοῖς κακοῖς γ' εἶναι καλά.

392–3 *τιτρώσκω   wound (703)

⁺σκοπέω   look, consider (ἐνέγκαιμι < *⁺φέρω, aor.¹ act. opt.; ὅπως . . . ἐνέγκαιμι, the opt. stands for an original interrog. subjv. in indirect question after a secondary tense: GMT #1490; κάλλιστα, adv. superl.: S #1609) – 'I considered how I might best bear it.'

394 ἐκ τοῦδε   *enjambment*; = 'So I began with this'

395 ⁺γλῶσσα, ἡ   tongue (γλώσσῃ, dat. of possess.: S #1476; it is quasi-personified here) – 'for [there is no trust in the tongue] the tongue cannot be trusted'

θῠραῖος (3/2)   outside the door (409)

396 φρόνημα, ατος, τό   mind, will, spirit (ἀνδρῶν, subj. gen.: S #1328, 1330) [1x *Hipp.*]

νουθετέω   (⁺νοῦς, *⁺τίθημι) bring to mind, warn, admonish, advise; – 'on the one hand, it knows how to admonish the thoughts of others [other men]' (724)

397 πλεῖστος (3)   very much (superl. of ⁺πολύς) (959)

*⁺κτάομαι   acquire; pf.: possess

ὑφ' αὑτῆς   by herself (αὑτῆς = ἑαυτῆς, reflex. pron.: S #329; gen. of agent: S #1493) – 'on the other hand, it causes by its own [doing] abundant trouble'

398–9 ⁺δεύτερος (3)   second (adv. acc.: see line 46; τὸ δεύτερον, subst. use of artic. with an adv.: S #1153e: 'secondly')

ἄνοια, ἡ   folly [1x *Hipp.*]

τῷ σωφρονεῖν   by means of self-control (artic. inf.: S #2025, 2033; GMT #789, 799; as dat. of means: S #1507. For the characters' various takes on σωφροσύνη, see notes on lines 80, 384–6, σχολή.)

⁺νικάω   overcome, subdue, win (νικῶσα, pres. act. ptc. of attendant circumstance, coincidental with προυνοησάμην; see ὁράω in line 4) – 'overcoming,' 'subduing'

προ-νοέω　　　　　　　　take care of, plan, devise beforehand (προυνοησάμην = προενοησάμην: S #449b) – 'Secondly, I intended to bear the
folly well by subduing it with self-control' (685)

400　τοισίδε　　　　　　= τοῖσδε (⁺τρίτον, adv. acc.: see line 46. The
deictic ῑ adds emphasis: S #333g; it always gets the accent.)

ἐξανύω/ἐξανύτω　　　　　accomplish, fulfill [1x *Hipp.*]

401　Κύπριν κρατῆσαι　emphatic *enjambment*; with κατθανεῖν:
consonance

⁺κατα-*⁺θνήσκω　　　　die; in aor. and pf.: to be dead (κατθανεῖν =
κατα-θανεῖν, aor.² inf. act.; *syncope*)

402　κράτιστος (3)　　strongest (irreg. superl. of ἀγαθός) [1x *Hipp.*]

ἀντερῶ　　　　　　　　　speak against, deny (fut. without any pres. in
use) [1x *Hipp.*]

⁺βούλευμα, ατος, τό　resolution, plan, design; – 'And third, when I
was unable to overpower Cypris with these means, it seemed to me
good to die, the best of plans (no one will deny).'

403　*⁺λανθάνω　　　　escape notice, lie hidden (ἐμοί, dat. of feel-
ing/ethical: S #1486; εἴη, independent opt. without ἄν expresses a wish: S
#1814; GMT #721.I, 722) (289)

404　⁺μάρτῦς, ῠρος, ὁ/ἡ　witness (δρώσῃ < *⁺δράω, pres. act. ptc. fem.
dat. sg., governs καλά and αἰσχρά; ptc. of attendant circumstance, see ὁράω
in line 4) – 'For may I not escape notice when I do good things, nor have
witnesses when I do shameful ones.'

405–7　⁺ἔργον, τό　　act, deed

δυσκλεής, ές　　　　　infamous, shameful (ἤδη < *⁺οἶδα)

οὖσα　　　　　　　　　　(**⁺εἰμί) (supplem. ptc. in indir. disc. after verb
of knowing, ἐγίγνωσκον: S #2106)

μίσημα, ατος, τό　　an object of hatred (μίσημα πᾶσιν, emphatic
enjambment) – 'I knew that the act and the disease are disgraceful, and
in addition I knew that I was a woman, an object of hatred to everyone.'
[1x *Hipp.*]

παγκάκως (adv.)   all miserably (ὄλοιτο < *⁺ὄλλυμι, aor.² mid. opt. of wish, usually introduced by εἰ γάρ, εἴθε not ὡς: S #1814; GMT #721.I, 722) [1x *Hipp.*]

408 *⁺**αἰσχύνω**   shame, disgrace (λέχη < λέχος, the pl. might come from repeated intercourse; see SS 6 §3 on the pl. of γάμος) – 'May she perish most miserably, whoever first began to shame her bed with other men.'

410 **θῆλυς, εια, υ**   of female (adj. used substantively without artic.; see σοφός in line 90; τόδε . . . κακόν, note the emphatic *asyndeton*) – 'This evil started for the female sex from noble households.' (624)

411–2 **ὅταν . . . δοκῇ**   indef. temporal clause for the fut. with subjv. and ἄν (S #2399, 1768; SS 294 §4; εἶναι καλά goes with both δοκῇ and δόξει in personal construction: S #1983)

⁺ἦ ⁺κάρτα   very much; – 'for whenever shameful things seem fine to the noble, they will very much seem good to the base ones.'

> μισῶ δὲ καὶ τὰς σώφρονας μὲν ἐν λόγοις,
> λάθρᾳ δὲ τόλμας οὐ καλὰς κεκτημένας·
> αἳ πῶς ποτ᾽, ὦ δέσποινα ποτνία Κύπρι,   415
> βλέπουσιν ἐς πρόσωπα τῶν ξυνευνετῶν
> οὐδὲ σκότον φρίσσουσι τὸν ξυνεργάτην
> τέραμνά τ᾽ οἴκων μή ποτε φθογγὴν ἀφῇ
> ἡμᾶς γὰρ αὐτὸ τοῦτ᾽ ἀποκτείνει φίλαι,
> ὡς μήποτ᾽ ἄνδρα τὸν ἐμὸν αἰσχύνασ᾽ ἁλῶ,   420
> μὴ παῖδας οὓς ἔτικτον· ἀλλ᾽ ἐλεύθεροι
> παρρησίᾳ θάλλοντες οἰκοῖεν πόλιν
> κλεινῶν Ἀθηνῶν, μητρὸς οὕνεκ᾽ εὐκλεεῖς.
> δουλοῖ γὰρ ἄνδρα, κἂν θρασύσπλαγχνός τις ἦ,
> ὅταν ξυνειδῇ μητρὸς ἢ πατρὸς κακά.   425
> μόνον δὲ τοῦτό φασ᾽ ἁμιλλᾶσθαι βίῳ,
> γνώμην δικαίαν κἀγαθὴν ὅτῳ παρῇ·
> κακοὺς δὲ θνητῶν ἐξέφην᾽, ὅταν τύχῃ,
> προθεὶς κάτοπτρον ὥστε παρθένῳ νέᾳ
> χρόνος· παρ᾽ οἷσι μήποτ᾽ ὀφθείην ἐγώ.   430

Xo.   φεῦ φεῦ, τὸ σῶφρον ὡς ἀπανταχοῦ καλὸν
             καὶ δόξαν ἐσθλὴν ἐν βροτοῖς καρπίζεται.

414 **λάθρᾳ** (adv.)   secretly [1x *Hipp.*]

⁺τόλμᾰ, ἡ   boldness, daring (κεκτημένας < κτάομαι, pf.
mid. ptc. of attendant circumstance, see ὁράω in line 4) – 'I also hate
those who are chaste in words, but in secret possess darings that are not
pretty'

415 **αἵ**   they (sentences often begin with a relat. pron.
to enhance the connection with what has been said)

416 **συν-ευνέτης, ου, ὁ**   bedfellow, husband, consort [1x *Hipp.*]

417 **φρίσσω**   shudder (855)

συν-εργάτης [ᾰ], ὁ   fellow worker, partner [1x *Hipp.*]

418 **⁺τέραμνον, τό**   anything closely shut, room, chamber (used
only in pl.)

φθογγή, ἡ   voice [1x *Hipp.*]

⁺ἀφ-⁺**ίημι**   send forth (ἀφ-ῇ, aor.² subjv. act. 3 sg.;
μή ... ἀφῇ, fear clause after φρίσσουσι, subjv. in 1st sequence:
S #2210b; GMT #365) – 'How in the world, oh Lady Cypris, mistress
of the Sea, do they look at the faces of their husbands and not shudder lest the darkness, their accomplice, and the chambers of the house
might at some point sound their voice?'

419 **⁺ἀπο-**⁺**κτείνω**   kill, slay

420 *⁺**ἁλίσκομαι**   be captured; be convicted (ἁλῶ, aor.² act.
subjv.; ὡς μήποτε ... ἁλῶ, final clause in 1st sequence: S #2193, 2196; αἰ-
σχύνασα, pres. act. ptc. of attendant circumstance, coincidental with ἁλῶ,
see ὁράω in line 4; τὸν ἐμὸν, resolution in 6th position)

421 **⁺τίκτω**   give birth, bear; – 'For this very thing that is
killing me, my friends, so that I may never be caught disgracing my husband or my children to whom I gave birth.'

⁺ἀλλά (conj.)   rather (S #2776)

⁺ἐλεύθερος (3/2)   free

422 παρρησία, ἡ   free speech [1x *Hipp.*]

θάλλω   bloom, flourish (θάλλοντες, pres. act. ptc. of attendant circumstance, coincidental with οἰκοῖεν, see ὁράω in line 4; ⁺οἰκοῖεν, independent opt. without ἄν expresses a wish: S #1814; GMT #721.I, 722) [1x *Hipp.*]

⁺πόλις, εως, ἡ   city

423 ⁺κλεινός (3)   renowned

⁺Ἀθῆναι, αἱ   Athens

⁺οὕνεκα   + gen., usually postpos.; on account of, for the sake of (improper prep.; see ἔσω in line 2) – 'rather may they dwell flourishingly in the renowned city of Athens as free men with free speech, with good repute in regard to their mother.'

424 δουλόω   enslave (the subj. is the ὅταν clause in line 425) [1x *Hipp.*]

κἄν   = καὶ ἐάν, although, even if (ᾖ, subjv. in concessive clause: S #2372)

θρᾰσύ-σπλαγχνος (2)   bold-hearted [1x *Hipp.*]

425 συν-είδω   share in the knowledge of, be conscious of (ξυνειδῇ, pf. act. subjv., pf. with pres. sense; ὅταν ξυνειδῇ, subjv. with ἄν in indef. temporal clause for the fut.: S #2399, 1768; SS 294 §4) – 'For this enslaves a man, even one who is bold-hearted, whenever he is conscious of his mother's and father's wrongdoings.' [1x *Hipp.*]

426 ἁμιλλάομαι   compete, contend (μόνον ... τοῦτο ... ἁμιλλᾶσθαι, acc. and inf. in indir. disc. following φασί) (971)

427 γνώμην δικαίαν κἀγαθήν   (parallels the acc. in the indir. disc.)

παρῇ   (⁺πάρ-*⁺ειμι, pres. act. subjv.; ὅτῳ = ᾧτινι: S #339, 339b; ἄν in general relat. clauses with subjv. is sometimes omitted) – 'One thing only, they say, competes in life, a just and good mind, for whomever it is present.'

428 ἐξέφηνα   (⁺ἐκ-*⁺φαίνω, aor.[1] act. indic.; gnomic aor. expressing general truth is best translated as a pres.: S #1931; the subj. is χρόνος, enjambed in line 430) ὅταν τύχῃ   (*⁺τυγχάνω, aor.² act. subjv. with ἄν in indef. temporal clause for the fut.: S #2399, 1768; SS 294 §4) – 'whenever it (i.e., time) happens,' i.e., 'sooner or later'

429–30 κάτοπτρον, τό   mirror (προθείς < ⁺προ-*τίθημι, aor.² act. ptc., coincidental/modal with ἐξέφανη; see λύσασα in line 290; οἷσι = οἷς) [1x *Hipp.*]

ὀφθείην   (*⁺ὁράω, aor. pass. opt. of wish, without introductory pcl.: S #1814; GMT #721.1, 722) – 'But time, sooner or later, reveals the base among mortals, placing [before them] a mirror as to a young maiden; may I never be seen in company with these.'

431 ἀπανταχοῦ (adv.)   everywhere [1x *Hipp.*]

⁺ὡς (adv.)   exclamatory: how (in independent direct exclamatory sentence: S #2682, 2998)

432 ⁺δόξα, ἡ   reputation, opinion, judgment

καρπίζω   pluck fruit; mid.: reap; – 'Ah! Ah! Moderation [is] a fine thing everywhere and reaps an excellent reputation among mortals!' [1x *Hipp.*]

Τρ.   δέσποιν', ἐμοί τοι συμφορὰ μὲν ἀρτίως
         ἡ σὴ παρέσχε δεινὸν ἐξαίφνης φόβον·
         νῦν δ' ἐννοοῦμαι φαῦλος οὖσα, κἂν βροτοῖς   435
         αἱ δεύτεραί πως φροντίδες σοφώτεραι.
         οὐ γὰρ περισσὸν οὐδὲν οὐδ' ἔξω λόγου
         πέπονθας· ὀργαὶ δ' ἐς σ' ἀπέσκηψαν θεᾶς.
         ἐρᾷς (τί τοῦτο θαῦμα;) σὺν πολλοῖς βροτῶν·
         κἄπειτ' ἔρωτος οὕνεκα ψυχὴν ὀλεῖς;   440
         οὔ τἄρα λύει τοῖς ἐρῶσι τῶν πέλας
         ὅσοι τε μέλλουσ', εἰ θανεῖν αὐτοὺς χρεών.
         Κύπρις γὰρ οὐ φορητὸν ἢν πολλὴ ῥυῇ,
         ἣ τὸν μὲν εἴκονθ' ἡσυχῇ μετέρχεται,
         ὃν δ' ἂν περρισὸν καὶ φρονοῦνθ' εὕρῃ μέγα,   445
         τοῦτον λαβοῦσα πῶς δοκεῖς καθύβρισεν.

433 ἀρτίως   just, exactly (907)

⁺συμφορά . . . ἡ σή   (The artic. and the attr. follow the noun. In this arrangement the emphasis is on the noun, and the attr. possess. adj. is added by way of explanation. Not a common arrangement [S #1158].)

434 ἐξαίφνης (adv.)   all of a sudden, suddenly (παρ-έσχε < παρ-*⁺έχω, aor.² act. indic.) [1x *Hipp.*]

⁺φόβος, ὁ   fear, fright; – 'My lady, just now this misfortune of yours suddenly gave me a terrible fright'

435 ἐννοέω   act. and mid.: think of, have in one's mind, consider, ponder [1x *Hipp.*]

οὖσα   (supplem. ptc. in indir. disc. after verb of knowing; represents the impf. = ὅτι ἦ/ἦν [S #2106])

φαῦλος (3/2)   shallow, simple-minded, silly, foolish (989)

436 ⁺πως (indef. adv.)   somehow, in any way

φροντίς, ίδος, ἡ   thought (σοφώτεραι, compar. of σοφός) – 'Now I realize that I was foolish, and among mortals second thoughts are somehow wiser' [1x *Hipp.*]

437 ⁺περισσός (3)   above measure, superior

438 πέπονθας   emphatic *enjambment* (*⁺πάσχω, pf. act. indic.)

⁺ὀργή, ἡ   wrath, impulse, feeling, passion

ἀπο-σκήπτω   strike against, dash against [1x Eur.]

439 θαῦμα, ατος, τό   wonder, marvel; astonishment (906)

440 κἄπειτ'   = καὶ ἔπειτα: and then; – 'and will you then destroy your life on account of love?'

441 ἄρα (pcl.)   τἄρα = τε ἄρα (S #2787: "a connective, confirmatory, and inferential pcl. marking the immediate connection and succession of events and thoughts." Not always translatable.)

⁺λύει   = λυσιτελεῖ (LSJ v.2) it is profitable, advantageous (τοῖς ἐρῶσι < ⁺ἐράω, pres. act. ptc. dat. pl. masc.; artic. subst. ptc., see πάρειμι in line 184) τῶν πέλας   'those nearby' (supply ἀνθρώπων; an adv. with an artic. may be used to qualify a noun that is often omitted: S #1153e; gen. following ἐρῶσι)

442 θανεῖν αὐτούς   follows *⁺χρέων in acc. and inf. construction (S #1972) – 'There is surely then no benefit to those who desire those close to them, and all those who are going to do so, if they must die [for it]'

443 φορητός (3/2) (verbal adj.) bearable (S #472: verbal adjs. "have the meaning of a perfect participle"; supply ἐστί) [1x *Hipp.*]

⁺**πολλή**   adj. used as predicate; here virtually adv. (cf. S #1040)

*****ῥέω, ἐρρύην**   flow (ἤν = ἐάν; [ἐστί] . . . ῥύῃ, aor.² act. subj.; pres. general condition: S #2297, 2337; GMT #462) [1x *Hipp.*]

444 εἴκω   submit, obey, follow (εἴκοντα, pres. act. ptc.; artic. subst.; see πάρειμι in line 184) [1x *Hipp.*]

ἡσύχη (adv.)   quietly, gently, mildly [1x *Hipp.*]

μετ-*⁺ἔρχομαι   + acc.: go after [1x *Hipp.*]

445 *⁺εὑρίσκω   find (ὃν . . . ἂν . . . εὕρῃ, pres. general conditional relat. clause: S #2567; GMT #532)

446 *⁺λαβοῦσα . . . καθύβρισεν (λαβοῦσα, aor. ptc. of attendant circumstance; aor. ptc. is generally antecedent to the main verb, here καθύβρισεν, which is a gnomic aor.; see line 428)

καθ-υβρίζω   mistreat badly, abuse; – 'For Cypris is unbearable when she flows greatly; she goes gently after the one who submits [to her], but if she finds someone superior or thinking big, she seizes him, and you can imagine how she mistreats him.' [1x *Hipp.*]

φοιτᾷ δ' ἀν' αἰθέρ', ἔστι δ' ἐν θαλασσίῳ
κλύδωνι Κύπρις, πάντα δ' ἐκ ταύτης ἔφυ·
ἥδ' ἐστὶν ἡ σπείρουσα καὶ διδοῦσ' ἔρον,
οὗ πάντες ἐσμὲν οἱ κατὰ χθόν' ἔκγονοι.   450
ὅσοι μὲν οὖν γραφάς τε τῶν παλαιτέρων
ἔχουσιν αὐτοί τ' εἰσὶν ἐν μούσαις ἀεί,

ἴσασι μὲν Ζεὺς ὥς ποτ᾽ ἠράσθη γάμων
Σεμέλης, ἴσασι δ᾽ ὡς ἀνήρπασέν ποτε
ἡ καλλιφεγγὴς Κέφαλον ἐς θεοὺς Ἕως   455
ἔρωτος οὕνεκ᾽ · ἀλλ᾽ ὅμως ἐν οὐρανῷ
ναίουσι κοὐ φεύγουσιν ἐκποδὼν θεούς,
στέργουσι δ᾽, οἶμαι, ξυμφορᾷ νικώμενοι.
σὺ δ᾽ οὐκ ἀνέξῃ; χρῆν σ᾽ ἐπὶ ῥητοῖς ἄρα
πατέρα φυτεύειν ἢ ᾽πὶ δεσπόταις θεοῖς   460
ἄλλοισιν, εἰ μὴ τούσδε γε στέρξεις νόμους.
πόσους δοκεῖς δὴ κάρτ᾽ ἔχοντας εὖ φρενῶν
νοσοῦνθ᾽ ὁρῶντας λέκτρα μὴ δοκεῖν ὁρᾶν;

447 **αἰθήρ, έρος, ὁ**   open air, upper air (178)

θᾰλάσσιος (3)   of the sea (*⁺ἔστι, existential: S #187b) [1x *Hipp.*]

448 **κλύδων, ωνος, ὁ**   wave, billow, surge, swell; – 'Cypris roams through the air. She is [lives] in the swell of the sea, everything is born from her.' (1213)

449 ***⁺σπείρω**   sow; engender, beget (ἡ σπείρουσα, ἡ *⁺διδοῦσα, artic. subst. ptcs.; see πάρειμι in line 184)

ἔρος, ὁ   poetic form of ⁺ἔρως, love, desire (337)

450 **ἔκγονος, ον**   sprung, descendant from; – 'she is the one who sows and gives desire, from which all of us upon earth are begotten.' [1x *Hipp.*]

451 **μὲν οὖν**   now, on the one hand

⁺γρᾰφή, ἡ   writing, painting

πᾰλαίτερος (3)   older (irreg. compar. of παλαιός formed from the adv. ⁺πάλαι: of old) [1x *Hipp.*]

452 **Μοῦσα, ἡ**   Muse, goddess of song, music, poetry, dancing, and the fine arts; pl. arts (1135)

453–4 **ἴσασι**   (<*⁺οἶδα, pf. act. indic. 3 pl.; ἠράσθη < *⁺ἔραμαι, aor. pass. indic. 3 sg.)

Σεμέλη, ἡ   Semele, mother of Dionysus. She was loved by Zeus, by whom she conceived Dionysus. When she asked to see her lover in his divine splendor, she was consumed by his lightning, but the child was saved. (Σεμέλη, resolution of the 1st anceps in a trimeter, is common with proper names; emphatic *enjambment*.) – 'Now, on the one hand, those who own the writings of ancient authors, and who are versed in poetry all the time, know how (ὡς) Zeus once desired union with Semele'

ἀν-αρπάζω   snatch up, abduct [1x *Hipp.*]

455   καλλιφεγγής, ές   beautiful-shining [1x *Hipp.*]

Κέφαλος, ὁ   Cephalus (husband of Procris, daughter of Erechtheus; Eos fell in love with him) [1x *Hipp.*]

Ἕως, ἡ   Dawn goddess (note the *hyperbaton* ἡ . . . Ἕως, which hugs the line and underscores the name of the goddess) [1x *Hipp.*]

456   ⁺ἔρωτος ⁺οὕνεκα   emphatic *enjambment*; – 'and they know how (ὡς) the beautiful-shining Eos once snatched Cephalus up to the company of the gods for passion's sake.'

457   ἐκποδών (adv.)   out of the way (708)

458   στέργω   be content, satisfied (⁺νικώμενοι, ptc. of attendant circumstance, see ὁράω in line 4) – 'but still [ἀλλ' ⁺ὅμως] they dwell in heaven and do not flee out of the way of the [other] gods, content, I think, being overcome by [this] misfortune' (461)

459–61   χρῆν . . . ⁺πατέρα φυτεύειν   (*⁺χρῆν = χρὴ ἦν, impf., indicates an unfulfilled obligation: 'should'; with acc. and inf.: S #1562, 1985b; cf. line 253)

ῥητός (3)   (ἐρῶ, speak) spoken of, specified, settled; ἐπί ῥητοῖς 'on set terms,' 'on fixed conditions' (846)

φυτεύω   beget [1x *Hipp.*]

ἢ 'πὶ   = ἢ ἐπί, *aphaeresis* (the elision of ε at the beginning of a word after a word ending in a long vowel or diphthong: S #76; δεσπόταις, predicative noun 'as masters') – 'And you will not

endure it? Then your father should have begotten you on set terms or
with other gods as masters, if you will not put up with these laws.'

462–3 πόσος (3)   how many, how much

εὖ *+ἔχειν τινός   to be well off in something (πόσους . . . ἔχοντας . . . ὁρῶντας . . . μὴ δοκεῖν, acc. and inf. following δοκεῖς; ἔχοντας . . . ὁρῶντας, circumstantial ptcs. of attendant circumstance, see
ὁράω in line 4; νοσοῦντα . . . λέκτρα, supplem. ptc. in indir. disc. following a verb of perception, ὁρῶντας: S #2110, 2111; GMT #904) –
'How many men (being well off in their mind) of sound mind do you
think see their marriages are sick and pretend not to see it?'

πόσους δὲ παισὶ πατέρας ἡμαρτηκόσιν
συνεκκομίζειν Κύπριν; ἐν σοφοῖσι γὰρ   465
τόδ᾿ ἐστὶ θνητῶν, λανθάνειν τὰ μὴ καλά.
οὐδ᾿ ἐκπονεῖν τοι χρὴ βίον λίαν βροτούς·
οὐδὲ στέγην γὰρ ᾗ κατηρεφεῖς δόμοι
καλῶς ἀκριβώσαις ἄν· ἐς δὲ τὴν τύχην
πεσοῦσ᾿ ὅσην σύ, πῶς ἂν ἐκνεῦσαι δοκεῖς;   470
ἀλλ᾿ εἰ τὰ πλείω χρηστὰ τῶν κακῶν ἔχεις,
ἄνθρωπος οὖσα κάρτα γ᾿ εὖ πράξειας ἄν.
ἀλλ᾿, ὦ φίλη παῖ, λῆγε μὲν κακῶν φρενῶν,
λῆξον δ᾿ ὑβρίζουσ᾿, οὐ γὰρ ἄλλο πλὴν ὕβρις
τάδ᾿ ἐστί, κρείσσω δαιμόνων εἶναι θέλειν,   475
τόλμα δ᾿ ἐρῶσα· θεὸς ἐβουλήθη τάδε·
νοσοῦσα δ᾿ εὖ πως τὴν νόσον καταστρέφου.
εἰσὶν δ᾿ ἐπῳδαὶ καὶ λόγοι θελκτήριοι·
φανήσεταί τι τῆσδε φάρμακον νόσου.
ἦ τἄρ᾿ ἂν ὀψέ γ᾿ ἄνδρες ἐξεύροιεν ἄν,   480
εἰ μὴ γυναῖκες μηχανὰς εὑρήσομεν.

464 πόσους . . . πατέρας supply δοκεῖς (πατέρας, resolution in 6th position; note the *consonance* of π in the line)

+ἡμαρτηκόσιν   lit.: 'erring sons' (+ἁμαρτάνω, pf. act. ptc.;
attr. ptc., see λεχθεῖσι in line 299)

465–6 συν-εκ-κομίζω   help in effecting (πόσους . . . πατέρας . . . συνεκκομίζειν, indir. disc. in acc. and inf. construction following

δοκεῖς) – 'How many fathers do you think help their erring sons in consummating Cypris?' [1x *Hipp.*]

⁺λανθάνω   act.: escape notice, lie hidden (⁺σοφοῖσι is neut., according to B.; λανθάνειν τὰ μὴ καλά stands in apposition to τόδε) – 'this is one of the wise principles among mortals, let what is not good lie hidden'

467 ⁺ἐκπονεῖν ... ⁺βροτούς   acc. and inf. following **⁺χρή** (S #1562, 1985b) – 'Nor should mortals [try to] perfect their lives too much'

468 στέγη, ἡ   roof (ῇ, dat. of means: S #1507) [1x *Hipp.*]

κατηρεφής, ές   overhanging, overarched [1x Eur.]

469 ἀκρῑβόω   make exact, arrange precisely (ἀκριβώσαις, aor.¹ act. opt.; potential opt. with ἄν: S #1824) – 'for no more would you make fine and exact the roof with which your house is overarched' [1x *Hipp.*]

470 ὅσην σύ   supply ἔπεσες (πεσοῦσα < **⁺πίπτω**, aor.² act. ptc., circumstantial causal ptc.: S #2064)

ἐκ-⁺νέω   swim out, swim to land (aor.¹ inf., ἐκνεῦσαι, with ἄν may be equivalent either to the aor. indic. with ἄν, indicating a potential sense, or to the aor. opt. with ἄν: S #1845, 1784; GMT #207, 243) – 'Since you've plunged into as much misfortune as you have, how do you think you could swim to the shore?' (823)

471 πλείω   = πλείονα, more (compar. of **⁺πολύς**; τῶν κακῶν, compar. gen.: S #1069) (641)

472 εὖ ⁺πράσσω   fare well (εἰ ... ἔχεις ... εὖ πράξειας ἄν, mixed condition: pres. indic. in protasis and a potential opt. in the apodosis; each clause has its proper force: GMT #503) – 'But if, being human, you have more good than bad, you would surely be very well off.'

473–4 ὑβρίζω   outrage, treat despitefully, commit outrage, assault (1073)

⁺λήγω   stop, cease from (λῆγε, λῆξον, *anaphora*; the pres. impv. focuses on subsequent continuance: 'no more ...,' while the aor. impv. focuses on immediate stopping. λήγω often takes a supplem. ptc., ὑβρίζουσα: S #2098.) – 'no more of your bad thinking, stop your presumption'

⁺πλήν (adv.)   besides, except

475 ⁺κρείσσω   = κρείσσονα, better, mightier, stronger (irreg. compar. of ἀγαθός: S #319; acc. sg. subj. of εἶναι; δαιμόνων, gen. of comparison: S #1431) – 'for it is nothing other than presumption to be mightier than the gods'

476 τολμάω   dare, endure (τόλμα = τόλμαε, pres. act. impv. 2 sg.; τολμάω takes the ptc., ἐρῶσα: S #2127) [1x *Hipp.*]

477 κατα-στρέφω   mid.: subdue (καταστρέφου, impv. mid.; νοσοῦσα, circumstantial concessive ptc.: S #2066; GMT #842) – 'and even if you are ill, somehow in a good way subdue your illness.' [1x Eur.]

478 ἐπῳδή, ἡ   incantation, charm, spell [1x *Hipp.*]

θελκτήριος, ον   charming, enchanting; – 'There are charms and bewitching words; some cure will appear for this sickness.' (509)

480 ἦ τάρ'   = ⁺ἦ ⁺τοι ἄρα: most assuredly, then

ὀψέ (adv.)   after a long time, late

ἐξ-*⁺ευρίσκω   find out, discover, invent (ἐξεύροιεν, aor.² act. potential opt.: S #1824; see ἄν . . . ἄν in line 270) (918)

481 μηχανή, ἡ   contrivance (εἰ εὑρήσομεν . . . ἐξευροῖεν, emotional condition: S #2297; εἰ with fut. indic. in the protasis and fut. indic. or equivalent in the apodosis, here a potential opt. with ἄν: S #1824, 1828) – 'Most assuredly, men would be late to invent contrivances if we women do not find them.' (1305)

Χο.   Φαίδρα, λέγει μὲν ἥδε χρησιμώτερα
             πρὸς τὴν παροῦσαν ξυμφοράν, αἰνῶ δὲ σέ.
             ὁ δ' αἶνος οὗτος δυσχερέσρερος λόγων
             τῶν τῆσδε καί σοι μᾶλλον ἀλγίων κλυεῖν.   485
Φα.   τοῦτ' ἔσθ' ὃ θνητῶν εὖ πόλεις οἰκουμένας
             δόμους τ' ἀπόλλυσ', οἱ καλοὶ λίαν λόγοι·

οὐ γάρ τι τοῖσιν ὠσὶ τερπνὰ χρὴ λέγειν
ἀλλ' ἐξ ὅτου τις εὐκλεὴς γενήσεται.
Τρ.   τί σεμνομυθεῖς; οὐ λόγων εὐσχημόνων   490
δεῖ σ' ἀλλὰ τἀνδρός. ὡς τάχος διιστέον,
τὸν εὐθὺν ἐξειπόντας ἀμφὶ σοῦ λόγον.
εἰ μὲν γὰρ ἦν σοι μὴ 'πὶ συμφοραῖς βίος
τοιαῖσδε, σώφρων δ' οὖσ' ἐτύγχανες γυνή,
οὐκ ἄν ποτ' εὐνῆς οὕνεχ' ἡδονῆς τε σῆς   495
προῆγον ἄν σε δεῦρο· νῦν δ' ἀγὼν μέγας
σῶσαι βίον σόν, κοὐκ ἐπίφθονον τόδε.

482 χρήσιμος (3/2)   (χράομαι, use) useful (compar.) [1x *Hipp.*]

483 παροῦσαν   (⁺πάρειμι) (ptc. qualifies the noun as an attr. adj.; see λεχθεῖσι in line 299)

484–5 αἶνος, ὁ   praise [1x *Hipp.*]

δυσ-χερής, ές   (δυσ-, χείρ, hand) unpleasant, troublesome (λόγων τῶν τῆσδε, demon. pron. in attr. position; the emphasis is on the noun: S #1159; G #963; λόγων, gen. of comparison: S #1431; see κλυεῖν, aor.² act. inf. in line 119) [1x *Hipp.*]

ἀλγίων, ον, -ονος   more painful (irreg. compar. of ἀλγεινός formed from ἄλγος, τό, pain; ἀλγίων = ἀλγίονα, adv. acc. pl. neut.: S #1606; μᾶλλον ἀλγίων, pleonasm/redundancy: the compar. may be strengthened by μᾶλλον: S #1084. Note that in these four spoken lines the Chorus are using four words that occur only once in the play.) – 'Phaedra, on the one hand, what she says is more useful for the present circumstance, but I praise you. On the other hand, this praise is more unpleasant than her words, and more painful for you to hear.' [1x *Hipp.*]

488 ⁺οὖς, ὠτός, τό   ear

489 ἐξ ὅτου   = ἐξ οὗτινος, from what (S #339; gen. of source: S #1410; γενήσεται < *⁺γίγνομαι, fut. dep.) – 'For [it is not necessary to speak] one should not say what is pleasant for the ears, but from what one becomes glorious'

490 σεμνομῦθέω   talk in solemn speech [1x Eur.]

εὐσχήμων, ον, -ονος   graceful, elegant, becoming [1x *Hipp.*]

491 δεῖ σε   'you have the need of' + gen. (τἀνδρός = τοῦ ἀνδρός)

ὡς τάχος   'as swiftly as possible'

διιστέον   it is necessary to have a clear understanding (verbal adj. < δι-ειδέναι: S #358.2b; supply ἐστί) [1x *Hipp.*]

492 ⁺εὐθύς, εῖα, ύ   straightforward, plain, honest (τὸν εὐθύν . . . λόγον, emphatic *hyperbaton*)

ἐξ-εῖπον   speak out, utter, avow (ἐξειπόντας, ptc. of attendant circumstance, see ὁράω in line 4. B.: "The participle in apposition to the unexpressed agent of an impersonal -τέον is commonly in acc.") (658)

⁺ἀμφί (prep.)   + gen.: about, concerning; – 'Why are you preaching? What you need is not elegant words, but the man. We must understand things clearly as soon as possible, speaking out about you with honesty.'

493–7 εἰ μὲν γὰρ ἦν . . . προῆγον ἄν   contrary-to-fact condition for the present time (S #2297; GMT #410; μὴ 'πὶ = μὴ ἐπί, *aphaeresis*; σοι, dat. of possess.: 'your life': S #1476; τοιαῖσδε, *enjambment* underscoring συμφοραῖς)

*⁺ἐτύγχανες   with οὖσα, as supplem. ptc., which tells what the main action is and is often translated as the finite verb with an adv. phrase: – ('you happened to be') 'you really were'

⁺εὐνή, ἡ   bed

προ-*ἄγω   lead onward; carry forward; advance [1x *Hipp.*]

ἀγών, νος, ὁ   contest, competition, struggle (1016)

*⁺σώζω   save (σῶσαι, aor.¹ inf. act.)

ἐπί-φθονος, ον   prone to envy or jealousy; be begrudged; – 'If your life were not now in such circumstances and you were really a chaste woman, I would never for the sake of the pleasure of your bed be leading you to this point; but now the contest is a great one—to save your life, and this should not be begrudged.' [1x *Hipp.*]

Φα.   ὦ δεινὰ λέξασ᾽, οὐχὶ συγκλήσεις στόμα
        καὶ μὴ μεθήσεις αὖθις αἰσχίστους λόγους;

Τρ.   αἴσχρ', ἀλλ' ἀμείνω τῶν καλῶν τάδ' ἐστί σοι·   500
        κρεῖσσον δὲ τοὔργον, εἴπερ ἐκσώσει γέ σε,
        ἢ τοὔνομ', ᾧ σὺ κατθανῇ γαυρουμένη.

Φα.   ἃ μή σε πρὸς θεῶν, εὖ λέγεις γὰρ αἰσχρὰ δέ,
        πέρα προβῇς τῶνδ'· ὡς ὑπείργασμαι μὲν εὖ
        ψυχὴν ἔρωτι, τἀσχρὰ δ' ἢν λέγῃς καλῶς   505
        ἐς τοῦθ' ὃ φεύγω νῦν ἀναλωθήσομαι.

Τρ.   εἴ τοι δοκεῖ σοι . . . χρῆν μὲν οὔ σ' ἁμαρτάνειν,
        εἰ δ' οὖν, πιθοῦ μοι· δευτέρα γὰρ ἡ χάρις.
        ἔστιν κατ' οἴκους φίλτρα μοι θελκτήρια
        ἔρωτος, ἦλθε δ' ἄρτι μοι γνώμης ἔσω,   510
        ἅ σ' οὔτ' ἐπ' αἰσχροῖς οὔτ' ἐπὶ βλάβῃ φρενῶν
        παύσει νόσου τῆσδ', ἢν σὺ μὴ γένῃ κακή.
        [δεῖ δ' ἐξ ἐκείνου δή τι τοῦ ποθουμένου
        σημεῖον, ἢ πλόκον τιν' ἢ πέπλων ἄπο,
        λαβεῖν συνάψαι τ'ἐκ δυοῖν μίαν χάριν.]   515

498–9 λέξασα   (*⁺λέγω, aor.[1] act. circumstantial ptc. denoting time; see ἐλθόντα in line 24)

συγ-*κλείω   shut up, close (οὐ . . . μή; see at 213) – 'Oh! You've spoken horrid things, won't you shut your mouth and let go of such shameful words from now on?!' [1x *Hipp.*]

500 ἀμείνων, ον,-ονος   better (ἀμείνω = ἀμείνονα; irreg. compar. of ἀγαθός; τῶν καλῶν, gen. of comparison: S #1431; σοι, dat. of advantage: S #1481) – 'Shameful; but better for you than the fine ones [i.e., words].' [1x *Hipp.*]

501 εἴπερ γε   if indeed, if really (98)

502 *⁺κατθανῇ   (fut. indic. 2 sg.; *syncope*)

γαυρόομαι   exult in (γαυρουμένη, ptc. of attendant circumstance, see ὁράω in line 4) – 'the deed is better, if it will save you, than the name in which you (will die exulting =) will exult and be dead' [1x *Hipp.*]

504 πέρᾱ   + gen.: beyond, further (improper prep.; see ἔσω in line 2) (1033)

ὑπ-*⁺εργάζομαι   work under, prepare for sowing (ὑπείργασμαι, pf. dep. indic.) [1x *Hipp.*]

505–6 ⁺ψυχήν   acc. of respect (S #1600)

ἐς εἰς/ἐς (prep.)   + acc.: in regard to

ἀν-*⁺αλίσκω   use up, spend; kill, destroy (ἀναλωθήσομαι,
fut. pass. indic.; ἤν [= ἐάν] λέγῃς . . . ἀναλωθήσομαι, fut. more vivid
condition: S #2297, 2321, 2323) – 'Oh no, in gods' name, you speak
well but [say] shameful things; do not go any further, (I am all made
ready in respect to my soul =) my soul is all made ready by desire, and
if you keep speaking nicely about shameful things, very soon I will be
exhausted upon the very thing I am fleeing.' (1336)

507 χρῆν   *⁺χρῆν = χρὴ ἦν, impf., was necessary (δοκεῖ . . . χρῆν, mixed condition: pres. indic. in the protasis, and χρῆν, a
potential indic. without ἄν, in the apodosis. χρῆν takes acc. and inf.: σὲ
ἁμαρτάνειν, S #503, 1562, 1985b; cf. line 253.)

508 εἰ δ'οὖν   GP 465: "Particularly used when a speaker hy-
pothetically grants a supposition which he denies, doubts, or reprobates";
'but if so and so *did* happen'

πιθοῦ   obey (*⁺πείθω, aor.² mid. impv., 2 sg.) – '(If this
seems to you so =) If you think so, you should have not erred, but since
you have erred, obey me, for this favor [of obeying] is second best.'

509 φίλτρον, τό   love charm, love medicine (μοι, dat. of possess.: S #1476) [1x *Hipp.*]

510 ⁺ἔρωτος   emphatic *enjambment*

ἄρτι (adv.)   just now (804)

511 βλαβή, ἡ   hurt, damage, harm [1x *Hipp.*]

512 παύσει . . . ἦν (= ἐάν) μὴ γένῃ   (fut. more vivid condition:
S #2297, 2321, 2323) – 'I have love charms in the house, enchantments for
passion—I just thought of this now—which will relieve you from this malady without disgrace or harm to your mind, if you do not become cowardly.'

Stockert square-brackets lines 513–15 following Nauck. B. does not.

513 ποθέω   desire (artic. subst. ptc.; see πάρειμι in line
184) (912)

514 σημεῖον, τό   mark, token, trace [1x *Hipp.*]

πλόκος, ὁ   lock or curl of hair [1x *Hipp.*]

⁺πέπλος, ὁ   full robe worn by a woman; man's cloak or
robe (ἄπο, *anastrophe*)

515 συν-*⁺ἅπτω   tie together, join together, bring together, attach (187)

δύο   two (δυοῖν, gen. dual: S #349) – '(But there is a
need =) But we need to obtain from the one who is desired some token,
either a lock of hair or something from his garments, and join together
one delight from two.' (387)

Φα.	πότερα δὲ χριστὸν ἢ ποτὸν τὸ φάρμακον;
Τρ.	οὐκ οἶδ'· ὄνασθαι, μὴ μαθεῖν βούλου τέκνον.
Φα.	δέδοιχ' ὅπως μοι μὴ λίαν φανῇς σοφή.
Τρ.	πάντ' ἂν φοβηθεῖσ' ἴσθι· δειμαίνεις δὲ τί;
Φα.	μή μοί τι Θησέως τῶνδε μηνύσῃς τόκῳ.	520
Τρ.	ἔασον, ὦ παῖ· ταῦτ' ἐγὼ θήσω καλῶς.
	μόνον σύ μοι, δέσποινα ποτνία Κύπρι,
	συνεργὸς εἴης. τἄλλα δ' οἷ' ἐγὼ φρονῶ
	τοῖς ἔνδον ἡμῖν ἀρκέσει λέξαι φίλοις.

516 χριστός (3)   to be rubbed on, as with an ointment (πότερα,
resolution in 2nd position) [1x *Hipp.*]

ποτός (3)   for drinking (both adjs. stand in a predicate position: S #910b) – 'Is the charm rubbed on or a potion?' B.'s assumption that Phaedra must be thinking that the charm is an anti-aphrodisiac
to be applied to herself, not an aphrodisiac applied to Hippolytus, is
unacceptable. A love charm, as B. admits, needs to be administered
without the victim's knowledge, which precludes its being administered to Phaedra. Nor does this idea contradict lines 513–15. As Fitton
(1967, 21) suggests, since anointing and washing went together, adding a salve to his oil would be easily accomplished, as would having
the ointment smeared on his garment, as Medea did to the deadly robe
of Jason's bride (Eur. *Medea* 989). [1x *Hipp.*]

517 βούλου   wish (*⁺βούλομαι, pres. dep. impv.; *apokoinou*, a word of two syntactic functions: ὄνεσθαι βούλου, μὴ μαθεῖν βούλου) – 'wish to profit [from it], child, not to learn [about it]'

518 δείδω   fear (δέδοικα, pf. with pres. meaning) (924)

519 ⁺φοβέω   terrify (φοβηθεῖσα, aor.¹ pass. ptc.; ἂν φοβηθεῖσα ἴσθι, supplem. ptc. in indir. disc. after verb of knowing οἶδ᾽: S #2106;
ἴσθι, pf. act. impv. of *⁺οἶδα. ἄν with a ptc. represents here an opt., with ἄν
expressing potentiality: S #1845) – 'Know that you may be fearing everything'; i.e., 'Know this—you're afraid of everything'

   δειμαίνω   be afraid, be alarmed; – 'What are you afraid
   of?' [1x *Hipp.*]

520 Θησέως   (-εω- in Θησέως is pronounced as one syllable
by *synizesis*)

   μοί   (ethical dat. or dat. of feeling to denote the
   speaker's interest; common with impv., in this case an ardent wish to
   avert the cause of fear; not always translated: S #1486; GMT #366)

   μή . . . ⁺μηνύσῃς   lest you reveal (⁺μηνύω, aor.¹ act. subjv.; a fear
   clause following δειμαίνεις: S #2221a; GMT #365) – '[I fear] lest you
   reveal some of this to the son of Theseus.'

521 ⁺ἔασον   [ᾱ] (⁺ἐάω, aor.¹ act. impv.) – 'let it be'

   **⁺τίθημι   put (fut. act. indic.) – 'let [it] be, child, I will
   arrange these things well.'

523 συνεργός, ον   working together; as subst.: partner, helper, accomplice (*⁺εἴης, pres. opt. 2 sg.; opt. of wish: S #1814; GMT #721.I, 722)
– 'Only may you, Cypris, Lady of the Sea, be my helper.' (676)

524 *ἀρκέω   assist, suffice, be of use (λέξαι < *⁺λέγω, aor.¹
act. inf.) (1036)

   ἔνδον (adv.)   inside (τοῖς ἔνδον . . . φίλοις, an adv. may
   serve as an adj. when it stands in an attr. position: S #1096; emphatic
   hyperbaton; ἡμῖν, *majestic plural*: S #1006. Does the Nurse imitate
   Phaedra's recurrent use of this literary device?) – 'The other things I
   have in mind, it will be enough for me to tell my friends within.' (649)

The Nurse exits into the palace.

FIRST STASIMON LINES 525–64

The first stasimon fills out the interval between the Nurse's exit to find a cure for her mistress's affliction and the disclosure that she has revealed her mistress's passion to Hippolytus. Phaedra and the Chorus stay in the orchestra. The Chorus reflect in lyric mode on what has occurred up to now, focusing on the main theme that has set everything in motion: the destructive power of Eros. The ode consists of two strophic pairs, with each pair having a parallel metrical structure. The first pair (525–44) considers the destructive power of Eros to the extent that the Chorus pray it will never come upon them in spite of the pleasure it can instill. The second pair (545–64) exemplifies the destructive power of Aphrodite by the tales of Heracles' unbridled passion for Iole, which killed her father, Eurytus, king of Oechalia, and destroyed her city, and Zeus' desire for Bacchus' mother, Semele, which brought upon her a fiery death.

Both pairs have direct relevance to the plot. The first pair sings of the potential pleasures of Eros, on the one hand; and on the other hand, its militant and ruinous power reminds us of the all-powerful desire that "wounded" Phaedra (392), as well as of the violence it will bring about. The warning of the first antistrophe, that mankind foolishly ignores Eros' ritual, might refer to Hippolytus' ill-considered refusal to honor Aphrodite, Eros' mother. The examples of the crushing effects of passion in the second pair parallel Phaedra's own tale. Not only does her desire bring about her own death, but it also causes the death of Hippolytus and the devastation of Theseus.

ΧΟΡΟΣ

Ἔρως Ἔρως, ὁ κατ' ὀμμάτων	[στρ.	Eros, Eros, you who drip
	α 525	desire down
στάζων πόθον, εἰσάγων γλυκεῖαν		into the eyes, bringing sweet
		pleasure to the
ψυχᾷ χάριν οὓς ἐπιστρατεύσῃ,		soul[s] [of those] against
		whom you campaign,
μή μοί ποτε σὺν κακῷ φανείης		may you never show yourself
		to me with harm
μηδ' ἄρρυθμος ἔλθοις.		nor come without due mea-
		sure. For neither

οὔτε γὰρ πυρὸς οὔτ᾽ ἄστρων   530   the shaft of fire nor that of the
ὑπέρτερον βέλος   stars is mightier
οἶον τὸ τᾶς Ἀφροδίτας ἵησιν ἐκ χερῶν   than that of Aphrodite [which]
                                              Eros, the son
Ἔρως ὁ Διὸς παῖς.   of Zeus, sends forth from his
                                              hands.

ἄλλως ἄλλως παρά τ᾽ Ἀλφεῷ   [ἀντ. α 535 In vain, in vain along the
                                             Alpheus, and
Φοίβου τ᾽ ἐπὶ Πυθίοις τεράμνοις   by the Pythian chambers of
                                             Phoebus, the
βούταν φόνον Ἑλλὰς ⟨αἶ᾽⟩ ἀέξει,   ⟨land⟩ of Hellas increases the
                                             bovine slaughter,
Ἔρωτα δέ, τὸν τύραννον ἀνδρῶν,   but Eros, the tyrant of men,
                                             the doorkeeper
τὸν τᾶς Ἀφροδίτας   of Aphrodite's dearest cham-
                                           bers, [him] we do
φιλτάτων θαλάμων κληδοῦχον,   540 not honor, the one who de-
οὐ σεβίζομεν,   stroys mortals
πέρθοντα καὶ διὰ πάσας ἱέντα   and who sends every kind of
συμφορᾶς
θνατοὺς ὅταν ἔλθῃ.   disaster whenever he comes.

525 = 535	⏓ – ⏓ – ⏑ ⏑ – ⏑ –	glyconic
526 = 536	– – ⏑ ⏑ – ⏑ – ⏑ – –	telesillean + bacchiac
527 = 537	– – ⏑ ⏑ – ⏑ – ⏑ – –	telesillean + bacchiac
528 = 538	⏑ – ⏑ ⏑ – ⏑ – ⏑ – –	telesillean + bacchiac
529 = 539	– – ⏑ ⏑ – –	reizianum
530–1 = 540–1	– ⏑ – ⏑ ⏑ – – – ⏑– ⏑– ⏑ –	pherecratean + lecythion
532–3 = 542–3	– – ⏑ – ⏑ ⏑ – – ⏑ –⏑ –⏑ –	wilamowitzian + lecythion
534 = 544	⏓ – ⏑ ⏑ – –	reizianum

525 ὅ   = ὅς (ὅ for the relat. pron. ὅς appears only here
in tragedy, but is found in epic and lyric poetry)

    κατά (prep.)   + gen.: down, down over, toward, down upon
(B.: "That sexual desire manifests itself in the eyes is a commonplace
of Greek poetry.")

526 στάζω   fall drop by drop, drip, distill (descriptive ptc.,
see ὁράω in line 4) (122)

πόθος, ὁ   longing, desire (234)

εἰσ-*άγω   lead into, bring into (descriptive ptc., see ὁράω
in line 4) [1x *Hipp.*]

γλŭκύς, εῖα, ύ   sweet [1x *Hipp.*]

527 οὕς   (Supply ἐκείνων as an antecedent. One would
expect here the dat. οἷς, but the acc. is also found with ἐπιστρατεύω.)

ἐπι-στρᾰτεύω   march against, campaign against (ἐπιστρατεύσῃ, fut. for pres.: S #1915; the mid. voice underscores Eros' self-in-
terest) [1x *Hipp.*]

528–9 μή ... φανείης ... ἔλθοις   (impv. opt.: S #1820; *+φαίνω,
aor.¹ opt. act.; *+ἔρχομαι, aor.² opt. act.)

ἄρρυθμος, ον   (ἀ privat., ῥυθμός, proportion, order) without
due measure and order [1x Eur.]

530–1 πῦρ, πῠρός, ὁ   fire (684)

ἄστρον, τό   star (ἄστρων, gen. of comparison: S #1431)
[1x *Hipp.*]

ὑπέρτερος (3)   stronger, mightier, superior (compar. adj. of
ὑπέρ) [1x *Hipp.*]

βέλος, εος, τό   shaft, arrow, dart (a noun without an article
may be followed by the artic. and attr. gen.: S #1161n1) [1x *Hipp.*]

τᾶς Ἀφροδίτᾱς   = τῆς Ἀφροδίτης (note that the Chorus sing
now not of Eros' destructive power, but of Aphrodite's)

*+ἵημι   send forth, throw, hurl (ἵησι, pres. act. indic.
3 sg.) (1125)

+οἷον   B.: "As though preceded not by ὑπέρτερον but
by τοιοῦτον."

534 Ἔρως ὁ Διὸς παῖς   Eros' paternity is saved up to the end of the
stanza for emphasis. In Hesiod, Eros has no parents: he came into being together with Chaos and Earth as one of the three primeval beings (*Theogony*
116–20, 201).

535 Ἀλφειός, ὁ   -ε- instead of -ει-, for metrical convenience. Alpheios, a river that flows though Olympia, was one of Zeus' chief shrines and the site of Olympic games. [1x *Hipp.*]

536 Φοῖβος, ὁ   Phoebus, an epithet of Apollo; (as adj.) pure, bright, radiant, beaming (15)

Πύθιος (3)   [ῠ] Pythian, i.e., Delphian, an epithet of Apollo
[1x *Hipp.*]

537 βούτης, ου, ὁ   herdsman, cowherd (βούταν = βούτην; the noun is used here as an adj. = βόειος, slaughter of cattle) [1x *Hipp.*]

φόνος, ὁ   slaughter, murder, homicide (1449)

538 Ἑλλάς, άδος, ἡ   Hellas, Greece [1x *Hipp.*]

⁺αἶα, ἡ   earth, land (poetic for γαῖα, γῆ; ⟨αἶ'⟩ = αἶ(α). B.: "The strophe shows that a syllable has fallen out after Ἑλλάς; this can be only αἶ[α].")

ἀέξω   make grow, increase, foster, strengthen (only in pres. and impf.) [1x *Eur.*]

540–3 θάλᾰμος, ὁ   an inner room, chamber, bedroom (182)

κληδοῦχος, ον   (κλεῖς, ἔχω) holding the keys [1x *Hipp.*]

σεβίζω   worship, honor [1x *Hipp.*]

πέρθω   destroy, ravage ([τὸν] πέρθοντα 'the one who destroys'; [τὸν] ‡⁺ἱέντα < *⁺ἵημι, pres. act. ptc., 'the one who sends'; ptcs. as subst. without an artic.: S #2049, 2052a; GMT #827)

544 ὅταν ‡⁺ἔλθη   (*⁺ἔρχομαι, aor.² act. subjv.) indef. relat. temporal clause with subjv. (S #2410)

τὰν μὲν Οἰχαλίᾳ	[στρ. β 545 The filly in Oechalia
πῶλον ἄζυγα λέκτρων,	not yoked to a marriage bed,
ἄνανδρον τὸ πρὶν καὶ ἄνυμφον, οἴκων	manless, and previously unwed,
ζεύξασ' ἀπ' Εὐρυτίων	yoking her away from Eurytus' house

δρομάδα ναῖδ᾽ ὅπως τε βάκ-	550	like a fleeing Naiad or a Bacchant,
χαν σὺν αἵματι, σὺν καπνῷ, φονίοισι νυμφείοις		with bloodshed, with smoke, with murderous wedding, Cypris gave
Ἀλκμήνας τόκῳ Κύπρις ἐξέδωκεν· ὦ		away in marriage to the son of Alcmene;
τλάμων ὑμεναίων.		Oh unhappy in her marriage!
ὦ Θήβας ἱερὸν	[ἀντ. β 555	Oh holy wall of Thebes,
τεῖχος, ὦ στόμα Δίρκας,		source of Dirce's fountain, you
συνείποιτ᾽ ἂν ἁ Κύπρις οἷον ἕρπει.		may confirm how Cypris comes.
βροντᾷ γὰρ ἀμφιπύρῳ		For betrothing to the all-flaming thunder
τοκάδα τὰν διγόνοιο Βακ-	560	the mother of the twice-born Bacchus
χου νυμφευσαμένα πότμῳ φονίῳ κατηύνασεν.		she lulled her to sleep in a bloody doom.
δεινὰ γὰρ τὰ πάντ᾽ ἐπιπνεῖ, μέλισσα δ᾽ οἵ- α τις πεπόταται.		She blows terribly over all, and like a bee she flits.

545 = 555	– ⏝ – ⏑ ⏑ – –	Aeolic hexasyllable or dodrans
546 = 556	– ⏑ – ⏑ ⏑ – –	pherecratean
547–8 = 557–8	⏑ ⏑ – – ⏑ – ⏑ ⏑ – ⏑ –	wilamowitzian + bacchiac
549 = 559	– – ⏑ – ⏑ ⏑ –	Λ wilamowitzian
550 = 560	⏑ ⏑ ⏑ – ⏑ ⏑ – ⏑ –	glyconic +
551 = 561	– ⏝ – ⏑ ⏑ – ⏑ –	glyconic
552 = 562	⏑ ⏑ – ⏑ – – –	telesillean *a* (B.)
553 = 563	– – – ⏑ – ⏑ ⏑ – ⏑ – ⏑ –	wilamowitzian + iambic +
554 = 564	– – ⏑ ⏑ – –	reizianum

545–6 μέν surely, indeed, really (μέν *solitarium*, i.e., without a corresponding δέ clause, is emphatic; here stressing the idea that no one can disagree with the sad story of Iole: S #2896–8; GP I. 359–60)

Οἰχᾰλία, ἡ   Oechalia, a city in Euboea. (πῶλος 'filly' refers to Iole, daughter of King Eurytus of Oechalia. Heracles sacked Oechalia and killed Eurytus, because Eurytus refused to give him Iole as a concubine. Cf. Soph. *Trachiniai* 358–68.) [1x *Hipp.*]

ἄ-ζυξ, ῦγος, ὁ/ἡ   unyoked, unmarried (λέκτρων, gen. of explanation: S #1322) (1425)

547–8 ἄν-ανδρος   (ἀ privat., ἀνήρ, man, husband) without a husband [1x *Hipp.*]

ἄ-νυμφος, ον   (ἀ privat., νύμφη, bride) unwedded [1x *Hipp.*]

549 ζεύγνυμι   join (ζεύξασα, aor.[1] act. ptc., coincidental/modal with ἐξέδωκεν; see λύσασα in line 290: 'yoking,' not 'having yoked') (111)

Ἐυρύτιος (3)   of Eurytus, king of Oechalia and father of Iole
[1x Eur.]

550 δρομάς, άδος, ὁ/ἡ   (δραμεῖν, run) running, whirling [1x *Hipp.*]

Νᾱΐς, ΐδος, ἡ   (for vᾱιάς) Naiad, a river or water nymph. (Lawall: "On the evidence of vase paintings one may assume that the nymph is running from a satyr or Pan desiring to rape her. The image is thus appropriate to the story of Iole and Heracles.") [1x Eur.]

Βάκχη, ἡ   (Βάκχος, Bacchus) Bacchant [1x *Hipp.*]

551 κάπνος, ὁ   smoke (954)

552 φόνιος (3/2)   bloody (562)

νυμφεῖος (3)   bridal, nuptial [1x *Hipp.*]

553–4 Ἀλκμήνη, ἡ   Alcmene, mother of Heracles (Ἀλκμήνας = Ἀλκμήνης; τλάμων = ⁺τλήμων) [1x *Hipp.*]

ἐκ-*⁺δίδωμι   give out of one's house in marriage [1x *Hipp.*]

ὑμέναιος, ὁ   wedding song, sung by the bride's attendants as they lead her to the bridegroom's house (ὑμεναίων, gen. of cause in exclamation: S #1407, here explaining τλάμων) [1x *Hipp.*]

555 Θηβαί, ὧν αἱ   Thebes (Θήβας is gen. sg.; the sg. is inherited
from Homer and is rare in Euripides, according to B.) [1x *Hipp.*]

ἱερός (3/2)   relating to gods, holy; unnatural (1206)

556 τεῖχος, εος, τό   wall [1x *Hipp.*]

Δίρκη, ης, ἡ   Dirce, one of the springs near Thebes [1x
Hipp.]

557–8 συν-*⁺εῖπον   agree with, confirm (συνείποιτε ἄν, aor.² act.
opt.; potential opt. used to indicate a polite request: S #1824) [1x Eur.]

ἕρπω   creep, crawl, move slowly (B. claims: "merely
a synonym of ἔρχεται," but there seems to be a sinister implication in
the verb; ⁺οἷον, acc. of manner: S #1608: how, in what manner) [1x
Hipp.]

559 βροντή, ἡ   thunder (1201)

ἀμφι-πῦρος, ον   surrounded by fire, with fire all around [1x
Hipp.]

560 τοκάς, άδος, ἡ   one who gave birth (τάν = τήν; the artic. and the
attr. gen. Βάκχου follow the noun, in an explicatory manner: S #1161n1)
[1x *Hipp.*]

δίγονος, ον   (δις, *γένω) twice-born (διγόνοιο = διγόνου,
epic gen.; once by Semele and once from Zeus' thigh. The idea of
giving birth to the 'twice-born' Bacchus is proleptic. Bacchus' second
birth will occur after his mother dies.) [1x *Hipp.*]

561 νυμφεύω   to betroth (νυμφευσάμενα = νυμφευσαμένη;
aor.¹ mid. ptc., coincidental/modal with κατηύνασεν: see λύσασα in
line 290. The mid. mode stresses Aphrodite's interest in the union.)
[1x *Hipp.*]

⁺πότμος, ὁ   fate, doom

562 κατ-ευνάζω, κατηύνασα   lull to sleep [1x *Hipp.*]

563 ἐπι-πνέω   blow upon (⁺δεινά = δεινή, Doric alpha)

μέλισσα, ἡ   (μέλι, honey) bee (⁺οἷα, like) (77)

564 ποτάομαι   fly about, flit, hover (πεπόταται = πεπότηται; pf. dep. indic.). The association of the bee with both a potential sting and honey connects her with the former claim that Eros/Aphrodite is destructive but also brings pleasure. (1272)

SECOND EPISODE LINES 565–731

At some point during the choral song, Phaedra, intrigued by the voices inside the palace, rises from her couch and eavesdrops at the door. She swiftly realizes that Hippolytus is rebuking her Nurse. She demands that the Chorus stop their song and relays to them what is being said in the palace in lines 565–95. Euripides tends to present a contrast in emotion between speakers by using meter. Aristotle considered the iambic trimeter most suitable for speech (*Poetics* 1449a18); songs, on the other hand, are sung in a variety of lyric meter, which reflects the degree of the singer's excitement (Roisman 2000a). One would expect here, therefore, that Phaedra, upset by what she hears, would use lyrical meter, while the Chorus remain calm. Euripides, however, reverses the norm. As if resigned to what she might have expected, Phaedra keeps her calm and speaks in iambs. The Chorus, on the other hand, are up in arms. They begin in spoken trimeters (566, 568), but once they realize the extent of the calamity they are witnessing, they break into the agitation of dochmiacs; then, calming down, they end in spoken iambs (598).

After Phaedra concludes that she must die as quickly as possible, Hippolytus and the Nurse emerge from the palace. Phaedra remains on stage silent, witnessing what unfolds between Hippolytus and the Nurse. After a brief *stichomythia* (601–15) between Hippolytus and the Nurse, in which the Nurse implores Hippolytus to keep silent, Hippolytus plunges into a misogynistic tirade against women (616–68), expresses his contempt for Phaedra, and declares that he will keep his oath but will watch Phaedra and the Nurse closely when Theseus returns. The episode ends with Phaedra's recriminations against the Nurse and her exchange with the Chorus leader before exiting to her death (669–731).

Φα.	σιγήσατ᾽, ὦ γυναῖκες· ἐξειργάσμεθα.	565
Χο.	τί δ᾽ἐστί, Φαίδρα, δεινὸν ἐν δόμοισί σοι;	
Φα.	ἐπίσχετ᾽, αὐδὴν τῶν ἔσωθεν ἐκμάθω.	
Χο.	σιγῶ· τὸ μέντοι φροίμιον κακὸν τόδε.	

Φα.	ἰώ μοι, αἰαῖ·	
	ὦ δυστάλαινα τῶν ἐμῶν παθημάτων.	570
Χο.	τίνα θροεῖς αὐδάν; τίνα βοᾷς λόγον;	
	ἔνεπε, τίς φοβεῖ σε φήμα, γύναι,	
	φρένας ἐπίσσυτος;	
Φα.	ἀπωλόμεσθα· ταῖσδ' ἐπιστᾶσαι πύλαις	575
	ἀκούσαθ' οἷος κέλαδος ἐν δόμοις πίτνει.	
Χο.	σὺ παρὰ κλῇθρα, σοὶ μέλει πομπίμα	
	φάτις δωμάτων·	
	ἔνεπε δ' ἔνεπέ μοι, τί ποτ' ἔβα κακόν;	580
Φα.	ὁ τῆς φιλίππου παῖς Ἀμαζόνος βοᾷ	
	Ἱππόλυτος, αὐδῶν δεινὰ πρόσπολον κακά.	
Χο.	ἰὰν μὲν κλύω, σαφὲς δ' οὐκ ἔχω·	585
	γεγώνει δ' οἷα διὰ πύλας ἔμολεν	
	ἔμολέ σοι βοά.	
Φα.	καὶ μὴν σαφῶς γε τὴν κακῶν προμνήστριαν,	
	τὴν δεσπότου προδοῦσαν ἐξαυδᾷ λέχος.	590
Χο.	ὤμοι ἐγὼ κακῶν· προδέδοσαι φίλα.	
	τί σοι μήσομαι;	
	τὰ κρύπτ' ἐκπέφηνε, διὰ δ' ὄλλυσαι,	
	αἰαῖ ἒ ἔ, πρόδοτος ἐκ φίλων.	

569	ᴗ – – ᴗ –	dochmiac
571	ᴗ ᴗᴗ – – – ᴗ ᴗᴗ – ᴗᴗ	2 dochmiacs
572/573	ᴗ ᴗᴗ – ᴗ – ᴗ – – ᴗ –	2 dochmiacs
574	ᴗ ᴗᴗ – ᴗ –	dochmiac
577/578	ᴗ ᴗᴗ – – ᴗ – – – ᴗ –	2 dochmiacs
579	ᴗ – – ᴗ –	dochmiac
580/581	ᴗ ᴗᴗ ᴗᴗ ᴗ – ᴗ ᴗᴗ – – –	2 dochmiacs
585	ᴗ – – ᴗ – ᴗ – – ᴗ –	2 dochmiacs
586/587	ᴗ – – – – ᴗ ᴗᴗ – ᴗ ᴗᴗ	2 dochmiacs
588	ᴗ ᴗᴗ – ᴗ –	dochmiac
591/592	– ᴗᴗ – ᴗ – ᴗ ᴗᴗ – ᴗ –	2 dochmiacs
593	ᴗ – – ᴗ –	dochmiac
594	ᴗ – – ᴗ – ᴗ ᴗᴗ – ᴗ –	2 dochmiacs
595	– – ᴗ – | ᴗᴗ ᴗ – ᴗ –	2 dochmiacs (one catalectic and one full)

565 ἐξ-*ἐργάζομαι   undo, destroy; pass.: am destroyed (ἐξειργά-σμεσθα = ἐξειργάσμεθα, for metrical convenience: S #465d; pf. pass. indic.) – 'we are undone' [1x *Hipp.*]

567 ἐπ-*⁺ἔχω   stop (ἐπίσχετε, aor.² act. impv.) [1x *Hipp.*]

ἔσωθεν (adv.)   from within (τῶν ἔσωθεν, substantive-making power of the artic. with advs.: S #1153e) [1x *Hipp.*]

ἐκ-*⁺μανθάνω, ἐκ-ἔμαθον   learn thoroughly; examine closely (ἐκμάθω, aor.² act. subjv. B.: "This voluntative 1st pers. subjv. [i.e., hortatory subjv.] . . . is used freely in the pl.. . . but in the sg. it is (when affirmative) used only after an impve. [ἐπίσχετε] requesting the compliance required"; S #1797b.) – 'Stop! Let me fully learn the voice of those inside.' [1x *Hipp.*]

568 φροίμιον, τό   (= προοίμιον) introduction, opening, beginning; – 'I am silent, but this opening bodes ill.' [1x *Hipp.*]

570 ⁺δυσ-τάλᾱς, αινα, ᾰν most miserable

πάθημα, ατος, τό   suffering, misfortune (gen. of cause in exclamation: S #1407, here explaining τάλαινα) [1x *Hipp.*]

571 θροέω   shriek, cry aloud, cry out (τίνα . . . αὐδάν, cognate acc.: S #1567.II) (212)

⁺βοάω   utter a cry (βοᾶς λόγον, cognate acc.: S #1567.II)

574 ἐπίσσυτος, ον   rushing upon, hurrying, gushing; – 'What utterance are you crying out, what word are you shrieking out? Tell us, what news scares you, lady, rushes upon your mind?' [1x Eur.]

575 *⁺ἀπωλόμεσθα   (= ἀπωλόμεθα, aor.² mid. indic.; metrical convenience: S #465d; ἐπιστᾶσαι < *ἐφίστημι, aor.² act. ptc. fem. pl.; ptc. of attendant circumstance: S #2068; GMT #843, or circumstantial/modal; see λύσασα in line 290)

576 ⁺ἀκούω   listen, hear

κέλαδος, ὁ   noise, din, shouting (πίτνει = *⁺πίπτει) – 'We are ruined. (Standing =) Stand at the door and hear what kind of clamor is falling in the house.' [1x *Hipp.*]

578 κλῇθρον, τό   (= κλεῖθρον, τό) a bolt or a bar closing a door;
a door (generally pl.) – 'You are by the door' (808)

    πόμπῐμος (3/2)   (πέμπω, send) sent, brought (πομπίμα = πο-
μπίμη) [1x *Hipp.*]

579 φάτις, ἡ   (⁺φημί, say) speech report (only in nom., voc.,
and acc.) (130)

    ⁺δῶμα, ατος, τό   house (lit.: 'news sent from the house is your
concern'; B.: "a recherché way of saying σοὶ μέλει φάτιν πέμπειν δωμάτων, it is your job to convey to us tidings about what is going on in
the house")

580 *⁺ἔβα   (= ἔβη < *⁺βαίνω, aor.² act. indic.) – 'Tell us,
tell us, what evil has come [upon us]?'

581 φίλ-ιππος, ον   fond of horses (probably a *hypallage*; the epithet should go with παῖς) [1x *Hipp.*]

584 ὁ ... Ἱππόλυτος   (emphatic *hyperbaton* placing Ἱππόλυτος in an
emphatic *enjambment*; αὐδῶν, "elevated synonym of λέγων" [B.]; κακά,
cognate acc./internal obj. modified by δεινά: S #1554, 1567) – 'The child
of the horse-loving Amazon, Hippolytus, is shouting, uttering horrible in-
sults at my servant.'

585 ἰά, ἡ   voice, cry; – 'I hear the voice, but I have nothing sure.' [1x *Hipp.*]

586 γεγωνέω   make noise (γεγώνει, pres. act. impv. 2 sg.)
[1x *Hipp.*]

    *⁺βλώσκω, ἔμολον   go, come

    ⁺βοή, ἡ   shout (βοά = βοή) – 'call out aloud what kind
of a cry has come, has come to you through the doors.'

589 καὶ μήν ... γε   Yes! Indeed! (translation according to the context; καὶ μήν "in replies usually confirms the last remark, accedes to a request, or denotes hearty assent"; γε "emphasizes the word or words with
which it is immediately connected," here σαφῶς; in replies "*and indeed,
and yet*, or *oh, but*": S #2921; GP 147b)

προμνήστρια, ἡ   matchmaker (κακῶν, gen. of explanation: S #1322) – 'matchmaker of evil' [1x Eur.]

590 ἐξ-αυδάω   speak out, call (τήν . . . προδοῦσαν, < ⁺προ-ᵗ⁺δίδωμι, aor.² act. ptc.; subst. power of the artic.; see πάρειμι in line 184) – 'Yes, he clearly calls [her] a matchmaker of evil, a betrayer of her master's marriage bed.' (1239)

591–5 ὤμοι ἐγὼ κακῶν   (κακῶν, gen. of cause in exclamation: S #1407) – 'woe's me for these ills'

μήδομαι   devise, resolve, plan, intend (the pf. ⁺προδέδοσαι underscores Phaedra's current unfortunate situation; τὰ κρυπτά, subst. power of the artic.; see νέος in line 114; ⁺ἐκ-ᵗ⁺πέφνη < ⁺ἐκφάινω, aor.² act. indic.) (1400)

⁺δι-ᵗ⁺όλλυμι   destroy utterly (διὰ . . . ὄλλυσαι, pres. mid./ pass.; *tmesis*)

πρόδοτος, ον   (προδίδωμι, betray) betrayed, abandoned (ἐκ φίλων = ὑπὸ φίλων, gen. of agent: S #1678) – 'You are betrayed, my friend! What can I devise for you? The hidden has been revealed, and you are utterly ruined! Ai ai! Betrayed by friends!' [1x Eur.]

Φα.	ἀπώλεσέν μ' εἰποῦσα συμφορὰς ἐμάς,
	φίλως καλῶς δ' οὐ τήνδ' ἰωμένη νόσον.
Χο.	πῶς οὖν; τί δράσεις, ὦ παθοῦσ' ἀμήχανα;
Φα.	οὐκ οἶδα πλὴν ἕν, κατθανεῖν ὅσον τάχος,
	τῶν νῦν παρόντων πημάτων ἄκος μόνον. 600
Ἱπ.	ὦ γαῖα μῆτερ ἡλίου τ' ἀναπτυχαί,
	οἵων λόγων ἄρρητον εἰσήκουσ' ὄπα.
Τρ.	σίγησον, ὦ παῖ, πρίν τιν' αἰσθέσθαι βοῆς.
Ἱπ.	οὐκ ἔστ' ἀκούσας δειν' ὅπως σιγήσομαι.
Τρ.	ναί, πρός σε τῆσδε δεξιᾶς εὐωλένου. 605
Ἱπ.	οὐ μὴ προσοίσεις χεῖρα μηδ' ἅψῃ πέπλων;
Τρ.	ὦ πρός σε γονάτων, μηδαμῶς μ' ἐξεργάσῃ.
Ἱπ.	τί δ', εἴπερ, ὡς φής, μηδὲν εἴρηκας κακόν;
Τρ.	ὁ μῦθος, ὦ παῖ, κοινὸς οὐδαμῶς ὅδε.
Ἱπ.	τά τοι κάλ' ἐν πολλοῖσι κάλλιον λέγειν. 610
Τρ.	ὦ τέκνον, ὅρκους μηδαμῶς ἀτιμάσῃς.
Ἱπ.	ἡ γλῶσσ' ὀμώμοχ', ἡ δὲ φρὴν ἀνώμοτος.

Τρ.   ὦ παῖ, τί δράσεις; σοὺς φίλους διεργάσῃ;
Ἱπ.   ἀνέπτυσ᾽· οὐδεὶς ἄδικός ἐστί μοι φίλος.
Τρ.   σύγγνωθ᾽· ἁμαρτεῖν εἰκὸς ἀνθρώπους, τέκνον.   615

596–8 ἰάομαι   heal (*⁺εἰποῦσα, aor.² ptc., coincidental/modal
with ἀπώλεσεν: see λύσασα in line 290; ἰωμένη, conative pres. ptc. expressing attempted or intended action: S #1878a) – 'She has destroyed me
by speaking of my misfortunes, trying to cure my disease as a friend but
improperly.' [1x *Hipp.*]

   ἀ-μήχᾰνος, ον   (ἀ privat., μηχᾰνή, device) helpless, inexplica-
   ble (παθοῦσα < *⁺πάσχω, aor.² act. circumstantial ptc., coincidental
   with the leading verb, see ὁράω in line 4) – 'What then? What will you
   do having suffered the impossible?' (643)

599–600 τάχος, εος, τό   swiftness, speed (ὅσον τάχος, acc. of manner:
S #1608) (973)

   ἄκος, εος, τό   cure, relief, remedy (⁺κατθανεῖν = κατα-
   *⁺θανεῖν, aor.² act. inf.; *syncope*; τῶν . . . ⁺παρ-*⁺όντων πημάτων, obj.
   gen.: S #1331; attr. ptc., see λεχθεῖσι in line 299) – 'I don't know,
   except for one thing, to die at once, the only remedy for my present
   troubles.' [1x *Hipp.*]

Hippolytus, followed by the Nurse, enters from the palace. Phaedra with-
draws from the palace doors but does not exit.

601 ἀναπτῠχή, ἡ   an opening, unfolding, expanse [1x *Hipp.*]

602 ἄρ-ρητος (3/2)   (ἀ privat., ῥηθῆναι, speak) unspeakable
[1x *Hipp.*]

   εἰσ-*ακούω   listen (712)

   ὄψ, οπός, ἡ   voice, word (λόγων, gen. of explanation:
   S #1322) – 'Oh earth and open sunlight (the unfoldings of the sun), the
   uttering of what unspeakable words I've heard!' [1x *Hipp.*]

603 *⁺αἰσθάνομαι   + gen.: take notice of, perceive (see πρίν + inf.
in line 29; τινα, subj. of the inf.) – 'Be quiet, child, before someone hears
your shout!'

604 οὐκ ἔστι... ὅπως   lit.: 'it is not... how,' i.e., 'it is not possible that' (ἔστι, quasi-impersonal with accent on penult, meaning 'it is possible'; ἀκούσας, aor.[1] act. circumstantial ptc. denoting time; see ἐλθόντα in line 24) – 'It is not possible that I will be silent after hearing such horrible things' (893)

605 ναί (adv.)   yes, yea, verily [1x *Hipp.*]

εὐ-ώλενος, ον   (εὖ, ὠλένη, arm) fair-armed; – 'Yes, [I implore you] by this fair [strong?] right arm [of yours]'; cf. line 200 [1x Eur.]

606 προσ-**⁺φέρω   apply to, lay upon (οὐ μὴ προσοίσεις; see γη-ρύω in line 213) (282)

**⁺ἅπτω   fasten, kindle; mid.: touch + gen. (ἅψῃ, fut. mid. indic. 2 sg.; οὐ... μηδ' ἅψῃ; see προσοίσεις above) – 'Don't bring your hand near to me, don't touch my cloak!'

607 γόνυ, γόνατος, τό   knee (γονάτων, resolution in 4th position; ritual supplication was done by embracing the knees of the person with one hand and touching his/her chin with the other) (326)

μηδαμῶς (adv.)   in no way (see μηδαμῶς ⁺ἀτιμάσῃς in line 611) – 'Oh, [I beg you] by your knees, do not destroy me!' [1x *Hipp.*]

608 τί (adv.)   why? how? wherefore? (τί δέ, 'why [do you say that]?' 'how so?'; a frequent expression conveying surprise, often introducing a further question, as in this case: GP 175.IVa) – 'How so? If, as you say, you have said nothing bad?'

609 ⁺κοινός (3)   common, shared, public, for all to hear

οὐδἄμῶς (adv.)   in no wise; – 'The story, child, was absolutely not for all to hear!' [1x *Hipp.*]

610 κάλλιον   (compar. of ⁺καλόν, neut. nom. sg.; supply ἐστί; note the *consonance* of λ in the line; τοι, 'surely,' expresses contempt; λέγειν, limiting/explanatory inf. often translated in English in pass.: S #2006; SS 238–9 §3a) – 'Surely, fine things are better told among many.'

611 ⁺ὅρκος, ὁ   oath

⁺ἀτῑμάζω   slight, dishonor (ἀτιμάσῃς, aor.¹ act. subjv.;
prohibitive subjv.: S #1800, 1840) – 'Oh child! Do *not* dishonor your
oath!'

612 *⁺ὄμνῡμι   wear (ὀμώμοχ'= ὀμώμοκε)

ἀν-ώμοτος   (ἀ privat., ὄμνῡμι) not bound by oath, unsworn
(supply ἐστί. A famous line in antiquity, three times parodied by Aristophanes [*Thesmophoriazousai* 276, *Frogs* 101–2, 1471] and even
quoted in the court of law [Aristotle *Rhetoric* 1416a 28ff.]. Cicero,
who approved of the sentiment that oaths are not always binding, rendered the line into Latin: *iuravi lingua, mentem iniuratam gero* [*De
Officiis* 3.108].) – 'My tongue swore, but my mind is unsworn.' [1x
Hipp.]

614 ἀπο-πτύω   spit away, reject (ἀπ-έπτυσα, aor.¹ act. indic.,
dramatic aor. used in the 1st pers. in drama "to denote a state of mind or an
act expressing a state of mind.. . . In translation the present is employed":
S #1937; μοι, dat. of possess.: S #1476) – 'I spit [it = the word 'friends']
out! No unjust man is a friend of mine!' [1x *Hipp.*]

⁺ἄ-δῐκος, ον   (ἀ privat., δίκη) doing wrong, unjust (ἄδῐκος,
resolution in 6th position)

615 συγ-*⁺γιγνώσκω   yield, concede; grant, allow (σύγγνωθι, aor.²
act. impv. 2 sg.) [1x *Hipp.*]

εἰκός   (neut. ptc. of ἔοικα, be like, seem) probable,
reasonable, proper (εἰκός [ἐστί] 'it is likely'+ inf.) – 'Forgive! Humans
tend to err, child!' (1434)

Ἱπ.   ὦ Ζεῦ, τί δὴ κίβδηλον ἀνθρώποις κακὸν
           γυναῖκας ἐς φῶς ἡλίου κατῴκισας;
           εἰ γὰρ βρότειον ἤθελες σπεῖραι γένος,
           οὐκ ἐκ γυναικῶν χρῆν παρασχέσθαι τόδε,
           ἀλλ' ἀντιθέντας σοῖσιν ἐν ναοῖς βροτοὺς   620
           ἢ χαλκὸν ἢ σίδηρον ἢ χρυσοῦ βάρος
           παίδων πρίασθαι σπέρμα του τιμήματος,
           τῆς ἀξίας ἕκαστον, ἐν δὲ δώμασιν
           ναίειν ἐλευθέροισι θηλειῶν ἄτερ.
           [νῦν δ' ἐς δόμους μὲν πρῶτον ἄξεσθαι κακὸν   625

μέλλοντες ὄλβον δωμάτων ἐκτίνομεν.]
τούτῳ δὲ δῆλον ὡς γυνὴ κακὸν μέγα·
προσθεὶς γὰρ ὁ σπείρας τε καὶ θρέψας πατὴρ
φερνὰς ἀπῴκισ᾽, ὡς ἀπαλλαχθῇ κακοῦ.
ὁ δ᾽ αὖ λαβὼν ἀτηρὸν ἐς δόμους φυτὸν   630
γέγηθε κόσμον προστιθεὶς ἀγάλματι
καλὸν κακίστῳ καὶ πέπλοισιν ἐκπονεῖ
δύστηνος, ὄλβον δωμάτων ὑπεξελών.

616 τί δή   'Why, pray?' (intensive/emphatic δή, which
with impvs. and questions adds urgency: S #2843a; GP 210, 5.I. Hippolytus' wish that mortals were able to have children without the female sex is
a figure of speech termed an *adynaton*; see p. 31; cf. 1074–1075. Phaedra
and Theseus similarly turn to *adynaton* when in distress; see lines 208–31
and 928–31.)

  κίβδηλος, ον   base, spurious; counterfeit, deceitful (κίβδηλον, predicative, 'counterfeit evil'; κακόν, subst. without artic., 'evil':
  see σοφός in line 90; ἀνθρώποις, dat. of disadvantage/incommodi: S
  #1481) [1x *Hipp.*]

617 κατ-οικίζω   bring into a dwelling; – 'Oh Zeus! Why, pray,
did you bring women, a counterfeit evil for men, into the light of the sun?'
[1x *Hipp.*]

618–20 ἀντι-*⁺τίθημι   deposit in exchange (σπεῖραι < *⁺σπείρω, aor.¹
act. inf.; see ⁺χρῆν in line 253, + inf. and acc.: [σε] παρασχέσθαι; παρασχέσθαι < ⁺παρ-*⁺έχω, aor.² mid. inf.; ἀντιθέντας, aor.² act. ptc. of attendant
circumstance; see προκόπτω in line 23) [1x *Hipp.*]

621 χαλκός, ὁ   bronze, copper [1x *Hipp.*]

  χρυσός, ὁ   [ῠ] gold [1x *Hipp.*]

622 πρίασθαι   buy (aor.² mid. inf. of ὠνέομαι) [1x *Hipp.*]

  σπέρμα, ατος, τό   seed (note the *consonance* of π) [1x *Hipp.*]

  τίμημα, ατος, τό   estate's estimate, worth, prize [1x *Eur.*]

623 ἀξία, ἡ   price, worth (τῆς ἀξίας, gen. of value, following πρίασθαι: S #1336) [1x *Hipp.*]

624 θῆλυς, εια, υ   female (adj. used substantively without artic.;
see σοφός in line 90) (410)

ἄτερ (prep. + gen.)   without; – 'For if you wanted to propagate the
human race, you should have not provided this from women, but men
should have deposited in your temples either bronze or iron or a weight
of gold to buy a seed of children, each at the value of his estate, and
dwell in their homes free from females.' [1x *Hipp.*]

[625–6] The two lines are considered an interpolation on several
grounds—among others, because the lines refer to bride-price and as such
are incompatible with the following lines 627–9, which talk about dowry.
The assumption is that one should not conflate two customs. Second, μὲν
πρῶτον in 625 is not answered by ἔπειτα δέ or equivalent. Third, ἐκτίνομεν
is unmetrical: – ⌣ ⌣ ⌣ should have been – – ⌣ ⌣̲.

*ἄγω   lead; ἄγεσθαι γυναῖκα, to take to oneself a wife
(ἄξεσθαι, fut. mid. inf.; μέλλοντες, pres. act. ptc. of attendant circum-
stance/descriptive, coincidental with the leading verb, see ὁράω in line
4. Fut. inf. with μέλλω usually occurs as a verb of thinking: S #1959a;
see line 390.) (1269)

ὄλβος, ὁ   wealth (1112)

ἐκ-τίνω   pay out, pay in full; – 'But, as things are, when
we intend on leading an evil into our house, we pay out the wealth of
our house.' [1x *Hipp.*]

627 δῆλος (3/2)   clear, evident certain (τούτῳ, dat. of means:
S #1507; lit.: 'by this' refers to what is following) [1x *Hipp.*]

628 ⁺προσ-*⁺τίθημι   give in addition, apply, attribute, impute to
(προσ-θείς, aor.² act. ptc., coincidental/modal here with ἀπῴκισε; see λύσασα in line 290; ὁ σπείρας, θρέψας, ptcs. qualifying the noun as attr. adjs.;
see λεχθεῖσι in line 299)

629 φερνή, ἡ   (φέρω) dowry [1x *Hipp.*]

ἀπ-οικίζω   send away (see ἐξέφηνα [gnomic aor.] in line
428, which is considered as primary tense; ἀπαλλαχθῇ < ⁺ἀπ-αλάττω, aor.¹
pass. subj. in final clause: S #2193, 2196) – 'And from this it is clear that
a woman is a great evil: a father who has begotten and reared her sends
her away with a dowry added, so he can be rid of the evil.' [1x *Hipp.*]

630 ἀτηρός (3)   (ἄτη, delusion, ruin) baneful, ruinous [1x *Hipp.*]

φῦτον, τό   creature (ὁ λαβών, artic. subst. ptc.; see πάρειμι in line 184) [1x *Hipp.*]

631 γηθέω   rejoice (γέγηθε, pf. act. indic.; προστίθεις, pres. act. ptc. of attendant circumstance, coincidental with the leading verb, see ὁράω in line 4) [1x *Hipp.*]

κόσμος, ὁ   finery, decoration, dress, raiment [1x *Hipp.*]

633 ὑπ-εξ-*⁺αιρέω   take out from under, steal away, undermine (ὑπεξελών, aor.² act. ptc. of attendant circumstance, see ὁράω in line 4) – 'And he who brings the ruinous creature to his home rejoices in adding lovely finery to the worst statue/image and decks her with clothing, wretched, having undermined the wealth of the house.'

[ἔχει δ' ἀνάγκην· ὥστε κηδεύσας καλῶς
γαμβροῖσι χαίρων σῴζεται πικρὸν λέχος,   635
ἢ χρηστὰ λέκτρα πενθεροὺς δ' ἀνωφελεῖς
λαβὼν πιέζει τἀγαθῷ τὸ δυστυχές.]
ῥᾷστον δ' ὅτῳ τὸ μηδέν· ἀλλ' ἀνωφελὴς
εὐηθίᾳ κατ' οἶκον ἵδρυται γυνή.
σοφὴν δὲ μισῶ· μὴ γὰρ ἔν γ' ἐμοῖς δόμοις   640
εἴη φρονοῦσα πλείον' ἢ γυναῖκα χρή.
τὸ γὰρ κακοῦργον μᾶλλον ἐντίκτει Κύπρις
ἐν ταῖς σοφαῖσιν· ἡ δ' ἀμήχανος γυνὴ
γνώμῃ βραχείᾳ μωρίαν ἀφῃρέθη.
χρῆν δ' ἐς γυναῖκα πρόσπολον μὲν οὐ περᾶν,   645
ἄφθογγα δ' αὐταῖς συγκατοικίζειν δάκη
θηρῶν, ἵν' εἶχον μήτε προσφωνεῖν τινα
μήτ' ἐξ ἐκείνων φθέγμα δέξασθαι πάλιν.
νῦν δ' †αἱ μὲν ἔνδον δρῶσιν αἱ κακαὶ† κακὰ
βουλεύματ', ἔξω δ' ἐκφέρουσι πρόσπολοι.   650

[634–7] The lines are considered an interpolation because they do not follow the main thrust of Hippolytus' speech about the worthlessness of women and admit that there are good wives. In addition, the mention of in-laws is irrelevant to Hippolytus' point. For a fuller discussion of the Greek, see B.

κηδεύω   ally oneself in marriage to (κηδεύσας, χαίρων, λαβών, circumstantial ptcs. of attendant circumstance according to their tenses, see ὁράω in line 4; see προκόπτω in line 23) [1x *Hipp.*]

γαμβρός, ὁ   father-in-law [1x *Hipp.*]

⁺πικρός (3/2)   bitter, sharp

πενθερός, ὁ   father-in-law; pl. parents-in-law

ἀνωφελής, ές   (ἀ privat., ὠφελέω, help) useless; hurtful, harmful, pernicious

πιέζω   stifle, press, suppress, squeeze, crush (τῷ ἀγαθῷ, τὸ δυστυχές, subst. power of the artic.; see νέος in line 114) – 'This must happen (there is a necessity): either after allying himself well with in-laws, enjoying [them] he preserves a bitter marriage, or having acquired a good marriage but harmful in-laws he crushes the bad fortune with the good.' [1x *Hipp.*]

638–9 ῥᾶστος (3)   (irreg. superl. of ⁺ῥάδιος) most easy (1047)

εὐ-ήθια, ἡ   simplicity, silliness (dat. of cause; see πάθος in line 139) [1x *Hipp.*]

τὸ ⁺μηδέν   nothingness

ἱδρύω   set up a statue (ἵδρυται, pf. pass.; the verb continues the metaphor of ⁺ἄγαλμα in line 631 [B.]) – 'A nonentity is the easiest for a man; but a woman set up as an idol in one's house is harmful due to her silliness.' (33)

640–1 μὴ ... εἴη   (opt. of wish; see κάμπτω in line 87)

πλεῖον'   = πλείονα, more (compar. of *⁺πολύς; *⁺χρή with acc. and inf.: see γυναῖκα [εἶναι] in line 641. Note that Hippolytus does not rule out marriage for himself.) – 'And I abhor a clever woman; may there never be in my house a woman more clever (thinking bigger) than a woman should be.' (471)

642–4 κᾰκ-οῦργος, ον   (⁺κακός, evil; *ἔργω, do) doing ill, knavish, villainous [1x *Hipp.*]

ἐν-τίκτω   engender, create, cause in (ἐν ταῖς σωφαῖσιν, *enjambment*) [1x *Hipp.*]

μωρία, ἡ   silliness, folly, absurdity (γνώμη βραχείᾳ, dat. of cause; see πάθος in line 139) [1x *Hipp.*]

⁺ἀφ-*⁺αιρέω, ἀφηρέθην   + double acc.: deprive X (acc.) of Y (acc.) (ἀφηρέθη, aor.¹ pass. indic. When the verb is in pass., X becomes the subj., and Y is the retained acc.: μωρίαν; gnomic aor.; see ἐξέφανη in line 428.) – 'For Cypris engenders mischief more in the clever ones; the helpless woman is deprived of folly due to her slight understanding.'

645–8   *⁺χρῆν   B. on 467: "χρή simply states the obligation, χρῆν (when used of a present obligation) regrets that it is not fulfilled."

περάω   pass, cross, go (περᾶν, pres. act. inf. in acc. and inf. structure after χρῆν; see lines 640–1) (782)

ἄ-φθογγος, ον   (ἀ privat., φθέγγομαι, utter a sound) voiceless [1x *Hipp.*]

συγ-κατ-οικίζω   settle in a place along with [1x *Eur.*]

δάκος, εος, τό   an animal whose bite is dangerous; bite (ἄφθογγα . . . δάκη θηρῶν, *hyperbaton*, *hypallage*: 'speechless bites of beasts,' i.e., 'speechless biting beasts') [1x *Hipp.*]

*⁺ἔχω + inf.   be able to (εἶχον, impf. act. indic.; impf. or aor. indic. is used in final clauses with ἵνα when the action of the leading clause is unfulfilled whether in past or present, here expressed by χρῆν: GMT #333–6; S #2185. The unreality is not always shown in translation.)

προσ-φωνέω   call by name, address [1x *Hipp.*]

⁺φθέγμα, ατος, τό   sound, word; – 'And no servant should ever go inside to a woman; speechless biting beasts should dwell with them, so that they would not be able to speak to anyone nor receive a word back.' (1215)

649–51   The text of 649 is thought to be corrupt, as δρῶσιν βουλεύματα 'do plans' cannot be right. The verb needs to indicate 'devise' or 'plot,' since Hippolytus' point is that some plot and the others execute.

ἔνδον (adv.)   inside (αἱ μὲν ἔνδον, subst. use of artic. with an adv.; see πρίν in line 302) (524)

ἐκ-*⁺φέρω   carry out (βουλεύματα, *enjambment*) – 'But as it is now, wicked women make wicked plots inside, and their servants carry them out [in the open]' [1x *Hipp.*]

ὡς καὶ σύ γ᾽ ἡμῖν πατρός, ὦ κακὸν κάρα,
λέκτρων ἀθίκτων ἦλθες ἐς συναλλαγάς·
ἀγὼ ῥυτοῖς νασμοῖσιν ἐξομόρξομαι
ἐς ὦτα κλύζων. πῶς ἂν οὖν εἴην κακός,
ὃς οὐδ᾽ ἀκούσας τοιάδ᾽ ἁγνεύειν δοκῶ;   655
εὖ δ᾽ ἴσθι, τοὐμόν σ᾽ εὐσεβὲς σῴζει, γύναι·
εἰ μὴ γὰρ ὅρκοις θεῶν ἄφαρκτος ᾑρέθην,
οὐκ ἄν ποτ᾽ ἔσχον μὴ οὐ τάδ᾽ ἐξειπεῖν πατρί.
νῦν δ᾽ ἐκ δόμων μέν, ἔστ᾽ ἂν ἐκδημῇ χθονὸς
Θησεύς, ἄπειμι, σῖγα δ᾽ ἕξομεν στόμα·   660
θεάσομαι δὲ σὺν πατρὸς μολὼν ποδὶ
πῶς νιν προσόψῃ καὶ σὺ καὶ δέσποινα σή.
[τῆς σῆς δὲ τόλμης εἴσομαι γεγευμένος.]
ὄλοισθε. μισῶν δ᾽ οὔποτ᾽ ἐμπλησθήσομαι
γυναῖκας, οὐδ᾽ εἴ φησί τίς μ᾽ ἀεὶ λέγειν·   665
ἀεὶ γὰρ οὖν πώς εἰσι κἀκεῖναι κακαί.
ἤ νύν τις αὐτὰς σωφρονεῖν διδαξάτω
ἢ κἄμ᾽ ἐάτω ταῖσδ᾽ ἐπεμβαίνειν ἀεί.

Hippolytus ceases the soliloquy and addresses the Nurse.

651–2 ἡμῖν   (μοί) *majestic plural* (poetic), to lend dignity
to himself and opposing the sg. σύ. Phaedra tends to use pl. for herself
(e.g., 331, 343, 349).

  ⁺κάρᾱ, τό   [ᾰ] head, poetic for κεφαλή (ὦ κακὸν κάρα, an
  emotional address; ὦ φίλον κάρα is more commonly used for affection)

  ἄ-θικτος, ον   (ἀ privat., θιγγάνω, touch) untouched (1002)

  συναλλᾰγή, ἡ   interchange; – 'Just as *you* have come to me,
  you wicked thing, for the commerce of the inviolable marriage bed of
  my father' [1x *Hipp.*]

653–5 ἀγώ   = ἃ ἐγώ (ἃ: the things that the Nurse has been
saying)

  ῥῠτός (3/2)   (ῥέω, flow) running, flowing (124)

  νασμός, ὁ   a flowing current, a stream, spring (dat. of
  means; see κύων in line 18) (225)

  ἐξ-*ομόργνῡμι, -ομόρξομαι   mid.: wipe off of oneself [1x *Hipp.*]

κλύζω   wash, splash (κλύζων, ptc. of attendant cir-
cumstance/descriptive, coincidental with the leading verb, see ὁράω
in line 4; *enjambment*) – 'These things I will wipe off of myself with
running stream water, splashing [it] into my ears.'

πῶς ἄν . . . εἴην   (potential opt. in independent clause with ἄν
for a timeless reference to the fut.: S #1824)

τοιόσδε, τοιάδε, τοιόνδε   of such nature (1455)

ἀγνεύω   (ἁγνός, chaste, pure) be pure, chaste (ἀκούσας,
ptc. of attendant circumstance, coincidental with the leading verb, see
ὁράω in line 4; δοκῶ ἁγνεύειν, when the subj. of the inf. and of the
governing verb is the same, the nom. can be omitted: S #1973) – 'How
could I be base, [I] who even only having heard such things, cannot
think I am chaste.' [1x *Hipp.*]

656–8 ἴσθι   do know (⁺οἶδα, pf. impv. act. 2 sg.; τὸ εὐσε-
βές. Note the *consonance* of -σ- in the line.) – 'Do know well, woman, my
piety saves you!' (304, 519)

ἄ-φαρκτος, ον   (ἀ privat., φράσσω, fence, defend) unfenced,
unguarded (θεῶν, *synizesis*; ἡρέθην < *⁺αἱρέω, aor.¹ pass. indic.)
[1x Eur.]

εἰ μὴ ἡρέθην . . . οὐκ ἄν ποτ' ἔσχον   (contrary-to-fact condition for
the past, aor. in both protasis and apodosis: S #2305; GMT #410)

ἐξ-εῖπον   speak out, utter, avow (μὴ οὐ with inf.; an inf.
that takes μή takes μὴ οὐ if dependent on a negated verb, here οὐκ ἄν
ποτ' ἔσχον. The οὐ is untranslatable: S #2745; G #1616; cf. line 49; μὴ
οὐ, *synizesis*.) – 'If I had not been taken off guard by oaths to the gods,
I would not have kept from declaring this to my father.' (492)

659–60 ἔστ(ε) (conj.)   while [1x *Hipp.*]

ἐκ-δημέω   go abroad (supply ἐστί; ἐκδημῇ, pres. act.
subjv. When ἔστε refers to the fut. and depends on a verb of fut. time
[ἕξομεν], it takes ἄν and the subjv., like a conditional relat. clause:
S #2399, 2423a; GMT #617, 613.3. See ἕξομεν, *majestic plural*, in
line 660.) [1x Eur.]

ἀπ-*⁺ειμι   (ἀπό, εἶμι) go away, depart (the pres. serves
mostly as fut.; Θησεύς, *enjambment*) [1x *Hipp.*]

σῖγα (adv.)   silently; – 'But as things are, I will go away
from the house, and as long as Theseus is abroad, I will keep my mouth
silent.' [1x *Hipp.*]

661–2 θεάομαι   [ᾱ] view, gaze (μολών < *⁺βλώσκω, aor.² act.
ptc. denoting time; see ἐλθόντα in line 24)

⁺πούς, ποδός, ὁ   foot [1x *Hipp.*]

προσ-*⁺οράω   look at (προσόψῃ, fut. dep. indic. 2 sg.) – 'But
I shall return with my father's coming (foot), and see how you meet his
eye and that mistress of yours too.' [1x *Hipp.*]

Line 663 is suspected of being an interpolation on the basis that it is anticlimactic after the emphatic phrase 'you and that mistress of yours' in
the previous line, and that if we remove line 663, the following, 'may you
perish,' flows wonderfully. However, we may ask if it is impossible to see
Hippolytus reverting to the misdoing of the Nurse. Although he assumes
that Phaedra is the primary cause, it was the Nurse who approached him
and made him take an oath, which he regrets right now, and his burning ire
is directed toward her. Giving him a line that does not necessarily follow
rhetorical logic would just expose the spectators to the inner emotional
struggle the youth is embroiled in.

663 γεύομαι   taste (εἴσομαι < *⁺οἶδα, fut. dep. indic.; εἴσομαι γεγευμένος, supplem. ptc. in indir. disc. after verb of knowing; see
ἀνοίγνυμι in line 56) – 'I will know that I have tasted your effrontery.'
[1x *Hipp.*]

664–5 ἐμ-*⁺πίμπλημι   fill full of a thing (ἐμπλησθήσομαι, fut.
pass. indic.; μισῶν, ptc. of attendant circumstance, coincidental with
the leading verb, see ὁράω in line 4; γυναῖκας stands in an emphatic
enjambment) – 'May you perish! I will never be satisfied enough
with hating women, not even if someone says that I always say [this].'
[1x *Hipp.*]

666–8 γὰρ οὖν   GP 446: "οὖν adds to γάρ the idea of importance and essentiality."

ἤ . . . ἤ   either . . . or (*⁺διδαξάτω; *⁺ἐάτω, aor.¹ act.
impv. 3 sg.; pres. act. impv. 3 sg.)

ἐπ-εμ-*⁺βαίνω   step upon, tread upon; – 'For they too are somehow always evil. Either let someone teach them to be chaste, or let me tread upon them forever!' [1x *Hipp.*]

Hippolytus exits. Phaedra, who has been listening in silence and whom Hippolytus must have seen, moves forward and sings the following lament.

The following antistrophe is a responsion to the choral stanza in lines 362–72. This is Phaedra's last song before she commits suicide.

Φα. τάλανες ὦ κακοτυχεῖς	[ἀντ.	Oh wretched [and] unfortunate
γυναικῶν πότμοι·		destinies of women!
τίν᾿ ἢ νῦν τέχναν ἔχομεν ἢ λόγον	670	What means or words do we have now after/since
σφαλεῖσαι κάθαμμα λύειν †λόγου†;		we have been tripped up to loosen the knot of words.
ἐτύχομεν δίκας· ἰὼ γᾶ καὶ φῶς.		We've met with what is deserved! Oh earth, oh light!
πᾷ ποτ᾿ ἐξαλύξω τύχας;		How will I escape my plight?
πῶς δὲ πῆμα κρύψω, φίλαι;		How will I hide my hurt, friends?
τίς ἂν θεῶν ἀρωγὸς ἢ τίς ἂν βροτῶν	675	Who among gods will appear as a helper? Who of
πάρεδρος ἢ ξυνεργὸς ἀδίκων ἔργων		mortals? Sitting beside me or partaking
φανείη; τὸ γὰρ παρ᾿ ἡμῖν πάθος		in unjust deeds? For the trouble that is
πέραν δυσεκπέρατον ἔρχεται βίου.		upon me goes across the boundary of life.
κακοτυχεστάτα γυναικῶν ἐγώ.		I am the most unfortunate of women!

669a	⏑⏑⏑ – ⏑⏑ ⏑ –	creticus + creticus
669b	⏑ – – ⏑ –	dochmiac
670	⏑ – – ⏑ – ⏑⏑⏑ – ⏑⏑	2 dochmiacs (the second is catalectic)
671	⏑ – – ⏑ – ⏑ – – ⏑ –	2 dochmiacs
672	⏑ ⏑⏑ – – ⏑ – ⏑ – – –	2 dochmiacs
673	– ⏑ – ⏑ – – ⏑ –	creticus + dochmiac

674	– ◡ – ◡ – – ◡ –	creticus + dochmiac
675	◡ – ◡ – ◡ – ◡ – ◡ –	3 iambs
676	◡ ◡◡ – ◡ – ◡ ◡◡ – – –	2 dochmiacs
677	◡ – – ◡ – ◡ – – ◡ –	2 dochmiacs
678	◡ – ◡ – ◡ – ◡ – ◡ –	3 iambs
679	◡ ◡◡ – ◡ – ◡ – – ◡ –	2 dochmiacs

669–7 Most manuscripts assign 669–71 to the Chorus and 672–9 to Phaedra. The error of attributing 669–71 to the Chorus probably resulted from the fem. pl. σφαλεῖσαι, which was assumed to indicate plurality of speakers. Phaedra speaks here of women in general; hence the pl. lines 669–79 are a metrical responsion to 362–72. Phaedra reacts to what she has just heard in what B. calls "heartbroken despair."

669 κᾰκο-τῠχής, ές   unfortunate (in *asyndeton* with τάλανες) (679)

670–1 ⁺τέχνη, ἡ   means, device (τέχναν = τέχνην)

κάθαμμα, ατος, τό   knot (σφαλεῖσαι < *⁺σφάλλω, aor.² pass. circumstantial causal ptc.; see ἐράω in line 32)

†λόγου†   There seems to be no need for the daggers: gen. of explanation/apposition; see αἷμα in line 35.

672–4 δίκας   = δίκης (gen. following *⁺τυγχάνω, meet with; γᾶ = γῆ)

πᾷ (interrog. pcl.)   = πῇ; how? which way? where? (877)

ἐξ-αλύσκω   shun, escape, avoid [1x *Hipp.*]

675–8 ἄν ... φανείη   (< *⁺φαίνω, aor.² pass. opt.; potential opt. see line 89; *hyperbaton* and *enjambment*)

ἀρωγός, ὁ   helper (predicative after φανείη) [1x *Hipp.*]

πάρ-εδρος, ον   (παρά, ἕδρα, a seat) sitting beside; next to, near (predicative after φανείη) [1x *Hipp.*]

συν-εργός, όν   associate, partner, helper, accomplice (predicative after φανείη) (523)

πέρᾱν (adv.)   = πέρην; + gen.: on the other side of, across (improper prep.; see ἔσω in line 2; πέραν ... βίου, *hyperbaton*) (1053)

δυσ-εκ-πέρᾱτος, ον   (δυσ-, ἐκπεράω, pass through) hard to get out from, hard to escape (883)

Χο.   φεῦ φεῦ, πέπρακται, κοὐ κατώρθωνται τέχναι,   680
δέσποινα, τῆς σῆς προσπόλου, κακῶς δ᾽ ἔχει.
Φα.   ὦ παγκακίστη καὶ φίλων διαφθορεῦ,
οἷ᾽ εἰργάσω με. Ζεύς σε γεννήτωρ ἐμὸς
πρόρριζον ἐκτρίψειεν οὐτάσας πυρί.
οὐκ εἶπον,—οὐ σῆς προυνοησάμην φρενός;—   685
σιγᾶν ἐφ᾽ οἷσι νῦν ἐγὼ κακύνομαι;
σὺ δ᾽ οὐκ ἀνέσχου· τοιγὰρ οὐκέτ᾽ εὐκλεεῖς
θανούμεθ᾽. ἀλλὰ δεῖ με δὴ καινῶν λόγων·
οὗτος γὰρ ὀργῇ συντεθηγμένος φρένας
ἐρεῖ καθ᾽ ἡμῶν πατρὶ σὰς ἁμαρτίας,   690
ἐρεῖ δὲ Πιτθεῖ τῷ γέροντι συμφοράς,
πλήσει τε πᾶσαν γαῖαν αἰσχίστων λόγων.
ὄλοιο καὶ σὺ χὤστις ἄκοντας φίλους
πρόθυμός ἐστι μὴ καλῶς εὐεργετεῖν.

680–1 **κατ-ορθόω**   set up right; pass. intrans.: be successful (πέ-πρακται < ⁺πράττω, pf. pass. indic.; impersonal) – 'Pheu! Pheu! It is all over, mistress! The schemes of your servant have not succeeded; the situation is bad!' (1445)

682–4 **πάγ-κᾰκος, ον**   utterly bad (superl. παγκάκιστος) [1x *Hipp.*]

διαφθορεύς, έως, ὁ   destroyer, corrupter, seducer [1x Eur.]

οἷ᾽(α) εἰργάσω με   'what have you done to me!' (*⁺ἐργάζομαι, aor.² mid. indic. + double acc.)

γεννήτωρ, ορος, ὁ   parent (Zeus was the father of Minos, Phaedra's father) [1x *Hipp.*]

πρόρ-ριζον (adv.)   (πρό, ῥίζα, root) by the roots, root and branch

ἐκ-*τρίβω   destroy completely (see κάμψαιμι, aor.¹ act. opt. of wish, in line 87) [1x *Hipp.*]

οὐτάζω   wound, strike (οὐτάσας, aor.¹ act. ptc.; descriptive ptc., coincidental/modal with that of the leading verb, ἐκτρίψειεν; see λύσασα in line 290; πυρί, dat. of means; see κύων in line 18) – 'May Zeus, my progenitor, destroy you root and branch by striking you with his thunderbolt!' [1x *Hipp.*]

685–6 προ-νοέω   + gen.: observe beforehand (προυνοησάμην = προενοησάμην: S #449b) (399)

κἀκύνομαι   be reproached, reviled (ἐφ᾽ οἷσι, [those things] 'on account of which') – 'Didn't I tell [you]—didn't I anticipate your thinking?—to keep silent [about those things] on account of which I am now reviled?' [1x *Hipp.*]

687–8 τοιγάρ (conj.)   inferential: therefore (S #2987) [1x *Hipp.*]

καινός (3)   new (θανούμεθα, emphatic *enjambment, majestic plural*, see line 660; δεῖ με . . . καινῶν λόγων in lines 490–91. Note Phaedra's focus on 'words.') – 'But you could not contain yourself! Therefore, I will no longer die with a good name! Oh! I need new words.' (370)

689–92 συν-θήγω   sharpen (ὀργῇ, dat. of means: S #1507; συντεθηγμένος, pf. pass. ptc. of attendant circumstance, coincidental with the leading verb, see ὁράω in line 4; φρένας, acc. of respect, see καρδία in line 27) [1x Eur.]

γέρων, οντος, ὁ   old person (Pittheus is the father of Aethra, Theseus' mother; see line 11) (797)

*πίμπλημι   + gen.: fill up; – 'For this man, whetted by anger in his mind, will denounce me to his father for your errors, and he will tell my misfortune to old Pittheus, and will fill the whole land with most shameful tales.' (1253)

693–4 ἄκων, ἄκουσα, ἄκον   against one's will, perforce (ὄλοιο < *⁺ὄλλυμι, aor.² mid. opt., impv. opt., see lines 528–9; χὤστις = καὶ ὅστις) (1433)

πρό-θῡμος, ον   ready, willing, eager (1006)

εὐ-εργετέω   do well, do good; – 'May you perish, you and whoever is eager to improperly benefit friends against their will.' [1x *Hipp.*]

Τρ.   δέσποιν᾽, ἔχεις μὲν τἀμὰ μέμψασθαι κακά,   695
τὸ γὰρ δάκνον σου τὴν διάγνωσιν κρατεῖ·
ἔχω δὲ κἀγὼ πρὸς τάδ᾽, εἰ δέξῃ, λέγειν.
ἔθρεψά σ᾽ εὔνους τ᾽ εἰμί· τῆς νόσου δέ σοι
ζητοῦσα φάρμαχ᾽ ηὗρον οὐχ ἀβουλόμην.
εἰ δ᾽ εὖ ἔπραξα, κάρτ᾽ ἂν ἐν σοφοῖσιν ἦ·   700

πρὸς τὰς τύχας γὰρ τὰς φρένας κεκτήμεθα.

Φα.   ἦ γὰρ δίκαια ταῦτα κἀξαρκοῦντά μοι,
      τρώσασαν ἡμᾶς εἶτα συγχωρεῖν λόγοις;
Τρ.   μακρηγοροῦμεν· οὐκ ἐσωφρόνουν ἐγώ.
      ἀλλ' ἔστι κἀκ τῶνδ' ὥστε σωθῆναι, τέκνον.   705
Φα.   παῦσαι λέγουσα· καὶ τὰ πρὶν γὰρ οὐ καλῶς
      παρῄνεσάς μοι κἀπεχείρησας κακά.
      ἀλλ' ἐκποδὼν ἄπελθε καὶ σαυτῆς πέρι
      φρόντιζ'· ἐγὼ γὰρ τἀμὰ θήσομαι καλῶς.
      ὑμεῖς δέ, παῖδες εὐγενεῖς Τροζήνιαι,   710
      τοσόνδε μοι παράσχετ' ἐξαιτουμένη,
      σιγῇ καλύπτειν ἀνθάδ' εἰσηκούσατε.

695–7 μέμφομαι   blame, upbraid (ἔχω + inf., especially of a verb
of saying—μέμψασθαι, λέγειν—denotes ability: 'I can': S #2000a) (1402)

⁺δάκνω   bite, sting (δάκνον, pres. act. ptc., artic.: 'the
sting'; see νέος in line 114)

διάγνωσις, εως, ἡ   discerning between, distinguishing; – 'Mistress, you can blame me for my mistakes, for that which is stinging
you overpowers your judgment, but I can speak against these charges,
if you'll accept.' (926)

698–701 εὔνους, ουν   well-minded, devoted, loyal [1x *Hipp.*]

ζητέω   search (ζητοῦσα, ptc. of attendant circumstance, see ὁράω in line 4. ἀβουλόμην = ἁ ἐβουλόμην, 'the ones [the
remedies] I was wanting to'; ἦ = ἦν < *⁺εἰμί, impf. indic. 1 sg.; εἰ
ἔπραξα . . . ἂν . . . ἦ, contrary-to-fact, with different tenses in protasis
and apodosis. The protasis indicates past time, the apodosis denotes
present time: GMT #410; S #2303–4.) – 'I reared you and am devoted
to you; seeking a remedy for this disease of yours, what I found was
not what I wished [to find]. Had I succeeded, I would be surely reck-
oned (now) among the wise, for we possess intelligence in proportion
to our luck.' [1x *Hipp.*]

702–3 ἦ γάρ   expresses surprise and here also indignation:
'What?'

ἐξ-αρκέω   be enough for; with ptc.: be satisfied with doing (attr. ptc.; see λεχθεῖσι in line 299) (278)

εἶτα (adv.)   then, after [1x *Hipp.*]

συγχωρέω   come to terms, agree, compromise (299)

τρῶσασαν ... συγχωρεῖν   acc. and inf. construction (τιτρώσκω, aor.¹ act. ptc. denoting time; see ἐλθόντα in line 24; ἡμᾶς, *majestic plural*) – 'What! Is this justice and satisfaction for me, that first you wounded me and now make concessions in words?' (392)

704–5 μακρηγορέω   speak at great length (ἔστι + inf.: 'it is possible'; ὥστε is unnecessary here) – 'We are talking too much. I was not restrained. But, oh child, it is possible to be saved from this.' [1x *Hipp.*]

706–7 παρ-*⁺αινέω   advise, recommend, counsel (παῦσαι, aor.¹ act. impv. 2 sg. with supplem. ptc.; see τυγχάνω in line 281. τὰ πρίν, subst. use of artic. with an adv.: S #1153e; cf. πρίν in line 302.)

ἐπι-χειρέω   make an attempt; – 'Stop talking! You did not advise me well before, and what you attempted was wrong.' [1x *Hipp.*]

708–9 ἐκποδών (adv.)   (ἐκ, ποδῶν) out of the way (457)

*⁺ἀπ-έρχομαι   go away, depart from (ἄπελθε, 2 sg. aor.² act. impv.; πέρι, *anastrophe*; τἀμά = τὰ ἐμά) – 'get out of my way and take care of yourself. I will arrange my affairs well.' (333)

The Nurse exits into the palace.

710–12 ἐξ-αιτέω   mid.: beg for oneself (859)

καλύπτω   cover, conceal, hide (ἐξαιτουμένη, ptc. of attendant circumstance, see ὁράω in line 4; σιγῇ, dat. of manner: S #1516) (251)

ἐνθάδε (adv.)   here, now (ἀνθάδ' = ἃ ἐνθάδε)

εἰσ-*ακούω   listen; – 'And you, noble daughters of Troezen, grant me, I beg you, this request, to conceal in silence what you have heard here.' (602)

Χο.   ὄμνυμι σεμνὴν Ἄρτεμιν, Διὸς κόρην,
            μηδὲν κακῶν σῶν ἐς φάος δείξειν ποτέ.
Φα.   καλῶς ἐλέξαθ'· ἐν δὲ †προτρέπουσ' ἐγὼ   715
            εὕρημα† δή τι τῆσδε συμφορᾶς ἔχω
            ὥστ' εὐκλεᾶ μὲν παισὶ προσθεῖναι βίον

αὐτή τ᾽ ὄνασθαι πρὸς τὰ νῦν πεπτωκότα.
οὐ γάρ ποτ᾽ αἰσχυνῶ γε Κρησίους δόμους
οὐδ᾽ ἐς πρόσωπον Θησέως ἀφίξομαι   720
αἰσχροῖς ἐπ᾽ ἔργοις οὕνεκα ψυχῆς μιᾶς.

Χο.   μέλλεις δὲ δὴ τί δρᾶν ἀνήκεστον κακόν;
Φα.   θανεῖν· ὅπως δέ, τοῦτ᾽ ἐγὼ βουλεύσομαι.
Χο.   εὔφημος ἴσθι. Φα. καὶ σύ γ᾽ εὖ με νουθέτει.

ἐγὼ δὲ Κύπριν, ἥπερ ἐξόλλυσί με,   725
ψυχῆς ἀπαλλαχθεῖσα τῇδ᾽ ἐν ἡμέρᾳ
τέρψω· πικροῦ δ᾽ ἔρωτος ἡσσηθήσομαι.
ἀτὰρ κακόν γε χἀτέρῳ γενήσομαι
θανοῦσ᾽, ἵν᾽ εἰδῇ μὴ 'πὶ τοῖς ἐμοῖς κακοῖς
ὑψηλὸς εἶναι· τῆς νόσου δὲ τῆσδέ μοι   730
κοινῇ μετασχὼν σωφρονεῖν μαθήσεται.

713–14 σεμνὴν Ἄρτεμιν by holy Artemis (acc. with verbs of swearing: S #1596) – 'I swear by holy Artemis, the daughter of Zeus, to never reveal any of your ills to the light.'

715–18 The second half of line 715 and the first half of 716 are baffling and difficult to understand; hence they are daggered by Stockert. The text is entirely a matter of conjecture. For possible emendation and explanation, see B. I offer a translation close to the unemended text.

προ-τρέπω   turn, urge forward (ptc. of attendant circumstance, see ὁράω in line 4) [1x Eur.]

εὕρημα, ατος, τό   that which was found, unexpected gain, windfall [1x *Hipp.*]

⁺ὥστε (**conj.**)   so as, so that (with the inf. implies a possible or intended result or tendency rather than actual fact: GMT #587; S #2011; εὐκλεᾶ . . . βίον, *hyperbaton* emphasizing πεπτωκότα)

προσ-⁺⁺τίθημι   offer, put forward (τὰ . . . πεπτωκότα, artic. as subst. ptc.; see τὰ λελεγμένα in line 244) – 'You spoke well. Turning to the one way I've found, I am able [to do] something for this misfortune, so that I can offer my children a reputable life and myself benefit considering how things have fallen out now.'

719–21 αἰσχυνῶ   < *⁺αἰσχύνω, fut. act. indic. (αἰσχροῖς ἐπ[ὶ] ἔργοις 'with shameful deeds.' Has Phaedra actually done anything? To what 'deeds' might she be referring? Cf. Eur. *Andromache* 833–39, where Hermione likewise feels guilty about her thoughts and intended but not executed acts.) – 'For I will not shame my Cretan home, nor will I come before the face of Theseus with shameful deeds, for the sake of one life.'

722–3 ἀν-ήκεστος, ον   (ἀ privat., ἀκέομαι, heal) incurable, not to be healed, deadly; – Chorus: 'What incurable harm do you intend to do?' Phaedra: 'To die, but how, this I will devise.' [1x *Hipp.*]

724 εὔ-φημος, ον   (⁺εὖ, φήμη, words, speech) abstaining from inauspicious words (i.e., religiously silent; ἴσθι < *⁺εἰμί) [1x *Hipp.*]

νουθετέω   (⁺νοῦς, *⁺τίθημι, put) bring to mind, warn, admonish, advise; – Chorus: 'No words of ill omen!' Phaedra: 'And you advise me well!' (396)

725–7 ὄσ-περ, ἥ-περ, ὅ-περ   the very person who/the thing which [1x *Hipp.*]

τέρπω   please, delight (*enjambment*; ἀπαλλαχθεῖσα < *ἀπαλάττω, aor.¹ pass. ptc., coincidental/modal; see λύσασα in line 290) (262)

ἡσσάομαι   + gen. (πικροῦ ἔρωτος) be beaten, worsted, defeated; – 'I will delight Cypris, the very one who destroys me, by being freed of my life on this day. I will be worsted by a bitter love.' (976)

728–31 ⁺ἀτάρ (conj.)   but, yet (introduces an objection)

χάτέρῳ   = καὶ ἑτέρῳ (θανοῦσα < *⁺θνῄσκω, aor.² act. ptc., coincidental/modal; see λύσασα in line 290) – 'But by/in dying, I will be a bane for another'

ὑψηλός (3)   high; metaph.: proud (εἰδῇ < *⁺οἶδα, pf. subjv., final clause in 1st sequence, γενήσομαι: S #2196) – 'so he may learn not to be haughty over my ills'

κοινῇ (adv.)   in common

μετ-έχω, μετέσχον   + gen.: have a share of (μετασχών, aor.² act. ptc. of attendant circumstance, see ὁράω in line 4) – 'and in common with me, having shared in my disease, he will learn moderation.' (Hippolytus' 'sharing' in her disease will be her fabrication of his culpability.) (306)

SECOND STASIMON LINES 732–75

The second stasimon ends the first part of the play. Phaedra has exited to her death. The stasimon consists of two strophic pairs. In the first two stanzas, the Chorus sing an escape song imbued with utopian and mythological imagination. In the first stanza, the tears of Phaëthon's sisters transform into the amber sap of poplar trees (739–41), and the second stanza ends with the blissful marriage of Zeus and Hera. The second pair focuses on the human aspect as they sing of the ship that brought Phaedra from Crete to Athens, alluding to the mortal marriage of Phaedra and Theseus, the consequences of which lead the Chorus to predict Phaedra's suicide.

		[στρ. α
Χο. ἠλιβάτοις ὑπὸ κευθμῶσι γενοίμαν,		If only I were under the hidden
ἵνα με πτεροῦσσαν ὄρνιν		clefts of steep mountains,
		where a god might make me
θεὸς ἐν ποταναῖς		a winged bird
ἀγέλαις θείη·		among the flying flocks!
ἀρθείην δ' ἐπὶ πόντιον	735	If only I could fly over the sea
κῦμα τᾶς Ἀδριηνᾶς		waves of the Adriatic shore
ἀκτᾶς Ἠριδανοῦ θ' ὕδωρ,		and the waters of Eridanus, where
ἔνθα πορφύρεον σταλάσ-		the unhappy daughters [of their father]
σουσ' ἐς οἶδμα [πατρὸς] τάλαιναι		in their grief for Phaëthon drip
κόραι Φαέθοντος οἴκτῳ δακρύων	740	into the deep-blue billows the
τὰς ἠλεκτροφαεῖς αὐγάς.		amber-gleaming rays of their tears.

Ἑσπερίδων δ' ἐπὶ μηλόσπορον ἀκτὰν	[ἀντ. α	May I reach the apple-bearing shore
ἀνύσαιμι τᾶν ἀοιδῶν,		of the Hesperides, the singers,
ἵν' ὁ πορφυρέας πον-		where the ruler
τομέδων λίμνας		of the deep-blue shallows
ναύταις οὐκέθ ὁδὸν νέμει,	745	no longer allows passage to sailors,
σεμνὸν τέρμονα κυρῶν		setting the sacred boundary of
οὐρανοῦ, τὸν Ἄτλας ἔχει,		heaven, which Atlas holds,

κρῆναί τ' ἀμβρόσιαι χέον-
ται Ζηνὸς [μελάθρων] παρὰ κοίταις,

ἵν' ὀλβιόδωρος αὔξει ζαθέα

χθὼν εὐδαιμονίαν θεοῖς.

and divine streams flow near the
marriage bed [in the halls] of
Zeus,

750 where the earth, bounteous and
very

holy, increases prosperity for
the gods.

732 = 742	– ◡◡ – ◡◡ – – ◡◡ – –	choriamb + 2 ionics
733 = 743	◡◡ – – ◡ – ◡ – –	2 ionics (anaclastic)
734 = 744	◡◡ – – ◡ – –	2 ionics (catalectic; or anapest + bacchiac)
734a = 744a	◡◡ – – – –	2 ionics Λ (syncopated; or anapests)
735 = 745	– – – ◡◡ – ◡ –	glyconic
736 = 746	– ◡̲ – ◡◡ – –	pherecratean
737 = 747	– ◡̲ ◡◡ – ◡ –	glyconic
738 = 748	– ◡̲ – ◡◡ – ◡ –	glyconic
739 = 749	– ◡̲ – ◡[◡ –]◡ – –	pherecratean (749 = – – – – [◡◡ –] ◡◡ – –)
740 = 750	◡ – ◡◡ – ◡ – – ◡◡ –	telesillean + choriamb
741 = 751	– – – ◡◡ – ◡̅ –	glyconic

732 **ἡλίβᾰτος, ον**   steep [1x *Hipp.*]

    κευθμών, ῶνος, ὁ   hiding place, lair, hole [1x *Hipp.*]

    *⁺γενοίμαν   = γενοίμην (aor.² opt. mid. opt. of wish; see
    κάμπτω in line 87)

733 **⁺ἵνα (adv.)**   where

    πτερόεις, εσσα, εν   furnished with feathers or wings [1x *Hipp.*]

    ⁺ὄρνις, ὄρνιθος, ὁ/ἡ   bird (acc. sg. ὄρνιν and ὄρνῑθα)

734 **ποτᾱνός (3)**   winged, flying [1x *Hipp.*]

734a–5 **ἀγέλη, ἡ**   (ἄγω, lead) herd (*⁺θείη < *⁺τίθημι, aor.² act.
opt. 3 sg.; opt. of wish, see κάμπτω in line 87; *⁺ἀρθείην < *⁺αἴρω, aor.¹
pass. opt. 1 sg.; opt. of wish, see κάμπτω in line 87) [1x *Hipp.*]

    ἐπί (prep.)   + acc.: toward, to, over

736 ⁺κῦμα, ατος, τό   anything swollen, swell, wave, billow

Ἀδριηνός (3)   of the Adriatic sea [1x Eur.]

737 ⁺ἀκτή, ἡ   (ἄγνυμι, break) the place where the waves break, seashore

Ἠρῐδᾰνός, ὁ   Eridanos, a mythic river in the west, beyond the Gulf of Venice, later identified with the Po, Rhone, or Rhine [1x *Hipp.*]

738 ἔνθᾰ   where (correl. relat. adv. taking the place of οὗ), when (75)

στᾰλάσσω   let fall in drops, drip [1x *Hipp.*]

739 οἶδμα, ατος, τό   the swell of the sea, a wave, billow ([πατρός] and in line 749 [μελάθρων] are not included in the scansion in square brackets; it would not be possible to make lines 739 and 749 respond if these words were included)

740 Φαέθων, ὁ   (properly ptc. of φαέθω, shine) Phaëthon, son of Apollo, famous for upsetting the chariot of the sun

οἶκτος, ὁ   an expression of pity or grief, weeping (1089)

741 ἠλεκτρο-φᾱής, ές   (ἤλεκτρον, amber; φάος, light) amber-gleaming [1x Eur.]

αὐγή, ἡ   bright light, ray [1x *Hipp.*]

742 Ἑσπερίδες, αἱ   (ἑσπερίς, ίδος, ἡ, evening) the Hesperides, daughters of the Evening, who dwelled on the western island of the ocean and guarded a garden with golden apples [1x *Hipp.*]

μηλό-σπορος, ον   apple-bearing [1x Eur.]

ἀνύ(τ)ω   complete (my journey) (ἀνύσαιμι, aor.[1] opt. mid. opt. of wish; see κάμπτω in line 87) [1x *Hipp.*]

743 ἀοιδός, ὁ   singer (masc./fem.; modifies the Hesperides; τᾶν -τῶν, Doric for gen. fem.) [1x *Hipp.*]

744 ποντο-μέδων, οντος, ὁ   (πόντος, sea; μέδω, rule) lord of the sea
[1x Eur.]

λίμνη, ἡ   marsh, shallow wave (148)

745 ναύτης, ου, ὁ   (ναῦς, ship) seaman, sailor (157)

νέμω   assign, allot [1x *Hipp.*]

746 κυρόω   settle, establish, set (κῡρῶν, pres. act. ptc. of
attendant circumstance/descriptive, coincidental with the finite verb νέμει;
see ὁράω in line 4) (1421)

747 τόν   = ὅν (demon. ὁ, ἡ, τό used as a relat. in tragedy
mainly to avoid hiatus or to produce position: S #1105; G #940)

748 κρήνη, ἡ   spring [1x *Hipp.*]

ἀμ-βρόσιος (3)   divine, immortal [1x *Hipp.*]

*χέω   pour forth, flow, stream [1x *Hipp.*]

750 ὀλβιό-δωρος, ον   bestowing bliss, bounteous [1x Eur.]

αὐξάνω/αὔξω   increase, make grow (172)

ζά-θεος (3/2)   very divine, holy, hallowed [1x *Hipp.*]

751 εὐδαιμονία, ἡ   prosperity, happiness [1x *Hipp.*]

ὦ λευκόπτερε Κρησία   [στρ. β   Oh white-winged Cretan
                                         vessel that

   πορθμίς, ἃ διὰ πόντιον   brought my mistress
                                         over the

   κῦμ' ἁλίκτυπον ἅλμας   roaring sea wave of the deep
                                         from a

ἐπόρευσας ἐμὰν ἄνασσαν   755   happy home; a most unhappy
ὀλβίων ἀπ' οἴκων   bridal
κακονυμφοτάταν ὄνασιν.   blessing. For indeed from both
                                         sides

ἦ γὰρ ἀπ' ἀμφοτέρων †ἦ†   it was a bad omen: when she
Κρησίας ⟨τ'⟩ ἐκ γᾶς   flew from
   δυσόρνις   the land of Crete to glorious
                                         Athens and

ἔπτατο κλεινὰς Ἀθήνας	760	when they tied the plaited ends of the
Μουνίχου τ᾽ ἀκ-		
ταῖσιν ἐκδήσαντο πλεκτὰς		mooring cables on Munichus'
πεισμάτων ἀρ-		shore and
χὰς ἐπ᾽ ἀπείρου τε γᾶς ἔβασαν.		stepped onto the boundless mainland.
ἀνθ᾽ ὧν οὐχ ὁσίων ἐρώ-	[ἀντ. β	For this reason, she was broken
των δεινᾷ φρένας Ἀφροδί-	765	in her soul by a terrible malady of
τας νόσῳ κατεκλάσθη·		unholy passion from Aphrodite;
χαλεπᾷ δ᾽ ὑπέραντλος οὖσα		and being overwhelmed by grievous
συμφορᾷ τεράμνων		
ἄπο νυμφιδίων κρεμαστὸν		misfortune, from the beams of
ἅψεται ἀμφὶ βρόχον λευκᾷ	770	her bridechamber she will
καθαρμόζουσα δειρᾷ,		fasten a
δαίμονα στυγνὸν καταιδεσθεῖσα τάν τ᾽ εὔ-		hanging noose, fitting [it]
δοξον ἀνθαιρουμένα φήμαν ἀπαλλάσ-		around her
		white neck, ashamed of her dreadful
σουσά τ᾽ ἀλγεινὸν φρενῶν	775	fate, choosing instead a good
ἔρωτα.		reputation, and ridding her heart of painful passion.

752 = 764	– – ‿ ‿‿ – ‿ –	glyconic
753 = 765	– ‿ – ‿‿ – ‿ –	glyconic
754 = 766	– ‿ – ‿‿ – –	pherecratean
755–6 = 767–8	‿‿ – ‿‿ – ‿ – ‿ | – ‿ – ‿ – –	enoplian + ithyphallic
757 = 769	‿‿ – ‿‿ – ‿ – ‿	enoplian
758–9 = 770–1	– ‿‿ – ‿‿ – | – – ‿ – | – – ‿ – –	hemiepes + 2 epitrites +
760–1 = 772–3	– ‿ – – | – ‿ – – | – ‿ – –	3 epitrites
762 = 774	– ‿ – – – ‿ – – – ‿ – –	3 epitrites
763 = 775	– ‿ – – | – ‿ – ‿ – ‿	epitrite + ithyphallic

752 λευκό-πτερος, ον   (λευκός, white; πτερόν, wing) white-winged
[1x *Hipp.*]

753 πορθμίς, ίδος   a ferry, a strait (ἅ = ἥ, relat. pron.) [1x *Hipp.*]

754 ἁλί-κτυπος, ον   (ἅλς, lump of salt; κτυπέω, crush) roaring over
the sea [1x *Hipp.*]

755 πορεύω   bring, carry (1156)

ὄλβιος (3/2)   happy, blessed (1440)

756 κακό-νυμφος, ον   (κακός, bad; νυμφή, bride) ill-wedded, unhappy bride (κακονυμφοτάταν = κακονυμφοτάτην, superl.) [1x *Hipp.*]

ὄνησις, εως, ἡ   profit, advantage (κακονυμφοτάταν ὄνασιν, acc. in apposition to the sentence, an offshoot of internal acc.:
S #1554a1) [1x *Hipp.*]

757–8 ἀμφότερος (3)   both [1x *Hipp.*]

759 δύσορνις, ῑθος, ὁ/ἡ   boding ill [1x *Hipp.*]

760 πέτομαι   fly, dart (according to B., the subj. is Phaedra,
not the ship) [1x *Hipp.*]

Μούνιχος, ὁ   the eponymous hero of the original Athenian
harbor, Munichia [1x Eur.]

761 ἐκ-δέω   bind to, tie to (the subj. is the crew; ἐκδήσαντο:
in tragedy the augment is sometimes omitted in choral odes and messen-
gers' speeches, seldom in dialogue: S #438a; G #549) [1x *Hipp.*]

762 πεῖσμα, ατος, τό   mooring cable [1x *Hipp.*]

ἀρχή, ἡ   beginning (272)

763 ἄ-πειρος, ον   (ἀ privat., πεῖρα, trial) without trial; boundless
[1x *Hipp.*]

764 ἀνθ' ὧν   wherefore, for which reason (connecting Phaedra's desire with the bad omen, on the one hand, and what we know of
Aphrodite's intent, on the other, exempts Phaedra from any responsibility
for her infatuation, as far as the Chorus are concerned)

ὅσιος (3)   sanctioned or approved by law of nature (1081)

765 φρένας   acc. of respect (see line 27)

766 κατα-κλάω   break down, snap, overcome (κατεκλάσθη, aor.
pass. indic. 3 sg. There is no reason for the subjv. κατεκλάσθη as Stockert
prints; I follow Musgrave, B., and Diggle.) [1x Eur.]
οὖσα   (< *⁺εἰμί, pres. act. ptc. of attendant
circumstance/descriptive, coincidental with the finite verb ἅψεται; see
ὁράω in line 4)

768 χᾰλεπός (3)   hard to bear, grievous, difficult, sore (259)
ὑπέρ-αντλος, ον   overwhelmed, borne down [1x Eur.]

769 νυμφίδιος (3)   (νυμφή, marriageable maiden, bride) bridal
(1140)
⁺κρεμαστός (3)   hung, hanging (subst. adj. without artic.:
G #932.1; S #1021; SS 163 §1)

770–1 ⁺ἀμφί (prep.)   + dat.: around
⁺βρόχος, ὁ   noose
καθαρμόζω   join to, fit to (καθορμόζουσα, pres. act. ptc. of
attendant circumstance/descriptive, coincidental with the finite verb
ἅψεται; see ὁράω in line 4) [1x *Hipp.*]
δειρή, ἡ   (Attic: δέρη, ἡ) neck (781)

772–3 κατ-αιδέομαι   feel shame (καταιδεσθεῖσα, aor.[1] pass. ptc.
fem. sg.; ptc. of attendant circumstance/descriptive, coincidental with the
finite verb ἅψεται; see ὁράω in line 4) [1x *Hipp.*]
εὔ-δοξος, ον   (εὖ, good; δόξα, reputation) of good report,
glorious [1x *Hipp.*]

774 ἀνθ-αιρέομαι   mid.: choose instead, prefer (ἀνθαιρου-
μένα = ἀνθαιρουμένη, pres. dep. ptc. of attendant circumstance/de-
scriptive, coincidental with the finite verb ἅψεται; see ὁράω in line 4)
[1x *Hipp.*]

775 ἀλγεινός (3)   (ἄλγος, pain) giving pain, painful, grievous (348)

THIRD EPISODE LINES 776–1101

Part I and Kommos: 776–898

In the second part of the play, the focus moves from Phaedra and Hippolytus to Theseus and Hippolytus. A servant announces Phaedra's suicide. Theseus arrives garlanded, having accomplished a successful visit to the Delphic oracle. Having been told about Phaedra's suicide, he erupts into a lament structured by a pair of strophic stanzas (817–33 = 836–51) and framed by the brief dochmiac lyrics (811–16, 852–5) of the Chorus or its leader and articulated by the leader's two iambic lines (834–5). The sung lament (termed *kommos*, a lyrical lament sung by the Chorus and actors) is an exchange between Theseus and the Chorus or its leader. It alternates between dochmiacs and iambic trimeter in a set pattern for each stanza that consists of four sections: three sets of two lines of dochmiacs (two to a line) followed by two lines of iambic trimeter; the fourth part is composed of seven dochmiacs. The change in meter is used to indicate the shift in Theseus' mood. While the dochmiacs that contain apostrophe and self-address (817, 822, 826, 827, 837, 841, 844, 848–9) and exclamations (817, 830, 844, 845, 848, except for the iambic 819) indicate Theseus' emotional utterances, the iambs point to intellectual reflection. Note the emphasis Theseus puts on his own suffering that emanates from Phaedra's death. After ten lines (856–65) of iambic trimeter, during which he finds the tablet hanging from Phaedra's hand, there is another *kommos* (866–84) between Theseus and the Chorus.

Note the use of Doric for Attic in the *kommos* (811–84), as is common in choral odes: e.g., τόλμας = τόλμης, σᾶς = σῆς, ζόαν = ζώην, μάκιστα = μήκιστα, τύχα = τύχη, τύχαν = τύχην, σάν = σήν, ἔβα = ἔβη, ἀρίστα = ἀρίστη, τύχᾳ = τύχη, ἁλίοιο = ἡλίοιο, σᾷ = σῇ, πᾷ = πῇ, γᾶς = γῆς, τλάμων = τλήμων.

ΤΡΟΦΟΣ (ἔσωθεν)

      ἰοὺ ἰού·
      βοηδρομεῖτε πάντες οἱ πέλας δόμων·
      ἐν ἀγχόναις δέσποινα, Θησέως δάμαρ.

Xo.   φεῦ φεῦ, πέπρακται· βασιλὶς οὐκέτ' ἔστι δὴ
      γυνή, κρεμαστοῖς ἐν βρόχοις ἠρτημένη.

Τρ.   οὐ σπεύσετ'; οὐκ οἴσει τις ἀμφιδέξιον   780
      σίδηρον, ᾧ τόδ' ἄμμα λύσομεν δέρης;

Xo.   φίλαι, τί δρῶμεν; ἦ δοκεῖ περᾶν δόμους

λῦσαί τ᾽ ἄνασσαν ἐξ ἐπισπαστῶν βρόχων;
— —   τί δ᾽; οὐ πάρεισι πρόσπολοι νεανίαι;
το πολλὰ πράσσειν οὐκ ἐν ἀσφαλεῖ βίου.   785
Τρ.   ὀρθώσατ᾽ ἐκτείναντες ἄθλιον νέκυν·
πικρὸν τόδ᾽ οἰκούρημα δεσπόταις ἐμοῖς.
Χο.   ὄλωλεν ἡ δύστηνος, ὡς κλύω, γυνή·
ἤδη γὰρ ὡς νεκρόν νιν ἐκτείνουσι δή.

The Nurse heard from the palace.

776 βοηδρομέω   run, on hearing a cry (βοηδρομεῖτε, pres. impv.
2 pl.; πάντες οἱ πέλας δόμων – 'anyone near the palace.' Subst. use of artic.
with improper prep.: S #1153c.) [1x *Hipp.*]

777 ⁺ἀγχόνη, ἡ   throttling, strangling, hanging; noose; – 'is in
the noose,' i.e., hanging

778 βᾰσῐλίς, ίδος, ἡ   queen (see πέπρακται in line 680; resolution in
6th position, βᾰσῐλίς) (267)

οὐκέτ᾽ ἔστι   'is no more,' i.e., she is dead. (Note the accent
that gives existential meaning to the usually enclit. verb; cf. S #187b;
emphatic δή used mostly in tragedy). GP 214 (8): "The emphasis conveyed by δή with verbs is for the most part pathetic in tone . . . in the
great crises of drama, above all at moments when death or ruin is present or imminent."

779 γυνή   an emphatic *enjambment*

⁺ἀρτάω   fasten; pass.: be hung, be fitted, prepared (ἠρτημένη, pf. mid. descriptive ptc.) – 'the queen is no more, suspended
in a hanging noose.'

780–1 σπεύδω   hasten, hurry (182)

ἀμφι-δέξιος, ον   with two right hands, ambidextrous (ἀμφιδέξιον σίδηρον, metaph.: 'two-edged blade'; σίδηρον, *enjambment*)
[1x Eur.]

ἄμμα, ατος, τό   (*⁺ἄπτω, fasten) noose, knot; – 'Won't you
hurry up? Won't someone bring a two-edged blade with which we will
release the knot from her neck?' [1x *Hipp.*]

782 *⁺δρῶμεν   deliberative subjv.: S #2639; GMT #287; –
'what should we do?'

⁺ἦ (pcl.)   (untranslatable interrog. pcl. used, according
to B., "when a speaker, after asking a question, himself suggests the
answer in a second question": GP 283)

783 ἐπισπαστός (3)   drawn upon itself, tight-drawn; – 'Does it seem
right to cross to the palace and release the queen from the tightly drawn
noose?' [1x *Hipp.*]

784 – –   The dashes mark what the editor thinks is a
change of speaker. Lines 782–3 were probably spoken by the leader of the
Chorus; 784–5 are spoken by another member of the Chorus who is reluc-
tant to interfere in what is going on in the palace.

νεᾱνίας, ου, ὁ   young man, youth; as masc. adj. = youthful
(τί δ': see on τί in line 608) (43)

785 τὸ πολλὰ πράσσειν meddling/interference in things that do not
concern one (τὸ πράσσειν, artic. inf. as subj., see line 80; πολλά, internal
[effected] obj.: S #1554a)

ἀ-σφᾰλής, ές   (ἀ privat., σφάλλω, make fall, trip up) firm,
steadfast; safe; – 'why [do you say that]? Are there not young servants
nearby? Meddling [in other people's affairs] is not safe in life.' (968)

786 ἐκ-*τείνω   stretch along (ἐκτείναντες, aor.¹ act. ptc.; when
an aor. ptc. refers to the same action as the aor. finite leading verb, here in
impv., ὀρθώσατε, it is coincidental with the action of the leading verb [of
whatever mood]; see λύσασα in line 290. According to B., 'straighten' and
'stretch' describe the same action.) – 'straighten the miserable corpse as
you stretch it' (789)

⁺ἄθλιος (3/2)   wretched

νέκυς, ῠος, ὁ   corpse [1x *Hipp.*]

787 οἰκούρημα, τό   housekeeping; or one who keeps the house, a
stay-at-home (οἰκουρός is the wife who is in charge of the house when the
husband is away; δεσπόταις, dat. of disadvantage/incommodi: S #1481) –
'this is a bitter housekeeping for my masters' [1x *Hipp.*]

789 ⁺νεκρός, ὁ   dead body, corpse (for δή, see on οὐκέτ' ἔστι in
line 778)

Theseus enters from one of the *parodoi*. He has been to Delphi to consult
Apollo. His head is garlanded, which indicates a favorable reply from the
oracle.

ΘΗΣΕΥΣ

> γυναῖκες, ἴστε τίς ποτ' ἐν δόμοις βοὴ   790
> †ἠχὼ βαρεῖα προσπόλων† ἀφίκετο;
> οὐ γὰρ τί μ' ὡς θεωρὸν ἀξιοῖ δόμος
> πύλας ἀνοίξας εὐφρόνως προσεννέπειν.
> μῶν Πιτθέως τι γῆρας εἴργασται νέον;
> πρόσω μὲν ἤδη βίοτος, ἀλλ' ὅμως ἔτ' ἂν   795
> λυπηρὸς ἡμῖν τοῦσδ' ἂν ἐκλίποι δόμους.

Χο. οὐκ ἐς γέροντας ἥδε σοι τείνει τύχη,
> Θησεῦ· νέοι θανόντες ἀλγύνουσί σε.

Θη. οἴμοι, τέκνων μοι μή τι συλᾶται βίος;

790 *⁺ἴστε   (< *⁺οἶδα: pf. act. indic. 2 pl.)

791 ἠχώ, ἡ   reverberated sound (†ἠχὼ βαρεῖα προσπό-
λων†; the γάρ for lines 792–3 indicates that it follows directly after Theseus' question, and therefore, as B. states, "since the noms. βοή and ἠχώ
cannot coexist," one of them must be corrupt. For various solutions, see
B. One would also expect με with ἀφίκετο, which some eds. supply.) –
'Women, do you know what shout in the house †a heavy noise of servants†
reached [me]?' (1201)

792 θεωρός, ὁ   an ambassador, sent to consult an oracle (807)

ἀξιόω   deem worthy/fit (1044)

793 ἀνοίγνυμι   open (ἀνοίξας, aor.¹ act. ptc. of attendant circumstance; see ἐλθόντα in line 24) (56)

εὐφρόνως (adv.)   graciously [1x *Hipp.*]

προσ-εννέπω   address; – 'For the house has not deemed fit to
address me graciously as a successful envoy from the god by having
the doors open.' (99)

794 γῆρας, τό   old age (εἴργασται < *⁺ἐργάζομαι, pf. pass. 3
sg.; note the wordplay on γῆρας and νέον) – 'It can't be that something
untoward happened to old Pittheus, can it?' [1x *Hipp.*]

795–6 πρόσω (adv.)   far along (resolution in 6th position, βίοτος)
[1x *Hipp.*]

⁺**ἔτι** (adv.)   still

λῦπηρός (3)   painful (ἡμῖν, *majestic plural*, see ἡμῖν in line
43; ἐκλίποι, aor.² opt. act.; ἀλλ' ὅμως ἔτ' [εἶεν] ἂν λυπηρός ἡμῖν ἂν,
[εἰ] τούσδ' ἐκλίποι δόμους, fut. less vivid condition: S #2297, 2329;
GMT #392.2, with repeated ἂν to make the conditional force felt:
S #1765; GMT #223) – 'His life is far advanced, all the same it would
be painful to me if he should have left this house.'

797 γέρων, οντος, ὁ   old person (γέροντας and νέοι: generalizing
pl.; see on ἐχθρός in line 49) (691)

*****τείνω**   stretch; extend; tend, refer; τείνει ἐς, concerns
(LSJ B iii.2) [1x *Hipp.*]

798 ἀλγύνω   pain, grieve, distress (*θανόντες, aor.² act. ptc.
attr.; see λεχθεῖσι in line 299) – 'What has befallen you does not concern
the old, Theseus, it is the young [who are] dead that pain you.' (1297)

799 σῦλάω   strip off (μή, expressing the speaker's wish: B.:
"apprehensive, like μῶν in 794"; – 'It can't be that the life of my children
is plundered?') [1x *Hipp.*]

Xo.	ζῶσιν, θανούσης μητρὸς ὡς ἄλγιστά σοι.	800
Θη.	τί φής; ὄλωλεν ἄλοχος; ἐκ τίνος τύχης;	
Xo.	βρόχον κρεμαστὸν ἀγχόνης ἀνήψατο.	
Θη.	λύπῃ παχνωθεῖσ' ἢ ἀπὸ συμφορᾶς τίνος;	
Xo.	τοσοῦτον ἴσμεν· ἄρτι γὰρ κἀγὼ δόμους,	
	Θησεῦ, πάρειμι σῶν κακῶν πενθήτρια.	805
Θη.	αἰαῖ, τί δῆτα τοῖσδ' ἀνέστεμμαι κάρα	
	πλεκτοῖσι φύλλοις, δυστυχὴς θεωρὸς ὤν;	
	χαλᾶτε κλῇθρα, πρόσπολοι, πυλωμάτων,	
	[ἐκλύσαθ' ἁρμούς, ὡς ἴδω δυσδαίμονα]	809
	ἐκλύεθ' ἁρμούς, ὡς ἴδω πικρὰν θέαν	825
	γυναικός, ἥ με κατθανοῦσ' ἀπώλεσεν.	810

800 ἄλγιστος (3)   most painful (irreg. superl., see line 485; θανούσης μητρός, gen. abs. of opposition: S #2070a, c; σοί, dat. of disadvantage/incommodi: S #1481) – 'They live, but their mother has died—most painfully for you.' [1x *Hipp.*]

801 ⁺ἄ-λοχος, ἡ   (α copulative; λέχος, bed) partner of one's bed, wife (resolution in 6th position, ἄλοχος)

802–3 παχνόω   to strike chill (ἀγχόνης, adnominal gen. instead of adj.: S #1291; παχνωθεῖσα, aor.¹ pass. circumstantial ptc. denoting time or cause: S #2061, 2064; the action of the aor. ptc. is usually antecedent to that of the leading verb: S #1872c, here ἀνήψατο; λύπη, see κύων in line 18; ἀπό, resolution in 7th position) – 'She fastened for herself a pendant noose to hang herself. Having been chilled by grief, or from what misfortune?' [1x Eur.]

804–5 ἄρτι (adv.)   right now (510)

πενθήτρια (fem. of πενθητήρ)mourner   (σῶν κακῶν, obj. gen.: S #1331) – 'This is as much as we know; for I too came just now to your house, a mourner for your troubles.' [1x Eur.]

806 ἀνα-στέφω   to wreath (ἀνέστεμμαι, pf. pass. indic.; κάρα, acc. of respect: see line 27, καρδία) [1x *Hipp.*]

807 φύλλον, τό   leaf (πλεκτοῖσι φύλλοις, dat. of means; see ἔρως in line 28) – 'Why then is my head wreathed with these plaited leaves?' [1x *Hipp.*]

θεωρός, ὁ   an ambassador sent to consult an oracle (792)

808 χαλάω   loosen, release [1x *Hipp.*]

κλῆθρον, τό   a bolt or a bar closing a door; a door (generally in pl.). (578)

πύλωμα, ατος, τό   gate, gateway [1x *Hipp.*]

[809]/825 ἐκ-λύω   (ῡ) unstring, loosen. (This line appears in manuscripts after 824, where it is out of place; the line that appears after 808 and has been put in square brackets is a variant that does not quite fit. See B. at 808–10 for a full explanation.) (1336)

ἀρμός, ὁ   joining, fastening; – 'unbar the doors, servants! Loosen their bolts!' [1x *Hipp.*]

δυσ-δαίμων, ον   (gen. ονος) ill-fated (ἴδω < *⁺οἶδα, aor.² act.
subjv., final clause in 1st sequence,, ἐκλύσατε/ἐκλύετε: S #2196; impv.
mood counts as primary because it points to the fut.: S #1858a)

809   Line 809 must be an interpolation because δυσδαίμονα cannot be
followed by γυναικός.

θέᾱ, ἡ   (θεάομαι, gaze, behold) sight [1x *Hipp*.]

810 γυναικός   (emphatic *enjambment*; adnominal gen., see
ἀγχόνης in line 802) – 'sight of my wife'

*⁺κατθανοῦσα   (aor.² act. ptc.; -τθ-, *syncope*; a coincidental/
modal ptc.; see λύσασα in line 290) – 'in dying she destroyed me.'

As the Chorus sing, the *ekkyklēma* is rolled out into view with Phaedra's
corpse on a platform.

Kommos: Lines 811–84

Xo. ἰὼ ἰὼ τάλαινα μελέων κακῶν·   Alas, alas, poor woman for your
                                              wretched ills;

ἔπαθες, εἰργάσω   you've suffered, you did
τοσοῦτον ὥστε τούσδε συγχέαι δόμους,   so much, as to confound this
                                              house,

αἰαῖ τόλμας,   alas for your recklessness,
βιαίως θανοῦσ' ἀνοσίῳ τε συμ-   dying violently and in unholy
                                              misfortune,

    φορᾷ σᾶς χερὸς πάλαισμα μελέας.   815 the struggle of our own wretched
                                              hand.

τίς ἄρα σάν, τάλαιν', ἀμαυροῖ ζόαν;   Who, poor woman, dims your life?

811	◡ ◡◡ – ◡ – ◡ ◡◡ – ◡ –	2 dochmiacs
812	◡ ◡◡ – ◡ –	1 dochmiac
813	3 iambic metrons	
813a	◡ – – –	syncopated dochmiac
814	◡ – – ◡ – ◡ ◡◡ – ◡ –	2 dochmiacs +
815	◡ – – ◡ – ◡ – ◡ ◡◡ –	2 dochmiacs
816	◡ ◡◡ – ◡ – ◡ – – ◡ –	2 dochmiacs

811 ⁺μελέων ⁺κακῶν   (gen. of explanation/apposition; see αἷμα in line 35)

812 εἰργάσω   (*⁺ἐργάζομαι, aor.¹ mid. indic. 2 sg.)

813 συγ-*χέω   confound (συγχέαι, aor.¹ inf. act.; for ὥστε with the inf., see ὥστε [result clause] in line 50)

813a ⁺τόλμας   because of your recklessness (gen. of cause in exclamation: S #1407, here explaining αἰαῖ)

814 βιαίως (adv.)   perforce; violently (θανοῦσα, aor.¹ act. ptc.; coincidental/modal ptc., see λύσασα in line 290) [1x *Hipp.*]
   ἀν-όσιος (3/2)   (ἀ privat., ὅσιος, holy) unholy [1x *Hipp.*]

815 πάλαισμα, ατος, τό   fall in wrestling; subterfuge; struggle (the entire clause is in apposition to what precedes: acc. in apposition to the sentence, an offshoot of internal acc.: S #1554a1) [1x *Hipp.*]

816 ἀμαυρόω   dim; weaken, impair [1x *Hipp.*]
   ζωή, ἡ   life [1x *Hipp.*]

Θη. ὤμοι ἐγὼ πόνων· ἔπαθον, ὦ τάλας,   [στρ.   Alas for my misery; I, wretched man

τὰ μάκιστ᾽ ἐμῶν κακῶν. ὦ τύχα,   that I am, suffered the greatest of my woes.

ὥς μοι βαρεῖα καὶ δόμοις ἐπεστάθης,   Oh fate, how heavily have you come upon me

κηλὶς ἄφραστος ἐξ ἀλαστόρων τινός·   820   and upon the house, an unthinkable stain from

κατακονὰ μὲν οὖν, ἀβίοτος βίος·   some avenging divinities; no, rather destruction,

κακῶν δ᾽, ὦ τάλας, πέλαγος εἰσορῶ   life that is not to be lived! Oh wretch, I see a sea

τοσοῦτον ὥστε μήποτ᾽ ἐκνεῦσαι πάλιν   of troubles so great that I can never swim

μηδ᾽ ἐκπερᾶσαι κῦμα τῆσδε συμφορᾶς.   824   back out of it, nor pass through the wave of this

τίνι λόγῳ, τάλας, τίνι τύχαν σέθεν	826	misfortune. With what word, wife, with what
βαρύποτμον, γύναι, προσαυδῶν τύχω;		word, addressing your ill-starred fortune, can
ὄρνις γὰρ ὥς τις ἐκ χερῶν ἄφαντος εἶ,		I, wretched, hit the mark? For like a bird you
πήδημ᾽ ἐς Ἅιδου κραιπνὸν ὁρμήσασά μοι.		vanished from my hands, as you hastily leapt
αἰαῖ αἰαῖ, μέλεα μέλεα τάδε πάθη.		into the house of Hades. Alas! Alas! Terrible
πρόσωθεν δέ ποθεν ἀνακομίζομαι		are these sufferings. From somewhere long
τύχαν δαιμόνων ἀμπλακίαισι τῶν		ago I am reaping bad fortune from the
πάροιθέν τινος.		gods for faults of someone from the past.

Χο. οὐ σοὶ τάδ᾽, ὦναξ, ἦλθε δὴ μόνῳ κακά,		My lord, these ills did not come on you alone,
πολλῶν μετ᾽ ἄλλων δ᾽ ὤλεσας κεδνὸν λέχος.	835	you have lost your faithful wife with many others.

817 = 836	⏒ ⏑⏑ – ⏑ – ⏑ ⏑⏑ – ⏑ –	2 dochmiacs
818 = 837	⏑ – – ⏑ – ⏑ – – ⏑ –	2 dochmiacs
819 = 838	3 iambic metrons	
820 = 839	3 iambic metrons	
821 = 840	⏑ ⏑⏑ – ⏑ – ⏑ ⏑⏑ – ⏑ –	2 dochmiacs
822 = 841	⏑ – – ⏑ – ⏑⏑⏑– ⏑ –	2 dochmiacs
823 = 842	3 iambic metrons	
824 = 843	3 iambic metrons	
826 = 844	⏑ ⏑⏑ – ⏑ – ⏑ ⏑ ⏑ – ⏑ –	2 dochmiacs
828 = 846	3 iambic metrons	
829 = 847	3 iambic metrons	
830 = 848	⏑ ⏑⏑ – ⏑ ⏑⏑ ⏑ ⏑⏑ ⏑⏑ ⏑ –	2 dochmiacs
831 = 849	⏑ – – ⏑ ⏑⏑ ⏑ ⏑⏑ – ⏑ –	2 dochmiacs
832 = 850	⏑ – – – ⏑ – ⏑ ⏑⏑ – ⏑ –	2 dochmiacs
833 = 851	⏑ – – – ⏑ –|||	

817 ⁺πόνων   (gen. of cause in exclamation: S #1407, here explaining ὤμοι)

818 μήκιστος (3/2)   greatest (ἐμῶν κακῶν, superl. with partit. gen.: S #1306, 1315) [1x *Hipp.*]

819 ⁺βαρεῖα   (predicative adj.; ⁺ἐπ-*⁺εστάθης < ⁺ἐφ-*⁺ίστημι, aor.¹ pass. indic.)

820 κηλίς, ῖδος, ἡ   stain, spot; a blemish, disgrace [1x *Hipp.*]

  ἄ-φραστος, ον   (ἀ privat., φράζω, tell, declare) unutterable, unexpected [1x Eur.]

  ἀ-λάστωρ, ορος, ὁ   (ἀ privat., λανθάνομαι, forget) he who forgets not, avenger (partit. gen.: S #1306) [1x *Hipp.*]

821 κατ-ἄκονά, ἡ   destruction (μὲν οὖν = 'no, rather,' rejects what has been just said, τύχα βαρεῖα, as inadequate description and substitutes a stronger expression: κατἄκονά: GP 475–6, 478–9) [1x *Hipp.*]

  ἀ-βίοτος, ον   (ἀ privat., βίοτος, life) not to be lived, intolerable (ἀβίοτος βίος, *oxymoron*) (868)

822 πέλαγος, εος, τό   sea, open sea, high sea (κακῶν, gen. of explanation or contents: S #1322, 1323) (149)

823 ἐκ-*νέω   swim out, swim to land (ἐκνεῦσαι, aor.¹ inf.; for ὥστε with inf., see ὥστε [result clause] in line 50; τοσοῦτον, emphatic *enjambment*) (470)

824 ἐκ-περάω   [ᾱ] pass through, pass over (ἐκπερᾶσαι, aor.¹ inf.; for ὥστε with inf., see ὥστε [result clause] in line 50; συμφορᾶς, gen. of explanation: S #1322) [1x *Hipp.*]

826 τίνι λόγῳ   (dat. of means; see ἔρως in line 28. Note the *consonance* of the sound τ/θ in the line, as well as the wordplay on τύχαν/τύχω.)

827 βαρύ-ποτμος, ον   with heavy fate, ill-starred, ill-fated [1x *Hipp.*]

προσ-αυδάω   speak to, address (προσαυδῶν, pres. act. ptc.; supplem. ptc., which tells what the main action is, while the finite verb tells something about how the action is occurring: S: #2096a; *⁺τύχω < *⁺τυγχάνω, aor.² act. deliberative subjv.: S #2639; GMT #287) [1x *Hipp.*]

828 ἄ-φαντος, ον   (ἀ privat., φαίνομαι, appear) invisible, forgotten. (Is Theseus' viewing Phaedra as held/captured in his hands suggestive?) [1x *Hipp.*]

829 πήδημα, ατος, τό   leaping, bounding (internal acc. with ὁρμήσασα: S #1554a) [1x *Hipp.*]

   ἐς Ἅιδου   'into the [house] of Hades'

   κραιπνός (3)   tearing, sweeping, rushing [1x Eur.]

   ὁρμάω   hasten, rush on (ὁρμήσασα, aor.¹ act. ptc., coincidental/modal with ἄφαντος εἶ; see λύσασα in line 290) – 'you are gone/vanished from my hands . . . as you hastened a leap' (1152)

831–3 ποθεν (enclit. adv.) from some place or other [1x *Hipp.*]

   ἀνα-κομίζομαι   bring/take back with one, take up (⁺δαιμόνων, subj. gen.: S #1330; – 'the fate from [= sent by] the gods'; ἀμπλακίαισι, dat. of cause: S #1517; for τῶν πάροιθεν, see Ὄλυμπος in line 71) [1x Eur.]

834 ἄναξ   = ὦ ἄναξ (note the *assonance* of -o- in the line)

Θη. τὸ κατὰ γῆς θέλω, τὸ κατὰ γῆς κνέφας	[ἀντ.	I wish to take the darkness below the earth
μετοικεῖν σκότῳ θανών, ὦ τλάμων,		as my new abode, below the earth, dead in the
τῆς σῆς στερηθεὶς φιλτάτης ὁμιλίας·		gloom. Oh unhappy me, because I am bereft of your
ἀπώλεσας γὰρ μᾶλλον ἢ κατέφθισο.		most beloved companionship; you have destroyed [me] more than you have perished yourself.
†τίνος κλύω† πόθεν θανάσιμος τύχα,	840	From where did it come, my poor wife, this

γύναι, σάν, τάλαιν᾽, ἔβα, καρδίαν;   fortune deadly to your heart?
                                      Could someone
εἴποι τις ἂν τὸ πραχθέν, ἢ μάτην ὄχλον   tell me what happened? Or does
                                      the royal house shelter a throng
στέγει τύραννον δῶμα προσπόλων ἐμῶν;   of my servants for nothing?
ὤμοι μοι ⟨   ⟩ σέθεν,   Alas! ⟨. . . . .⟩ because of you,
μέλεος, οἷον εἶδον ἄλγος δόμων,   845   unhappy me, what pain have I
                                         seen of my house,
οὐ τλητὸν οὐδὲ ῥητόν. ἀλλ᾽ ἀπωλόμην·   unbearable! unspeakable! Oh, I
                                         am undone;
ἔρημος οἶκος, καὶ τέκν᾽ ὀρφανεύεται.   my house is deserted, my chil-
                                         dren are orphaned.
⟨αἰαῖ αἰαῖ,⟩ ἔλιπες ἔλιπες, ὦ φίλα   <Alas! Alas!> You've left!
                                         You've left! Oh beloved
γυναικῶν ἄριστα θ᾽ ὁπόσας ὁρᾷ   among women and the best of as
                                         many as the
φέγγος θ᾽ ἀλίοιο καὶ νυκτὸς ἀ-   850   light of the sun and the starry
                                         brightness of
    στερωπὸν σέλας.   the night see.

836 κνέφᾱς, τό   darkness, dusk at nightfall [1x *Hipp.*]

837 μετ-οικέω   change one's abode, remove to a place [1x
Hipp.]

838 στερέω   deprive (στερηθείς, aor.[1] pass. ptc.; circumstantial ptc. denoting cause: S #2061. The action of the aor. ptc. is usually
antecedent to that of the leading verb, here θέλω; see προκόπτω in line 23.)
(1460)

   φίλτατος (3)   most loved (irreg. superl. of φίλος)

839 κατα-φθίω   ruin, destroy; pass.: be destroyed (κατεφθίσο,
aor.[2] pass. indic.) [1x *Hipp.*]

840 †τίνος κλύω†   B.: "corrupt beyond remedy."
   πόθεν (interrog. adv.)   where from (1205)
   θᾰνάσῐμος (3)   deadly (1438)

842 ⁺μάτην (adv.)   in vain (*⁺εἴποι < *⁺λέγω, aor.² potential opt. with ἄν: S #1824; τὸ πραχθέν < ⁺πράττω, aor.¹ pass. artic. ptc. as subst., see πάρειμι in line 184)

843 στέγω   cover [1x *Hipp.*]

844–5 a lacunose line; hence the dots (σέθεν could possibly be gen. of cause in exclamation: S #1407, explaining ὤμοι μοι; ⁺δόμων, subj. gen.: S #1330)

846 τλητός (3)   (‡τλάω, suffer) suffering; to be endured, sufferable (875)

   ῥητός (3)   (ἐρῶ, speak) spoken of, specified, settled (τλητός, ῥητός: B.: "deliberate assonance") (459)

847 ἔρημος (3/2)   deserted (1198)

   ὀρφανεύω   mid./pass.: be an orphan [1x *Hipp.*]

849 ὁπόσος (3) (relat. adj.)   as many as (γυναικῶν, [πασῶν] ὁπόσας, partit. gen.: S #1306, 1315) [1x *Hipp.*]

850 ἀστερ-ωπός, ον   (ἀστήρ, star; ὤψ, eye) starry, starlike, bright [1x *Hipp.*]

   σέλας, αος, τό   bright light, brightness [1x *Hipp.*]

Xo.	ὦ τάλας, ὅσον κακὸν ἔχει δόμος·		Oh miserable Theseus, your house holds such a great grief;
	δάκρυσί μου βλέφαρα καθαχυθέντα τέγ-		my eyes, drenched with tears, are melting
	γεται σᾷ τύχᾳ.		at your misfortune. I've been shuddering
	τὸ δ' ἐπὶ τῷδε πῆμα φρίσσω πάλαι.	855	for some time at the calamity to follow.

852	– ◡ – ◡ – ◡ ◡◡ – ◡ –	hypodochmiac, dochmiac
853	◡ ◡◡ – ◡ ◡◡ ◡ ◡◡ – ◡ –	2 dochmiacs
854	◡ – – ◡ –	dochmiac
855	◡ ◡◡ – ◡ – ◡ – – ◡ – |||	2 dochmiacs

853–4 βλέφᾰρον, τό   (*⁺βλέπω, see) eyelid (here: eye, *synecdoche*; δάκρυσί, dat. of means, see ἔρως in line 28; σᾷ τύχᾳ, dat. of cause: S #1517) [1x *Hipp.*]

κατα-*χέω   pour down, shed upon/over (καταχυθέντα, aor.¹ pass. ptc. of attendant circumstance/descriptive, antecedent to or coincidental with the finite verb τέγγεται: S #1872) [1x *Hipp.*]

855 φρίσσω   shudder (417)

Θη.   ἔα ἔα·
       τί δή ποθ’ ἥδε δέλτος ἐκ φίλης χερὸς
       ἠρτημένη; θέλει τι σημῆναι νέον;
       ἀλλ’ ἦ λέχους μοι καὶ τέκνων ἐπιστολὰς
       ἔγραψεν ἡ δύστηνος, ἐξαιτουμένη;
       θάρσει, τάλαινα· λέκτρα γὰρ τὰ Θησέως   860
       οὐκ ἔστι δῶμά θ’ ἥτις εἴσεισιν γυνή.
       καὶ μὴν τύποι γε σφενδόνης χρυσηλάτου
       τῆς οὐκέτ’ οὔσης οἵδε προσσαίνουσί με.
       φέρ’ ἐξελίξας περιβολὰς σφραγισμάτων
       ἴδω τί λέξαι δέλτος ἥδε μοι θέλει.   865

856 ⁺ἔα   a cry of surprise; here it is *extra metrum* that makes it more emphatic.

⁺δέλτος, ἡ   writing tablet

857 ⁺ἠρτημένη   *enjambment* (⁺ἀρτάω, pf. mid. ptc. of attendant circumstance/descriptive, see ὁράω in line 4) – 'What is this? What is this tablet hanging from her dear hand?'

⁺σημαίνω   signal, declare (aor.¹ act. inf.; Theseus personifies the tablet)

858 ἀλλ’ ἦ   marks an idea that suddenly dawns on one as true: 'What?! Why?!' (λέχους, τέκνων, obj. gen.: S #1331 with ἐπιστολάς)

ἐπιστολή, ἡ   message; letter (according to B., always pl. in tragedy) [1x *Hipp.*]

859 γράφω   write (1311)

ἐξ-αιτέω   mid.: beg for oneself (ἐξαιτουμένη, ptc. of attendant circumstance/descriptive, see ὁράω in line 4) – 'Has the poor woman written to me about our marriage and children, pleading [something] for herself?' (711)

860–1 θαρσέω   be of good courage, be of good cheer (pres. impv. act.) (203)

εἴσ-ειμι   go into, go in (ἔστι, existential use of εἰμί; λέ-κτρα and δῶμα are inside the ἥτις clause: οὐκ ἔστι γυνὴ ἥτις εἴσεισιν λέκτρα δῶμά τε. Ironically, Hippolytus avowed the same commitment.) – 'Cheer up, poor woman: there is no woman (wife) who will come to Theseus' bed and house.' (1067)

862 τύπος, ὁ   print mark, imprint, impress of a seal (see καί μήν . . . γε in line 589; γε emphasizes τύποι) [1x *Hipp*.]

σφενδόνη, ἡ   sling; ring in which a stone or seal is set [1x *Hipp*.]

χρῡσήλατος, ον   of beaten gold, wrought of gold [1x *Hipp*.]

863 προσσαίνω   to please, to greet fawningly (τῆς οὐκέτ' οὔ-σης, pres. act. artic. ptc. as subst.; see πάρειμι in line 184) – 'Yes, indeed the imprint of the gold-wrought seal of that one who is no more greets me.' [1x Eur.]

864–5 φέρε   come, now, well (impv. of *⁺φέρω with *⁺ἴδω< *⁺ὁράω, aor.² act. hortatory subjv.: S #1797b; GMT #257)

ἐξ-ελίσσω   unwind, unfold (ἐξελίξας, aor.¹ act. circumstantial ptc. denoting time: S #2061. The action of the aor. ptc. is usually antecedent to that of the leading verb, here ἴδω; see προκόπτω in line 23; λέξαι < *⁺λέγω.) [1x *Hipp*.]

περιβολή, ἡ   coverings, strings (resolution in 6th position, περιβολάς). [1x *Hipp*.]

σφράγισμα, ατος, τό   impression of a signet ring, seal (gen. of explanation: S #1322; or possess.: S #1297) – 'Now, let me unfold the seal's wrappings and see . . .' [1x *Hipp*.]

Χο. φεῦ φεῦ· τόδ' αὖ νεοχμὸν   Oh! Oh! God is sending in addi-
ἐκδοχαῖς   tion this

ἐπεισφρεῖ θεὸς κακόν. †ἐμοὶ [μὲν οὖν novel evil . . .
    ἀβίοτος βίου]

                                        . . .
τύχα πρὸς τὸ κρανθὲν εἴη τυχεῖν·†   . . .
ὀλομένους γάρ, οὐκέτ' ὄντας, λέγω,   For I claim the house of my king
                                            has perished,
φεῦ φεῦ, τῶν ἐμῶν τυράννων δόμους. 870 alas! Alas! [Oh spirit, if it is
                                            somehow possible,
[ὦ δαῖμον, εἴ πως ἔστι, μὴ σφήλῃς   do not make this house fall, but
δόμους,   listen to me
αἰτουμένης δὲ κλῦθί μου· πρὸς γάρ   praying; for from somewhere,
τινος   like a prophet
οἰωνὸν ὥστε μάντις εἰσορῶ κακόν].   I see a bird of bad omen.]
Θη. οἴμοι, τόδ' οἷον ἄλλο πρὸς   Alas! What evil upon evil is this!
κακῷ κακόν,
οὐ τλητὸν οὐδὲ λεκτόν· ὦ τάλας 875   Unbearable and unspeakable! Oh
ἐγώ.   wretched me!
Χο. τί χρῆμα; λέξον, εἴ τί μοι   What is it? Tell me, if it can be
λόγου μέτα.   shared with me at all.

866	– – ⏑ – ⏑ ⏑⏑ – ⏑ –	iamb and dochmiac
867	⏑ – – – ⏑ – ⏑ ⏑ † ⏑ – – ⏑ – ⏑ ⏑ ⏑ – ⏑ – †	(dochmiacs)
868	† ⏑ – – – ⏑ – ⏑ – – – ⏑ – †	(2 dochmiacs)
869	⏑ ⏑ ⏑⏑ – ⏑ – – ⏑ – – ⏑ –	2 dochmiacs
870	– – – ⏑ – ⏑ – – ⏑ –	2 dochmiacs
871–6	iambic trimeters	

866 νεοχμός, ον   new, fresh; novel, unusual (τόδ' . . . νεοχ-
μόν . . . κακόν, meaningful *hyperbaton* effecting tension) [1x *Hipp.*]

ἐκδοχή, ἡ   succession [1x Eur.]

†**867–8**† ἐπ-εισφρέω   introduce besides, send in; – 'Oh! Oh! God is
sending in addition this novel evil.' [1x *Hipp.*]

*⁺κραίνω   bring to pass, accomplish, complete (κρανθέν,
aor.¹ pass. ptc. The ends of lines 867 and 868 are corrupted; see B. for
a variety of reading possibilities.)

869–73 *⁺ὀλομένους . . . *⁺ὄντας . . . δόμους   emphatic   *hyperba-*
ton (descriptive ptcs., see ὁράω in line 4, or supplem. ptc. in indir. disc.:
S #2092)
A scholiast states that lines 871–3 are omitted in some copies. See B. for
discussion.

μὴ *⁺σφήλῃς   (< *⁺σφάλλω, aor.¹ act. subjv.; prohibitive
subjv.: S #1800)

⁺κλῦθι   (< ⁺κλύω, aor.² impv. act.; αἰτουμένης μου,
gen. required by κλύω; descriptive ptc., see ὁράω in line 4)

οἰωνός, ὁ   a bird of omen; omen [1x *Hipp.*]

875 λεκτός (3)   (*⁺λέγω, speak) able to be spoken [1x *Hipp.*]

876 ⁺χρῆμα, ατος, τό   business, affair; often strengthening a phrase,
e.g., τὶ χρῆμα for τί: 'what?'

μέτα   = μέτεστι + gen.; there is a share of

Θη. βοᾷ βοᾷ δέλτος ἄλαστα·	The tablet cries out, cries out dire
πᾷ φύγω	things!
βάρος κακῶν; ἀπὸ γὰρ ὀλόμενος	How can I escape the weight of
οἴχομαι,	ills: for I am
οἷον οἷον εἶδον [ἐν] γραφαῖς	completely ruined, such a song
μέλος	I saw uttered
φθεγγόμενον τλάμων. 880	by means of her letter,
	wretched me!
Χο. αἰαῖ, κακῶν ἀρχηγὸν	You are revealing a word that is
ἐκφαίνεις λόγον.	the beginning of ills.
Θη. τόδε μὲν οὐκέτι στόματος	No longer will I hold within the
ἐν πύλαις	gates of
καθέξω δυσεκπέρατον ὀλοὸν	my mouth this inexpressible
	destructive
κακόν· ἰὼ πόλις.	evil. Oh city!

877	◡ – ◡ – – ◡ ◡ – ◡ – ◡ –	iamb choriamb iamb
878	◡ – ◡ – ◡ ◡◡ ◡ ◡◡ ◡ – ◡ –	3 iambs
879	– ◡ – ◡ – – ◡ – ◡ –	2 hypodochmiacs
880	– ◡◡ – – –	dochmiac

881	iambic trimeter	
882	⌣ ⌣⌣ – ⌣ – ⌣ ⌣⌣ – ⌣ –	2 dochmiacs
883	⌣ – – ⌣ – ⌣ – ⌣⌣ ⌣ –	2 dochmiacs
884	⌣ ⌣⌣ – ⌣ – |||	dochmiac

877 ἄ-λαστος, ον   (ἀ privat., *⁺λανθάνομαι, forget) not to be forgotten, dire, insufferable [1x *Hipp.*]

πῇ (interrog. pcl.)   how (*⁺φύγω, aor.² act. deliberative subjv.: S
#2639; GMT #287) (673)

878 κακῶν   (gen. of explanation: S #1322)

ἀπὸ . . . ὀλόμενος   (< *⁺ἀπόλλυμι, aor.² supplem. ptc., which tells
what the main action is, while the finite verb οἴχομαι tells something
about how the action is occurring: S #2088, 2099; *tmesis*)

οἴχομαι   be gone, have gone (pres. for pf.: S #1886) [1x
Hipp.]

μέλος, εως, τό   song, strain (1178)

880 φθέγγομαι   utter a sound (γραφαῖς, dat. of means; see ἔρως
in line 28. The ἐν is an interpolation by someone who did not realize the
dat.'s function. B.: a song "giving utterance by means of the writing"; note
the incongruity of senses: sight and hearing.) (300)

881 ἀρχηγός, ον   (ἄρχω, begin; ἡγέομαι, lead) beginning, originating, leading; as a subst.: leader (ἀρχηγόν, predicative adj.: – '[which is]
a beginning of ills'; κακῶν, gen. of explanation: S #1322) (152)

882 μέν   surely, indeed, really (μέν *solitarium*, i.e., with
no corresponding δέ clause, is emphatic but not always translatable; here
stressing and affirming the idea of the verb: S #2896–8; GP 359–60)

883–4 δυσ-εκπέρᾱτος, ον   (δυσ-, ἐκπεράω, pass through) hard to pass
out from, hard to escape (678)

ὀλοός (3)   destructive (κακόν, emphatic *enjambment*)
[1x *Hipp.*]

Ἱππόλυτος εὐνῆς τῆς ἐμῆς ἔτλη θιγεῖν   885
βίᾳ, τὸ σεμνὸν Ζηνὸς ὄμμ᾽ ἀτιμάσας.

ἀλλ᾽, ὦ πάτερ Πόσειδον, ἃς ἐμοί ποτε
ἀρὰς ὑπέσχου τρεῖς, μιᾷ κατέργασαι
τούτων ἐμὸν παῖδ᾽, ἡμέραν δὲ μὴ φύγοι
τήνδ᾽, εἴπερ ἡμῖν ὤπασας σαφεῖς ἀράς.   890
Χο.   ἄναξ, ἀπεύχου ταῦτα πρὸς θεῶν πάλιν,
      γνώσῃ γὰρ αὖθις ἀμπλακών· ἐμοὶ πιθοῦ.
Θη.   οὐκ ἔστι· καὶ πρός γ᾽ ἐξελῶ σφε τῆσδε γῆς·
      δυοῖν δὲ μοίραιν θατέρᾳ πεπλήξεται·
      ἢ γὰρ Ποσειδῶν αὐτὸν εἰς Ἅιδου δόμους   895
      θανόντα πέμψει τὰς ἐμὰς ἀρὰς σέβων
      ἢ τῆσδε χώρας ἐκπεσὼν ἀλώμενος
      ξένην ἐπ᾽ αἶαν λυπρὸν ἀντλήσει βίον.

885 *‡τλάω*   take upon oneself; + inf.: dare (pres. form never found; Ἱππόλυτος, resolution in 2nd position; ⁺θιγεῖν < ⁺θιγγάνω, aor.² inf. act.) (1073)

886–7 ⁺βία, ἡ   force, might, violence (βίᾳ, dat. of means, see ἔρως in line 28; emphatic *enjambment*)

ὄμμα, ατος, τό   eye (1438)

⁺ἀτιμάσας   (< ⁺ἀτιμάζω, aor.¹ act., ptc. coincidental with the action of the leading verb also in aor., in whatever mood, ἔτλη: S #1872c2; see λύσασα in line 290) – 'Hippolytus dared to touch my marriage bed by violence, slighting the revered eye of Zeus.'

888 ⁺ἀρά, ἡ   prayer, curse

ὑπισχνέομαι   promise (ὑπέσχου, aor.² mid. indic.; the antecedent is drawn into the case of the relat. clause: S #2540: ἀραὶ τρεῖς ἃς ἐμοί ποτε ὑπέσχου) [1x *Hipp.*]

τρεῖς, οἱ, αἱ, τρία, τά   three [1x *Hipp.*]

κατ-*⁺εργάζομαι   effect, accomplish; destroy, dispatch (κατέργασαι, aor.¹ dep. impv.; μίᾳ, dat. of means, see ἔρως in line 28. Theseus has joint paternity: divine, Poseidon, and human, Aegeus.)

889 τούτων   (partit. gen.: S #1306) – 'by one of these curses destroy my son'

μὴ *⁺φύγοι   (< *⁺φεύγω, aor.² act. opt.; opt. of wish; see κάμπτω in line 87)

890 ὀπάζω   make to follow, give, grant (τήνδε, emphatic *enjambment*; σαφεῖς, predicative adj.) – 'that my son may not escape this very day, if indeed you gave me curses that are reliable' [1x *Hipp.*]

891 ἀπ-εύχομαι   wish a thing away; – 'Oh lord, by the gods, take this wish back' [1x *Hipp.*]

892 ἀμπλακίσκω   miss, fail, fall short (ἀμπλακών, aor.[2] act. ptc. supplem. in indir. disc.: S #2106 with *[+]γνώσῃ < *[+]γιγνώσκω) – 'for in time you will realize that you've made a mistake; obey me!' [1x *Hipp.*]

893 ἐξ-*ἐλαύνω   drive out, banish (οὐκ ἔστι = it is impossible)
(1052)

[+]πρός (adv.)   in addition to (σφε = αὐτόν. Theseus thus imposes a double punishment. By adding banishment to his prayer to Poseidon, he indicates that he only half believes in his divine paternity, as indeed his claim in lines 1169–70 shows. See Knox 1986 [1952], 222.)

894 [+]μοῖρα, ἡ   fate, one's portion in life, destiny, apportionment (δυοῖν μοίραιν, dual partit. gen.)

ἕτερος (3)   one of two (θατέρᾳ = τῇ ἑτέρᾳ) (349)

***πλήττω**   strike (πεπλήξεται, fut. pf. pass.) [1x *Hipp.*]

897 ἐκ-*[+]πίπτω   be driven out (ἐκπεσών, aor.[2] act. ptc. of time) [1x *Hipp.*]

ἀλάομαι   wander (descriptive ptc., coincidental with the finite verb ἀντλήσει; see ὁράω in line 4)

898 λυπρός (3)   wretched (1049)
ἀντλέω   exhaust, drain (1049)

Part II: Lines 899–1101

Hippolytus rushes onto the stage together with his huntsmen. He is innocent, self-satisfied with the solicitude he shows to his father, as is reflected in the speed with which he comes as soon as he hears his father shouting. He is ready to help in any way he can. He is surprised by Phaedra's death but does not go back on his oath of silence even when Theseus accuses him of a sex crime. It is clear that even if Hippolytus had broken his oath, his father would have not believed him. Theseus banishes him. Hippolytus makes a formal reply along the lines of classical rhetorical principles, addressing Theseus as if they were in a public meeting. He protests his virginity, which would make the crime he is accused of impossible. Although Theseus is still unbending, he reveals some underlying uncertainty. Hippolytus pauses before the statue of Artemis as he goes to exile.

Hippolytus, accompanied by his huntsmen, rushes onto the stage through the same *eisodos* through which he departed.

Χο.	καὶ μὴν ὅδ᾽ αὐτὸς παῖς σὸς ἐς καιρὸν πάρα	
	Ἱππόλυτος· ὀργῆς δ᾽ ἐξανεὶς κακῆς, ἄναξ	900
	Θησεῦ, τὸ λῷστον σοῖσι βούλευσαι δόμοις.	
Ἱπ.	κραυγῆς ἀκούσας σῆς ἀφικόμην, πάτερ,	
	σπουδῇ· τὸ μέντοι πρᾶγμ᾽ ὅτῳ στένεις ἔπι	
	οὐκ οἶδα, βουλοίμην δ᾽ ἂν ἐκ σέθεν κλυεῖν.	
	ἔα, τί χρῆμα; σὴν δάμαρθ᾽ ὁρῶ, πάτερ,	905
	νεκρόν· μεγίστου θαύματος, τόδ᾽ ἄξιον·	
	ἦν ἀρτίως ἔλειπον, ἢ φάος τόδε	
	οὔπω χρόνος παλαιὸς εἰσεδέρκετο.	
	τί χρῆμα πάσχει; τῷ τρόπῳ διόλλυται;	
	πάτερ, πυθέσθαι βούλομαι σέθεν πάρα.	910
	σιγᾷς; σιωπῆς δ᾽ οὐδὲν ἔργον ἐν κακοῖς·	
	[ἡ γὰρ ποθοῦσα πάντα καρδία κλυεῖν	
	κἂν τοῖς κακοῖσι λίχνος οὖσ᾽ ἁλίσκεται.]	
	οὐ μὴν φίλους γε, κἄτι μᾶλλον ἢ φίλους,	
	κρύπτειν δίκαιον σάς, πάτερ, δυσπραξίας.	915

899–901 καὶ μήν   introducing a new point: 'why look' (πάρα = πάρεστι; Ἱππόλυτος, resolution in 2nd position)

καιρός, ὁ   right time; right measure, appropriate; – 'Hippolytus himself is here, at just the right moment' (386)

ἐξ-αν-*⁺ίημι   + gen.: let go, dismiss (ἐξανείς, aor.² act. ptc.; coincidental/modal ptc. with aor.¹ impv. βούλευσαι; see λύσασα in line 290) [1x *Hipp.*]

λῷστος (3)   best (superl. of λῷων) – 'once you give up your anger, my lord Theseus, deliberate what is best for your house' [1x *Hipp.*]

902 κραυγή, ἡ   cry, shout (ἀκούσας, aor.¹ act. ptc.; coinci-
dental/modal ptc. with aor.² ἀφικόμην, see λύσασα in line 290) – 'I came
quickly, father, as I heard your cry' [1x *Hipp.*]

903 σπουδή, ἡ   haste, speed (σπουδῇ, dat. of manner: S #1516;
emphatic *enjambment* underscores Hippolytus' solicitude for his father;
ἔπι, *anastrophe*, governs ὅτῳ) (1152)

904 *⁺βουλοίμην ἄν   (potential opt. used to indicate a polite request,
see βουλόμαι in line 270; see κλυεῖν in line 119) – 'And yet, I don't know
the matter about which you are groaning, but I would like to hear from you.'

906 θαῦμα, ατος, τό   wonder, marvel; astonishment; – ['this thing is
worthy of the greatest surprise'] = 'this is extremely surprising' (439)

907 ἀρτίως   just, exactly (ἔλειπον, according to B., is impf.
rather than aor. "because Hipp. is picturing the scene to himself: 'it was
only a moment ago that I was leaving her'") (433)

908 οὔ-πω (adv.)   not yet [1x *Hipp.*]

    πᾰλαιός (3)   old, aged (B.: "οὔπω χρόνος παλαιὸς sc. ἐστι:
    'it is no long time ago'") (1380)

    εἰσ-δέρκομαι   look upon; – 'she who not long ago was look-
    ing on this light of day' [1x *Hipp.*]

909 ⁺τρόπος, ὁ   way, manner, fashion (τῷ τρόπῳ, dat. of manner: S #1516; πάσχει, διόλλυται, historical presents, see λείπω in line 34.
Note the many short questions and appeals, indicating his inner havoc, and
the stillness of his father.) – 'what happened? How did she die?'

910 πάρα   = παρά, *anastrophe*

911 σιωπή, ἡ   silence; – 'But silence is no use in troubles!'
[1x *Hipp.*]

[912–13] ποθέω   desire (These two lines censure the very act of
curiosity that Hippolytus exhibits and seem out of place; hence they are in
square brackets. ποθοῦσα, descriptive ptc., see ὁράω in line 4; see κλυεῖν
in line 119.) (513)

λίχνος (3)   greedy (οὖσα, supplem. ptc. in direct discourse
with ἁλίσκεται: S #2046C, 2113a) – 'For the heart desiring to hear
everything, even in troubles is caught being greedy' [1x *Hipp.*]

914 ⁺μήν (pcl.)   in truth, surely (asseverative: S #2920)

915 δυσ-πραξία, ἡ   ill success, ill luck (double acc. following κρύπτειν) – 'It is really not right, father, to hide your ill luck from your friends
and [from those who are] even more than friends.' (1405)

Θη.   ὦ πόλλ' ἁμαρτάνοντες ἄνθρωποι μάτην,
            τί δὴ τέχνας μὲν μυρίας διδάσκετε
            καὶ πάντα μηχανᾶσθε κἀξευρίσκετε,
            ἓν δ'οὐκ ἐπίστασθ' οὐδ' ἐθηράσασθέ πω,
            φρονεῖν διδάσκειν οἷσιν οὐκ ἔνεστι νοῦς;   920
Ἱπ.   δεινὸν σοφιστὴν εἶπας, ὅστις εὖ φρονεῖν
            τοὺς μὴ φρονοῦντας δυνατός ἐστ' ἀναγκάσαι.
            ἀλλ' οὐ γὰρ ἐν δέοντι λεπτουργεῖς, πάτερ,
            δέδοικα μή σου γλῶσσ' ὑπερβάλλῃ κακοῖς.

916–18 μυρίος (3)   numberless, countless (ἁμαρτάνοντες, attr.
ptc.; see λεχθεῖσι in line 299) (1179)

    ἐξ-*⁺ευρίσκω   find out, discover, invent (480)

919 θηράω   hunt [1x *Hipp.*]

    πω (enclit. pcl.)   to this time, yet, ever (mostly with negatives;
note that antithetically to the short sentences and appeals of Hippolytus, Theseus answers in one long, thought-out sentence) – 'Oh mankind who so often are useless, why on the one hand, you devise and
discover everything, but on the other hand, one thing you do not understand nor have you yet hunted down: how to teach sense [to those]
in whom there is no sense'? (76)

920 οἷσιν   supply the antecedent τούτους (note the *assonance* of the repeated 2nd pl., -τε, -σθε in lines 916–20)

921 σοφιστής, οῦ, ὁ   one who is clever [1x *Hipp.*]

922 δυνατός (3)   able (τοὺς μὴ φρονοῦντας, artic. as subst. ptc.;
see πάρειμι in line 184)

   ἀναγκάζω   compel, force [1x *Hipp.*]

923 δέον, οντος, τό   that which is right, proper (neut. ptc. of the impersonal ⁺δεῖ; ἐν δέοντι, supply καιρῷ 'at the appropriate time')

   λεπτουργέω   quibble, deal subtly [1x *Hipp.*]

924 δείδω   fear (δέδοικα, pf. with pres. meaning) (518)

   ὑπερβάλλω   exceed the limits, go too far (ὑπερβάλλῃ, subjv.
in a fear clause following δέδοικα; see εὐλαβέομαι in line 100) – 'But
since you are subtle at an inappropriate moment, father, I fear lest your
tongue might go too far because of your troubles.' [1x *Hipp.*]

Θη.   φεῦ, χρῆν βροτοῖσι τῶν φίλων τεκμήριον   925
      σαφές τι κεῖσθαι καὶ διάγνωσιν φρενῶν,
      ὅστις τ' ἀληθής ἐστιν ὅς τε μὴ φίλος,
      δισσάς τε φωνὰς πάντας ἀνθρώπους ἔχειν,
      τὴν μὲν δικαίαν τὴν δ' ὅπως ἐτύγχανεν,
      ὡς ἡ φρονοῦσα τἄδικ' ἐξηλέγχετο   930
      πρὸς τῆς δικαίας, κοὐκ ἂν ἠπατώμεθα.
Ἱπ.   ἀλλ' ἤ τις ἐς σὸν οὖς με διαβαλὼν ἔχει
      φίλων, νοσοῦμεν δ' οὐδὲν ὄντες αἴτιοι;
      ἔκ τοι πέπληγμαι· σοὶ γὰρ ἐκπλήσσουσί με
      λόγοι, παραλλάσσοντες ἔξεδροι φρενῶν.   935

925 τεκμήριον, τό   sign, token (χρῆν = χρὴ ἦν, impf., it was necessary; indicates an unfulfilled present obligation: 'should,' with acc. and
inf.; cf. line 253) [1x *Hipp.*]

926 κεῖμαι   lie down, be established (1200)

   διάγνωσις, εως, ἡ   discerning between, distinguishing; – 'There
should have been for mortals some clearly established sign of friends and
discernment of minds, to tell who is a true friend and who isn't' (696)

928–9 φωνή, ἡ   voice; – 'and all men ought to have two voices,
one just and one however it happened [τὴν δ' ὅπως ἐτύγχανεν]'; B.: "Every

man ought to have an honest voice in addition to the one he would have had anyhow (which might be dishonest or not)." [1x *Hipp.*]

930–1 ⁺ἐξ-ελέγχω   test, refute, convict, expose (ὡς ἐξηλέγχετο aor.² or impf. indic. are used in final clauses with ὡς/ἵνα when the action of the leading clause is unfulfilled, whether past or pres., here expressed by χρῆν: GMT #333–6; S #2185c. The unreality is not always shown in translation.) (944)

    ἀπᾰτάω   cheat, trick, beguile (κοὐκ ἂν ἠπατώμεθα, this is a statement independent of the initial χρῆν) – 'so that the [voice] thinking unjust thoughts [τὰ ἄδικα] would be exposed by the just [voice] [πρὸς τῆς δικαίας] and we would not be deceived.' It is note-worthy that both Phaedra and Hippolytus also turn to *adynaton* when faced with distress; see lines 208–31, 616–24, 1074–6. [1x *Hipp.*]

932 ἀλλ' ᾗ̈   see line 858 (The *majestic plural* that Hippoly-tus uses serves here as an attempt more to lessen his self-importance than to underscore it.)

    δια-*⁺βάλλω   accuse falsely, slander (διαβαλὼν ἔχει, *periph-rasis* of resultative pf.: S #599b) [1x *Hipp.*]

933 αἴτιος (3)   guilty, blamable (ὄντες, circumstantial conces-sive ptc.: see νοσοῦσα in line 477) – 'am I in trouble, even though I am not guilty at all?' (1149)

934 ⁺ἐκ ... *πέπληγμαι   *tmesis* (wordplay with ἐκπλήσσουσι)

935 παρ-αλλάσσω   deviate, turn from the path, go astray (ptc. of attendant circumstance/descriptive, see ὁράω in line 4) – 'for your words astonish me, going astray out of their senses' [1x Eur.]

    ἔξ-εδρος, ον   away from home, strange, extraordinary [1x *Hipp.*]

Θη.   φεῦ τῆς βροτείας—ποῖ προβήσεται;—φρενός.
       τί τέρμα τόλμης καὶ θράσους γενήσεται;
       εἰ γὰρ κατ' ἀνδρὸς βίοτον ἐξογκώσεται,
       ὁ δ' ὕστερος τοῦ πρόσθεν εἰς ὑπερβολὴν
       πανοῦργος ἔσται, θεοῖσι προσβαλεῖν χθονὶ   940

ἄλλην δεήσει γαῖαν ἢ χωρήσεται
τοὺς μὴ δικαίους καὶ κακοὺς πεφυκότας.
σκέψασθε δ᾽ ᾽ἐς τόνδ᾽, ὅστις ἐξ ἐμοῦ γεγὼς
ᾔσχυνε τἀμὰ λέκτρα κἀξελέγχεται
πρὸς τῆς θανούσης ἐμφανῶς κάκιστος ὤν.　　　945
δεῖξον δ᾽, ἐπειδή γ᾽ ἐς μίασμ᾽ ἐλήλυθα,
τὸ σὸν πρόσωπον δεῦρ᾽ ἐναντίον πατρί.
σὺ δὴ θεοῖσιν ὡς περρισὸς ὢν ἀνὴρ
ξύνει; σὺ σώφρων καὶ κακῶν ἀκήρατος;
οὐκ ἂν πιθοίμην τοῖσι σοῖς κόμποις ἐγὼ　　　950
θεοῖσι προσθεὶς ἀμαθίαν φρονεῖν κακῶς.

936 τῆς βροτείας ... φρενός (*hyperbaton*; gen. of exclamation: SS 71–2 §35; ποῖ προβήσεται is inserted parenthetically, cf. line 401) – 'Oh human mind! How far will it go?'

937 θράσος, εως, τό impudence, rashness [1x *Hipp.*]

938 ἐξ-ογκόω make swell, inflate; pass. metaph.: be puffed up; swell, rise high (resolution in 6th position, βίοτον) [1x *Hipp.*]

939 ⁺ὕστερος (3) coming after, latter (ὁ δ᾽ ὕστερος, noun-making power of the artic. with advs.; see Ὄλυμπος in line 71)

πρόσθεν (adv.) before, formerly (τοῦ πρόσθεν, noun-making power of the artic. with advs.; gen. of comparison) (1228)

ὑπερβολή, ἡ passing over [1x *Hipp.*]

940–2 πᾰν-οῦργος, ον; ὁ/ἡ ready to do anything (mostly negatively); knave, villain, rogue; – 'For if it [the mind] swells in the course of a man's life, and the man who comes after surpasses his predecessor in wickedness' (1400)

προσ-*⁺βάλλω attach, add (θεοῖσι, *synizesis*; τοὺς ... πεφυκότας < *φύω, artic. pf. act. ptc., see πάρειμι in line 184) – 'it will be necessary for the gods to add another land to the world, which will contain those unjust and vile by nature' [1x *Hipp.*]

943–5 γεγώς (< **⁺γίγνομαι, circumstantial concessive pf. dep. ptc.: see νοσοῦσα in line 477; ὤν < εἰμί, pres. supplem. ptc. in indir. disc. after verb of showing, ἐξελέγχεται: S #2106)

ἐμφανῶς (adv.)   clearly; – 'Look at this one who, in spite of being begotten by me, shamed my marriage bed and is clearly being convicted by the dead woman of being most evil.' [1x *Hipp.*]

Theseus addresses Hippolytus directly. Hippolytus must have been averting his face.

946–7   ἐπειδή γ᾽ ἐς μίασμ᾽ ἐλήλυθα is parenthetically inserted between δεῖξον and line 947. As far as Theseus is concerned, his son has committed a horrible crime and has thus already contaminated him because he, his father, came close to him and looked at him.

ἐναντίος (3)   against, opposite (δεῖξον < δείκνῦμι, aor.[1] impv. 2 sg.) – 'Since I've already come into [your] pollution, right here show your face to your father.' (1078)

950–1   **κόμπος, ὁ**   boasting (οὐκ ἂν πιθοίμην, aor.[2] mid. opt., potential opt. with ἄν; pres. and aor. opts. are used for fut. time: S #1824, 1828) [1x *Hipp.*]

προσθείς   (< ⁺προστίθημι, aor.[2] act. ptc. circumstantial describing φρονεῖν κακῶς: S #2060)

ἀμαθία, ἡ   foolishness, ignorance (φρονεῖν, final-consecutive inf.: S #2008; GMT #775) – 'I would not be persuaded by your boasting to think falsely, imputing folly to the gods.' [1x *Hipp.*]

> ἤδη νυν αὔχει καὶ δι᾽ ἀψύχου βορᾶς
> †σίτοις† καπήλευ᾽, Ὀρφέα τ᾽ ἄνακτ᾽ ἔχων
> βάκχευε πολλῶν γραμμάτων τιμῶν καπνούς·
> ἐπεί γ᾽ ἐλήφθης. τοὺς δὲ τοιούτους ἐγὼ   955
> φεύγειν προφωνῶ πᾶσι· θηρεύουσι γὰρ
> σεμνοῖς λόγοισιν, αἰσχρὰ μηχανώμενοι.
> τέθνηκεν ἥδε· τοῦτό σ᾽ ἐκσώσειν δοκεῖς;
> ἐν τῷδ᾽ ἁλίσκῃ πλεῖστον, ὦ κάκιστε σύ·
> ποῖοι γὰρ ὅρκοι κρείσσονες, τίνες λόγοι   960
> τῆσδ᾽ ἂν γένοιντ᾽ ἄν, ὥστε σ᾽ αἰτίαν φυγεῖν;
> μισεῖν σε φήσεις τήνδε καὶ τὸ δὴ νόθον
> τοῖς γνησίοισι πολέμιον πεφυκέναι;
> κακὴν ἄρ᾽ αὐτὴν ἔμπορον βίου λέγεις,
> εἰ δυσμενείᾳ σῇ τὰ φίλτατ᾽ ὤλεσεν.   965

952 αὐχέω   feel confident [1x *Hipp.*]

ἄ-ψῡχος, ον   (ἄ privat., ψῡχή, ἡ, breath, life) lifeless [1x *Hipp.*]

βορά, ἡ   meat, food [1x *Hipp.*]

953 †σῖτος, ὁ†   (irreg. pl. σῖτα, τά) food, meal (there is no reason to suspect corruption here) (109)

καπηλεύω   be a retail dealer [1x Eur.]

'Ορφεύς, έως, ὁ   Orpheus, a legendary bard of Thrace. The Orphics of the fifth century, with their peculiar beliefs and practices, were the notorious ascetics of the period, and many considered them impostors. They were vegetarians. Theseus claims that Hippolytus' alleged purity is now revealed also as a sham.

954 βακχεύω   inspire with frenzy [1x *Hipp.*]

καπνός, ὁ   smoke; – 'and honoring many vaporous writings, play the Bacchant with your lord Orpheus' (551)

955 *⁺ἐλήφθης   (< *⁺λαμβάνω, aor.² pass. indic.) – 'for you are caught'

956–7 προ-φωνέω   declare [1x *Hipp.*]

θηρεύω   hunt, run down; – 'and I declare to everyone to shun (run away from) such men; for they hunt [you] down with their saintly words while devising vile things.' [1x *Hipp.*]

958–9 ⁺πλεῖστον (adv.)   to the greatest extent (ἥδε, B.: "deictic; he makes a gesture toward her body"; *⁺ἁλίσκομαι is the regular term for being 'convicted, found guilty') – 'in this above all you are found guilty.'

961 αἰτία, ἡ   charge, accusation (1036)

ἄν ... ἄν   for the repetition of ἄν, see line 270 (γένοιντ[ο] ἄν, potential opt. with ἄν: GMT #286, S #1824; τῆσδε, deictic and gen. of comparison; ὥστε with inf. for probable result, see line 50)

962–3 τὸ νόθον, [τὸ] πολέμιον (collective neut.: S #1024; B.)

πολέμιος (3/2)   (πόλεμος, war) hostile, ill-disposed, adversarial (indicates a public enemy, a political or military foe, while ἐχθρός points to a private enemy; μισεῖν σε, πολέμιον πεφυκέναι: accs. and infs. following *⁺φήσεις) (43)

964–5 ἔμ-πορος, ον   trader [1x *Hipp.*]

δυσμένεια, ἡ   ill-will, enmity (σῇ, the possess. adj. serves as an obj. gen.) – 'you claim that she is a poor bargainer in life, if she lost what is most dear to her (i.e., her life) out of enmity to you.' [1x *Hipp.*]

ἀλλ' ὡς τὸ μῶρον ἀνδράσιν μὲν οὐκ ἔνι,
γυναιξὶ δ' ἐμπέφυκεν; οἶδ' ἐγὼ νέους
οὐδὲν γυναικῶν ὄντας ἀσφαλεστέρους,
ὅταν ταράξῃ Κύπρις ἡβῶσαν φρένα·
τὸ δ' ἄρσεν αὐτοὺς ὠφελεῖ προσκείμενον.   970
νῦν οὖν—τί ταῦτα σοῖς ἁμιλλῶμαι λόγοις
νεκροῦ παρόντος μάρτυρος σαφεστάτου;—
ἔξερρε γαίας τῆσδ' ὅσον τάχος φυγάς,
καὶ μήτ' Ἀθήνας τὰς θεοδμήτους μόλῃς
μήτ' εἰς ὅρους γῆς ἧς ἐμὸν κρατεῖ δόρυ.   975
εἰ γὰρ παθών γέ σου τάδ' ἡσσηθήσομαι,
οὐ μαρτυρήσει μ' Ἴσθμιος Σίνις ποτὲ
κτανεῖν ἑαυτὸν ἀλλὰ κομπάζειν μάτην,
οὐδ' αἱ θαλάσσῃ σύννομοι Σκιρωνίδες
φήσουσι πέτραι τοῖς κακοῖς μ' εἶναι βαρύν.   980

966 ἀλλ(ά) ὡς   or (will you say) (GP 9, II.ii; S #2785; *hypophora*, a rhetorical device for proposing and rejecting successive suggestions, popular with the orators and with Euripides: S #3029; GP 10–11, II.iv; 'or (will you say)' needs to be added in translation, but is an ellipse in Greek)

μῶρος (3)   stupid, silly, foolish (adj. used substantively in neut. with an artic. when the subst. idea is thing in general: S #1023; ἐνί = ἔνεστι) [1x *Hipp.*]

967 ἐμ-*⁺φύω (ῠ)   cling to, be in, be inherent; – 'Or [will you say] that folly is absent in men, but naturally inherent in women?' [1x *Hipp.*]

968 ἀ-σφᾰλής, ές   (ἀ privat., σφάλλω, make fall, trip up) firm, steadfast; safe (οἶδα νέους ὄντας ἀσφαλεστέρους, indir. disc. with supplem. ptc.: S #2123, 2139) (785)

969 ταράττω   disturb; stir up, rouse (ὅταν ταράξῃ, subjv., indef. temporal clause: S #2394, 2409a) [1x *Hipp.*]

ἡβάω   young; pubescent; vigorous; – 'whenever Cypris stirs up their young mind' (note how many times both Hippolytus and Theseus use words found only once in the play) [1x *Hipp.*]

970 ἄρσην, ενος, ὁ   male, masculinity (τὸ ἄρσεν, collective neut.: S #1024) (295)

ὠφελέω   help, assist [1x *Hipp.*]

πρόσ-κειμαι   belonging to, involved in, joined with; – 'but the masculinity belonging to [them] helps them' (i.e., they get away with it) [1x *Hipp.*]

971–2 ἁμιλλάομαι   compete, contend (426)

ταῦτα   'in this way' (internal acc., see line 21; νεκροῦ . . . σαφεστάτου, gen. abs., see ἱκνέομαι in line 330)

973 ἐξ-έρρω   go out [1x Eur.]

τάχος, εος, τό   swiftness, speed (ὅσον τάχος, 'at once,' 'with all speed,' 'as fast as possible,' acc. of manner: S #1608) (599)

⁺φυγάς, άδος, ὁ, ἡ   an exile, fugitive, banished man ('as a fugitive')

974–5 θεό-δμητος, ον   god-built (the noun Ἀθήνας takes no artic. before it, but is followed by the artic. and attr.; not always translatable: S #1159; μήτε *⁺μόλῃς, prohibitive subjv.: S #1800) [1x *Hipp.*]

ὅρος, ὁ   boundary, border [1x *Hipp.*]

δόρυ, τό   spear; – 'nor to the borders of the land over which my spear rules' [1x *Hipp.*]

976 ἡσσάομαι   + gen. (σου) be beaten, worsted, defeated by (727)

977–8 μαρτυρέω   be a witness (followed by indir. disc. in the form of acc. and inf.: μ' . . . κτανεῖν . . . κομπάζειν. Sinis was a robber who plagued travelers at the Isthmus. Bending a pine tree to the earth, he would force a traveler to help him hold it down. He would then let go, and the traveler would be propelled to his death.) [1x *Hipp.*]

κομπάζω   boast, brag; – 'For if, after having suffered [these things], I am to be bested by you, Isthmian Sinis will never bear witness that I killed him but that I boast in vain' [1x *Hipp.*]

979 θάλασσα, ἡ   the sea (305)

σύν-νομος, ὁ, ἡ   partner [1x *Hipp.*]

Σκίρων, ὁ   Sciron, another robber whom Theseus killed. Sciron used to make travelers wash his feet, and when a person was doing this, with a kick Sciron would hurl him from the cliff down into the sea. The Scironian rocks, named after Sciron, were a cliff on the Saronic Gulf coast of the Isthmus. (οὐδ᾽ . . . φήσουσι with indir. disc. in the form of acc. and inf.: μ᾽ εἶναι βαρύν) – 'nor will the Scironian rocks, partners with the sea, say that I am hard on evildoers.'

Χο.   οὐκ οἶδ᾽ ὅπως εἴποιμ᾽ ἂν εὐτυχεῖν τινα
           θνητῶν· τὰ γὰρ δὴ πρῶτ᾽ ἀνέστραπται πάλιν.
Ἱπ.   πάτερ, μένος μὲν ξύντασίς τε σῶν φρενῶν
           δεινή· τὸ μέντοι πρᾶγμ᾽, ἔχον καλοὺς λόγους,
           εἴ τις διαπτύξειεν οὐ καλὸν τόδε.   985
           ἐγὼ δ᾽ ἄκομψος εἰς ὄχλον δοῦναι λόγον,
           ἐς ἥλικας δὲ κὠλίγους σοφώτερος·
           ἔχει δὲ μοῖραν καὶ τόδ᾽· οἱ γὰρ ἐν σοφοῖς
           φαῦλοι παρ᾽ ὄχλῳ μουσικώτεροι λέγειν.
           ὅμως δ᾽ ἀνάγκη, ξυμφορᾶς ἀφιγμένης,   990
           γλῶσσάν μ᾽ ἀφεῖναι. πρῶτα δ᾽ ἄρξομαι λέγειν
           ὅθεν μ᾽ ὑπῆλθες πρῶτον ὡς διαφθερῶν
           οὐκ ἀντιλέξοντ᾽. εἰσορᾷς φάος τόδε
           καὶ γαῖαν· ἐν τοῖσδ᾽ οὐκ ἔνεστ᾽ ἀνὴρ ἐμοῦ,
           οὐδ᾽ ἢν σὺ μὴ φῇς, σωφρονέστερος γεγώς.   995

981–2 εὐ-τυχέω   be lucky, prosper (*⁺εἴποιμ᾽ ἂν, potential opt. with ἄν: GMT #286, S #1824) (1018)

ἀνα-στρέφω   turn upside down, turn back (θνητῶν, *enjambment*) – 'I don't know how I can say that anyone of mortals is fortunate, for even the foremost things are now overthrown' (1176)

983 μένος, εος, τό   force [1x *Hipp.*]

σύντᾰσις, εως, ἡ   (= ξύστασις) composition, straining together, harshness [1x *Hipp.*]

984 ἔχον καλοὺς λόγους 'even though it [the affair] has fine words' (*⁺ἔχον, concessive pres. act. ptc. neut. sg.; see νοσοῦσα in line 477)

985 δια-πτύσσω unfold, disclose (mixed condition, protasis of less vivid condition, with a missing pres. indic. in the apodosis [ἐστί], pointing to a fut.: GMT #500b: "if one should unfold [it], it is not/won't be fine") [1x Eur.]

986 ἄ-κομψος, ον unadorned simple, plain [1x *Hipp.*]

987 ἧλιξ, ικος, ὁ/ἡ of the same age (1180)

988–9 *⁺ἔχει ⁺μοῖραν 'is natural' (B.: "is in accordance with, is a matter of a natural apportionment")

φαῦλος (3/2) shallow, simpleminded, silly, careless (435)

μουσῐκός (3) harmonious, elegant (λέγειν, limiting/explanatory inf.: S #2002; SS 238–9 §3a–b) – 'And this is perfectly natural, for those who are of no account among the wise are more elegant speakers before a crowd' [1x *Hipp.*]

990–1 (⁺ἀνάγκη, supplement ἐστί with acc. and inf.: μ' ⁺ἀφεῖναι <⁺ἀφίημι; ⁺συμφορᾶς *⁺ἀφιγμένης, gen. abs.) – 'However, it is necessary, since disaster has come, that I loosen my tongue.'

992 ὑπ-έρχομαι go into secretly; come upon; undermine (ὡς *⁺διαφθερῶν, fut. act. ptc. of purpose/final: S #2065; GMT #840) (1089)

993 ἀντι-*⁺λέγω reply (ἀντιλέξοντα, fut. act. descriptive ptc. sequential to ὑπῆλθες parallel to διαφθερῶν. Hippolytus claims that Theseus' expectation in making the attack was to overwhelm Hippolytus; believing him guilty, Theseus did not imagine that he would reply.) – 'I will first begin to speak from where you first ambushed me in order to destroy me, expecting that I would not reply.' [1x Eur.]

995 οὐδ(ε) ἤν = ἐάν: 'not even if you do deny it' (B.: "he cannot really believe that Theseus is convinced of his wickedness." γεγώς < *⁺γίγνομαι, pf. act. descriptive ptc., coincidental with ἔνεστι; see ὁράω in line 4.) – 'You see this light and earth; in these there is no man, not even if you do deny it, that is of more virtuous nature than I am.'

ἐπίσταμαι γὰρ πρῶτα μὲν θεοὺς σέβειν
φίλοις τε χρῆσθαι μὴ ἀδικεῖν πειρωμένοις
ἀλλ᾽ οἷσιν αἰδὼς μήτ᾽ ἐπαγγέλειν κακὰ
μήτ᾽ ἀνθυπουργεῖν αἰσχρὰ τοῖσι χρωμένοις,
οὐκ ἐγγελαστὴς τῶν ὁμιλούντων, πάτερ,   1000
ἀλλ᾽ αὐτὸς οὐ παροῦσι κἀγγὺς ὢν φίλοις.
ἑνὸς δ᾽ ἄθικτος, ᾧ με νῦν ἔχειν δοκεῖς·
λέχους γὰρ ἐς τόδ᾽ ἡμέρας ἁγνὸν δέμας.
οὐκ οἶδα πρᾶξιν τήνδε πλὴν λόγῳ κλύων
γραφῇ τε λεύσσων· οὐδὲ ταῦτα γὰρ σκοπεῖν   1005
πρόθυμός εἰμι, παρθένον ψυχὴν ἔχων.
†καὶ δὴ† τὸ σῶφρον τοὐμὸν οὐ πείθει σ᾽ ἴσως·
δεῖ δή σε δεῖξαι τῷ τρόπῳ διεφθάρην.

996–9   πειρωμένοις   (*⁺πειράομαι, ptc. as subst. without an artic.:
S #2052a; GMT #827; πρῶτα μέν = πρῶτον μέν, adv., the μέν is answered
by δέ in line 1002; μήτ᾽. . . μητ᾽ = 'not to either . . . or')

ἐπ-*αγγέλλω   command (οἷσιν, dat. of possess.: S #1476;
κακά, acc. as internal obj.: S #1573, 1554) [1x *Hipp.*]

ἀνθ-υπουργέω   return a kindness (αἰσχρά, acc. as internal obj.:
S #1573, 1554; τοῖσι χρωμένοις, artic. subst. ptc., see πάρειμι in line
184) – 'For I know first of all how to reverence the gods and how to
consort with friends who try to commit no wrong but who have the
sense of decency not to either give evil commands or return evil services to their friends' [1x Eur.]

1000   ἐγγελαστής, ου, ὁ   mocker, scorner (supply εἰμί) [1x Eur.]

ὁμιλέω   be together, in company with, associate
with (τῶν ὁμιλούντων, artic. subst. ptc.; see πάρειμι in line 184)
[1x *Hipp.*]

1001   ἐγγύς   + gen.: near (see ἔσω in line 2; αὐτός = ὁ αὐτός
in *hyperbaton* with ὤν; παροῦσι < ⁺πάρ-*⁺ειμι, pres. act. ptc. as subst. without an artic.: S #2052a; GMT #827; κἀγγύς = καὶ ἐγγύς; ὤν < *⁺εἰμί, pres.
act. ptc. denoting time: S #20161) – 'but I am the same toward friends who
are not present as [καί] when I am near them.' (1070)

1002–3   ἄ-θικτος, ον   (ἀ privat., θιγγάνω, touch); + gen.: untouched
by (⁺ἑνός < εἷς, antecedent to ᾧ, dat. of means) – 'But by one thing I am

untouched, by which you now think that you have me; for to this very moment (point of the day) my body is unsullied by sex.' (652)

1004–6 πρᾶξις, εως, ἡ   deed (λόγῳ, γραφῇ, dats. of means) [1x *Hipp.*]

⁺λεύσσω   look (κλύων, λεύσσων, descriptive ptcs.)

πρό-θῦμος, ον   ready, willing, eager (ἔχων, pres. act. ptc. denoting cause; see line 838) – 'I don't know of this deed except by hearing it in a story or seeing it in a painting, because I am not eager to look at these things, for I have a virgin soul.' (694)

1007–8 †καὶ δή†   suppose that . . . (introduces an assumption: GP 253; S #2847. In lines 1007–20 Hippolytus refutes assertions that Theseus has not made. The daggers mark the pcls. καὶ δή as suspect because they repeat and thus clash with the manuscripts' ἴσως that qualifies the verb: – '*Suppose* my chastity *perhaps* does not convince you'; an adversative would be expected here instead; τὸ σῶφρον, neut. adj. with an artic., can denote an abstract noun: S #1023.)

ἴσως (adv.)   probably, perhaps (τῷ = τίνι, interrog.) – 'you need then to show in what way/how I was corrupted.' [1x *Hipp.*]

πότερα τὸ τῆσδε σῶμ᾽ ἐκαλλιστεύετο
πασῶν γυναικῶν; ἢ σὸν οἰκήσειν δόμον   1010
ἔγκληρον εὐνὴν προσλαβὼν ἐπήλπισα;
μάταιος ἄρ᾽ ἦν, οὐδαμοῦ μὲν οὖν φρενῶν.
ἀλλ᾽ ὡς τυραννεῖν ἡδύ; τοῖσι σώφροσιν
ἥκιστά γ᾽ †εἰ μή† τὰς φρένας διέφθορεν
θνητῶν ὅσοισιν ἁνδάνει μοναρχία.   1015
ἐγὼ δ᾽ ἀγῶνας μὲν κρατεῖν Ἑλληνικοὺς
πρῶτος θέλοιμ᾽ ἄν, ἐν πόλει δὲ δεύτερος
σὺν τοῖς ἀρίστοις εὐτυχεῖν ἀεὶ φίλοις·
πράσσειν τε γὰρ πάρεστι, κίνδυνός τ᾽ ἀπὼν
κρείσσω δίδωσι τῆς τυραννίδος χάριν.   1020
ἐν οὐ λέλεκται τῶν ἐμῶν, τὰ δ᾽ ἄλλ᾽ ἔχεις·
εἰ μὲν γὰρ ἦν μοι μάρτυς οἷός εἰμ᾽ ἐγὼ
καὶ τῆσδ᾽ ὁρώσης φέγγος ἠγωνιζόμην,
ἔργοις ἂν εἶδες τοὺς κακοὺς διεξιών·
νῦν δ᾽ ὅρκιόν σοι Ζῆνα καὶ πέδον χθονὸς   1025
ὄμνυμι τῶν σῶν μήποθ᾽ ἅψασθαι γάμων
μηδ᾽ ἂν θελῆσαι μηδ᾽ ἂν ἔννοιαν λαβεῖν.

1009–10 καλλιστεύω   be the most beautiful (πότερα, resolution in 2nd position; πασῶν γυναικῶν, partit. gen.) [1x *Hipp.*]

ἔγ-κληρος, ον   having a lot or share in an inheritance (B.: "In Attic law a widow was never ἐπίκληρος; a man's property went to his legitimate children . . . and failing these to other blood relations. But in the heroic world marriage with a royal widow may well be a step to her husband's position [Aigisthos, Oedipus].") [1x *Hipp.*]

προσ-*⁺λαμβάνω   take hold of (προσλαβών, aor.² act. ptc. of manner: see on στένω in line 38; here describes the subj. of ἐπήλπισα) [1x *Hipp.*]

ἐπ-ελπίζω   bring to hope; hope; – 'Did her body excel in beauty above all women? Or had I the expectation of dwelling in your house by means of grabbing onto the bed of your heiress?' [1x Eur.]

1012 οὐδαμοῦ (adv.)   + gen.: nowhere; – 'Then I was a fool, (nowhere in my mind =) out of my mind.' [1x *Hipp.*]

1013–15 τυραννέω   rule [1x *Hipp.*]

ἥκιστα (adv.)   not at all (The text at the beginning of line 1014 is troubled. For an argument to remove lines 1012–15 altogether on the basis of their meaning, see B. on 1014–15.)

ἀνδάνω   please, delight [1x *Hipp.*]

μοναρχία, ἡ   rule, sovereignty; – 'But [would you say] that to rule is sweet? To those who are sensible, not at all, unless sovereignty has destroyed the minds of the mortals whom it pleases.'

1016–18 ἀγών, ῶνος, ὁ   contest, competition, struggle (ἀγῶνας, internal acc. with κρατεῖν, 'to win contests'; see θροέω in line 571) (496)

Ἑλληνικός (3)   Greek, Hellenic (θέλοιμ' ἄν, potential opt.; see ἄν . . . δέξαιο in line 89)

εὐτυχέω   be lucky, prosper; – 'I would like, on the one hand, to be first in winning contests in the Hellenic games; in the city, on the other hand, to be second and to always prosper with my noble friends.' (981)

1019–20 κίνδυνος, ὁ   danger (*⁺πράσσειν, here 'exercise political power'; ἀπών < ⁺ἄπειμι, pres. act. descriptive ptc., see ὁράω in line 4, coincidental with δίδωσι; ⁺κρείσσω = κρείσσονα; κρείσσω . . . χάριν, *hyperbaton*; τυραννίδος, gen. of comparison: S #1431) – 'For it is possible to exercise political power, and the absence of danger gives greater pleasure than rule.' [1x *Hipp.*]

1022–4 εἰ ἦν ... ἂν εἶδες (contrary-to-fact condition: S #2303; μοι, dat. of possess.: S #1476)

ἀγωνίζομαι   plead my case (lawcourts' technical term; τῆσδ' ὁρώσης, gen. abs.) [1x *Hipp.*]

δι-έξειμι   (δία, ἐξεῖμι) go out through, pass through; – 'Indeed, if I had a witness as to what sort of man I am and if I were debating while this woman still looked at the light, you would have seen who the culprits are, by going through the facts.' [1x Eur.]

1025–7 ὅρκιος (3/2)   of oaths [1x *Hipp.*]

πέδον, τό   plain, ground [1x *Hipp.*]

ἔννοια, ἡ   thought, intent (μηδ' ἂν θελῆσαι, μηδ᾽ἂν λαβεῖν, infs. in indir. disc. after ὄμνυμι, standing for finite verbs with ἂν reflecting unreality) – 'I never touched your marriage, never would have wished to, never would have had the thought.' [1x *Hipp.*]

> ἦ τἄρ' ὀλοίμην ἀκλεὴς ἀνώνυμος
> [ἄπολις ἄοικος, φυγὰς ἀλητεύων χθόνα,]
> καὶ μήτε πόντος μήτε γῆ δέξαιτό μου   1030
> σάρκας θανόντος, εἰ κακὸς πέφυκ'ἀνήρ.
> τί δ' ἥδε δειμαίνουσ᾽ ἀπώλεσεν βίον
> οὐκ οἶδ', ἐμοὶ γὰρ οὐ θέμις πέρα λέγειν.
> ἐσωφρόνησε δ' οὐκ ἔχουσα σωφρονεῖν,
> ἡμεῖς δ' ἔχοντες οὐ καλῶς ἐχρώμεθα.   1035
> Χο.   ἀρκοῦσαν εἶπας αἰτίας ἀποστροφὴν
>   ὅρκους παρασχών, πίστιν οὐ σμικράν, θεῶν.

1028–31 ἀ-κλεής, ές   without fame, inglorious, ignoble (τἄρ'= τοι ἄρα; *+ὀλοίμην, +δέξαιτο, opt. of wish: S #1814; GMT #721.I, 722, serves as apodosis to a simple protasis in indic.: +πέφυκα; resolution in 2nd and 6th positions, ἄπολις, φυγάς) [1x *Hipp.*]

Line 1029 is usually excised on various grounds—e.g., that it is anticlimactic after 1028, that it is a partial doublet of 1048, or that it is an intrusion into Hippolytus' self-curse—but in fact the line is very much in place after

1028, simply underscoring it. See Willink 1968, 34–6, who defends 1029 but suggests excising 1047–9.

ἄ-πολις, ιδος/εως   without a city [1x *Hipp.*]

ἄ-οικος, ον   homeless, without a home [1x Eur.]

ἀλητεύω   be a wanderer (1048)

⁺σάρξ, σαρκός, ἡ   flesh (**⁺θανόντος, gen. abs.) – 'and may earth not accept my body when I die'

1032 δειμαίνω   (used only in pres. and impf.) + acc.: fear a thing (δειμαίνουσα, ptc. of attendant circumstance/descriptive, see ὁράω in line 4)

1033 πέρᾱ (adv.)   beyond, further (improper prep.; see ἔσω in line 2) – 'What she feared that caused her to lose her life I don't know, for it is not right for me to say more.'

1034–5 ⁺ἐσωφρόνησε ... ⁺σωφρονεῖν emphatic wordplay on grammatical aspect; cf. lines 243–5 (ἔχουσα, pres. ptc., circumstantial concessive ptc.: see νοσοῦσα in line 477; **⁺ἔχοντες [σωφρονεῖν], circumstantial concessive pf. dep. ptc.; *majestic plural*) – 'She acted virtuously, even though she was unable to be virtuous, and I, in spite of having virtue, did not use [it] well.'

1036–7 *ἀρκέω   be strong enough (524)

αἰτία, ἡ   charge, accusation (961)

ἀποστροφή, ἡ   turning back, rebuttal [1x *Hipp.*]

⁺πίστις, εως, ἡ   assurance (⁺παρασχών, ptc. coincidental with εἶπας; see λύσασα in line 290) – 'you have spoken a sufficient rebuttal of the charge, providing oaths to the gods, not a small assurance.'

Θη.   ἆρ᾽ οὐκ ἐπῳδὸς καὶ γόης πέφυχ᾽ ὅδε,
    ὃς τὴν ἐμὴν πέποιθεν εὐοργησίᾳ
    ψυχὴν κρατήσειν, τὸν τεκόντ᾽ ἀτιμάσας;   1040
Ιπ.   καὶ σοῦ γε κάρτα ταῦτα θαυμάζω, πάτερ·
    εἰ γὰρ σὺ μὲν παῖς ἦσθ᾽, ἐγὼ δὲ σὸς πατήρ,
    ἔκτεινά τοί σ᾽ ἂν κοὐ φυγαῖς ἐζημίουν,
    εἴπερ γυναικὸς ἠξίους ἐμῆς θιγεῖν.

Θη.   ὡς ἄξιον τόδ᾽ εἶπας· οὐχ οὕτω θανῇ·   1045
       [ὥσπερ σὺ σαυτῷ τόνδε προύθηκας νόμον·]
       ταχὺς γὰρ Ἅιδης ῥᾷστος ἀνδρὶ δυστυχεῖ·
       ἀλλ᾽ ἐκ πατρῴας φυγὰς ἀλητεύων χθονὸς
       ξένην ἐπ᾽ αἶαν λυπρὸν ἀντλήσεις βίον.
       [μισθὸς γὰρ οὗτός ἐστιν ἀνδρὶ δυσσεβεῖ.]   1050
Ἱπ.   οἴμοι, τί δράσεις; οὐδὲ μηνυτὴν χρόνον
       δέξῃ καθ᾽ ἡμῶν, ἀλλά μ᾽ ἐξελᾷς χθονός;

1038–40 ἐπῳδός, ὁ/ἡ   enchanter [1x *Hipp.*]

   γοής, ητος, ὁ   wizard, sorcerer, cheat [1x *Hipp.*]

   εὐοργησία, ἡ   gentleness, mildness of temper (τὸν τέκοντα <
⁺τίκτω, aor.² act. artic. ptc.) – 'Isn't this one an enchanter and a sorcerer by nature, who is confident that by his mild manner he will win
over my spirit, even though he dishonored the one who begot him?'
[1x *Hipp.*]

1041–4 θαυμάζω   wonder, marvel at X (gen.) for Y (acc.) – 'I too
marvel very much at the same in you, father.' [1x *Hipp.*]

   ζημιόω   punish [1x *Hipp.*]

   ἀξιόω   deem   worthy   (εἰ . . . ἦσθα . . . ἔκτεινα
ἄν . . . εἴπερ . . . ἠξίους, contrary-to-fact conditions, the first one for
the past, the second for the present) – 'For if you were my son, and I
your father, I would have surely killed you and would not punish you
with exile if you dared to touch my wife' (792)

1045 ἄξιον   – 'worthy (of you)'

[1046]   There is no good reason to delete this line: it explains what is to
come. B. and Diggle keep it. – 'according to this rule [in line 1043] you
have just set for yourself.'

1047 ῥᾷστος (3)   (irreg. superl. of ⁺ῥᾴδιος) most easy (638)

1049 λῡπρός (3)   wretched (898)

   ἀντλέω   exhaust, drain (the line is identical to 898 except for the verb's pers.) (898)

[1050] μισθός, ὁ   wages [1x *Hipp.*]

δυσσεβής, ές   ungodly, impious (The scholiast reports that many manuscripts are without this line. B. and Diggle see it as spurious, but in fact it provides a nice gnomic conclusion for this short speech.) [1x *Hipp.*]

1051 μηνῡτής, οῦ, ὁ   (masc. adj.) bringing to light (μηνυτὴν χρόνον, 'Time as witness.' Personification of 'Time' as in lines 430 and 1322.) [1x *Hipp.*]

1052 ἐξ-*ελαύνω   drive out, banish (893)

Θη.   πέραν γε Πόντου καὶ τόπων Ἀτλαντικῶν,
      εἴ πως δυναίμην, ὡς σὸν ἐχθαίρω κάρα.
Ιπ.   οὐδ' ὅρκον οὐδὲ πίστιν οὐδὲ μάντεων   1055
      φήμας ἐλέγξας ἄκριτον ἐκβαλεῖς με γῆς;
Θη.   ἡ δέλτος ἥδε κλῆρον οὐ δεδεγμένη
      κατηγορεῖ σου πιστά· τοὺς δ'ὑπὲρ κάρα
      φοιτῶντας ὄρνις πόλλ' ἐγὼ χαίρειν λέγω.
Ιπ.   ὦ θεοί, τί δῆτα τοὐμὸν οὐ λύω στόμα,   1060
      ὅστις γ' ὑφ' ὑμῶν, οὓς σέβω, διόλλυμαι;
      οὐ δῆτα· πάντως οὐ πίθοιμ' ἂν οὕς με δεῖ,
      μάτην δ' ἂν ὅρκους συγχέαιμ' οὓς ὤμοσα.
Θη.   οἴμοι, τὸ σεμνὸν ὥς μ' ἀποκτεινεῖ τὸ σόν.
      οὐκ εἶ πατρῴας ἐκτὸς ὡς τάχιστα γῆς;   1065
Ιπ.   ποῖ δῆθ' ὁ τλήμων τρέψομαι; τίνος ξένων
      δόμους ἔσειμι, τῇδ' ἐπ' αἰτίᾳ φυγών;
Θη.   ὅστις γυναικῶν λυμεῶνας ἥδεται
      ξένους κομίζων καὶ ξυνοικούρους κακῶν.

1053–4 πέρᾱν   + gen.: on the other side of, across (improper prep.; see ἔσω in line 2) (678)

Ἀτλαντικός (3)   of Atlas; the boundaries of Atlas are located by the Straits of Gibraltar, the traditional western limit of the known world. (3)

ἐχθαίρω   hate, detest, loathe; – 'Yes, across the Euxine Sea and the places of Atlas, if somehow I could, so much do I loathe you.' [1x *Hipp.*]

1056 ἄ-κρῐτος, ον   (ἀ privat., κρίνω) unjudged, without a trial (ἄκρῐτος, resolution in 6th position)

ἐκ-*⁺βάλλω   throw out, cast out; – 'Having not even examined . . . you will throw' [1x *Hipp.*]

1057–9 κλῆρος, ὁ   lot, divination by lot (Seers practice divination by lot and also by observation of the behavior of birds; δεδεγμένη < *⁺δέχομαι, concessive pf. dep. ptc.; see νοσοῦσα in line 477.) [1x *Hipp.*]

κατ-ηγορέω   + gen.: speak against, accuse (⁺πιστά, adv. acc.; see μηδέν in line 46) – 'This tablet, although it contains no divination by lot, accuses you reliably' [1x *Hipp.*]

⁺ὄρνις   birds (= ὄρνιθας, acc. pl.; see πολλὰ χαίρειν λέγω in line 113. Cf. line 113 for the dismissive tone. Does Euripides intend to draw similarities between father and son?) – 'and as to the birds who fly above my head, I say a fond goodbye.'

1060–1 θεοί   (-εοι is pronounced as one syllable by *synizesis*)

ὅστις γε   (causal; ὅστις . . . διόλλυμαι, *hyperbaton*) – 'Oh gods! Why then do I not open my mouth, since I am being destroyed by you, whom I reverence?'

1062–3 πάντως (adv.)   in any case, wholly, altogether (*⁺πίθοιμ' ἄν, potential opt. with ἄν: S #1824) [1x *Hipp.*]

συγ-χέω   confound, make of no effect (ἄν . . . συγχέαιμι, πίθοιμ' ἄν, potential opt. with ἄν: S #1824) – 'No, I will not; in any case, I would not persuade those whom I must, and I would violate the oaths that I swore in vain.' (813)

1064–5 τὸ σεμνὸν . . . τὸ σόν   (subst. use of artic. with adj.; see νέους in line 114)

⁺πατρῷος (3)   of a father

ἐκτός   + gen.: out of (improper prep.; see ἔσω in line 2; εἶ < εἶμι) – 'Oh my! Your saintliness will be the death of me! Won't you get out of your father's land as quickly as possible?' [1x *Hipp.*]

1066–7 τρέπω   turn (246)

εἴσ-ειμι   go into, go in (φυγών, aor.² act. descriptive
ptc.) – 'exiled on this charge.' (861)

1068–9 λῦμεών, ῶνος, ὁ a destroyer, spoiler [1x *Hipp*.]

*⁺ἥδομαι   + dat.: enjoy oneself, take pleasure in, be
pleased (κομίζων, supplem. ptc. with verb of emotion: S #2100)
(1260)

συν-οίκουρος, ον   keeping house together; metaph. συν-οικουρός
κακῶν, 'a partner in mischief' (note the *consonance* of ξ, κ, and ζ)
– 'Whoever enjoys keeping company with guests who are defilers of
their wives and partners in wickedness.' [1x *Hipp*.]

Ἱπ.	αἰαῖ, πρὸς ἧπαρ· δακρύων ἐγγὺς τόδε,	1070
	εἰ δὴ κακός γε φαίνομαι δοκῶ τε σοί.	
Θη.	τότε στενάζειν καὶ προγιγνώσκειν σ' ἐχρῆν	
	ὅτ' ἐς πατρῷαν ἄλοχον ὑβρίζειν ἔτλης.	
Ἱπ.	ὦ δώματ', εἴθε φθέγμα γηρύσαισθέ μοι	
	καὶ μαρτυρήσαιτ' εἰ κακὸς πέφυκ' ἀνήρ.	1075
Θη.	ἐς τοὺς ἀφώνους μάρτυρας φεύγεις σοφῶς·	
	τὸ δ' ἔργον, οὐ λέγον, σε μηνύει κακόν.	
Ἱπ.	φεῦ·	
	εἴθ' ἦν ἐμαυτὸν προσβλέπειν ἐναντίον	
	στάνθ', ὡς ἐδάκρυσ' οἷα πάσχομεν κακά.	
Θη.	πολλῷ γε μᾶλλον σαυτὸν ἤσκησας σέβειν	1080
	ἢ τοὺς τεκόντας ὅσια δρᾶν δίκαιος ὤν.	
Ἱπ.	ὦ δυστάλαινα μῆτερ, ὦ πικραὶ γοναί·	
	μηδείς ποτ' εἴη τῶν ἐμῶν φίλων νόθος.	
Θη.	οὐχ ἕλξετ' αὐτόν, δμῶες; οὐκ ἀκούετε	
	πάλαι ξενοῦσθαι τόνδε προυννέποντά με;	1085

1070 ἧπαρ, ἄτος, τό   liver (seat of the passions, especially anger and
love) – 'Ah! To the heart!' [1x *Hipp*.]

ἐγγύς   + gen.: near (improper prep.; see ἔσω in line 2)

1072–3 τότε (adv.)   then, at that time (302)

στενάζω   groan, moan, wail (The argument makes little
sense. Why should Hippolytus have wailed in the past, when allegedly
he was attacking Phaedra?) [1x *Hipp*.]

προ-γιγνώσκω   realize (ἐχρῆν, B.: "the original impf. of χρή was χρῆν; in the 5th cent, it began to acquire an augment, ἐχρῆν") [1x Eur.]

ὑβρίζω   treat despitefully, commit outrage, assault (ὅτ'= ὅτε; ὅτι never elides) (474)

*‡τλάω   take upon oneself; + inf.: dare (885)

1074–5 γηρύω   utter, speak, say (*adynaton*) (213)

μαρτὕρέω   be a witness (γηρύσαισθε, μαρτυρήσαιτε, opt. of wish: see κάμπτω in line 87) (977)

1076–7 ἄ-φωνος, ον   (ἀ privat., φωνή) voiceless, speechless (σοφῶς, Theseus keeps harping on Hippolytus' alleged sophistic rhetoric; cf. 1038, 1045, 1064) [1x *Hipp.*]

*μηνύω   inform, reveal, make known, disclose (οὐ λέγον, concessive ptc.: see νοσοῦσα in line 477) – 'Cleverly you flee to voiceless witnesses, but the deed, although mute, reveals you as evil.'

1078–9 προσ-βλέπω   look at, look upon (εἴθ' ἦν, 'if only it were possible to stand opposite and look upon myself') [1x *Hipp.*]

ἐναντίος (3)   against, opposite (see στάντα < *⁺ἵστημι, descriptive ptc., coincidental with ἦν, see ὁράω in line 4; *enjambment*) (947)

δακρύω   weep (ὡς [= ἵνα] ἐδάκρυσα, aor. or impf. indic. is used in final clauses with ἵνα when the action of the leading clause is unfulfilled, whether past or pres., here expressed by εἴθ' ἦν: GMT #333–6; S #2185c. The unreality is not always shown in translation.) – 'so that I could cry over what I suffer.' [1x *Hipp.*]

1080–1 ἀσκέω   + inf.: make a practice of (τεκόντας, generalizing pl.; see ἐχθρός in line 49. He is of course thinking only of himself, not Hippolytē, but rhetorically the objectivity gained by the artificial generalization strengthens his statement; resolution in 6th position: ὅσια.) – 'Far more you've practiced worshiping yourself, rather than being righteous and acting piously toward your parents.' [1x *Hipp.*]

1082–3 γονή, ἡ   birth [1x *Hipp.*]

1084–5 ⁺ἕλκω   drag

ㅤ⁺δμώς, ωός, ὁ   slave

ㅤξενόω   pass.: go into exile [1x *Hipp.*]

ㅤπρο-εννέπω   proclaim (προυννέποντά με, supplem. ptc. in
indir. disc. after ἀκούετε: S #2112b) – 'Will you not drag him away,
servants? Have you not heard me long since proclaiming that this one
is an exile?' [1x *Hipp.*]

Ιπ.ㅤㅤㅤ κλαίων τις αὐτῶν ἆρ' ἐμοῦ γε θίξεται·
ㅤㅤㅤㅤσὺ δ' αὐτός, εἴ σοι θυμός, ἐξώθει χθονός.
Θη.ㅤㅤㅤ δράσω τάδ', εἰ μὴ τοῖς ἐμοῖς πείσῃ λόγοις·
ㅤㅤㅤㅤοὐ γάρ τις οἶκτος σῆς μ' ὑπέρχεται φυγῆς.
Ιπ.ㅤㅤㅤ ἄραρεν, ὡς ἔοικεν· ὦ τάλας ἐγώ,   1090
ㅤㅤㅤㅤὡς οἶδα μὲν ταῦτ', οἶδα δ' οὐχ ὅπως φράσω.
ㅤㅤㅤㅤὦ φιλτάτη μοι δαιμόνων Λητοῦς κόρη,
ㅤㅤㅤㅤσύνθακε, συγκύναγε, φευξούμεσθα δὴ
ㅤㅤㅤㅤκλεινὰς Ἀθήνας. ἀλλὰ χαιρέτω πόλις
ㅤㅤㅤㅤκαὶ γαῖ' Ἐρεχθέως· ὦ πέδον Τροζήνιον,   1095
ㅤㅤㅤㅤὡς ἐγκαθηβᾶν πόλλ' ἔχεις εὐδαίμονα,
ㅤㅤㅤㅤχαῖρ'· ὕστατον γάρ σ' εἰσορῶν προσφθέγγομαι.
ㅤㅤㅤㅤἴτ', ὦ νέοι μοι τῆσδε γῆς ὁμήλικες,
ㅤㅤㅤㅤπροσείπαθ' ἡμᾶς καὶ προπέμψατε χθονός·
ㅤㅤㅤㅤὡς οὔποτ' ἄλλον ἄνδρα σωφρονέστερον   1100
ㅤㅤㅤㅤὄψεσθε, κεἰ μὴ ταῦτ' ἐμῷ δοκεῖ πατρί.

1086–7 κλαίω   cry, weep, lament (1175)

ㅤθυμός, ὁ   soul, heart, desire [1x *Hipp.*]

ㅤἐξ-ωθέω   thrust out; – 'Any of them that will touch me
will lament [it], but you yourself, if you have the heart to, thrust me out
of the land.' [1x *Hipp.*]

1088–9 οἶκτος, ὁ   expression of pity or grief, weeping (740)

ㅤὑπ-*⁺έρχομαι   go into secretly; come upon (φυγῆς, obj. gen.
with οἶκτος; see δαιμόνων in line 107) – 'I will do this, if you do not
obey my words; for no pity for your exile comes upon me.' (992)

1090–1   *ἀραρίσκω   fasten, fit [1x *Hipp.*]

φράζω   tell; – 'It is settled, as it seems. Oh wretched
me, since [ὡς] I know these things [i.e., the truth], but I don't know
how to tell [it].' [1x *Hipp.*]

1093–4 σύν-θᾱκος, ον   sitting with or together (συνθᾱκε, voc.; *consonance* of the sound -s- in line 1093, and *assonance* of α in line 1094)
[1x *Hipp.*]

συγ-κυνᾱγός, ὁ, ἡ [ῠ]   fellow hunter, fellow huntress (συγκύναγε,
voc.; the *asyndeton* renders his address emphatic; emphatic δή is used
mostly in tragedy; GP 214 [8]: "The emphasis conveyed by δή with
verbs is for the most part pathetic in tone . . . in the great crises of
drama, above all at moments when death or ruin is present or imminent." B.: "The son of the Athenian king must in Attic tragedy think of
himself primarily as an Athenian.") [1x *Hipp.*]

1096–7 ἐγ-καθηβάω   to pass one's youth in (ὡς exclamatory with
πολλά; ἐγκαθηβᾶν, final-consecutive inf.: GMT #770; S #2008) – 'how
many blessings you hold [for those who] pass their youth in you.' [1x *Eur.*]

ὕστατος (3)   last (see ὕστατον, adv. acc., in line 46)
[1x *Hipp.*]

προσ-φθέγγομαι   address; – 'farewell, for I address you, looking
at you for the last time.' [1x *Hipp.*]

1098–1101 ὁμῆλιξ, ικος, ὁ, ἡ   of the same age; as subst.: comrade
[1x *Hipp.*]

προς-εῖπον   speak to, address [farewell to] (προσείπαθ'=
προσείπατε) [1x *Hipp.*]

προ-πέμπω   send forth; – 'Come, oh my young age-mates
of this land, say farewell to me and send me forth from the land, for
you will never see another man more virtuous, even if it does not seem
so to my father.' [1x *Hipp.*]

Hippolytus and his comrades exit by the *eisodos* opposite the one by which
they entered. Theseus exits into the palace.

Third Stasimon Lines 1102–50

This last full stasimon of the play, just before the heartbreaking account of Hippolytus' wreck, provides an emotional commentary on Hippolytus' lot. As usual, the first two stanzas provide a general principle: human condition has no stability; we can only pray for a flexible life without distress where things are ephemeral. The second two stanzas give Hippolytus' misfortune as an example for this principle.

Χο.	ἦ μέγα μοι τὰ θεῶν μελεδήμαθ', ὅταν φρένας ἔλθῃ,	[στρ. α	Indeed, the concern of gods, whenever it comes to my mind, greatly relieves my distress;
	λύπας παραιρεῖ· ξύνεσιν δέ τις ἐλπίδι κεύθων λείπεται ἔν τε τύχαις θνατῶν καὶ ἐν ἔργμασι λεύσσων·	1105	but anyone shrouding his understanding in hope is left abandoned when looking amid the fortunes and the deeds of mortals;
	ἄλλα γὰρ ἄλλοθεν ἀμείβεται, μετὰ δ' ἵσταται ἀνδράσιν αἰὼν		for things come and go from one direction and another, men's life is shift- ing, ever
	πολυπλάνητος αἰεί.	1110	roaming.
	εἴθε μοι εὐξαμένᾳ θεόθεν τάδε μοῖρα παράσχοι, τύχαν μετ' ὄλβου καὶ ἀκήρατον ἄλγεσι θυμόν· δόξα δὲ μήτ' ἀτρεκὴς μήτ' αὖ παράσημος ἐνείη, ῥᾴδια δ' ἤθεα τὸν αὔριον μεταβαλλομένα χρόνον αἰεὶ	[ἀντ. α 1115	If only, in answer to my prayer, destiny would give me these things from the gods: fortune, prosperity, and a heart untouched by pain; and may the thought within me be neither rigid nor counterfeit,
	βίον συνευτυχοίην.		but changing my easy customs every morning, may I always share in a life of good fortune.

1102 s. = 1111 s.	– ⌣⌣ – ⌣⌣ – ⌣⌣ – ⌣⌣ – ⌣⌣ – –	5 dactyls + 1 spondee (dactylic hexameter)
1104 s. = 1113 s.	⏓ – ⌣ – – ⌣⌣ – ⌣⌣ – ⌣⌣ – –	2 iambs + 3 dactyls + 1 spondee
1106 s. = 1115 s.	– ⌣⌣ – ⌣⌣ – – – ⌣⌣ – ⌣⌣ – –	5 dactyls + 1 spondee (dactylic hexameter)
1108 s. = 1117 s.	– ⌣⌣ – ⌣⌣| ⌣ – ⌣ – ⌣⌣ – ⌣⌣ – ⌣⌣ – –	2 dactyls | iamb + paroemion
1110 = 1119	⌣ – ⌣ – ⌣ – – |||	2 iambs catalectic

1102 μελέδημα ατος, τό   care, anxiety, concern [1x Eur.]

μέγα   adv. with παραιρεῖ (θεῶν, subj. gen.; see ὅταν ἔλθῃ in line 544) [1x *Hipp.*]

1105–7 παρ-αιρέω   take away from, lessen (λύπας = λύπης, partit. gen.) (1316)

σύνεσις, Attic: ξύνεσις, εως, ἡ   (συν-ίημι) joining together; understanding, judgment, intelligence [1x *Hipp.*]

κεύθω   hide, shroud (κεύθων, λεύσσων, circumstantial ptcs. of time or condition) [1x *Hipp.*]

1108–10 ἄλλοθεν (adv.)   from another place (ἄλλα . . . ἄλλοθεν, *figura etymologica*, 'some from one place, others from another') [1x *Hipp.*]

ἀμείβομαι   mutually exchange places; come and go; answer, reply; converse with (85)

μεθ-*⁺ίστημι   change, shift, withdraw (μετὰ . . . ἵσταται, *tmesis*)

αἰών, ῶνος, ὁ   lifetime, life (1426)

πολυ-πλάνητος, ον   (πολύς, πλάνάομαι, wander) oft-wandering [1x *Hipp.*]

1111–14 *⁺εὔχομαι   (εὐξαμένᾳ = εὐξαμένῃ, ptc. of attendant circumstance/descriptive, see ὁράω in line 4; εἴθε . . . παράσχοι, opt. of wish, see line 87; *hyperbaton*) (1455)

ὄλβος, ὁ   wealth (626)

1115–19 ἀτρεκής, ές   real, true, exact, rigid

παρά-σημος, ον   (παρά, σῆμα) falsely stamped, counterfeit
[1x *Hipp.*]

ἦθος, εος, τό   custom, habit (1219)

αὔριον (adv.)   tomorrow [1x *Hipp.*]

μετα-*βάλλομαι   change [1x *Hipp.*]

συν-ευτὕχέω   be fortunate along with *or* together ([εἴθε] . . .
συνευτυχοίην, opt. of wish, see line 87; *hyperbaton*) [1x *Hipp.*]

After Hippolytus and his friends exit by the parodos and Theseus enters the
palace, the Chorus continue their third stasimon.

οὐκέτι γὰρ καθαρὰν φρέν' ἔχω,	[στρ. β 1120	For I don't have a clear
παρὰ δ' ἐλπίδ' ἃ λεύσσω·		mind anymore
		beyond all hope are the things
ἐπεὶ τὸν Ἑλλανίας φανερώτατον	1123	that I see; because we saw,
ἀστέρ' †ἀθήνας†		we saw
εἴδομεν εἴδομεν ἐκ πατρὸς ὀργᾶς		the brightest star of Greek †Athena†
ἄλλαν ἐπ' αἶαν ἱέμενον.	1125	rushing to another land as a result of
ὦ ψάμαθοι πολιήτιδος ἀκτᾶς,		his father's anger. Oh sands of the
ὦ δρυμὸς ὄρεος ὅθι κυνῶν		city's shore, Oh mountain thicket,
ὠκυπόδων [ἐπέβας θεᾶς] μέτα		where with his swift-footed hounds
θῆρας ἔναιρεν		
Δίκτυνναν ἀμφὶ σεμνάν.	1130	he used to kill beasts in the company of holy Diktynna.
οὐκέτι συζυγίαν πώλων Ἐνετᾶν	[ἀντ. β	No longer will you mount a yoked
ἐπιβάσῃ		team of Enetian fillies,
τὸν ἀμφὶ Λίμνας τρόχον κατέχων		holding the
ποδὶ γυμνάδος ἵππου·		track around this lagoon with the

μοῦσα δ᾽ ἄυπνος ὑπ᾽ ἄντυγι χορδᾶν	1135	trained horse's foot; and the music
λήξει πατρῷον ἀνὰ δόμον·		sleepless beneath the strings' frame will
ἀστέφανοι δὲ κόρας ἀνάπαυλαι		cease in your father's house;
Λατοῦς βαθεῖαν ἀνὰ χλόαν·		ungarlanded the spots where Leto's
νυμφιδία δ᾽ ἀπόλωλε φυγᾷ σᾷ	1140	daughter rests in the deep greenery; the
λέκτρων ἄμιλλα κούραις.		contest for your bridal bed is to the maidens because of your exile.

1120 s. = 1131 s.	– ⌣⌣ – ⌣⌣ – – ‿‿ – ⌣⌣ – –	6 dactyls
1122 s. = 1133 s.	⌣ – ⌣ – ⌣ –⌣ – | ⌣⌣ – ⌣⌣ – ⌣⌣	iamb, creticus,
	– –	paroemion
1124 = 1135	– ⌣⌣ – ⌣⌣ – ⌣⌣ – –	4 dactyls
1125 = 1136	– – ⌣ – ⌣ ⌣⌣ ⌣ ⌣ ||	2 iambs
1126 = 1137	– ⌣⌣ – ⌣⌣ – ⌣⌣ – –	4 dactyls
1127 = 1138	– – ⌣ ‿‿ ⌣ ⌣⌣ ⌣ –	2 iambs
1128 = 1140	– ⌣⌣ – ⌣⌣ – ⌣⌣ – –	4 dactyls
1130 = 1141	– – ⌣ – ⌣ – –	2 iambs catalectic

1120 κᾰθᾰρός (3)   clear, pure (209)

1123 Ἑλλήνιος (3)   Greek (Ἑλλανίας = Ἑλλανίης; Ἑλλα-νίας . . . †ἀθήνας†, *hyperbaton*; †ἀθήνας†, possibly corrupt. Athena does not appear at all in the play.) [1x *Hipp.*]

φανερός (3)   visible (1289)

ἀστήρ, έρος, ὁ   star [1x *Hipp.*]

†ἀθήνας†   corrupt "Greek Athena"

1124–5 ⁺ἐκ (prep.)   from; here with the sense of 'resulting from' (πατρός, subj. gen.; εἴδομεν, εἴδομεν, emphatic emotional repetition)

**⁺ἵημι   send forth, throw (ἱέμενον, mid. pres. ptc. of attendant circumstance/descriptive, coincidental with the finite verb εἴδομεν; see ὁράω in line 4) (533)

1126–30 ψάμᾰθος, ἡ   sandy shore, the sands (234)

[πολιῆτις,] ιδος, ἡ   LSJ: adj., of the city, < πολιήτης, εω, ὁ, variant of πολίτης: citizen [1x Eur.]

δρῦμός, ὁ   thicket [1x *Hipp.*]

ὠκύ-πους, ὁ, ἡ, -πουν τό, ποδος   swift-footed

[ἐπι-βαίνω]   + gen.: set foot on (ἐπέβας θεᾶς, corrupt addition)

*ἐναίρω   slay, kill (unaugmented in impf.) [1x *Hipp.*]

Δίκτῡνα/Δίκτυννα, ἡ   Diktynna, Cretan divinity of wildwood, identified with Artemis (145)

1131–4 συζύγιος, [ῠ] (3)   yoked together, joined, united [1x *Hipp.*]

Ἐνετός (3)   Venetian (Ἐνετᾶν, Doric fem. gen. pl. The Venetians lived near the Adriatic Sea and were famed for their horses.) (231)

τρόχος, ὁ   racecourse [1x *Hipp.*]

κατ-*+έχω   restrain, tread; occupy, hold [1x *Hipp.*]

γυμνάς, άδος   (fem. form of γυμνός: LSJ) (3) naked, trained, exercised

1135–6 Μοῦσα, ἡ   Muse, goddess of song, music, poetry, dancing, and the fine arts; pl.: arts (452)

ἄ-υπνος, ον   (ἀ privat., ὕπνος) sleepless [1x *Hipp.*]

+ἄντυξ, ῡγος, ἡ   rim of a chariot front (here the frame of a lyre)

χορδή, ἡ   string of a lyre (χορδᾶν = χορδῶν, Doric fem. pl.) [1x *Hipp.*]

1138–9 ἀ-στέφᾰνος, ον   (ἀ privat., στέφᾰνος) ungarlanded [1x *Hipp.*]

ἀνάπαυλα, ης, ἡ   rest, repose [1x *Hipp.*]

βαθύς, βαθεῖα, βαθύ   deep [1x *Hipp.*]

χλόη, ἡ   greenery [1x *Hipp.*]

1140–1 νυμφίδιος (3)   (νύμφη, marriageable maiden, bride) bridal (769)

ἄμιλλα, ἡ   contest [1x *Hipp.*]

ἐγὼ δὲ σᾷ δυστυχίᾳ	ἐπῳδ.	But because of your ill fortune
δάκρυσιν διοίσω		I will endure with tears
πότμον ἄποτμον· ὦ τάλαινα μᾶτερ,		my ill-fated fate; Oh unhappy mother,
ἔτεκες ἀνόνατα· φεῦ,	1145	you gave birth in vain; pheu!
μανίω θεοῖσιν.		I am angry at the gods.
ἰὼ ἰώ·		You yoked Graces, why are
συζύγιαι Χάριτες, τί τὸν τάλαν' ἐκ		you sending this unhappy man, in no way
πατρίας γᾶς		
οὐδὲν ἄτας αἴτιον		guilty of this disaster, out of his
πέμπετε τῶνδ' ἀπ' οἴκων;	1150	fatherland, away from this house?

1142	◡ – ◡ – – ◡◡ –	iamb, choriamb
1143	– ◡ – ◡ – –	ithyphallic
1144	◡◡ ◡ ◡◡| – ◡– ◡– ◡||	creticus, ithyphallic
1145	◡◡ ◡ ◡◡ – ◡ –	creticus + creticus
1146	– ◡ – ◡– ◡ ||	ithyphallic
1147	◡ – ◡ –	iamb
1148	– ◡ ◡ – ◡ ◡ – ◡ – ◡ ◡ – ◡ ◡ – –	hemiepes ◡ hemiepes –
1149	– ◡ – – – ◡ –	lecythus
1150	– ◡ ◡ – – ◡ – –	aristophanean

1142–7 δυστυχία, ἡ   ill luck, ill fortune [1x *Hipp.*]

δια-*⁺φέρω   bear through, endure (πότμον ἄποτμον, *oxymoron*) [1x *Hipp.*]

ἀν-όνητος, ον   (ἀ privat., ὀνίνημι) profitless (acc. neut. pl. as an adv.: 'in vain,' or internal acc.)

μηνίω   be enraged, be angry at, rage at (μᾱνίω = μηνίω). [1x *Hipp.*]

αἴτιος (3)   guilty, blamable (933)

Fourth Episode Lines 1151–1267

The fourth episode contains the speech of one of Hippolytus' companions, who reports Hippolytus' accident, with injuries that soon will prove fatal, and how it was caused by a miraculous bull from the sea. 'Messenger' (ἄγγελος) is the regular designation of any minor character whose sole function is to report events that have happened off stage. Euripides generally commits an entire scene to a messenger's speech, which usually runs for about eighty lines and is preceded by a brief dialogue. The scene often concludes with a dialogue proposing an immediate response to the event.

A companion of Hippolytus enters from a parodos.

– – – καὶ μὴν ὀπαδὸν Ἱππολύτου τόνδ' εἰσορῶ
       σπουδῇ σκυθρωπὸν πρὸς δόμους ὁρμώμενον.

ΑΓΓΕΛΟΣ
          ποῖ γῆς ἄνακτα τῆσδε Θησέα μολὼν
          εὕροιμ' ἄν, ὦ γυναῖκες; εἴπερ ἴστε μοι
          σημήνατ'· ἆρα τῶνδε δωμάτων ἔσω;   1155
Χο.   ὅδ' αὐτὸς ἔξω δωμάτων πορεύεται.
Αγ.   Θησεῦ, μερίμνης ἄξιον φέρω λόγον
          σοὶ καὶ πολίταις οἵ τ' Ἀθηναίων πόλιν
          ναίουσι καὶ γῆς τέρμονας Τροζηνίας.
Θη.   τί δ' ἔστι; μῶν τις συμφορὰ νεωτέρα   1160
          δισσὰς κατείληφ' ἀστυγείτονας πόλεις;
Αγ.   Ἱππόλυτος οὐκέτ' ἔστιν, ὡς εἰπεῖν ἔπος·
          δέδορκε μέντοι φῶς ἐπὶ σμικρᾶς ῥοπῆς.
Θη.   πρὸς τοῦ; δι' ἔχθρας μῶν τις ἦν ἀφιγμένος
          ὅτου κατῄσχυν' ἄλοχον ὡς πατρὸς βίᾳ;   1165

1151 – – –   The dashes mark what the editor thinks is a change of speaker.

ὀπᾱδός, ὁ   attendant (Ἱππόλυτον, resolution in 6th position). [1x *Hipp.*]

1152 σπουδή, ἡ   haste, speed (903)

σκυθρ-ωπός, ον (3)   (σκυθρός, sullen; ὤψ, face) sullen, of a sad countenance [1x *Hipp.*]

ὁρμάω   hasten, rush on (ὁρμώμενον, ptc. of attendant circumstance/descriptive, see ὁράω in line 4; σπουδῇ . . . ὁρμώμενον, *hyperbaton*) (829)

1153–5 ποῖ . . . μολὼν εὕροιμ'ἄν   'where should I go to find' (μολών < *⁺βλώσκω, ptc. of time; εὕροιμ'ἄν < *⁺εὑρίσκω, potential opt. with ἄν; lit.: 'having arrived, how can I find'; σημήνατε, *enjambment*)

1157 μέριμνᾰ, ἡ   concern, care (1429)

1161 κατα-*⁺λαμβάνω   seize upon, lay hold of, befall (δισσὰς . . . πόλεις, *hyperbaton*) [1x *Hipp.*]

1162 ὡς εἰπεῖν ἔπος   so to speak, virtually (*figura etymologica*)

1163 σμῑκρός (3)   μῑκρός (3) small, little [1x *Hipp.*]
ῥοπή, ἡ   inclination; balance, turn of the scales; – 'he
still sees the light, but with a delicate balance'

1164 πρὸς τοῦ   = πρὸς τινός 'by whom' (as if οὐκέτ' ἔστιν
meant that he has been killed)
ἐχθρά, ἡ   hatred, enmity (ἀφιγμένος < *⁺ἀφικνέομαι)
[1x *Hipp.*]

1165 κατ-αισχύνω   shame, disgrace, dishonor (ἄλοχον, resolution
in 6th position) – 'Could it be someone whose wife he disgraced forc-
ibly as he did his father's, arrived into a state of hatred [toward him]?'
[1x *Hipp.*]

Αγ.	οἰκεῖος αὐτὸν ὤλεσ' ἁρμάτων ὄχος
	ἀραί τε τοῦ σοῦ στόματος, ἃς σὺ σῷ πατρὶ
	πόντου κρέοντι παιδὸς ἠράσω πέρι.
Θη.	ὦ θεοὶ Πόσειδόν θ'· ὡς ἄρ' ἦσθ'ἐμὸς πατὴρ
	ὀρθῶς, ἀκούσας τῶν ἐμῶν κατευγμάτων. 1170
	πῶς καὶ διώλετ'; εἰπέ, τῷ τρόπῳ Δίκης
	ἔπαισεν αὐτὸν ῥόπτρον αἰσχύναντά με;
Αγ.	ἡμεῖς μὲν ἀκτῆς κυμοδέγμονος πέλας
	ψήκτραισιν ἵππων ἐκτενίζομεν τρίχας
	κλαίοντες· ἦλθε γάρ τις ἄγγελος λέγων 1175
	ὡς οὐκέτ' ἐν γῇ τῇδ' ἀναστρέψοι πόδα
	Ἱππόλυτος, ἐκ σοῦ τλήμονας φυγὰς ἔχων.
	ὁ δ' ἦλθε ταὐτὸν δακρύων ἔχων μέλος
	ἡμῖν ἐπ' ἀκτάς, μυρία δ' ὀπισθόπους
	φίλων ἅμ' ἔστειχ' ἡλίκων ⟨θ'⟩ ὁμήγυρις. 1180

1166–8 οἰκεῖος (3/2)   belonging to the house, domestic, one's own
[1x *Hipp.*]

⁺ὄχος, εος, ὁ   chariot (ἁρμάτων ὄχος, Hamilton: "chariot of chariots," i.e., "chariot team")

κρέων, οντος   ruler, master [1x *Hipp.*]

ἀράομαι   curse (ἀραί . . . ἠράσω, *figura etymologica*; note the emphasis on Theseus' responsibility through σοῦ, σύ, σῷ, and πατρί, to remind him of his parenthood. The long *hyperbaton* of τοῦ . . . παιδός emphasizes this as well; στόματος, resolution in 6th position; πέρι, *anastrophe*.) [1x *Hipp.*]

1169–70 θεοί   *synizesis* (see note on line 893)

ἄρ(α) (pcl.)   'after all' (GP 35–6: expresses "the surprise attendant upon disillusionment" with a verb in the present or in the past. Here, with the imperfect ἦν, indicates a fact just realized. Did Theseus not believe in his divine paternity after all?)

ὀρθῶς (adv.)   rightly, justly, truly, really (*enjambment*; ἀκούσας, causal ptc. = 'because you have listened . . .') (94)

κάτευγμα, ατος, τό   (κατ-εύχομαι) always pl.; vows, prayers, curses [1x Eur.]

1171–2 πῶς καί   just how . . . ?

παίω   smite [1x *Hipp.*]

ῥόπτρον, τό   club, cudgel (αἰσχύναντά, causal/time ptc.) [1x *Hipp.*]

1173 κῦμο-δέγμων, ον, ονος   (κῦμα, δέχομαι) receiving/meeting the wave [1x Eur.]

1174–7 ψήκτρα, ἡ   scraper, strigil [1x Eur.]

κτενίζω   comb [1x Eur.]

θρίξ, τρῐχός, ἡ   hair [1x *Hipp.*]

κλαίω   cry, weep, lament (κλαίοντες, *enjambment*; ἀναστρέψοι, the fut. opt. reflects the fut. indic. of the reported direct discourse; Ἱππόλυτον, resolution in 2nd position) – 'that Hippolytus no longer will set foot in this land' (1086)

1178–80 μέλος, εος, τό song, strain; – 'and he came to us on the shore with the same strain of tears' (879) μυρίος (3)   numberless, countless (917)

ὀπισθό-πους, ὁ, ἡ, πουν   attendant, following behind

⁺στείχω   come, go, walk

ἧλιξ, ικος, ὁ/ἡ   of the same age (987)

ὀμ-ήγῠρις, ιος, ἡ   (ὁμός, like; ἄγῠρις, gathering) assembly, meeting; throng, gathering; – 'and following behind him came a countless throng of friends [and] age-mates' [1x *Hipp.*]

χρόνῳ δὲ δή ποτ' εἶπ' ἀπαλλαχθεὶς γόων·
Τί ταῦτ' ἀλύω; πειστέον πατρὸς λόγοις.
ἐντύναθ' ἵππους ἅρμασι ζυγηφόρους,
δμῶες· πόλις γὰρ οὐκέτ' ἔστιν ἥδε μοι.
τοὐνθένδε μέντοι πᾶς ἀνήρ ἠπείγετο,   1185
καὶ θᾶσσον ἢ λέγοι τις ἐξηρτυμένας
πώλους παρ' αὐτὸν δεσπότην ἐστήσαμεν.
μάρπτει δὲ χερσὶν ἡνίας ἀπ' ἄντυγος,
αὐταῖς ἐν ἀρβύλαισιν ἁρμόσας πόδας.
καὶ πρῶτα μὲν θεοῖς εἶπ' ἀναπτύξας χέρας·   1190
Ζεῦ, μηκέτ' εἴην, εἰ κακὸς πέφυκ' ἀνήρ·
αἴσθοιτο δ' ἡμᾶς ὡς ἀτιμάζει πατὴρ
ἤτοι θανόντας ἢ φάος δεδορκότας.
κἂν τῷδ' ἐπῆγε κέντρον ἐς χεῖρας λαβὼν
πώλοις ἁμαρτῇ· πρόσπολοι δ' ὑφ' ἅρματος   1195
πέλας χαλινῶν εἰπόμεσθα δεσπότῃ
τὴν εὐθὺς Ἄργους κἀπιδαυρίας ὁδόν.

1181–2 γόος, ὁ   weeping, wailing, groaning (gen. of separation; χρόνῳ, dat. of time: S #1447; ἀπαλλαχθείς, circumstantial ptc. of time) – 'In time, after having stopped weeping, he said . . .' [1x *Hipp.*]

ἀλύω   be distraught, rave, wander in one's wits (ταῦτα, internal acc. 'in this way') [1x *Hipp.*]

πειστέον> (verbal adj.) (πείθω) one must obey [1x *Hipp.*]

1183–4 ἐντύνω   equip, get ready + acc. + dat. (ἐντύνατε, aor.[1] impv.) [1x Eur.]

ζῠγη-φόρος, ον   bearing a yoke (δμῶες, *enjambment*; ἥδε is the subj., πόλις, predicative; μοι, dat. of possess.) – 'slaves, get the yoke horses ready for the chariot; for this is no longer my city' [1x *Hipp.*]

1185–7 ἐνθένδε (adv.)   hence, from this time (τοὐνθένδε = τὸ ἐνθένδε) (1314)

ἐπείγω   pass. absolute: hurry, hasten, speed [1x *Hipp.*]

θάσσων, ον   swifter, quicker (compar. of ⁺ταχύς; λέγοι, potential opt. without ἄν, occasional in Homeric epic: S #1821) (1323)

ἐξ-αρτύω   mid.: get ready (ἐξηρτυμένας, attr. pf. pass. ptc.) – 'and then from that point every man hastened, and faster than one could say [it], we had set the horses all readied right by our master' [1x *Hipp.*]

1188–9 μάρπτω   grasp, hold, catch (historical pres.; see line 34, here standing for the aor.) [1x *Hipp.*]

ἡνία, ἡ   rein [1x *Hipp.*]

ἄντυξ, ῦγος, ἡ   rail (on the front and the sides of a chariot; the reins were fastened to the rail when the horses were held standing) (1135)

ἀρβύλη, ἡ   shoe, boot, footstall (here a fitting on the chariot's floor made to hold the driver's feet) [1x *Hipp.*]

ἁρμόζω   fit (ἁρμόσας, aor. act. ptc. of attendant circumstance/descriptive; according to B., the ptc. is coincidental with μάρπτει: "He does it so swiftly that seizing the reins and mounting seem part of the same action.") – 'With his hands he seizes the reins from the rail, fitting his feet right into the footstalls' [1x *Hipp.*]

1190–3 ἀνα-πτύσσω   unfold (ἀναπτύξας, aor. act. ptc. of attendant circumstance/descriptive, coincidental with the finite verb εἶπε; see λύσασα in line 290; the Greeks prayed with their arms raised and palms turned upward; εἴην, αἴσθοιτο < *⁺αἰσθάνομαι, opt. of wish; ἡμᾶς, θανόντας, δεδορκότας, *majestic plural*) [1x *Hipp.*]

1194–7 ἀπ-άγω   bring upon (ἐπῆγε, inceptive impf.; λαβών, aor.² act. ptc. of attendant circumstance/descriptive, coincidental with the finite verb εἶπε; see λύσασα in line 290) [1x *Hipp.*]

ἁμαρτῇ (adv.)   (ἅμα) together at the same time, at once (a mark of skill) – 'And at this [moment], taking the goad into his hands, he began to strike all the horses at the same time' [1x *Hipp.*]

χᾰλῑνός, ὁ   bridle [1x *Hipp.*]

Ἄργος, εος, τό   Argos, a major city in eastern Peloponnese

Ἐπιδαυρία, ἡ   Epidauros (κἀπιδαυρίας = καὶ Ἐπιδαυρίας) –
'and we servants followed our master beside the chariot near the bridles along the road straight forward to Argos and Epidauros' [1x Eur.]

ἐπεὶ δ' ἔρημον χῶρον εἰσεβάλλομεν,
ἀκτή τις ἔστι τοὐπέκεινα τῆσδε γῆς
πρὸς πόντον ἤδη κειμένη Σαρωνικόν.   1200
ἔνθεν τις ἠχὼ χθόνιος, ὡς βροντὴ Διός,
βαρὺν βρόμον μεθῆκε, φρικώδη κλυεῖν·
ὀρθὸν δὲ κρᾶτ' ἔστησαν οὖς τ' ἐς οὐρανὸν
ἵπποι, παρ' ἡμῖν δ' ἦν φόβος νεανικὸς
πόθεν ποτ' εἴη φθόγγος. ἐς δ' ἁλιρρόθους   1205
ἀκτὰς ἀποβλέψαντες ἱερὸν εἴδομεν
κῦμ' οὐρανῷ στηρίζον, ὥστ' ἀφῃρέθη
Σκίρωνος ἀκτὰς ὄμμα τοὐμὸν εἰσορᾶν,
ἔκρυπτε δ' Ἰσθμὸν καὶ πέτραν Ἀσκληπιοῦ.
κἄπειτ' ἀνοιδῆσάν τε καὶ πέριξ ἀφρὸν   1210
πολὺν καχλάζον ποντίῳ φυσήματι
χωρεῖ πρὸς ἀκτὰς οὗ τέθριππος ἦν ὄχος.

1198–1200 ἔρημος (3/2) deserted (847)

εἰσ-*⁺βάλλω   throw into (τοὐπέκεινα = τὸ ἐπέκεινα, beyond
+ gen.) [1x *Hipp.*]

Σαρωνικός (3)   Saronic (πόντον . . . Σαρωνικόν, *hyperbaton*.
Ferguson: "The Saronic Gulf or the Gulf of Aegina, is the more open water between the Peloponnese and Attica, in contrast with the more enclosed bay of Methana which H. was skirting.") [1x *Hipp.*]

1201–5 ἠχώ, οὖς, ἡ   tumultuous noise (of a crowd), roar (of the
sea) (791)

χθόνιος (3/2)   of/from the earth (χθόνιος, resolution in
6th position) (791)

βρόντη, ἡ   thunder (559)

βρόμος, ὁ   any loud noise or roaring (note the *consonance*
of β in lines 1201–2) [1x *Hipp.*]

φρῑκ-ώδης, ες   (φρίξ, εἶδος) that causes shuddering (see κλυ-εῖν, aor.[2] act. inf., in line 119; see limiting inf. in line 610: 'such that one shuddered to hear') (1216)

ὀρθός (3)   straight [1x *Hipp.*]

κράς, κρᾱτός   (LSJ: "gender rarely determinate") head (ἵπ-ποι, *enjambment*) – 'the horses stood their heads and ears straight toward the heavens' [1x *Hipp.*]

νεᾱνῐκός (3)   youthful, i.e., vigorous, wild [1x *Hipp.*]

φθόγγος, ὁ   sound (εἴη opt. after secondary tense in indirect question: S #2677b) – 'and there was a vigorous/serious fear among us [about] where the noise came from' [1x *Hipp.*]

1205–9 **ἁλίρροθος, ον**   roaring with waves, sea-beaten [1x *Hipp.*]

ἀπο-*⁺βλέπω   look steadfastly, gaze at (ἀποβλέψαντες, ptc. of time) [1x *Hipp.*]

ἱερός (3/2)   relating to gods, holy; supernatural (555)

στηρίζω   stand fast/firm, fixed to stand fast (στηρίζον, attr. ptc.; for the syntactical construction of ἀφηρέθη, see line 644; the retained acc. is εἰσορᾶν; ἔκρυπτε, B.: "The aor. would say what happened [the Isthmus vanished from sight]; the impf. pictures the scene [the Isthmus was invisible].") – 'And when we gazed at the sea-beaten shore we saw an unnatural wave fixed in the heavens, so that my eye was deprived of the sight of Sciron's coast, and it hid the Isthmus and the rock of Asclepius.' [1x *Hipp.*]

1210–12 **ἀν-οιδέω**   swell up (ἀνοιδῆσαν, aor. act. neut. sg. descriptive ptc.) [1x Eur.]

πέριξ (adv.)   all around [1x *Hipp.*]

ἀφρός, ὁ   foam, froth [1x *Hipp.*]

καχλάζω   dash, plash, bubble (of the sound of liquid) (καχλάζον, pres. act. neut. sg. descriptive ptc.) [1x Eur.]

φύσημα, ατος, τό   roaring, raging [1x *Hipp.*]

οὗ (relat. adv.)   where

τέθρ-ιππος, ον   (τέτταρα, ἵππος) with four horses yoked abreast; – 'And then swelling up and churning deep foam all around with the raging of the sea, it advances toward where the four-horse chariot was.' [1x *Hipp.*]

αὐτῷ δὲ σὺν κλύδωνι καὶ τρικυμίᾳ
κῦμ' ἐξέθηκε ταῦρον, ἄγριον τέρας·
οὗ πᾶσα μὲν χθὼν φθέγματος πληρουμένη   1215
φρικῶδες ἀντεφθέγγετ', εἰσορῶσι δὲ
κρεῖσσον θέαμα δεργμάτων ἐφαίνετο.
εὐθὺς δὲ πώλοις δεινὸς ἐμπίπτει φόβος·
καὶ δεσπότης μὲν ἱππικοῖσιν ἤθεσιν
πολὺς ξυνοικῶν ἥρπασ' ἡνίας χεροῖν,   1220
ἕλκει δέ, κώπην ὥστε ναυβάτης ἀνήρ,
ἱμᾶσιν ἐς τοὔπισθεν ἀρτήσας δέμας·
αἱ δ' ἐνδακοῦσαι στόμια πυριγενῆ γνάθοις
βίᾳ φέρουσιν, οὔτε ναυκλήρου χερὸς
οὔθ' ἱπποδέσμων οὔτε κολλητῶν ὄχων   1225
μεταστρέφουσαι. κεἰ μὲν ἐς τὰ μαλθακὰ
γαίας ἔχων οἴακας εὐθύνοι δρόμον,
προυφαίνετ' ἐς τὸ πρόσθεν, ὥστ' ἀναστρέφειν,
ταῦρος, φόβῳ τέτρωρον ἐκμαίνων ὄχον·

1213–14 **κλύδων, ωνος, ὁ** wave, billow, surge, swell (448)

τρῐ-κῡμία, ἡ   a third wave, a huge overwhelming surge
[1x *Hipp.*]

ἐκ-*⁺τίθημι   put forth [1x *Hipp.*]

τέρας, ατος, τό   portent, monster (1247)

ἄγριος (3/2)   wild, savage (note the *consonance* of ρ in line 1214) – 'and with its very swell and huge surge, the wave put forth a bull, a wild monster' [1x *Hipp.*]

1215–17 **πληρόω**   fill (οὗ, subj. gen.) (1329)

φρῑκ-ώδης, ες   that causes shuddering/horror, awful, terrible (internal acc., with ἀντιφθέγγετο) (1202)

ἀντι-φθέγγομαι   return a sound, reecho (for the impf., cf. line 1209; εἰσορῶσι [ἡμῖν], ptc. as an unarticulated subst.) [1x *Hipp.*]

θέᾱμα, ατος, τό   sight, spectacle [1x *Hipp.*]

δέργμα, ατος, τό   (δέρκομαι) a look, glance; – 'The whole earth, filled with its voice, gave a hair-raising roar in reply, and the sight [of it] appeared to us who were looking more than our gaze could bear.' [1x *Hipp*.]

1218–22 ἁρπάζω   seize and overpower (note the historical pres. ἐμπίπτει for vividness) [1x *Hipp*.]

ἦθος, εος, τό   custom, habit (1116)

συν-⁺οικέω   + dat.: dwell together, live together with; i.e., be familiar with (163)

κώπη, ἡ   oar [1x *Hipp*.]

ναυ-βάτης, ου, ὁ [ᾰ]   (ναῦς, βαίνω) seaman, mariner, sailor (155)

ἱμάς, άντος, ὁ   leather strap or thong (1245)

ὄπισθεν (adv.)   after, behind (τοὔπισθεν = τὸ ὄπισθεν, the hinder parts, rear, back) – 'Immediately a terrible fear falls on the horses; and the master, being well acquainted with the ways of horses, seizes the reins with his hands and pulls, the way a sailor [pulls] an oar, hanging his body backward on the straps' [1x *Hipp*.]

1223–6 ἐν-δάκνω   bite into, hold in the teeth (resolutions in positions 6 and 8) [1x *Hipp*.]

στόμιον, τό   bridle bit, bit [1x *Hipp*.]

πῠρῐ-γενής, ες   wrought or forged by fire [1x *Hipp*.]

γνάθος, ἡ   jaw, mouth [1x *Hipp*.]

ναύ-κληρος, ὁ   helmsman; as adj.: of the helmsman [1x *Hipp*.]

ἱππό-δεσμα, ων, τά   reins, a harness [1x Eur.]

κολλητός (3)   tight-glued, close-joined [1x Eur.]

μετα-στρέφω   turn aside; + gen.: care for, regard (ἐνδακοῦσαι, μεταστρέφουσαι, descriptive ptcs.) – 'but they, biting with their jaws on the fire-forged bits, carry [him] away by force, paying attention neither to their helmsman's hand, nor to the reins, nor to the tight-glued chariot.' [1x *Hipp*.]

1226–9 μαλθᾰκός (3)   soft [1x *Hipp*.]

οἴαξ, ᾱκος, ὁ   the tiller, helm [1x *Hipp*.]

εὐθύνω   direct, guide straight (εἰ . . . εὐθύνοι . . . προυφαίνετο, past general condition: S #2297) [1x *Hipp.*]

προ-φαίνομαι   appear before [1x *Hipp.*]

πρόσθεν (adv.)   before, formerly (cf. ὥστε ἀναστρέφειν, possible or intended result, cf. line 50) (939)

τέτρωρος, ον   four-horse (of a chariot) [1x *Hipp.*]

ἐκ-μαίνω   drive mad; – 'And whenever, holding the tiller, he would direct their course toward softer ground, the bull would appear in front so as to turn them back, driving the four-horse team mad with fear' [1x *Hipp.*]

εἰ δ᾽ ἐς πέτρας φέροιντο μαργῶσαι φρένας,   1230
σιγῇ πελάζων ἄντυγι ξυνείπετο,
ἐς τοῦθ᾽ ἕως ἔσφηλε κἀνεχαίτισεν
ἀψῖδα πέτρῳ προσβαλὼν ὀχήματος.
σύμφυρτα δ᾽ ἦν ἅπαντα· σύριγγές τ᾽ ἄνω
τροχῶν ἐπήδων ἀξόνων τ᾽ ἐνήλατα,   1235
αὐτὸς δ᾽ ὁ τλήμων ἡνίαισιν ἐμπλακεὶς
δεσμὸν δυσεξέλικτον ἕλκεται δεθείς,
σποδούμενος μὲν πρὸς πέτραις φίλον κάρα
θραύων τε σάρκας, δεινὰ δ᾽ ἐξαυδῶν κλυεῖν·
Στῆτ᾽, ὦ φάτναισι ταῖς ἐμαῖς τεθραμμέναι,   1240
μή μ᾽ ἐξαλείψητ᾽· ὦ πατρὸς τάλαιν᾽ ἀρά·
τίς ἄνδρ᾽ ἄριστον βούλεται σῶσαι παρών;
πολλοὶ δὲ βουληθέντες ὑστέρῳ ποδὶ
ἐλειπόμεσθα. χὠ μὲν ἐκ δεσμῶν λυθεὶς
τμητῶν ἱμάντων οὐ κάτοιδ᾽ ὅτῳ τρόπῳ   1245
πίπτει, βραχὺν δὴ βίοτον ἐμπνέων ἔτι·

1230–3 μαργάω   rage furiously (φρένας, acc. of respect)
[1x *Hipp.*]

πελάζω   draw near [1x *Hipp.*]

συν-έπομαι   follow close upon (εἰ . . . φέροιντο . . . ξυνείπετο, past general condition; see line 1227) [1x *Hipp.*]

ἀνα-χαιτίζω   overthrow, throw back [1x *Hipp.*]

ἀψίς, ῖδος, ἡ   felloe (the outer rim of the wheel; *synecdoche*)
[1x *Hipp.*]

ὄχημα, ατος, τό   chariot; – 'and whenever [the horses], maddened in their mind, rushed toward the rocks, it followed silently close
by the chariot rail, until in the end it tripped up [the chariot] and over-
threw [it], smashing the felloes (i.e., the wheels) of the chariot on a
rock.' (1356)

1234–5 σύμφυρτος, ον   kneaded/mixed together; metaph.: confounded,
confused [1x Eur.]

σῦριγξ, ιγγος, ἡ   the box/axle hole in the nave of the wheel [1x
Hipp.]

τροχός, ὁ   wheel [1x *Hipp.*]

πηδάω   spring, leap (ἐπήδων, 3 pl. impf. act.) (1352)

ἄξων, ονος, ὁ   axle [1x *Hipp.*]

ἐνήλᾰτον, τό   anything driven in; ἀξόνων ἐνήλατα: the pins
driven into the axle; – 'everything was confounded together; the
wheels' naves and the linchpins were leaping in the air' [1x *Hipp.*]

1236–9 ἐμπλέκω   weave in, implicate (ἐμπλακείς, aor. pass. ptc.)
[1x *Hipp.*]

δεσμός, ὁ   a tying, a binding; band, strap (1244)

δυσεξέλικτος, ον   hard to unravel [1x *Hipp.*]

*δέω   bind, tie, fasten (ἕλκεται, historical pres.; δε-
σμὸν . . . δεθείς, *hyperbaton*, *figura etymologica*, internal acc.) – 'and
the wretched man himself, entangled in the reins, bound in a binding
hard to unravel, was dragged' (160)

σποδέω   pound, smite [1x *Hipp.*]

θραύω   break, smash, shatter [1x *Hipp.*]

ἐξ-αυδάω   speak out, call out (see κλυεῖν in line 119; for
limiting inf., see line 610) – 'smashing his head upon the rocks and
shattering his flesh, screaming out things dreadful to hear' (590)

1240–2 φάτνη, ἡ   manger (τεθραμμέναι < ‡⁺τρέφω, pf. pass. ptc.,
descriptive) [1x *Hipp.*]

ἐξ-αλείφω   wipe out, destroy (μή . . . ἐξαλείψητε, prohibitive subjv. It is unclear how Hippolytus knows about his father's
curse; cf. lines 1349, 1362, 1378, 1411. The assumption is that such

pedantic observations did not matter to the ancient playwrights, and most such minor inconsistencies probably went unnoticed by the spectators.) – 'Who that is present [παρών] wishes to save the best of men?' [1x *Hipp.*]

1245–6 τμητός (3)   well-cut (χὢ = καὶ ὅ) [1x Eur.]

ἐμ-πνέω   breathe, live (for the pathetic δή, see 778, βίοτον, internal acc.; resolution in 6th position) – 'and he, after being freed from the cut leather straps—I don't know how—falls, while still breathing a little life' [1x *Hipp.*]

	ἵπποι δ᾽ ἔκρυφθεν καὶ τὸ δύστηνον τέρας	
	ταύρου λεπαίας οὐ κάτοιδ᾽ ὅποι χθονός.	
	δοῦλος μὲν οὖν ἔγωγε σῶν δόμων, ἄναξ,	
	ἀτὰρ τοσοῦτόν γ᾽ οὐ δυνήσομαί ποτε,	1250
	τὸν σὸν πιθέσθαι παῖδ᾽ ὅπως ἐστὶν κακός,	
	οὐδ᾽ εἰ γυναικῶν πᾶν κρεμασθείη γένος	
	καὶ τὴν ἐν Ἴδῃ γραμμάτων πλήσειέ τις	
	πεύκην· ἐπεί νιν ἐσθλὸν ὄντ᾽ ἐπίσταμαι.	
Χο.	αἰαῖ· κέκρανται συμφορὰ νέων κακῶν,	1255
	οὐδ᾽ ἔστι μοίρας τοῦ χρεών τ᾽ ἀπαλλαγή.	
Θη.	μίσει μὲν ἀνδρὸς τοῦ πεπονθότος τάδε	
	λόγοισιν ἥσθην τοῖσδε· νῦν δ᾽ αἰδούμενος	
	θεούς τ᾽ ἐκεῖνόν θ᾽, οὕνεκ᾽ ἐστὶν ἐξ ἐμοῦ,	
	οὔθ᾽ ἥδομαι τοῖσδ᾽ οὔτ᾽ ἐπάχθομαι κακοῖς.	1260
Αγ.	πῶς οὖν; κομίζειν, ἢ τί χρὴ τὸν ἄθλιον	
	δράσαντας ἡμᾶς σῇ χαρίζεσθαι φρενί;	
	φρόντιζ᾽· ἐμοῖς δὲ χρώμενος βουλεύμασιν	
	οὐκ ὠμὸς ἐς σὸν παῖδα δυστυχοῦντ᾽ ἔσῃ.	
Θη.	κομίζετ᾽ αὐτόν, ὡς ἰδὼν ἐν ὄμμασιν	1265
	τὸν τἄμ᾽ ἀπαρνηθέντα μὴ χρᾶναι λέχη	
	λόγοις τ᾽ ἐλέγξω δαιμόνων τε συμφοραῖς.	

1247–8 λεπαῖος (3)   craggy (ἔκρυφθεν < *κρύπτω = ἐκρύφθησαν, epic 3rd pl.) [1x *Hipp.*]

ὅποι (relat. adv.)   + gen.: where; – 'the horses and the horrid monster of the bull had disappeared, I don't know where in the craggy land.' [1x *Hipp.*]

1252–4 κρέμᾰμαι   pass. of κρεμάννυμι, hang (δυνήσομαι . . . κρεμασθείη . . . πλήσειε, mixed condition, opt. in the twin protases and fut.
indic. in apodosis: GMT #499a) [1x *Hipp.*]

  Ἴδα, ἡ   Ida, the name of a mountain in Phrygia near
  Troy and another in Crete; the double reference lends emphasis to the
  statement.

  πεύκη, ἡ   fir, pine (collective sg., i.e., forest, *enjamb-*
  ment) (216)

  *πίμπλημι   + gen.: fill up; – 'not even if the whole female
  race should be hanged and someone will fill the pine forest upon Mount
  Ida with writing' (692)

1255–6 κραίνω   accomplish, complete (1345)

  ἀπαλλαγή, ἡ   deliverance, release; – 'and there is no escape
  from fate and necessity' [1x *Hipp.*]

1257–60 μῖσος, τό   hatred (μίσει, dat. of cause; ἥσθην, aor.[1] indic.
pass. 1 sg.; πεπονθότος < *⁺πάσχω, pf. act. ptc.) – 'Because of my hatred
for the man who suffered these things, I was pleased with your words' [1x
Hipp.]

  ἐπ-άχθομαι   be distressed at a thing; – 'since he is my son, I
  do not rejoice at these ills, nor do I feel distressed by them.' [1x Eur.]

1261–4 χαρίζομαι   + dat.: indulge, satisfy (χρή + acc. + inf.: δράσαντας ἡμᾶς . . . χαρίζεσθαι) – 'What now? Carry [him] here, or what
should we do with the poor man to satisfy your heart?' [1x *Hipp.*]

  ὠμός (3)   savage, cruel (χρώμενος, conditional ptc.
  reflecting the protasis of an emotional fut. more vivid condition: S
  #2323–4) – 'but if you take my advice, you will not be cruel toward
  your unfortunate son.' [1x *Hipp.*]

1265–7 ἀπ-αρνέομαι   deny utterly (τὸν ἀπαρνηθέντα, ptc. as artic.
subst.) [1x *Hipp.*]

  χραίνω   stain (μή, the redundant negative, is common
  after negative verbs of saying, here ἀπαρνηθέντα) – 'so that seeing
  before my eyes the man who denies that he has stained my bed, I will
  refute [him] with speech and calamities from the gods' (1438)

FOURTH STASIMON LINES 1268–81

The last choral ode in tragedy is often shorter than others, but this one is atypically brief (thirteen lines) and astrophic. We earlier heard a hymn to Eros and Aphrodite and their destructive power, when the Nurse went to approach Hippolytus (525–64), as a warning of what Phaedra's love might cause. Here it is clear that Aphrodite has achieved complete destruction, and the spectators are reminded of her eternal power. The symmetry evident in the structure of the play is reflected in this stasimon. The two halves on either side of the central point of Phaedra's suicide form mirror images of each other. Aphrodite's prologue is reflected in Artemis' epilogue. Aphrodite's presence is followed by a hymn to Artemis, and the process is reversed at the end of the play, where the Chorus sing a hymn to the victory of Aphrodite and Eros just before Artemis' entrance.

Χο. σὺ τὰν θεῶν ἄκαμπτον φρένα
καὶ βροτῶν
ἄγεις, Κύπρι, σὺν δ' ὁ ποι-

κιλόπτερος ἀμφιβαλὼν   1270
ὠκυτάτῳ πτερῷ·

ποτᾶται δὲ γαῖαν εὐάχητόν θ'

ἁλμυρὸν ἐπὶ πόντον,
θέλγει δ' Ἔρως ᾧ μαινομένᾳ κραδίᾳ

πτανὸς ἐφορμάσῃ χρυσοφαής ⟨   ⟩   1275

φύσιν ὀρεσκόων σκύμνων πελαγίων θ'

ὅσα τε γᾶ τρέφει

τά τ' αἰθόμενος ἅλιος δέρκεται

ἄνδρας τε· συμπάντων βασιληΐδα τι-   1280

μάν, Κύπρι, τῶνδε μόνα κρατύνεις.

Cypris, you drive the unyield-
ing heart of both
gods and mortals, and with
you the
one with many-colored wings,
encompassing them with his
swift wing.
He flies over the earth and
over the sweet-
booming briny sea,
and Eros bewitches [anyone]
against
whose maddened heart he
rushes,
winged and gold-gleaming,
<   > the nature
of cubs from the mountain
and of the sea
as many as the earth nurtures
and the
blazing sun looks upon, as
well as men;
over all these, Cypris, you
alone hold royal honor.

1268	◡ – – ◡ – – ◡◡ – ◡ –	2 dochmiacs
1269	◡ – – ◡ – ◡ –	bacchiac + iamb or dochmiac + iamb
1270	◡ – ◡◡ – ◡◡ –	◡ hemiepes
1271	– ◡ ◡ – ◡ –	dochmiac
1272	◡ – – ◡ – ◡ – – – –	2 dochmiacs
1273	– ◡◡ ◡◡ – –	dochmiac
1274	– – ◡ – – – ◡◡ – ◡◡ –	iambs + hemiepes or iamb + prosodiac
1275	– ◡◡ – – – – ◡◡ – < >	2 dochmiacs or dochmiac + choriamb
1276–7	◡ ◡◡ – ◡ – – – ◡◡ ◡ –	2 dochmiacs
1278	◡ ◡◡ – ◡ –	dochmiac
1279	◡ – ◡◡ ◡ – ◡ – – – ◡ – ‖	2 dochmiacs
1280	– – ◡ – – – ◡◡ – ◡◡ –	iambs + hemiepes or iamb + prosodiac
1281	– ◡ ◡ – ◡ ◡ – ◡ – –	alcaic decasyllable

1268–71 ἄ-καμπτος, ον   unbending, inexorable [1x Eur.]

σύν (adv.)   in company [with you]

ποικιλό-πτερος, ον   with variegated, many-colored wings [1x Eur.]

ἀμφι-*⁺βάλλω   surround, encompass [1x *Hipp.*]

ὠκύς, ὠκεῖα, ὠκύ   swift, fleet, speedy [1x *Hipp.*]

1272–3 ποτάομαι   fly about, flit, hover (564)

εὐάχητος, ον [ᾱ]   tuneful, well-sounding, whether loud or sweet
[1x *Hipp.*]

ἀλμῠρός (3)   salt, briny (ἐπί governs both γαῖαν and πόντον)
[1x *Hipp.*]

1274–5 θέλγω   bewitch, enchant [1x *Hipp.*]

πτηνός/πτανός (3)   feathered, winged (1292)

ἐφ-ορμάω   + dat.: rush upon, attack (ἐφορμάσῃ, subjv.
in general conditional relative sentence: GMT #532; ἄν is omitted)
[1x Eur.]

χρῡσο-φαής, ές   with golden light [1x *Hipp.*]

1276–9	ὀρέσ-κοος, ον	mountain-bred [1x *Hipp.*]
	σκύμνος, ὁ	young animal [1x *Hipp.*]
	πελάγιος (3)	of the sea [1x *Hipp.*]
	αἴθω	burn, blaze (cf. τά = ἄ, cf. line 747) [1x *Hipp.*]

1280 βᾰσῐλη̄ίς, ίδος, ἡ   royal [1x *Hipp.*]

Exodos Lines 1283–1466

Euripides favored divine epiphanies at the end of a play to resolve the plot's entanglement. Artemis, identifiable by her bow and arrows (1422), appears at the top of the stage building just when the spectators expect the arrival of Hippolytus. The meter of 1283–95 is anapestic (�’ �’ –�’ �’ –). See introduction to the first episode, lines 170–266.

ΑΡΤΕΜΙΣ

σὲ τὸν εὐπατρίδην Αἰγέως κέλομαι
παῖδ᾽ ἐπακοῦσαι·
Λητοῦς δὲ κόρη σ᾽ Ἄρτεμις αὐδῶ.   1285
Θησεῦ, τί τάλας τοῖσδε συνήδη,
παῖδ᾽ οὐχ ὁσίως σὸν ἀποκτείνας
ψευδέσι μύθοις ἀλόχου πεισθεὶς
ἀφανῆ; φανερὰν δ᾽ ἔσχεθες ἄτην.
πῶς οὐχ ὑπὸ γῆς τάρταρα κρύπτεις   1290
δέμας αἰσχυνθείς,
ἢ πτηνὸς ἄνω μεταβὰς †βίοτον†
πήματος ἔξω πόδα τοῦδ᾽ ἀνέχεις;
ὡς ἔν γ᾽ ἀγαθοῖς ἀνδράσιν οὔ σοι
κτητὸν βιότου μέρος ἐστίν.   1295
ἄκουε, Θησεῦ, σῶν κακῶν κατάστασιν.

1283–4	εὐ-πατρίδης, ου, ὁ	of a noble father/lineage (152)
	κέλομαι	call, command [1x *Hipp.*]
	ἐπ-ἄκούω	listen [1x *Hipp.*]

1286–9 συν-ήδομαι   + dat.: rejoice at (a thing) – 'why, wretched man, are you rejoicing at these things?' [1x *Hipp.*]

ὁσίως (adv.)   piously; with a negative = impiously [1x *Hipp.*]

ἀφᾰνής, ές   (ἀ privat., φανῆναι, appear) unseen, invisible; hidden, unknown (in addition to the dat. ψευδέσι μύθοις, πεισθεὶς takes ἀφανῆ, acc. neut. pl. of that of which one is persuaded; *enjambment*) – 'you have impiously killed your son because you were persuaded of uncertain things by the lying words of your wife' (346)

φανέρος (3)   visible (ἀφανῆ, φανεράν, wordplay; ἔσχθες, poetic for ἔσχες) (1123)

1290–3 Ταρτᾰρος, ὁ   Tartarus (irreg. pl. Τάρταρα) [1x *Hipp.*]

μετα-*⁺βαίνω   alter, undergo change; – 'How is it that in your shame you do not hide your body in Tartarus beneath the earth, or that having changed to a winged life above you do not take your foot out of [this] pain?' [1x *Hipp.*]

1295–6 κτητός (3)   acquired, possessed [1x *Hipp.*]

μέρος, εος, τό   share, part; – 'You have no possible (acquirable) share of life among good men.' [1x *Hipp.*]

κατᾰστασις, εως, ἡ   settling, appointing, state; – 'Hear, Theseus, the state of your misfortune.' [1x *Hipp.*]

καίτοι προκόψω γ᾽ οὐδέν, ἀλγυνῶ δέ σε·
ἀλλ᾽ ἐς τόδ᾽ ἦλθον, παιδὸς ἐκδεῖξαι φρένα
τοῦ σοῦ δικαίαν, ὡς ὑπ᾽ εὐκλείας θάνῃ,
καὶ σῆς γυναικὸς οἶστρον ἢ τρόπον τινὰ   1300
γενναιότητα. τῆς γὰρ ἐχθίστης θεῶν
ἡμῖν ὅσαισι παρθένειος ἡδονὴ
δηχθεῖσα κέντροις παιδὸς ἠράσθη σέθεν·
γνώμῃ δὲ νικᾶν τὴν Κύπριν πειρωμένη
τροφοῦ διώλετ᾽ οὐχ ἑκοῦσα μηχαναῖς,   1305
ἢ σῷ δι᾽ ὅρκων παιδὶ σημαίνει νόσον.
ὁ δ᾽, ὥσπερ οὖν δίκαιον, οὐκ ἐφέσπετο
λόγοισιν, οὐδ᾽ αὖ πρὸς σέθεν κακούμενος
ὅρκων ἀφεῖλε πίστιν, εὐσεβὴς γεγώς·
ἡ δ᾽ εἰς ἔλεγχον μὴ πέσῃ φοβουμένη   1310
ψευδεῖς γραφὰς ἔγραψε καὶ διώλεσεν
δόλοισι σὸν παῖδ᾽, ἀλλ᾽ ὅμως ἔπεισέ σε.

1297 καίτοι   and yet, although; – 'And yet I will accomplish nothing [by this], but I will cause you pain'; cf. προκόπτω in line 23 [1x *Hipp*.]

προ-κόπτω   intrans. in act.: make one's way forward, advance, make (23)

ἀλγύνω   pain, grieve, distress (798)

1298–9 ἐκ-*⁺δείκνῡμι   show off, display [1x *Hipp*.]

εὔκλειᾰ, ἡ   good fame, renown (θάνῃ, subjv., in final clause; θάνοι would have been expected depending on ἦλθον, but "her purpose continues into the present" [B.]) [1x *Hipp*.]

1300–1 οἶστρος, ὁ   madness, frenzied desire [1x *Hipp*.]

γενναιότης, ητος, ἡ   nobility; – 'and [to display] your wife's frenzy or, in a way, her nobility.' [1x *Hipp*.]

1305 μηχανή, ἡ   contrivance (μηχαναῖς, dat. of means) – 'by the contrivances of her Nurse' (481)

1307–9 ὥσπερ οὖν δίκαιον   'as indeed was just'

ἐφ-*έπομαι   + dat.: follow, pursue [1x *Hipp*.]

κακόω   pass.: be ill-treated (κακούμενος, concessive ptc.) – 'But he, as indeed was right, did not follow her arguments, nor did he retract the pledge of his oath even though he was ill-treated by you, because he was born pious' [1x *Hipp*.]

1310–12 ἔλεγχος, ὁ   trial, test, scrutiny, cross-examination (μὴ πέσῃ, subjv. in fear clause; γραφὰς ἔγραψε, emphatic *figura etymologica*) – 'but she, out of fear lest she be put to examination, wrote a lying letter and by tricks destroyed your son, but all the same she persuaded you.' (1337)

Θη.   οἴμοι.
Αρ.   δάκνει σε, Θησεῦ, μῦθος; ἀλλ᾽ ἔχ᾽ ἥσυχος,
       τοὐνθένδ᾽ ἀκούσας ὡς ἂν οἰμώξῃς πλέον.
       ἆρ᾽ οἶσθα πατρὸς τρεῖς ἀρὰς ἔχων σαφεῖς;   1315
       ὧν τὴν μίαν παρεῖλες, ὦ κάκιστε σύ,
       ἐς παῖδα τὸν σόν, ἐξὸν εἰς ἐχθρῶν τινα.

πατὴρ μὲν οὖν σοι πόντιος φρονῶν καλῶς
ἔδωχ' ὅσονπερ χρῆν, ἐπείπερ ἤνεσεν·
σὺ δ' ἔν τ' ἐκείνῳ κἀν ἐμοὶ φαίνῃ κακός,　　　　　1320
ὃς οὔτε πίστιν οὔτε μάντεων ὄπα
ἔμεινας, οὐκ ἤλεγξας, οὐ χρόνῳ μακρῷ
σκέψιν παρέσχες, ἀλλὰ θᾶσσον ἤ σ' ἐχρῆν
ἀρὰς ἐφῆκας παιδὶ καὶ κατέκτανες.

1313–14 ἥσυχος, ον　　　still, quiet (ἔχ' ἥσυχος, keep quiet) [1x *Hipp.*]

ἐνθένδε (adv.)　　　hence (τοὐνθένδε = ἐνθένδε) (1185)

οἰμώζω　　　groan (ἀκούσας, circumstantial ptc. denoting time; ὡς ἂν οἰμώξῃς, subjv. in final clause in 1st sequence: ἔχε) – 'but keep quiet, so you may groan more after hearing what follows.' (1405)

1315 οἶσθα ... ἔχων　　　(supplem. ptc. in indir. disc.: S #2106)

1316–17 παρ-*⁺αιρέω　　　take away from, lessen (ὧν, partit. gen.; ἐξόν, neut. ptc. from ἔξεστι, acc. abs., instead of the gen., when the verb is impersonal: S #2076A) – 'when it should have been possible [to use it] against some one of your enemies' (1105)

1321–4 ὄψ, ὀπός, ἡ　　　voice, word

σκέψις, εως, ἡ　　　examination, inquiry (ἔμεινας, *enjambment*; χρόνῳ μακρῷ σκέψιν = χρόνῳ μακρὰν σκέψιν, *hypallage* and personification of 'Time' as in lines 430 and 1051; see B. If χρόνῳ is not personified, it could be dat. of time.) [1x *Eur.*]

ἐφ-*⁺ίημι　　　(+ acc. and dat.) send against, launch; – 'you who did not wait for proof or the voice of prophets, you did not put [it] to the test, allow Time a long inquiry; but sooner than you should have, you hurled curses at your son and killed [him].' [1x *Hipp.*]

κατα-*⁺κτείνω　　　kill, put to death (1358)

Θη.　δέσποιν', ὀλοίμην.　　　　　1325
　　　　Αρ.　δείν' ἔπραξας, ἀλλ' ὅμως
ἔτ' ἔστι καί σοι τῶνδε συγγνώμης τυχεῖν·
Κύπρις γὰρ ἤθελ' ὥστε γίγνεσθαι τάδε,
πληροῦσα θυμόν. θεοῖσι δ' ὧδ' ἔχει νόμος·
οὐδεὶς ἀπαντᾶν βούλεται προθυμίᾳ　　　　　1330

τῇ τοῦ θέλοντος, ἀλλ᾽ ἀφιστάμεσθ᾽ ἀεί.
ἐπεί, σάφ᾽ ἴσθι, Ζῆνα μὴ φοβουμένη
οὐκ ἄν ποτ᾽ ἦλθον ἐς τόδ᾽ αἰσχύνης ἐγὼ
ὥστ᾽ ἄνδρα πάντων φίλτατον βροτῶν ἐμοὶ
θανεῖν ἐᾶσαι. τὴν δὲ σὴν ἁμαρτίαν   1335
τὸ μὴ εἰδέναι μὲν πρῶτον ἐκλύει κάκης·
ἔπειτα δ᾽ ἡ θανοῦσ᾽ ἀνήλωσεν γυνὴ
λόγων ἐλέγχους, ὥστε σὴν πεῖσαι φρένα.
μάλιστα μέν νυν σοὶ τάδ᾽ ἔρρωγεν κακά,
λύπη δὲ κἀμοί· τοὺς γὰρ εὐσεβεῖς θεοὶ   1340
θνήσκοντας οὐ χαίρουσι· τούς γε μὴν κακοὺς
αὐτοῖς τέκνοισι καὶ δόμοις ἐξόλλυμεν.

1326 συγγνώμη, ἡ   forgiveness (ἔστι, here 'it is possible,' note the accent; τῶνδε, obj. gen. with καί) – 'you have committed terrible things, but all the same, it is still possible for you to receive forgiveness even for these' (117)

1329–33 πληρόω   fill (ὥστε is unnecessary here; θεοῖσι, *synizesis*) (1215)

ἀπαντάω   + dat.: oppose [1x *Hipp.*]

ἀφ-*⁺ίσταμαι   stand off, stand aloof [1x *Hipp.*]

μὴ φοβουμένη ... ἂν ἦλθον   (contrary-to-fact condition for the past; cf. lines 657–8)

1335–7 ἐκ-λύω (ῡ)   unstring (a bow), loosen, release ([809]/825)

κάκη, ἡ   badness, wickedness [1x *Hipp.*]

ἀν-*⁺αλίσκω   use up, spend, i.e., do away with; kill, destroy; – 'secondly, your dead wife [i.e., your wife, by dying] prevented the cross-examination of her words, and thus persuaded your mind' (506)

1339–40 *ῥήγνυμι   break, burst, shatter; – 'These evils burst upon you mostly, but I too feel grief' [1x *Hipp.*]

1341–2 αὐτοῖς τέκνοισι καὶ δόμοις   'with their very children and houses' (dat. with αὐτός often indicates "the idea of accompaniment ... this use is common when the destruction of a person or thing is referred to": S #1525) – 'but we destroy the evil ones with their very children and houses.'

Hippolytus enters. Στείχει suggests that he is walking, even if supported by his servants. After the descriptions by the Messenger and Artemis, a litter might have been expected. It is possible that it is brought after Hippolytus' entrance.

Xo.   καὶ μὴν ὁ τάλας ὅδε δὴ στείχει,
        σάρκας νεαρὰς ξανθόν τε κάρα
        διαλυμανθείς. ὦ πόνος οἴκων,   1345
        οἷον ἐκράνθη δίδυμον μελάθροις
        πένθος θεόθεν καταληπτόν.

1343–7 νεᾰρός (3)   young [1x *Hipp.*]

    δια-λῡμαίνομαι   maltreat shamefully (1349)

    *κραίνω   accomplish, complete (1255)

    δίδῠμος (3/2)   double, twofold [1x *Hipp.*]

    καταληπτός (3)   (verbal adj. < κατα-*⁺λαμβάνω; usually pass.:
    seized; but here act.: 'seizing') [1x Eur.]

LINES 1348–88

Hippolytus' lament is divided into two parts differing in meter. The first part (1348–69) consists of non-lyric anapestic dimeter. In this part, Hippolytus bewails his ill fate while insisting that he is innocent. In the second part (1370–88), a more emotional lyric combination of anapests and iambs, his pain increases and he prays for death.

Ιπ.   αἰαῖ αἰαῖ·
        δύστηνος ἐγώ, πατρὸς ἐξ ἀδίκου
        χρησμοῖς ἀδίκοις διελυμάνθην.   1350
        ἀπόλωλα τάλας, οἴμοι μοι.
        διά μου κεφαλῆς ἄσσουσ᾽ ὀδύναι
        κατά τ᾽ ἐγκέφαλον πηδᾷ σφάκελος·
        σχές, ἀπειρηκὸς σῶμ᾽ ἀναπαύσω.
        ἒ ἔ·   1355

ὦ στυγνὸν ὄχημ᾽ ἵππειον, ἐμῆς
βόσκημα χερός,
διά μ᾽ ἔφθειρας, κατὰ δ᾽ ἔκτεινας.
φεῦ φεῦ· πρὸς θεῶν, ἀτρέμα, δμῶες.
χροὸς ἑλκώδους ἅπτεσθε χεροῖν.   1360
τίς ἐφέστηκεν δεξιὰ πλευροῖς;
πρόσφορά μ᾽ αἴρετε, σύντονα δ᾽ ἕλκετε
τὸν κακοδαίμονα καὶ κατάρατον
πατρὸς ἀμπλακίαις. Ζεῦ Ζεῦ, τάδ᾽ ὁρᾷς;
ὅδ᾽ ὁ σεμνὸς ἐγὼ καὶ θεοσέπτωρ,   1365
ὅδ᾽ ὁ σωφροσύνῃ πάντας ὑπερσχών,
προῦπτον ἐς Ἅιδην στείχω, κατ᾽ ἄκρας
ὀλέσας βίοτον, μόχθους δ᾽ ἄλλως
τῆς εὐσεβίας
εἰς ἀνθρώπους ἐπόνησα.   1370

1350 χρησμός, ὁ   oracle, divine pronouncement (the reference is
to Theseus' curse, which Hippolytus seems to know about) – 'I have been
shamefully maltreated by unjust divine pronouncements from an unjust
father.' [1x *Hipp.*]

1352–3 ἀΐσσω   shoot, dart, leap, rush (165)

ὀδύνη, ἡ   pain (1371)

ἐγ-κέφἄλος, ον   within the head [1x *Hipp.*]

πηδάω   spring, leap (1235)

σφάκελος, ὁ   spasm, convulsion [1x *Hipp.*]

1354 ἀπ-*⁺εῖπον   intrans., be worn out (ἀπειρηκός, neut. pf. attr.
ptc.) [1x *Hipp.*]

ἀνα-παύω   come a to stop (ἀναπαύσω, hortatory subjv.) –
'stop, I'm exhausted—let me rest my body.' (211)

1356 ὄχημα, ατος, τό   chariot (ὄχημ᾽ ἵππειον, *periphrasis* for
'horses') (1233)

1357 βόσκημα, ατος, τό   that which is fed; – 'Oh hateful chariot team
that fed from my hand.' [1x *Hipp.*]

1358   διά ... ἔφθειρας, κατα ... ἔκτεινας   *tmesis*

1359–60   ἀ-τρέμᾰ (adv.)   gently, calmly [1x *Hipp.*]

χρώς, ὁ, Ionic gen. χροός   skin, the body itself [1x *Hipp.*]

ἑλκ-ώδης, ες   like a wound, ulcerous; – 'Pheu, pheu; by the gods, servants, touch my wounded body gently' [1x Eur.]

1361–4   πλευρόν, τό   rib; pl.: side; – 'who is standing by my right side?' [1x *Hipp.*]

πρόσ-φορος, ον   convenient, suited to (πρόσφορα, inner acc. as adv.: fitly) (112)

σύντονος, ον   on the stretch, strained (σύντονα, acc. neut. pl. as adv.: in harmony, in unison) [1x *Hipp.*]

κατάρᾱτος, ον   accursed, abominable (πατρὸς ἀμπλακίαις, emphatic *enjambment*) – 'lift me properly, move me all together, ill-starred and accursed because of my father's errors' [1x *Hipp.*]

1365–9   θεο-σέπτωρ, ορος, ὁ   = θεοσεβής god-worshiping, devout (ὅδ', ὅδ', *anaphora*) [1x Eur.]

ὑπερ-*⁺ἔχω   be above, surpass (the aor.² ptc. indicates that "he is looking back on his life as already over" [B.])

προῦπτος, ον   = πρόοπτος, manifest, foreseen [1x Eur.]

ἄκρα, ἡ   highest point (κατ' ἄκρας, to destroy from top to bottom) – 'Here am I, the holy one, the god-worshiper, here am I, the one who surpassed everyone in chastity, clearly I am going to Hades, having totally lost my life, in vain have I toiled in labors of piety toward humankind.' [1x *Hipp.*]

αἰαῖ αἰαῖ·
καὶ νῦν ὀδύνα μ' ὀδύνα βαίνει·
μέθετέ με τάλανα,
καί μοι θάνατος παιὰν ἔλθοι.
†προσαπόλλυτέ μ' ὄλλυτε τὸν δυσδαί-   1375
     μονα·† ἀμφιτόμου λόγχας ἔραμαι,
διαμοιρᾶσαι κατά τ' εὐνᾶσαι
τὸν ἐμὸν βίοτον.
ὦ πατρὸς ἐμοῦ δύστανος ἀρά·

μιαιφόνον τι σύγγονον
παλαιῶν προγεννη-   1380
    τόρων ἐξορίζεται
κακὸν οὐδὲ μένει,
ἔμολέ τ᾽ ἐπ᾽ ἐμέ—τί ποτε, τὸν οὐ-
    δὲν ὄντ᾽ ἐπαίτιον κακῶν;
ἰώ μοί μοι.
τί φῶ; πῶς ἀπαλλά-   1385
    ξω βιοτὰν ἐμὰν
τοῦδ᾽ ἀνάλγητον πάθους;
εἴθε με κοιμάσειε τὸν
δυσδαίμον᾽ Ἄιδα μέλαι-
    να νύκτερός τ᾽ ἀνάγκα.

1371	– – – –	anapest
1372	– – ⌣ ⌣ – ⌣ ⌣ – – –	2 anapests
1373	⌣ ⌣ ⌣ ⌣ ⌣ ⌣ –	anapest
1374	– – ⌣ ⌣ – – – – –	2 anapests
1375	† ⌣ ⌣ – ⌣ ⌣ – ⌣ ⌣ – – –	2 anapests
1376	⌣ ⌣† – ⌣ ⌣ – – – ⌣ ⌣ –	2 anapests
1376a	⌣ ⌣ – – – ⌣ ⌣ – – –	2 anapests
1377	⌣ ⌣ – ⌣ ⌣ –	anapest
1378	– – ⌣ ⌣ – – – ⌣ ⌣ –	2 anapests
1379	⌣ – ⌣ – ⌣ – ⌣ –	2 iambs
1380	⌣ – – ⌣ – –	2 bacchiacs
1380a	⌣ – – – ⌣ – ⌣ –	bacchiac and iamb
1381	⌣ ⌣ – – ⌣ ⌣ –	anapest
1382	⌣ ⌣⌣ ⌣ ⌣⌣ ⌣ ⌣⌣ ⌣ –	2 iambs
1383	⌣ – ⌣ – ⌣ – ⌣ –	2 iambs
1384	⌣ – – –	*extra metrum*
1385	⌣ – – ⌣ – –	2 bacchiacs
1385a	– ⌣ ⌣ – ⌣ –	dodrans
1386	– ⌣ – – – ⌣ –	lecythion
1387	– ⌣ ⌣ – ⌣ – ⌣ –	choriamb and iamb
1388	– – ⌣ – – ⌣ –	iamb and creticus
1388a	⌣ – ⌣ – ⌣ – –	iamb and bacchiac

1374 παιάν, ᾶνος, ὁ   healer (ἔλθοι, opt. of wish) – 'may death come
to me as healer.' [1x *Hipp.*]

1375–7 προς-*⁺ἀπόλλῦμι destroy in addition (to the pain) (προσαπόλλυτέ, impv.; *⁺ὄλλυτε, the compound verb is often repeated by the simple one) [1x Eur.]

ἀμφι-τόμος, ον   two-edged [1x *Hipp.*]

λόγχη, ἡ   blade [1x *Hipp.*]

δια-μοιράω   rend asunder [1x *Hipp.*]

κατ-ευνάζω   lull to sleep (*tmesis*) – 'Destroy me completely, destroy the ill-fated one; I long for a double-edged blade to rend me asunder and lull my life to sleep.' [1x Eur.]

1379–83 μῖαι-φόνος, ον blood-stained, defiled with blood [1x *Hipp.*]

σύγ-γονος (2)   born with, connected by blood, akin, brother, sister (340)

πᾰλαιός (3)   old, aged (908)

προ-γεννήτωρ, ορος, ὁ forefather, ancestor [1x Eur.]

ἐξ-ορίζω   send beyond the frontier, banish [1x *Hipp.*]

ἐπ-αίτος, ον   blamed for, blamable, culpable; – 'some blood-stained kindred evil from ancient ancestors is sent beyond its bounds and does not stay in place, but has come upon me—why ever, when I am guilty of no evils?' [1x *Hipp.*]

1386–8 ἀν-άλγητος, ον without pain (ἀνάλγητον, proleptic: S #2182) – 'how will I free my life so it is painless of this suffering?' [1x *Hipp.*]

κοιμάω   put to bed, lull, soothe (κοιμάσειε, opt. of wish) – 'If only the night-dark necessity of Hades would put me, ill-fated, to rest.' [1x *Hipp.*]

LINES 1389–1461

Artemis addresses Hippolytus, who responds in ordinary iambic trimeter of dialogue. Theseus joins the conversation, and Artemis then addresses both Hippolytus and Theseus.

Αρ.   ὦ τλῆμον, οἵα συμφορᾷ συνεζύγης·
          τὸ δ᾽ εὐγενές σε τῶν φρενῶν ἀπώλεσεν.   1390

Ἱπ.   ἔα·
        ὦ θεῖον ὀσμῆς πνεῦμα· καὶ γὰρ ἐν κακοῖς
        ὢν ᾐσθόμην σου κἀνεκουφίσθην δέμας.
        ἔστ' ἐν τόποισι τοισίδ' Ἄρτεμις θεά.
Αρ.   ὦ τλῆμον, ἔστι, σοί γε φιλτάτη θεῶν.
Ἱπ.   ὁρᾷς με, δέσποιν', ὡς ἔχω, τὸν ἄθλιον;   1395
Αρ.   ὁρῶ· κατ' ὄσσων δ'οὐ θέμις βαλεῖν δάκρυ.
Ἱπ.   οὐκ ἔστι σοι κυναγὸς οὐδ' ὑπηρέτης.
Αρ.   οὐ δῆτ'· ἀτάρ μοι προσφιλής γ' ἀπόλλυσαι.
Ἱπ.   οὐδ' ἱππονώμας οὐδ' ἀγαλμάτων φύλαξ.
Αρ.   Κύπρις γὰρ ἡ πανοῦργος ὧδ' ἐμήσατο.   1400
Ἱπ.   οἴμοι· φρονῶ δὴ δαίμον' ἥ μ' ἀπώλεσεν.
Αρ.   τιμῆς ἐμέμφθη, σωφρονοῦντι δ' ἤχθετο.
Ἱπ.   τρεῖς ὄντας ἡμᾶς ὤλεσ', ᾔσθημαι, μία.
Αρ.   πατέρα γε καὶ σὲ καὶ τρίτην ξυνάορον.
Ἱπ.   ᾤμωξα τοίνυν καὶ πατρὸς δυσπραξίας.   1405
Αρ.   ἐξηπατήθη δαίμονος βουλεύμασιν.
Ἱπ.   ὦ δυστάλας σὺ τῆσδε συμφορᾶς, πάτερ.
Θη.   ὄλωλα, τέκνον, οὐδέ μοι χάρις βίου.
Ἱπ.   στένω σε μᾶλλον ἢ 'μὲ τῆς ἁμαρτίας.
Θη.   εἰ γὰρ γενοίμην, τέκνον, ἀντὶ σοῦ νεκρός.   1410
Ἱπ.   ὦ δῶρα πατρὸς σοῦ Ποσειδῶνος πικρά.
Θη.   ὡς μήποτ' ἐλθεῖν ὤφελ' ἐς τοὐμὸν στόμα.
Ἱπ.   τί δ'; ἔκτανές τἄν μ', ὡς τότ' ἦσθ' ὠργισμένος.
Θη.   δόξης γὰρ ἦμεν πρὸς θεῶν ἐσφαλμένοι.
Ἱπ.   φεῦ·
        εἴθ' ἦν ἀραῖον δαίμοσιν βροτῶν γένος.   1415

1389–90 συ-ζεύγνυμι   yoke together (συνεζύγης, aor.² pass.; τὸ εὐγε-
νές, adj. used substantively with artic.: 'your nobility') [1x *Hipp.*]

1391–2 ὀσμή, ἡ   scent [1x *Hipp.*]

πνεῦμα, ατος, τό   breath [1x *Hipp.*]

ἀνα-κουφίζω   pass. be lifted up, lightened in spirit (cf. δέμας,
acc. of respect, in line 274) – 'for even in this distress, I felt your presence and am eased in my body.' [1x *Hipp.*]

1396 ὄσσε, τώ   eyes (neut. dual). (1444)

1397   κῠν-ᾱγός, ὁ   hunter [1x *Hipp.*]

ὑπ-ηρέτης, ὁ   assistant, attendant; – 'You no longer have your hunter and attendant.' [1x *Hipp.*]

1398   προσ-φῑλής, ές   dear, beloved, friendly (Artemis' conduct toward Hippolytus seems pretty cold in spite of her pronounced love for her worshiper) [1x *Hipp.*]

1399   ἱππο-νόμας, ου, ὁ   keeper of horses [1x Eur.]

φύλαξ, ακος, ὁ   guardian [1x *Hipp.*]

1400   πᾰν-οῦργος, ὁ/ἡ   ready to do anything (mostly negatively); knave, villain, rogue (940)

μήδομαι   devise, resolve, plan, contrive (592)

1402   μέμφομαι   blame, upbraid (τιμῆς, gen. of cause) (695)

ἄχθομαι   be vexed, disgusted; – 'She decries you for your worship, and was disgusted by your chastity.' [1x *Hipp.*]

1403–4   συν-ήορος, ον wife (= ξυν-ᾱορος; πατέρα, resolution in 2nd position; note the opposed numbers encompassing the line, yielding predominance to Aphrodite). – 'She alone, I realize, ruined the three of *us*. **Art.:** Yes [γε], your father and you and his wife, third.' Was Hippolytus thinking of Phaedra or rather of Artemis as the third sufferer? See discussion in Roisman 1999, 150. [1x *Hipp.*]

1405–7   δυσ-πραξία, ἡ   ill success, misfortune (915)

οἰμώζω   groan (see line 614 for the dramatic aor.) (1314)

1412   ὀφείλω   (with inf. expresses an unattainable wish for the past: S #1781)

1413–14   ὀργίζω   make angry (τἄν = τοι ἄν) – 'Why?! You would have killed me anyway, you were so angry then! **Th.:** For we were tripped up in our judgment by the gods.' [1x *Hipp.*]

1415   ἀραῖος (3/2)   cursing; – 'If only the human race could curse the gods!' (The curse of a dying person was thought to be particularly potent. Gods were of course immune to human curses, and yet, after this statement by Hippolytus, Artemis intervenes.) [1x *Hipp.*]

Αρ. ἔασον· οὐ γὰρ οὐδὲ γῆς ὑπὸ ζόφον
     θεᾶς ἄτιμοι Κύπριδος ἐκ προθυμίας
     ὀργαὶ κατασκήψουσιν ἐς τὸ σὸν δέμας,
     σῆς εὐσεβείας κἀγαθῆς φρενὸς χάριν.
     ἐγὼ γὰρ αὐτῆς ἄλλον ἐξ ἐμῆς χερὸς   1420
     ὃς ἂν μάλιστα φίλτατος κυρῇ βροτῶν
     τόξοις ἀφύκτοις τοῖσδε τιμωρήσομαι.
     σοὶ δ᾽, ὦ ταλαίπωρ᾽, ἀντὶ τῶνδε τῶν κακῶν
     τιμὰς μεγίστας ἐν πόλει Τροζηνίᾳ
     δώσω· κόραι γὰρ ἄζυγες γάμων πάρος   1425
     κόμας κεροῦνταί σοι, δι᾽ αἰῶνος μακροῦ
     πένθη μέγιστα δακρύων καρπουμένῳ·
     ἀεὶ δὲ μουσοποιὸς ἐς σὲ παρθένων
     ἔσται μέριμνα, κοὐκ ἀνώνυμος πεσὼν
     ἔρως ὁ Φαίδρας ἐς σὲ σιγηθήσεται.   1430
     σὺ δ᾽, ὦ γεραιοῦ τέκνον Αἰγέως, λαβὲ
     σὸν παῖδ᾽ ἐν ἀγκάλαισι καὶ προσέλκυσαι·
     ἄκων γὰρ ὤλεσάς νιν· ἀνθρώποισι δὲ
     θεῶν διδόντων εἰκὸς ἐξαμαρτάνειν.
     καὶ σοὶ παραινῶ πατέρα μὴ στυγεῖν σέθεν,   1435
     Ἱππόλυτ᾽· ἔχεις γὰρ μοῖραν ᾗ διεφθάρης.
     καὶ χαῖρ᾽· ἐμοὶ γὰρ οὐ θέμις φθιτοὺς ὁρᾶν
     οὐδ᾽ ὄμμα χραίνειν θανασίμοισιν ἐκπνοαῖς·
     ὁρῶ δέ σ᾽ ἤδη τοῦδε πλησίον κακοῦ.

1416–19 ζόφος, ὁ   darkness (Κυπρίδος, resolution in 7th position)
[1x Eur.]

     ἄ-τῑμος, ον   unrevenged, unpunished [1x *Hipp.*]

     κατα-σκήπτω   fall upon, be hurled down upon; – 'For not even under the darkness of the earth will the anger of the goddess Cypris, born from her passion, fall upon your body unavenged, thanks to your piety and noble mind.' [1x *Hipp.*]

1420–2 κῠρέω   hit the mark, happen to be, be right (746)

     τόξον, τό   bow; in pl.: arrows [1x *Hipp.*]

ἄ-φυκτος, ον   unerring; – 'For with my own hand I will take
revenge with these unerring arrows on some other one, whoever happens to be the very dearest of mortals [to her].' [1x *Hipp.*]

1425–7 ἄ-ζυξ, ῦγος, ὁ/ἡ/τό   unyoked, unmarried (546)

πάρος (prep.)   + gen.: before [1x *Hipp.*]

*κείρω   shear, cut off [1x *Hipp.*]

αἰών, ῶνος, ὁ   lifetime, life (1109)

καρπόω   reap the fruits of, bear fruit; – 'for you . . . who
will enjoy the fruits of the great mourning of their tears' [1x *Hipp.*]

1428–9 μουσο-ποιός, ον   making poetry [1x *Hipp.*]

μέριμνᾰ, ἡ   concern, care (ἀνώνυμος, predicative; cf. note
on line 1) (1157)

1432–4 ἀγκάλη, ἡ   arm bent to cradle [1x *Hipp.*]

ἄκων, ἄκουσα, ἄκον   against one's will (θεῶν διδόντων, gen. abs.) (693)

εἰκός   (neut. ptc. of ἔοικα, be like, seem) probable,
reasonable, proper (εἰκός [ἐστί] 'it is likely' + inf.) (615)

ἐξ-*⁺ἁμαρτάνω   err greatly; – 'and it is likely for mortals to err
greatly when a god grants it.' [1x *Hipp.*]

1435–6 παρ-*⁺αινέω   advise, recommend, counsel (707)

στῠγέω   hate, loathe ('Ἱππόλυτ', resolution in 2nd position, *enjambment*) [1x *Hipp.*]

1437–9 φθιτός (3)   wasted, dead

ὄμμα, ατος, τό   eye (886)

χραίνω   stain (1266)

θᾱνάσῐμος (3)   deadly (840)

ἐκ-πνοή, ἡ   a breathing out, expiring [1x *Eur.*]

Artemis exits.

In.   χαίρουσα καὶ σὺ στεῖχε, παρθέν' ὀλβία·   1440
         μακρὰν δὲ λείπεις ῥᾳδίως ὁμιλίαν.

λύω δὲ νεῖκος πατρὶ χρῃζούσης σέθεν·
καὶ γὰρ πάροιθε σοῖς ἐπειθόμην λόγοις.
αἰαῖ, κατ᾽ ὄσσων κιγχάνει μ᾽ ἤδη σκότος·
λαβοῦ, πάτερ, μου καὶ κατόρθωσον δέμας.   1445

Θη. οἴμοι, τέκνον, τί δρᾷς με τὸν δυσδαίμονα;
Ἱπ. ὄλωλα καὶ δὴ νερτέρων ὁρῶ πύλας.
Θη. ἦ τὴν ἐμὴν ἄναγνον ἐκλιπὼν χέρα;
Ἱπ. οὐ δῆτ᾽, ἐπεί σε τοῦδ᾽ ἐλευθερῶ φόνου.
Θη. τί φῄς; ἀφίης αἵματος μ᾽ ἐλεύθερον;   1450
Ἱπ. τὴν τοξόδαμνον Ἄρτεμιν μαρτύρομαι.
Θη. ὦ φίλταθ᾽, ὡς γενναῖος ἐκφαίνῃ πατρί.
Ἱπ. ὦ χαῖρε †καὶ σύ†, χαῖρε πολλά μοι, πάτερ.
Θη. οἴμοι φρενὸς σῆς εὐσεβοῦς τε κἀγαθῆς.
Ἱπ. τοιῶνδε παίδων γνησίων εὔχου τυχεῖν.   1455
Θη. μή νυν προδῷς με, τέκνον, ἀλλὰ καρτέρει.
Ἱπ. κεκαρτέρηται τἄμ᾽· ὄλωλα γάρ, πάτερ.
     κρύψον δέ μου πρόσωπον ὡς τάχος πέπλοις,
Θη. †ὦ κλείν᾽ Ἀθῆναι Παλλάδος θ᾽ ὁρίσματα,†
     οἵου στερήσεσθ᾽ ἀνδρός. ὦ τλήμων ἐγώ,   1460
     ὡς πολλά, Κύπρι, σῶν κακῶν μεμνήσομαι.

1440–1 ὄλβιος (3/2)   happy, blessed (μακρὰν ... ὁμιλίαν, the *hyperbaton* emphasizes the length of their companionship antithetically to the ease with which she departs) (755)

1442 χρῄζω   desire, want (χρῃζούσης σέθεν, gen. abs.: because you wish [it]) [1x *Hipp.*]

1444 κιγχάνω   = κιχάνω; meet with, arrive at [1x *Hipp.*]

1445 κατ-ορθόω   set up right (cf. line 786). (680)

1447 νέρτερος (3)   infernal, underground; οἱ νέρτεροι = the dwellers of the Netherworld, realms of the dead (νερτέρων, adj. used substantively without artic.) [1x *Hipp.*]

1448 ἄν-αγνος, ον   impure, unchaste, unclean (predicative) – 'leaving my hand unclean.' [1x *Hipp.*]

1449 φόνος, ὁ   slaughter, murder, homicide (537)

1451 τοξόδαμνος, ον   subduing with the bow [1x *Hipp.*]

μαρτύρομαι   call as a witness, invoke [1x *Hipp.*]

1455 τοιόσδε, τοιάδε, τοιόνδε   of such nature; – 'Pray that your legitimate sons be such as I am.' Is this comment bitter or insecure? Proud,
honest, or all of the above? How might all of these emotions interact? (655)

1456–7 καρτερέω   endure, persevere (κεκαρτέρηται τὰ ἐμά, "my
enduring is done" [B.]) [1x *Hipp.*]

†**1459**† ὅρισμα, τό   boundary (This is a corrupt line; κλείν(α) cannot be construed grammatically with Ἀθῆναι, and 'Athens and the glorious
boundaries of Pallas' is a very peculiar expression. The alternate manuscript reading, Ἀθηνῶν, would give 'glorious boundaries of Athens and of
Pallas,' which does not make much more sense.) [1x *Hipp.*]

1460 στερέω   deprive (838)

1461 *μιμνήσκω   + gen.: remind; mid.: remember (πολλά, adv.
'how much,' 'how well,' 'how often') [1x *Hipp.*]

Xo.   κοινὸν τόδ᾽ ἄχος πᾶσι πολίταις
         ἦλθεν ἀέλπτως.
         πολλῶν δακρύων ἔσται πίτυλος·
         τῶν γὰρ μεγάλων ἀξιοπενθεῖς   1465
         φῆμαι μᾶλλον κατέχουσιν.

1462–6 ἄχος, εος, τό   grief, pain, distress [1x *Hipp.*]

ἀέλπτως (adv.)   unexpectedly [1x *Hipp.*]

πίτῠλος, ὁ   [ῐ] splash, splashing [1x *Hipp.*]

ἀξιο-πενθής, ές   worthy of lamentation; – 'This grief common
to all citizens came unexpectedly. There will be a splashing of many
tears; for tales worthy of lamentation about the great hold greater
power.' [1x Eur.]

Glossary

A

ἀγαθός (3)	*good, noble*
ἄγαλμα, ατος, τό	*image of a god as an object of worship, idol*
ἀγνός (3)	+ gen.: *pure (from a thing), chaste, unsullied (by)*
ἀγχόνη, ἡ	*throttling, strangling, hanging, noose*
ἄδῐκος, ον	*doing wrong, unjust*
ἀεί (adv.)	(ᾰ/ᾱ) *ever, always*
Ἀθῆναι, αἱ	*city of Athens*
ἄθλιος (3/2)	*wretched*
αἶα, ἡ	*earth, land* (poetic for γαῖα, γῆ)
αἰδέομαι	*respect, be ashamed of*
Ἅιδης, ου, ὁ	*Hades*
αἰδώς, οῦς, ἡ	*sense of shame, modesty, reverence*
αἷμα, ατος, τό	*blood*
*αἰνέω	*praise, speak in praise of*
*αἱρέω	*take;* mid.: *choose*
*αἴρω	*raise, lift up*
*αἰσθάνομαι	*perceive;* + gen.: *take notice of*
αἰσχρός (3/2)	*shameful, disgracing, ugly, ill-favored*
αἰσχύνη, ἡ	*shame*
*αἰσχύνω	*shame, disgrace*
ἀκήρᾰτος, ον	*untouched, pure*
ἀκτή, ἡ	(ἄγνυμι, *break*) *the place where the waves break, seashore*
ἄλγος, τό	*pain, sorrow, grief, distress*
*ἁλίσκομαι	*be captured, be convicted*

ἀλλά (conj.)   but, rather, or; with commands and exhortations:
                       well

ἄλλος (3)   *another, other*

ἄλλως (adv.)   *in vain, without purpose, at other times, in other*
                       circumstances

ἄλμη, ἡ   *water of the sea, brine*

ἄλοχος, ἡ   *one's bed partner, wife*

ἅμα   + dat. (improper prep.): *together with, at the same*
                       time with; adv.: *at the same time, at once*

Ἀμαζών, όνος, ἡ   *Amazon*

*ἁμαρτάνω   *err, miss the mark*

ἁμαρτία, ἡ   *failure, error, sin*

ἀμπλακία ἡ   *error, offense*

ἀμφί (prep.)   + acc.: *around, in attendance on, in the company*
                       of/with, against; + gen.: *about, concerning*; + dat.:
                       around

ἀνά (prep.)   + acc.: *through, throughout*

ἀνάγκη, ἡ   *force, constraint, necessity*

ἄναξ, ἄνακτος, ὁ   *lord, king, master* (applied to all gods)

ἀνάπαυσις, εως, ἡ   *rest, cessation, relief*

ἄνασσα, ἡ   *queen, lady, mistress*

ἀνα-στρέφω   *turn upside down, turn back, turn around/about*

ἀν-*+ἔχω   *continue to*; + ptc.: *hold up, lift up, hold in, keep in*;
                       mid.: *endure, hold out*

ἀνήρ, ἀνδρός, ὁ   *man*

ἄνθρωπος, ὁ   *man/woman, mortal*

ἄντυξ, ὕγος, ἡ   *a rim of a chariot front*

ἀνώνῠμος (2)   (ἀ privat. + ὄνυμα, Aeolic for ὄνομα) *without name,*
                       anonymous

ἄξιος (3)   *worthy*

ἀπαλάττω   *set free, release, get rid of*

ἄπ-*+ειμι   *be absent*

ἀπό (prep.)   + gen.: *from, off, away from, after, by, because, as a*
                       result of

ἀπο-*κτείνω   *kill, slay*

ἀπ-*όλλῡμι   act.: *destroy utterly*; mid.: ἀπ-όλλῡμαι, *perish, die,*
                       cease to exist

ἅπτω   *touch*; mid.: *fasten for oneself*

ἀρά, ἡ   *prayer, curse*

ἄρα (pcl.)	expresses "the surprise attendant upon disillusionment" with a verb in the present or in the past (GP 35–6).
ἆρα	interrog. pcl.: S #2650: "introduce[s] questions asking merely for information and impl[ies] nothing as to the answer expected (neither *yes* nor *no*)"; confirmative pcl.: S #2800, *therefore*
ἅρμα, ατος, τό	*chariot*
ἀρτάω	*fasten*; pass.: *be hung, be fitted*
Ἄρτεμις, ιδος, ἡ	*Artemis, daughter of Zeus and Leto* (acc. Ἄρτεμιν or Ἀρτέμιδα)
*ἄρχω	+ gen. or inf.: *begin, rule*
ἀτάρ (conj.)	*but, yet* (introduces an objection)
ἄτη, ἡ	*folly, delusion, temporary clouding of the mind, destruction, ruin*
ἀτῑμάζω	*slight, dishonor*
αὖ (adv.)	*again, now*
αὐδάω	+ double acc.: *speak, talk, say*
αὐδή, ἡ	*voice*
αὖθις (adv.)	*hereafter, from now on*
αὐτός, αὐτή, αὐτό	intensive pron.: *-self*; in oblique cases pers. pron. of 3rd pers.
ἀφ-*αιρέω, εῖλον	*take away, deprive* X (acc.) *of* Y (acc.)
ἀφ-*ίημι	*send forth*
*ἀφικνέομαι	*arrive*

B

*βαίνω	*go*
βάρος, εος, τό	*weight, burden*; metaph.: *misery*
βᾰρύς, εῖα, ύ	*heavy, burdensome*
βία, ἡ	*force, might, violence*
βίος, ὁ	*life, the course of life, lifetime*
βίοτος, ὁ	*life, way of life*
*βλέπω	*see, look*
*βλώσκω	*go, come*
βοάω	*utter a cry*
βοή, ἡ	*cry, shout*
βούλευμα, ατος, τό	*resolution, plan, design*
βουλεύω	*take counsel, give counsel, consider*

*βούλομαι   *wish, will*
βραχύς, εῖα, ύ   *short, brief*
βρότειος (3/2)   *human, mortal*
βροτός, ὁ   *mortal*
βρόχος, ὁ   *noose*

Γ

γαῖα, ἡ   poetic for γῆ, *earth, ground, soil*
γάμος, ὁ   [ἄ] *marriage, wedding*
γάρ (postpos. conj.) *for* (introducing a reason for the preceding state-
                     ment); explanatory: *the fact is that*
γε   *at least*; postpos. enclit. pcl., in limitative function,
                     used to emphasize a word, often untranslatable;
                     sometimes attached to the word, e.g., ἔμοιγε, *to me
                     at least*; in conversation to be translated "yes"
γενναῖος (3)   *suitable to one's birth or descent, noble*
γένος, ους, τό   *race, stock, kin*
γεραιός (3)   *old*
γῆ, ἡ   *earth, land*
*γίγνομαι   *become, be*
*γιγνώσκω   *know*
γλῶσσα, ἡ   *tongue*
γνήσιος (3)   *legitimate, highborn*
γνώμη, ἡ   *judgment, thought, mind*
γράμμα, ατος, τό   *letter, writing*
γρᾰφή, ἡ   *writing, painting*
γῠνή, γῠναῖκος, ἡ   *woman*

Δ

δαίμων, ονος, ὁ, ἡ   *deity, divinity*
δάκνω   *bite*
δάκρυ, υος, τό   poetic for δάκρυον, *a tear*
δάμαρ, αρτος, ἡ   *wife, spouse*
δέ (postpos. pcl.)   *and, but*
δεῖ   *it is necessary* (with dat. of pers. and gen. of thing)
*δείκνῡμι   *show, reveal*
δεινός (3)   *fearful, terrible, powerful*
δέλτος, ἡ   *writing tablet*
δέμας, τό   *body* (only in nom. and acc.)

δέξιος (3)   *on the right hand*
δέσποινα, ἡ   *mistress, lady*
δεσπότης, ου, ὁ   *master, lord*
δεῦρο (adv.)   *to this place, hither, over here*
δεύτερος (3)   *second*
*δέχομαι   *receive, accept*
δή (pcl.)   *of course, indeed, quite, naturally* (postpos.; adds
                              explicitness, i.e., marks something as immediately
                              present and clear to the mind: S #2840, 2841)
δῆτα (adv.)   (emphatic) *assuredly, really, in truth*; οὐ δῆτα, *in-
                              deed/certainly not* (in emphatic negative answers)
διά (prep.)   + gen. or acc.: *through, throughout*
δια-*φθείρω   *corrupt, destroy utterly*
διδάσκω   *teach* (+ double acc.)
*δίδωμι   *give*
δίκη, ἡ   *order, right, atonement, satisfaction, penalty,
                              retribution*
δι-*+όλλυμι   *destroy utterly*
δισσός (3)   *twofold, double*
δμώς, ωός, ὁ   *slave*
δοκέω   *form an opinion, think, imagine*; intrans.: *seem,
                              appear*; 3 sg.: *seems right, good*
δόμος, ὁ   *house, chamber* (often in pl. because the house con-
                              tains multiple rooms)
δόξα, ἡ   *reputation, opinion, judgment*
*δράω   *do, accomplish*
δυστάλᾱς, αινα, ἀν   *most miserable*
δύστηνος (2)   *wretched, unhappy, unfortunate*
δυστῠχής, ές   *unlucky, unfortunate*
δῶμα, ατος, τό   *house*

E

ἔα   a cry of surprise at something unexpected
*ἐάω   [ᾱ] *let, suffer, allow, permit*
ἐγώ (pers. pron.)   *I*
*ἐθέλω   = θέλω; *wish, be willing, desire*
*εἰμί, ἔσομαι, ἦν   *be* (S #768)
εἶμι   *I shall go* (S #773; serves as the fut. of ἔρχομαι:
                              S #774)

*εἶπον	*said*
εἰς/ἐς (prep.)	+ acc. only: *toward, into, up to, until, toward, to, for; in regard to*
εἷς, μία, ἕν	*one*
εἰσ-*οράω	*look at, look upon*
ἐκ, ἐξ (prep.)	+ gen. (ἐξ before a vowel): *out of, from, after, as the result of; by* = ὑπό + gen. of agent: *by*
ἔκ-δημος (2)	*abroad, away from home, foreign*
ἐκ-*+λείπω	*leave out, forsake, abandon*
ἐκ-*πλήττω	*strike out of one's senses, drive from one's senses (generally of any overpowering passion), scare, astound*
ἐκ-πονέω	*accomplish by means of toil, execute, carry out, bring to perfection*
ἐκ-*σώζω	*preserve, keep safe*
ἐκ-*+φαίνω	*bring to light, reveal*
ἑκών, ἑκοῦσα, ἑκόν	*willing*
ἐλέγχω	*examine, question, disagree, refute*
ἐλεύθερος (3/2)	*free, free from*
ἕλκω	*drag, pull*
ἐν (prep.)	+ dat. (locative): *in, at, near, by, on, among*
ἔν-*ειμι	*be within, be in or among*; impersonal: ἔνεστι τινί, *it is in one's power, one may* or *one can*
ἐνέπω	*see* ἐννέπω
ἐννέπω	*tell*
ἐξ-ελέγχω	*test, refute, convict, expose*
ἔξω	(ἐξ) + gen. (improper prep.): *away from, out of*
ἐπεί (conj.)	of time: *after, when, from time when*; of cause: *since, seeing that, for that*
ἐπει-δή (conj.)	*since*
ἐπί (prep.)	+ dat.: *over, for, near, with a view to, in addition to, on top of*; + acc.: *toward, to, over*
ἐπίσταμαι	*know*
ἕπομαι	*follow*
ἔπος, εος, τό	*word*
*ἐράω/ἔραμαι	*love, desire*
*ἐργάζομαι	*do (to), work, undo, destroy*
ἔργον, τό	*act, deed*
*ἔρχομαι	*come, go*

ἔρως, ωτος, ὁ	love, desire
ἐσθλός (3)	good
εἴσω/ἔσω	(improper prep. + gen.) within
ἕτερος (3)	the other one of two
ἔτι (adv.)	still
εὖ (adv.)	well
εὐγενής, ές	noble, of high descent
εὐθύς, εῖα, ύ	straightforward, plain, honest, straight
εὐκλεής, ές	of good fame, glorious, noble
εὐνή, ἡ	bed
*εὑρίσκω, ηὗρον	find
εὐσεβής, ές	pious, reverent
ἐφ-*+ίστημι	pres. impf. fut. and aor.[1]: set, place upon; mid./pass.: come against, come upon; aor.[2] pf. pass.: stand
*εὔχομαι	pray, boast
ἐχθρός (3)	hated, hateful, hostile; as subst.: ὁ ἐχθρός, one's enemy
*ἔχω	have, hold; in verse ἔχω is often used as κατέχω, hold back, curb; + gen.: keep away from; ἔχω + inf.: be able to

Z

*ζάω	live
Ζεῦς, ὁ	Zeus

H

ἦ	affirmative pcl.: in truth, truly, verily; interrog. pcl.: untranslatable, asking for information without implying anything about the answer expected ("yes" or "no")
ἤ (conj.)	disjunctive: or; interrog.: ἤ . . . ἤ, either . . . or, whether . . . or; compar.: than
ᾗ (adv.)	how, in what way, which way, where, in truth, verily, truly
ἤδη (adv.)	already, by this time, now, immediately, in the past
*ἥδομαι	+dat.: enjoy oneself, take pleasure in, be pleased
ἡδονή, ἡ	pleasure
ἡδύς, ἡδεῖα, ἡδύ	sweet, pleasant, welcome

ἥλιος, ὁ	*sun*
ἡμέρα, ἡ	*day*

Θ

θάνᾰτος, ὁ	*death*
θεά, ἡ	*goddess*
θέλω	= **ἐθέλω*
θέμις, θέμιστος, ἡ	*law, right* (agreed upon by common consent or pre-scription); θέμις ἐστί, *is right*
θεός, ὁ	*god*
θήρ, θηρός, ὁ	*wild beast of prey*
Θησεύς, έως, ὁ	*Theseus*
θιγγάνω	+ gen.: *touch*
*θνήσκω	*die*
θνητός (3/2)	*mortal*

I

ἵνα (adv.)	*where*
ἵνα (final conj.)	*so that*
Ἱππόλυτος, ὁ	*Hippolytus*
ἵππος, ὁ, ἡ	*horse*
*ἵστημι	*set, place, stand, make stand*

K

καί (conj.)	*and, also, too, even, as*
κακός (3)	*bad, evil in its kind, worthless*
καλός (3)	*fine, good, beautiful*
καλῶς (adv.)	*well*
κάρα, τό [ᾰ]	*head*
καρδία, ἡ	*heart*
κάρτα (adv.)	*very; very much*
κατά (prep.)	+ acc.: *over, throughout, according to, in relation to*; + gen.: *down, over, toward, down upon, against*
κατ-*+ἔχω	*seize*
κατα-*+θνήσκω	*die*
κέντρον, τό	*point, spike, sting*; metaph.: *spur, goad*
κεφαλή, ἡ	*head*
κλεινός (3)	*renowned, glorious*
κλύω	+ gen.: *hear, give ear, listen to*

κοιτή, ἡ — *bed*
κομίζω — *bring, carry, welcome*
κόρη, ἡ — (Ionic κούρη) *girl, daughter, maiden*
κραίνω — *bring to pass, accomplish, complete*
κρατέω — *prevail (over), win out, be best, hold sway*
κρείσσων, ον, gen.: ονος — *better, stronger, mightier*
κρεμαστός (3) — *hung, hanging*
Κρήσιος (3) — *Cretan*
*κρύπτω — *hide*
*κτάομαι — *acquire;* pf.: *possess*
*κτείνω — *kill, slay*
κῦμα, ατος, τό — *anything swollen, swell, wave, billow*
Κύπρις, ῖδος — *Cypris, a name of Aphrodite, from the island of Cyprus, where she was most worshiped*
κύων, κυνός, ὁ, ἡ — *a dog, a hound* (if "hound" it is usually fem.)

Λ

*λαμβάνω — *take*
*λανθάνω — act.: *escape notice, lie hidden*; mid. and pass. + gen.: *forget*
*λέγω — *say, state, proclaim*
λειμών, ῶνος, ὁ — *any moist grassy place, meadow*
*λείπω — *leave*
λέκτρον, τό — *couch, bed*; in pl. mostly: *marriage bed*
λεύσσω — *look*
λέχος, εος, τό — *marriage bed: a marriage*
λήγω — *stop, cease from*
Λητώ, όος/οῦς, ἡ — (Doric: Λᾱτώ) *Leto, mother of Apollo and Artemis*
λίαν (adv.) — *too much*
λίμνη, ἡ — *lagoon*
λόγος, ὁ — *word, report, rumor*
λύπη, ἡ — *pain, sorrow, distress*
λύω [ῡ] — *loosen, unfasten, release, relax, lay aside; be profitable*

M

*μαίνομαι — *be mad*
μακρός (3) — *long* (whether in space or time)

μᾶλλον	more; μᾶλλον ἤ, more than
*μανθάνω	learn by inquiry
μάντῐς, εως, ὁ	diviner, seer, prophet, prophetess
μάρτῠς, ῠρος, ὁ/ἡ	witness
μάταιος (3/2) [ᾰ]	unmeaning, trifling, in vain, thoughtless
μάτην (adv.)	in vain
μέγας, μεγάλη μέγα [ᾰ]	great; μέγα, adv.: very much, exceedingly
μέγιστος (3)	biggest, most important (superl. of μέγας)
μεθ-*ίημι	let go, give up, let loose, release, abandon
μείζων, μεῖζον	bigger (compar. of μέγας)
μέλαθρον, τό	cross-beam, rafter, roof; in pl.: house
μέλεος (3/2)	wretched, unhappy
*μέλλω	be about to, be on the point of doing, intend to
*μέλω	be an object of care or concern; μέλει, impersonal use with dat.: it is a care (to me); mid. in trans. sense + gen.: care for, turn one's thoughts to, tend to
μέν	surely, indeed, really (μέν solitarium)
μέντοι	(μέν + τοι) as an asseverative pcl.: certainly, surely, of course; as an adversative pcl.: however, yet
μέτα (prep.)	+ gen.: with, by means of
μηδείς, μηδέν	(indef. pronominal adj.) μηδέν, adv. acc.: not at all
μήν (pcl.)	adversative: however, yet, but; asseverative: in truth, surely
μήτηρ, μητρός, ἡ	mother
μηχανάομαι	contrive, devise, scheme
μίασμα, ατος, τό [ῐ]	stain, defilement, pollution
μῑσέω	hate
μοῖρα, ἡ	fate, one's portion in life, destiny, apportionment
μόνος (3)	only, alone; μόνον, adv.: only
μόχθος, ὁ	toil
μῦθος, ὁ	word, speech
μῶν (interrog. pcl.)	= μὴ οὖν; can/could it be that (used in questions when a negative answer is expected)

N

ναίω	dwell, inhabit
ναυβάτης, ου, ὁ [ᾰ]	seaman, sailor
νεκρός, ὁ	dead body, corpse

νέος (3)	*young, unexpected, untoward*
νικάω	*overcome, subdue, win*
νιν	enclit. acc. of 3rd pers. pron.
νόθος (3/2)	*illegitimate, born out of wedlock*
νόμος, ὁ	*custom, convention, law*
νοσέω	*be ill*
νόσος, ἡ	*sickness, disease, malady, illness*
νοῦς, νοῦ, ὁ	*mind, thought*
νυν (enclit. pcl. postpos.)	usually inferential: *then, therefore* (often best not translated)
νύξ, νυκτός, ἡ	*night*

Ξ

ξανθός (3)	*golden, auburn*
ξυν-	*see* συν-

Ο

ὅδε, ἥδε, τόδε	(demon. pron.) *this* (ὅ -δε points out what is present or before one)
ὁδός, ἡ	*path, way*
ὅθεν (adv.)	*from where, whence*
*οἶδα	*see with the mind's eye, know* (old pf. used as pres.)
οἰκέω	*live in, inhabit*
οἶκος, ὁ	*house, abode, dwelling* (pl. often stands for a single house)
οἴμοι	*woe's me!* (exclamation of pain, fright, pity, anger, surprise)
οἷος, οἵα, οἷον (pron.)	*such as, of such sort*
*ὄλλυμι	act.: *destroy, loose*; mid.: *perish*
ὁμῑλία, ἡ	*companionship, intercourse*
ὄμμα, ατος, τό	*eye*
*ὄμνῡμι	*swear*
ὅμως (adv.)	*nevertheless, still*; ἀλλ᾽ ὅμως = *but still, all the same, nonetheless*
*ὀνίνημι	*profit, benefit*
ὅπη (indef. interrog. adv.)	*in which way, where*

ὅπως (conj.)   with purpose clause: *so that*; compar.: *as*; time:
                                when
*ὁράω   *see*
ὀργή, ἡ   *wrath, impulse, feeling, passion*
ὀρθόω   *set straight, put right*
ὅρκος, ὁ   *oath*
ὄρνις, ὄρνιθος, ὁ/ἡ   *bird* (acc. sg. ὄρνιν and ὄρνῑθα)
ὄρος, τό   *mountain, hill*
ὅς, ἥ, ὅ (relat. pron.)   *which, that*
ὅσος, η, ον (relat.   *how much, as great as, as much as*; in pl.: *all that,*
   correl. pron.)   *as many as*
ὅστις, ἥτις, ὅ τι   *whoever, anyone who, anything, which*
   (indef. or
   general relat.
   pron.)
οὐδείς, οὐδεμία,   *no one, nothing*
   οὐδέν
οὐκέτι (adv.)   *no more, no longer, no further*
οὖν (conj.)   *so now, therefore, then, in fact, at all events* (inferen-
                                tial: marks transition to a new thought)
οὕνεκα (improper   *on account of, for the sake of;* + gen., usually postpos.
   prep.)
οὐρανός, ὁ   *heaven/sky, the seat of the gods*
οὖς, ὠτος, τό   *ear*
οὕτως/οὕτω (adv.)   *it is fitting, in this way, in this manner, thus*
ὄχλος, ὁ   *throng of people, crowd*
ὄχος, εος, τό   *chariot*

Π

πάθος, εος, τό   *suffering, misfortune, calamity*
παῖς, παιδός, ὁ/ἡ   *child*
πάλαι (adv.)   *long ago, formerly, before*
πάλιν (adv.)   *back, again*
παρά (prep.)   + acc.: *running along, beside, next to*; + dat.: *by the*
                                side of, beside, by
πάρ-*+ειμι   *be present/near, at hand*; + dat.: πάρεστι μοι, *it is in*
                                my power; impersonal absolute: *it is possible, it may*
                                be done, it is allowed
παρ-έχω   *hold beside, grant, supply*

παρθένος, ἡ	*virgin, maiden*
πάροιθε (adv.)	*before*
πᾶς, πᾶσα, πᾶν	*all, every, everything*
*πάσχω	*suffer, experience*
πατήρ, τρός, ὁ	*father*
πατρῷος (3)	*of a father*
*πείθω	*persuade*; mid.: *obey*
*πειράομαι	*try, attempt*
πέλας	(improper prep. mostly + gen., but also + dat.) *close, near*
πέμπω	*send, attend, escort, take*
πέπλος, ὁ	*full robe worn by a woman, man's cloak or robe*
περί (prep.)	+ gen.: *about, in regard to*
περισσός (3)	*above measure, superior*
πέτρα, ἡ	*rock, crag*
πῆμα, ατος, τό	*suffering, misery, woe*
πικρός (3/2)	*bitter, sharp*
*πίπτω	*fall, turn out, happen*
πίστις, εως, ἡ	*assurance*
πιστός (3)	*reliable, loyal, trustworthy*
Πιτθεύς, έως, ὁ	*Pittheus, Hippolytus' great-grandfather; father of Theseus' mother, Aethra*
πλεῖστος (3)	*very much, very great, most* (superl. of +πολύς)
πλεκτός (3)	*plaited, twisted, twined*
πλέον	*more*
πλήν (adv.)	*besides, except*
ποῖ (correl. adv.)	*whither? to what end?* (sometimes + gen.)
πόλις, εως, ἡ	*city*
πολίτης, [ῑ] ου, ὁ	*citizen*
πολύς, πολλή, πολύ	*great, large, mighty*
πόνος, ὁ	*hard work, toil, pain*
πόντιος (3/2)	*of/from/in the sea, ruling the sea*
πόντος, ὁ	*sea; in tragedy, sea in general and the Black Sea*
πορφύρεος (3)	*purple, dark, crimson*
Ποσειδῶν, ῶνος, ὁ	*Poseidon*
ποτέ (indef. adv.)	(enclit.) *at some time, once, erst*
πότερον/ πότερα . . . ἤ	*whether . . . or* (introduces direct alternative questions; frequently left untranslated in English)
πότμος, ὁ	*fate, doom*

πούς, ποδός, ὁ	*foot*
πρᾶγμα, ατος, τό	*deed, matter*
πράττω	*fare, do, work, achieve*
πρίν (conj.) [ῐ]	*before, formerly* (when subordinated to an affirmative clause, usually takes inf.)
προ-*+βαίνω	*go toward, go forward, advance*
προ-*δίδωμι	*betray, fail one*
προθῡμία, ἡ	*readiness, willingness, zeal; goodwill*
πρός (prep.)	+ acc.: *toward, to, upon, with, in proportion to*
πρός (adv.)	*in addition to*
πρὸς θεῶν	*please, in the name of the gods*
πρόσ-πολος, ὁ	*servant, attendant*
προσ-*+τίθημι	*apply, attribute, impute to*
προ-*τίθημι	*put/set before, prefer*
πρόσωθεν (adv.)	*from afar, from long ago*
πρόσωπον, τό	*face*
πρῶτος (3)	*first*
πύλη, ἡ [ῠ]	*gate*
πυνθάνομαι	+ gen.: *ask, inquire, learn*
πῶλος ὁ/ἡ	*a foal, whether a colt or a filly*; in poetry often *a young girl*
πῶς (interrog. adv.)	*how? in what way/manner?*
πως (indef. adv.)	*somehow, in any way*

Ρ

ῥᾴδιος (3)	*easy, easygoing*
ῥίπτω	*hurl, throw, cast out*

Σ

σάρξ, σαρκός, ἡ	*flesh*
σαφής, ές	*clear, sure, certain, reliable*
σέβω	*worship, honor*
σεμνός (3)	*august, holy, solemn, haughty, grand*
σημαίνω	*signal, declare*
σῑγάω	*be silent or still, keep silence*
σῑγή, ἡ	*silence*
σίδηρος, ὁ	*iron; anything made of iron, tool, implement, scythe*
σκοπέω	*look, consider*
σκότος, ὁ	*darkness, gloom*

σός (3)	*your*
σοφός (3)	*clever, wise, learned*
*σπείρω	*sow, engender, beget*
στείχω	*walk, go, come, approach*
στένω	*sigh*; trans.: *bemoan, lament, deplore, complain* (only in pres. and impf.)
στόμα, ατος, τό	*mouth, tongue*
στυγνός (3)	*hateful, sullen, sad, gloomy*
συμφορά, ἡ	*an event in either a good or a bad sense, mishap, misfortune*
σύν	prep., + dat.: *with*; adv.: *together, at once, jointly, besides, moreover*
‡συνείδω	*share in the knowledge* (σύνοιδα, pf. with pres. sense; the pres. of this stem does not exist)
σύν-*ειμι	*associate with, live with, consort with*
*σφάλλω	*make fall, trip up*; pass.: *get upset, slip from*
*σῴζω	*preserve, keep safe*
σῶμα, ατος, τό	*body*
σωφρονέω	*be of sound mind, practice self-control*
σώφρων, ονος, ὁ, ἡ, σῶφρον, τό	*of sound mind, prudent, chaste*

T

τᾶλας, τάλαινᾰ, τάλᾰν	(*τλάω, *suffer*) *suffering, wretched, enduring*
ταῦρος, ὁ	*bull*
ταύτῃ (adv.)	*in this way or manner*
ταχύς, εῖα, ύ	*quick, swift, fast*; ὡς τάχος, *as quickly as possible*
τε (enclit. pcl.)	*and*; τε . . . τε, *both . . . and, as . . . so, and . . . and*
τέγγω	*moisten, wet, soak, soften, melt*
τέκνον, τό	*child*
τέραμνον, τό	*anything closely shut, room, chamber* (used only in pl.)
τέρμα, ατος, τό	*end, goal, finish line*
τέρμων, ονος, ὁ	= τέρμα; *boundary, end, goal*
τερπνός (3)	*delightful, pleasant, agreeable, cheering*
τέχνη, ἡ	*means, device*
τῇδε (adv.)	*in this way, in this direction*
τί (adv.)	*why, how, wherefore, in any way, at all*
*τίθημι	*put*
τίκτω	*give birth*

τῑμάω	*hold worthy, honor, respect*
τῑμή, ἡ	*honor, esteem*
τίς, τί (interrog. pron.)	*who, which, what*
τὶς, τὶ (indef. pron.)	*anyone, someone, anything, something*
τλήμων, ονος, ὁ/ἡ	*suffering, wretched*
τοι (enclit. pcl. of inference)	(postpos.) *therefore, accordingly*; strengthening an assertion: *in truth, verily*
τόκος, ὁ	*offspring, young child*
τόλμᾰ, ἡ	*boldness, daring*
τόπος, ὁ	*place*
τοσοῦτος, -αύτη, -οῦτο (demon. pron.)	*so great, so large*
*τρέφω	*nourish, rear*
τρίτος (3)	*third*
Τροζήνιος (3)	(Τροιζ- codd.) *of Troezen*
τρόπος, ὁ	*way, manner, fashion*
τροφός, ὁ/ἡ	*rearer, nurse*
*τυγχάνω	*happen, hit the mark, obtain*
τύραννος, ὁ, ἡ [ῠ]	*master, mistress*; τύραννος, ον, *royal*
τύχη, ἡ	*fortune, chance, coincidence, misfortune*

Υ

ὕδωρ, ατος, τό	*water*
ὑπέρ (prep.)	+ gen.: *beyond, on behalf of*
ὑπό (prep.)	+ gen.: *by, under, through, from*; + dat.: *under*
ὕστερος (3)	*coming after, latter*

Φ

Φαίδρα, ἡ	*Phaedra*
*φαίνω	*bring to light, show, make known, reveal, disclose*
φάος, εος, τό	*light, daylight* (usually signifies life versus the darkness of the Netherworld)
φάρμακον, τό	*drug, medicine, remedy, charm*
φέγγος, εος, τό	*light, sunlight*
*φέρω	*bring, carry, bear, endure*
φεύγω	*flee, run away*

φήμη, ἡ	*rumor, news, voice, story, utterance*
*φημί	*say, assert*
φθέγμα, ατος, τό	*sound, word*
φίλος (3)	*loved, dear, friendly*
φοβέω	*terrify*
φόβος, ὁ	*fear, fright*
φοιτάω	*go to and fro, roam wildly about, wander*
φρήν, φρενός, ἡ	*heart, mind, sense*
φρονέω	*think*
φροντίζω	*think, consider, reflect, give heed*
φῦγάς, άδος, ὁ, ἡ	*an exile, fugitive, banished man/woman*
φῦγή, ἡ	*exile, banishment*
φύσις, εως, ἡ [ῠ]	*nature, inborn quality; natural origin*
*φύω [ῠ/ῡ]	*bring forth, produce*; aor.²: *grew, was*; pf.: *be by nature*
φῶς, ωτός, τό	(contraction of +φάος) *light*

X

*χαίρω	*rejoice, be glad, be delighted, be pleased; welcome, farewell*
χάρις, ἡ [ᾰ]	*grace, favor, delight*; χάριν + gen.: *for the sake of*
χείρ, χειρός, ἡ	*hand*
χθών, χθονός, ἡ	*the earth, ground*
χράομαι	+ dat.: *use, experience, engage in, practice*
χρεών (indecl.)	*that which must be*
*χρή	*it is necessary* (indecl. noun, "necessity," with ἐστί supplied); χρῆν = χρὴ ἦν, impf.: *it was necessary*
χρῆμα, ατος, τό	*business, affair*; τὶ χρῆμα = τί: *what?*
χρηστός (3)	*useful, good, favorable*; as subst. adj.: *good services, benefits*
χρόνος, ὁ	*time, span of time*
χωρέω	*make room for another, give way, go forward, advance, go, come*

Ψ

ψῡχή, ἡ	*spirit, soul, life*

Ω

ὡς   conj.: *so that, how*; exclamatory adv.: *how; just as*

ὥσπερ (conj.)   *just as, as* (introduces compar. clause of quality)

ὥστε   conj.: *so as, so that* (with the inf. implies a possible
                              or intended result or tendency rather than actual
                              fact); adv.: *as, like*

Index of Grammatical, Syntactical, Literary, and Rhetorical Figures

Cited by line number unless otherwise noted.

ABSTRACT FOR CONCRETE   11

ACCUSATIVE   *absolute* 1317; *adverbial* 22, 46, 66, 112, 113, 183, 205, 398, 400, 1058, 1059, 1097, 1361; *cognate* 571, 584, 1016; *double acc.* 21, 252, 352, 644, 683, 914–15; *of extent of time* 135–7; *in indirect discourse/acc. and inf.* 10–13, 16, 33, 41, 131–2, 135–40, 248, 254, 347, 426–7, 442, 460–3, 464–5, 467, 507, 618, 641, 645, 702–3, 925–6, 928, 962, 977–8, 980, 991, 1008, 1072, 1298–301, 1401; *internal* 21, 119, 223, 293, 584, 756 (in apposition), 785, 815 (in apposition), 829, 971, 998, 999, 1016, 1182, 1216, 1237, 1246; *of manner* 119, 557, 599, 973; *of respect* 27, 199, 274, 505, 689, 765, 806, 1230; *with verbs of swearing* 713

ADJECTIVE   *attributive with article* 33, 974; *neut. denoting abstract noun* 656, 1007; *predicative* 616, 675, 676, 819, 881, 890, 1429, 1447; *proleptic/anticipatory* 175; *used substantively with article* 114, 192, 380, 593, 637×2, 966, 1064, 1390; *used substantively without article* 90, 330, 410, 616, 624, 769, 967, 1008, 1447

ADVERB   *in attributive function and position* 288, 524; *substantivized* 302

ADYNATON   p. 31; 208–31, 616–24, 925–31, 1074–6

AMBIGUITY   376, 384–6

ANACOLUTHON   p. 31; 23, 40, 292

ANAPHORA   p. 31; 23–4, 182–3, 355, 473–4, 1364–5, 1395–6

ANASTROPHE   p. 32; 8, 32, 83, 92, 111, 312, 381, 514, 708–9, 903, 910, 1168

AORIST   *dramatic* 614, 1405; *gnomic* 428, 446, 629, 644, 708

APHAERESIS   p. 32; 459, 493

FUTURE AS PRESENT   527

GENDER   349; *collective neuter* 962; *generalizing neuter* 966

GENITIVE   *absolute* 330, 800, 972, 990, 1023, 1031, 1434, 1442;
accountability 147; *adnominal* 802, 810; *of cause* 366, 554, 570, 591,
813a, 817, 844, 1402, 1407; *of comparison* 120, 191, 265, 305, 471,
475, 484, 500, 530, 939, 961, 968, 995, 1020; *of disadvantage* 328;
of exclamation 936, 1454; *explanation/apposition* 35, 39, 52, 138,
139, 546, 560, 589, 602, 671, 811, 822, 824, 864, 878, 881, 925, 938,
948, 1169, 1248; *of material or content* 822, 864, 1178; *objective*
107, 130, 194, 195, 233, 338, 386, 600, 804, 858×2, 926, 1000, 1068,
1089, 1141, 1326; *partitive* 12, 13, 40, 54, 66, 94, 402, 520, 820, 832,
849, 888, 894, 933, 935, 982, 1010, 1083, 1086, 1092, 1105, 1182,
1317, 1318; *of personal agent* 8, 397, 594, 931, 945, 1061, 1164,
1414; *possession* 89, 864, 1171, 1174; *of separation* 18, 138, 357,
1181; *source/origin* 89, 122, 164, 489; *subjective* 136, 241, 396, 831,
845, 1102, 1124, 1215; *of value* 623; *with verbs of hearing/inquiring*
270, 363

HISTORICAL PRESENT   *see* present

HYPALLAGE   p. 32; 335, 581, 646–7, 1322–3

HYPERBATON   p. 32; 3–4, 10–12, 25, 36, 47–8, 54–5, 56, 92, 102,
135–8, 226–7, 250–1, 253–4, 258–9, 308–9, 332, 371, 373–4, 455,
492, 524, 583–4, 645–7, 675–7, 678, 717, 866, 869–71, 936, 970,
1001, 1020, 1061–2, 1093, 1098, 1111, 1119, 1123, 1152, 1161,
1167–8, 1200, 1232, 1237

HYPOPHORA   p. 32; 966–7

INDICATIVE   *in final clause* 648

INDIRECT DISCOURSE   13, 16, 33, 56, 131–2, 135–40, 173, 393,
405–7, 426–7, 435, 462–3, 465–6, 519, 663, 869–73, 892, 943–5,
968–9, 977–8, 979, 1026–7, 1085, 1176, 1205, 1315

INFINITIVE   *appositive* 46, 1228; *articular* 49 (obj.), 80 (subj.), 192
(gen. of comparison), 247 (subj.), 378 (subj.), 399 (dat. of means);
epexegetic 712; *final-consecutive* 294, 346, 961, 1096; *following* πρίν
29, 365, 1336; *in indirect discourse reflecting unreality* 1026–7; *limit-
ing/explanatory* 610, 989, 1202, 1239; *as object of indirect statement*
13; *potential* 470; *result (following* ὥστε) 50, 390, 717, 823, 824, 961,
1228; *as subject* 115, 785

LITOTES   p. 32; 1, 354, 371

MAJESTIC PLURAL (*pluralis maiestatis*)   *see* plural

μέν **solitarium**   1, 47, 545, 882

METER   1–120, 121–69, 170–524, 525–64, 565–731, 669–71, 856,
 1268–81, 1370–88a; *Meter and Prosody* pp. 23–25; *metrical convenience* 1, 31, 60, 116, 380, 535, 565, 575; *unmetrical* 141, 625–26

NEGATION   49. *See also* litotes

NOMINATIVE AND INFINITIVE   122, 655

OPTATIVE   *imperative* 528, 529, 693; *in indirect discourse* 1205;
 potential 89, 90, 228, 270 (politeness), 336 (politeness), 345, 469, 480,
 557 (politeness), 654, 675–7, 842, 904 (politeness), 950, 961, 981,
 1017, 1054, 1062–3, 1154, 1186; *of wish* 87, 105, 209, 230, 321, 345,
 364, 403, 407, 422, 430, 523, 640–41, 684, 732, 734, 735, 742, 889,
 1028, 1030, 1074–5, 1083, 1111, 1119, 1191, 1192, 1374, 1386, 1410

OXYMORON   p. 32; 17, 331, 821, 1144

PARTICIPLE   *attributive ptc.* 299, 464, 483, 600, 628x2, 702, 798,
 916, 970, 1036, 1059, 1187, 1207, 1337, 1354; *articular ptc. as substantive* 184, 244, 382, 441, 444, 449, 513, 590, 630, 696, 842, 863,
 922, 942, 945, 999, 1000, 1040, 1081, 1189, 1266, 1331; *unarticulated
 ptc. as substantive* 541, 967, 997, 1001, 1216; *circumstantial ptc.:*
 aorist coincidental/modal 290, 357, 429, 549, 561, 575, 596, 628, 684,
 726, 729, 786, 810, 814, 829, 886, 1036, 1190, 1194; *of attendant cir-
 cumstance/descriptive* 4, 8, 19, 23, 35, 52, 56, 108, 118, 122, 124, 128,
 131, 139, 158, 171, 192, 211, 214, 218, 221, 231, 233, 275, 276, 287,
 292, 306, 325, 387, 399, 404, 414, 420, 422, 446, 458, 462–3, 492,
 502, 526, 575, 598, 620, 626, 631, 633, 634, 635, 637, 654, 655, 664,
 689, 699, 731, 746, 768, 770, 772–5, 779, 793, 843, 857, 859, 869,
 872, 896, 897, 935, 948, 951, 953, 957, 993, 995, 1004–6, 1019, 1024,
 1032, 1034, 1035, 1048, 1056, 1067, 1079, 1081, 1097, 1105–6, 1111,
 1125, 1152, 1175x2, 1178, 1189, 1193, 1194, 1210, 1211, 1215, 1220,
 1223, 1226, 1227, 1231, 1236, 1238, 1239x2, 1240, 1242, 1246, 1257,
 1270, 1291x2, 1318, 1329, 1366, 1440; *causal* 32, 102, 470, 671, 803,
 838, 1006, 1170, 1172, 1177, 1288, 1303, 1309, 1310; *conative* 597;
 concessive 271, 313, 477, 933, 943, 984, 1034, 1035, 1040, 1057,
 1077, 1243, 1308; *conditional* 305, 332, 1005, 1006, 1263; *of manner*
 38, 786, 793, 1011; *of purpose/final* 992; *of time* 24, 37, 74, 111, 112,
 280, 290, 604, 661, 703, 803, 864, 897, 976, 1001, 1105, 1106, 1153,
 1164, 1172, 1181, 1206, 1216, 1244, 1314. *supplementary ptc.* 281,
 355, 388, 474, 494, 706, 827, 869, 878, 913, 1069; *supplementary ptc.
 in indirect discourse* 56, 305, 313, 393, 406, 435, 463, 476, 519, 663,
 892, 945, 968, 1085, 1315

LIST OF IRREGULAR GREEK VERBS

A

ἀγγέλλω, ἀγγελῶ, ἤγγειλα, ἤγγελκα, ἤγγελμαι, ἠγγέλθην   *announce*
ἄγω, ἄξω, ἤγαγον (ἀγαγ-), ἦχα, ἦγμαι, ἤχθην (ἀχθ-)   *lead*
ᾄδω, ᾄσομαι, ᾖσα, ᾖσμαι, ᾔσθην   *sing*
αἰνέω, usually in compounds with ἐπί, παρά, etc.: -αινέσω, -ήνεσα,
    -ήνεκα, ήνεμαι, -ήνεθην   *praise, speak in praise of*
αἱρέω, αἱρήσω, εἷλον (ἑλ-), ᾕρηκα, ᾕρμαι, ᾑρέσθην   *take;* mid.: *choose*
αἴρω, ἀρῶ, ἦρα, ἦρκα, ἦρμαι, ἤρθην   *raise, lift up*
αἰσθάνομαι, αἰσθήσομαι, ᾐσθόμην, ᾔσθμαι   *perceive*
αἰσχύνω, αἰσχυνῶ, ᾔσχυνα, ᾐσχύνθην   *disgrace;* mid.: *feel ashamed*
ἀκούω, ἀκούσομαι, ἤκουσα, ἀκήκοα, ἠκούσθην   *hear*
ἁλίσκομαι, ἁλώσομαι, ἑάλων/ἥλων, ἑάλωκα/ἥλωκα   *be captured*
ἀλλάττω, often compounded with ἀπό, διά, μετά: ἀλλάξω, ἤλλαξα,
    -λλαχα, ἤλλαγμαι, ἠλλάχθην/ἠλλάγην; fut. pass.: ἀπ-αλλαχθήσομαι/
    ἀπ-αλλαγήσομαι; fut. mid.: -αλλάξομαι   *change*
ἁμαρτάνω, ἁμαρτήσομαι, ἥμαρτον, ἡμάρτηκα, ἡμάρτημαι,
    ἡμαρτήθην   *err*
ἀπόλλῡμι, ἀπολῶ, ἀπώλεσα, ἀπωλόμην (aor.² mid.), ἀπολώλεκα/
    ἀπόλωλα   *destroy;* mid.: *perish*
ἅπτω, ἅψω, ἧψα, ἧμμαι, ἥφθην   *fasten, kindle;* mid.: *touch*
ἀραρίσκω, ἦρσα; aor.²: ἤραρον; pf.²: ἄρᾱρα; aor. pass.: ἤρθην   *fit, join*
ἀρκέω, ἀρκέσω, ἤρκεσα   *assist, suffice, be of use*
ἄρχω, ἄρξω, ἦρξα, ἦρχα, ἦργμαι, ἤρχθην   *begin, rule*
ἀφικνέομαι, ἀφίξομαι, ἀφικόμην, ἀφῖγμαι   *arrive*

B

βαίνω, βήσομαι, ἔβην, βέβηκα   *go*
βάλλω, βαλῶ, ἔβαλον, βέβληκα, βέβλημαι, ἐβλήθην   *throw, hit*

βλέπω, βλέψομαι, ἔβλεψα   *see*
βλώσκω, μολοῦμαι, ἔμολον, μέμβλωκα   *go, come*
βούλομαι, βουλήσομαι, βεβούλομαι, ἐβουλήθην   *wish, will*

Γ

γίγνομαι, γενήσομαι, ἐγενόμην, γέγονα (*I am*; pf. ptc.: γεγώς), γεγένημαι
    (late ἐγενήθην)   *become, be*
γιγνώσκω, γνώσομαι, ἔγνων, ἔγνωκα, ἔγνωσμαι, ἐγνώσθην   *know*

Δ

δείκνῡμι, δεικνύω, δείξω, ἔδειξα, δέδειχα, δέδειγμαι, ἐδείχθην   *show,*
    reveal
δέχομαι, δέξομαι, ἐδεξάμην, δέδεγμαι, -εδέχθην   *receive, await*
δέω, δήσω, ἔδησα, δέδεκα, δέδεμαι, ἐδέθην   *bind*
διαφθείρω, διαφθερῶ, διέφθειρα, διέφθαρκα and διέφθορα, διέφθαρμαι,
    διεφθάρην   *corrupt, destroy*; pf.[2]: *be ruined*
διδάσκω, διδάξω, ἐδίδαξα, δεδίδαχα, δεδίδαγμαι   *teach*
δίδωμι, δώσω, ἔδωκα, aor. pl.: ἔδομεν, δέδωκα, δέδωμαι, ἐδόθην   *give*
δράω, δράσω, ἔδρασα, δέδρακα, δέδραμαι, ἐδράσθην   *do, accomplish*

Ε

ἐάω (impf. εἴων), ἐάσω, εἴασα, εἴακα, εἴαμαι, εἰάθην   *permit, let alone*
ἐθέλω, ἐθελήσω, ἐθέλησα, ἐθέληκα   *be willing, wish*
εἰμί, ἔσομαι, ἦν   *be*
εἶπον, aor.[2]   *said* (*see under* λέγω)
ἐλαύνω, ἐλῶ, ἤλασα, -ελήλακα, ἐλήλαμαι, ἠλάθην   *drive*
ἐναίρω, aor.[2]; ἤναρον, aor.[1]; mid.: ἐνηράμην   *kill, slay*
ἕπομαι, ἕψομαι, ἑσπόμην   *follow*
ἐράω (impf. ἔρων), aor.: ἐράσθην   *love*
ἐργάζομαι, augments to ἠ and εἰ, reduplicates to εἰ, ἐργαζόμην, ἔργασμαι,
    ἠργασάμην, εἴργασμαι, ἠργάσθην   *work, do*
ἔρχομαι, ἐλεύσομαι, ἦλθον, ἐλήλυθα   *come, go*
εὑρίσκω, εὑρήσω, ηὗρον/εὗρον, ηὕρηκα/εὕρηκα, εὕρημαι, εὑρέθην   *find*
εὔχομαι, εὔξομαι, εὐξάμην/ηὐξάμην, ηὖγμαι   *pray, boast*
ἔχω (impf. εἶχον), ἕξω and σχήσω, ἔσχον (aor. stem σχ-), ἔσχηκα,
    -ἔσχημαι, ἐσχέθην   *have*

Z

ζάω, ζήσω/ζήσομαι, ἔζησα, ἔζηκα   *live*

H

ἥδομαι, ἡσθήσομαι, ἥσθην   *be pleased*

Θ

θνῄσκω, θανοῦμαι, ἔθανον, τέθνηκα (fut. pf. τεθνήξω)   *die*

I

ἵημι, -ήσω, -ἧκα, -εἷκα, -εἷμαι, εἵθην   *send*
ἱκνέομαι (*see under* ἀφικνέομαι)   *arrive, come to, come as a suppliant, beseech, entreat, implore*
ἵστημι, στήσω, ἔστησα and ἔστην, ἔστηκα (plupf. εἱστήκη, fut. pf. ἑστήξω), ἔσταμαι, ἐστάθην   *stand, make stand*

K

καλέω, καλῶ, ἐκάλεσα, κέκληκα, κέκλημαι, ἐκλήθην   *call*
κείρω, κερῶ, ἔκειρα, κέκραμαι   *shear*
κέλλω, κέλσω, ἔκελσα   *run ashore*
κλίνω, κλινῶ, ἔκλινα, κέκλικα; aor.² pass.: -εκλίνη; aor.¹ pass.: ἐκλίθην   *cause to recline*
κραίνω, κρανῶ, ἔκρᾱνα; pf. 3 sg. and pl.: κέκρανται, ἐκράνθην, κρανθήσομαι   *accomplish*
κρίνω [ῑ], κρινῶ, ἔκρῑνα, κέκρικα, κέκριμαι, ἐκρίθην   *judge*
κρύπτω, κρύψω, ἔκρυψα, κέκρυμμαι, ἐκρύφθην   *hide*
κτάομαι, κτήσομαι, ἐκτησάμην, κέκτημαι   *acquire*; pf.: *possess*
κτείνω, κτενῶ, ἔκτεινα, -έκτονα   *kill*

Λ

λαγχάνω, λήξομαι; aor.²: ἔλαχον; pf.²: εἴληχα, εἴληγμαι, ἐλήχθην   *obtain by lot*
λαμβάνω, λήψομαι, ἔλαβον, εἴληφα, εἴλημμαι, ἐλήφθην   *take*
λανθάνω, λήσω, ἔλαθον, λέληθα   *escape notice, lie hidden*; mid. and pass.: *forget*
λάσκω, λακήσομαι; aor.²: ἔλακον; pf.² as pres.: λέληκα/λέλᾱκα   *speak loudly, shout*

λέγω, λέξω and ἐρῶ, ἔλεξα and εἶπον, εἴρηκα, λέλεγμαι and εἴρημαι,
    ἐλέχθην and ἐρρήθην   *say, proclaim*
λείπω, λείψω, ἔλιπον, λέλοιπα, λέλειμμαι, ἐλείφθην   *leave*

M

μαίνομαι, ἔμηνα, μέμηνα, ἐμάνην   *be mad*
μανθάνω, μαθήσομαι, ἔμαθον, μεμάθηκα   *learn by inquiry*
μέλλω, μελλήσω, ἐμέλλησα   *be about to, be on the point of doing*
μέλω, μελήσω; pf.²: μέμηλα   *care for, concern*
μένω, μενῶ, ἔμεινα, μεμένηκα   *remain, await*
μιμνήσκω, -μνήσω,-έμνησα, μέμνημαι, ἐμνήσθην   *remind;* mid.:
    remember

N

νέω, νευσοῦμαι, -ένευσα, -νένεκα   *swim*

O

οἴγνῡμι, οἴξω, ᾦξα, ᾤχθην, οἰχθείς; ἀν-οιγνῡμι, -οίξω, -ᾦξα, -οίχθεις,
    ἔῳγα, ἔῳγμαι   *open, lay open*
οἶδα, plupf. ᾔδη, εἴσομαι   *know*
ὄλλῡμι   *see under* ἀπόλλῡμι
ὄμνῡμι, ὀμοῦμαι, ὤμοσα, ὀμώμακα, ὀμώμομαι, ὠμόθην   *swear*
ὀμόργνῡμι, with ἐξ in poetry: ἐξ-ομόρξομαι, -ωμορξάμην,
    -ωμόρηθην   *wipe*
ὁράω (impf. ἑώρων), ὄψομαι, εἶδον (aor. stem: ἰδ-), ἑόρακα/ἑώρακα,
    ἑώραμαι/ὦμμαι, ὤφθην   *see*

Π

πάσχω, πείσομαι, ἔπαθον, πέπονθα   *suffer, experience*
πείθω, πείσω, ἔπεισα (aor.²: ἔπιθον), πέπεικα/πέποιθα (*trust*), πέπεισμαι,
    ἐπείσθην   *persuade;* mid.: *obey*
πειράομαι, πειράσομαι, ἐπειρασάμην, πεπείραμαι, ἐπειράθην   *try*
πέμπω, πέμψω, ἔπεμψα; pf.²: πέπομφα, πέπεμμαι, ἐπεμφθην   *send*
πίμπλημι, -πλήσω, -έπλησα, -πέπληκα, -πέπλησομαι, -επλήσθην   *fill*
πίπτω, πεσοῦμαι, ἔπεσον, πέπτωκα   *fall, turn out, happen*
πλέω, πλεύσομαι/πλευσοῦμαι, ἔπλευσα, πέπλευκα, πέπλευσμαι   *sail*
πλήττω, often in compounds with ἐξ, ἐπί, κατά: -πλήξω, -έπληξα;
    pf.²: πέπληγα, πέπληγμαι; aor.² pass.: ἐπλήγην; but in compounds
    -επλάγην   *strike*

πράσσω, πράξω, ἔπραξα, πέπραχα/πέπραγα, πέπραγμαι,
   ἐπράχθην   *fare, do*
πυνθάνομαι, πεύσομαι, ἐπυθόμην, πέπυσμαι   *learn, inquire*

Ρ

ῥέω, ῥυήσομαι, ἐρρύην, ἐρρύηκα   *flow*
ῥήγνυμι, -ρήξω, ἔρρηξα, -έρρωγα, ἐρράγην   *break*

Σ

σπείρω, σπερῶ, ἔσπειρα, ἔσπαρμαι; aor.² pass.: ἐσπάρην   *sow*
σφάλλω, σφαλῶ, ἔσφηλα, ἔσφαλμαι; aor.² pass.: ἐσφάλην,
   σφαλήσομαι   *trip up, make fall*
σώζω, σώσω, ἔσωσα, σέσωκα, σέσωμαι, ἐσώθην   *save*

Τ

τείνω, τενῶ, -έτεινα, τέτακα, τέταμαι, -ετάθην   *stretch*
τίθημι, θήσω, ἔθηκα, τέθηκα, τέθειμαι, ἐτέθην   *put*
τιτρώσκω, τρώσω, ἔτρωσα, τέτρωμαι, ἐτρώθην   *wound*
‡τλάω: pres. form not found, τλήσομαι, ἐτάλασσα; epic aor.²: ἔτλην;
   τέτληκα   *endure;* + inf.:   *dare*
τρέφω, θρέψω, ἔθρεψα, τέτροφα, τέθραμμαι, ἐθρέφθην/
   ἐθράφην   *nourish*
τρίβω, τρίψω, ἔτρῑψα; pf.²: τέτριφα, τέτρῑμμαι, ἐτρέφθην   *rub*
τυγχάνω, τεύξομαι, ἔτυχον, τετύχηκα   *happen, hit the mark, obtain*

Φ

φαίνω, φανῶ, ἔφηνα, πέφαγκα/πέφηνα, πέφασμαι, ἐφάνθην/
   ἐφάνην   *show*
φέρω, οἴσω, ἤνεγκον/ἤνεγκα, ἐνήνοχα, ἐνήνεγμαι, ἠνέχθην   *carry, bear*
φεύγω, φεύξομαι/φευξοῦμαι, ἔφυγον, πέφευγα   *flee, run away*
φημί, φήσω, ἔφησα   *say*
φύω, φύσω, ἔφυσα/ἔφυν, πέφυκα   *produce;* aor.²: *grew, was;* pf.: *be by*
   nature

Χ

χαίρω, χαιρήσω, κεχάρηκα, ἐχάρην   *rejoice, farewell*
χράομαι, χρήσομαι, ἐχρησάμην, κέχρημαι, ἐχρήσθην   *use, experience*
χρή (subv.: χρῇ, opt.: χρείη, inf.: χρῆναι; impf.: χρῆν or ἔχρην)   *it is*
   necessary

Ιπποлυτος: *HIPPOLYTUS*—The Play

The commentary follows the Teubner text edited by W. Stockert, with minor alterations.

ΑΦΡΟΔΙΤΗ

Πολλὴ μὲν ἐν βροτοῖσι κοὐκ ἀνώνυμος
θεὰ κέκλημαι Κύπρις οὐρανοῦ τ᾿ ἔσω·
ὅσοι τε Πόντου τερμόνων τ᾿ Ἀτλαντικῶν
ναίουσιν εἴσω, φῶς ὁρῶντες ἡλίου,
τοὺς μέν σέβοντας τἀμὰ πρεσβεύω κράτη,   5
σφάλλω δ᾿ ὅσοι φρονοῦσιν εἰς ἡμᾶς μέγα.
ἔνεστι γὰρ δὴ κἀν θεῶν γένει τόδε·
τιμώμενοι χαίρουσιν ἀνθρώπων ὕπο.
δείξω δὲ μύθων τῶνδ᾿ ἀλήθειαν τάχα·
ὁ γάρ με Θησέως παῖς, Ἀμαζόνος τόκος,   10
Ἱππόλυτος, ἁγνοῦ Πιτθέως παιδεύματα,
μόνος πολιτῶν τῆσδε γῆς Τροζηνίας
λέγει κακίστην δαιμόνων πεφυκέναι·
ἀναίνεται δὲ λέκτρα κοὐ ψαύει γάμων,
Φοίβου δ᾿ ἀδελφὴν Ἄρτεμιν, Διὸς κόρην,   15
τιμᾷ, μεγίστην δαιμόνων ἡγούμενος,
χλωρὰν δ᾿ ἀν᾿ ὕλην παρθένῳ ξυνὼν ἀεὶ
κυσὶν ταχείαις θῆρας ἐξαιρεῖ χθονός,
μείζω βροτείας προσπεσὼν ὁμιλίας.
τούτοισι μέν νυν οὐ φθονῶ· τί γάρ με δεῖ;   20
ἃ δ᾿ εἰς ἔμ᾿ ἡμάρτηκε τιμωρήσομαι
Ἱππόλυτον ἐν τῇδ᾿ ἡμέρᾳ· τὰ πολλὰ δὲ
πάλαι προκόψασ᾿, οὐ πόνου πολλοῦ με δεῖ.

ἐλθόντα γάρ νιν Πιτθέως ποτ᾽ ἐκ δόμων
σεμνῶν ἐς ὄψιν καὶ τέλη μυστηρίων   25
Πανδίονος γῆν πατρὸς εὐγενὴς δάμαρ
ἰδοῦσα Φαίδρα καρδίαν κατέσχετο
ἔρωτι δεινῷ τοῖς ἐμοῖς βουλεύμασιν.
καὶ πρὶν μὲν ἐλθεῖν τήνδε γῆν Τροζηνίαν,
πέτραν παρ᾽ αὐτὴν Παλλάδος κατόψιον   30
γῆς τῆσδε, ναὸν Κύπριδος ἐγκαθείσατο,
ἐρῶσ᾽ ἔρωτ᾽ ἔκδημον· Ἱππολύτῳ δ᾽ ἔπι
τὸ λοιπὸν ὀνομάσουσιν ἱδρῦσθαι θεάν.
ἐπεὶ δὲ Θησεὺς Κέκροπίαν λείπει χθόνα
μίασμα φεύγων αἵματος Παλλαντιδῶν   35
καὶ τήνδε σὺν δάμαρτι ναυστολεῖ χθόνα
ἐνιαυσίαν ἔκδημον αἰνέσας φυγήν,
ἐνταῦθα δὴ στένουσα κἀκπεπληγμένη
κέντροις ἔρωτος ἡ τάλαιν᾽ ἀπόλλυται
σιγῇ· ξύνοιδεν οὔτις οἰκετῶν νόσον.   40
ἀλλ᾽ οὔτι ταύτῃ τόνδ᾽ ἔρωτα χρὴ πεσεῖν,
δείξω δὲ Θησεῖ πρᾶγμα κἀκφανήσεται.
καὶ τὸν μὲν ἡμῖν πολέμιον νεανίαν
κτενεῖ πατὴρ ἀραῖσιν ἃς ὁ πόντιος
ἄναξ Ποσειδῶν ὤπασεν Θησεῖ γέρας,   45
μηδὲν μάταιον ἐς τρὶς εὔξασθαι θεῷ.
ἡ δ᾽ εὐκλεὴς μὲν ἀλλ᾽ ὅμως ἀπόλλυται
Φαίδρα· τὸ γὰρ τῆσδ᾽ οὐ προτιμήσω κακὸν
τὸ μὴ οὐ παρασχεῖν τοὺς ἐμοὺς ἐχθροὺς ἐμοὶ
δίκην τοσαύτην ὥστε μοι καλῶς ἔχειν.   50
ἀλλ᾽ εἰσορῶ γὰρ τόνδε παῖδα Θησέως
στείχοντα, θήρας μόχθον ἐκλελοιπότα,
Ἱππόλυτον, ἔξω τῶνδε βήσομαι τόπων.
πολὺς δ᾽ ἅμ᾽ αὐτῷ προσπόλων ὀπισθόπους
κῶμος λέλακεν, Ἄρτεμιν τιμῶν θεὰν   55
ὕμνοισιν· οὐ γὰρ οἶδ᾽ ἀνεῳγμένας πύλας
Ἅιδου, φάος δὲ λοίσθιον βλέπων τόδε.

ΙΠΠΟΛΥΤΟΣ
ἕπεσθ᾽ ᾄδοντες ἕπεσθε
τὰν Διὸς οὐρανίαν
Ἄρτεμιν, ᾇ μελόμεσθα.   60

ΧΟΡΟΣ ΚΥΝΗΓΩΝ

πότνια πότνια σεμνοτάτα,
Ζηνὸς γένεθλον,
χαῖρε χαῖρέ μοι, ὦ κόρα
Λατοῦς Ἄρτεμι καὶ Διός,   65
καλλίστα πολὺ παρθένων,
ἃ μέγαν κατ'οὐρανὸν
ναίεις εὐπατέρειαν αὐ-
λάν, Ζηνὸς πολύχρυσον οἶκον.
χαῖρέ μοι, ὦ καλλίστα   70
καλλίστα τῶν κατ' Ὄλυμπον.

Ιπ.   σοὶ τόνδε πλεκτὸν στέφανον ἐξ ἀκηράτου
λειμῶνος, ὦ δέσποινα, κοσμήσας φέρω,
ἔνθ' οὔτε ποιμὴν ἀξιοῖ φέρβειν βοτὰ   75
οὔτ' ἦλθέ πω σίδηρος, ἀλλ'ἀκήρατον
μέλισσα λειμῶν' ἠρινὴ διέρχεται,
Αἰδὼς δὲ ποταμίαισι κηπεύει δρόσοις,
ὅσοις διδακτὸν μηδὲν ἀλλ' ἐν τῇ φύσει
τὸ σωφρονεῖν εἴληχεν ἐς τὰ πάντ' ἀεί,   80
τούτοις δρέπεσθαι, τοῖς κακοῖσι δ' οὐ θέμις.
ἀλλ', ὦ φίλη δέσποινα, χρυσέας κόμης
ἀνάδημα δέξαι χειρὸς εὐσεβοῦς ἄπο.
μόνῳ γάρ ἐστι τοῦτ' ἐμοὶ γέρας βροτῶν·
σοὶ καὶ ξύνειμι καὶ λόγοις ἀμείβομαι,   85
κλύων μὲν αὐδῆς, ὄμμα δ'οὐχ ὁρῶν τὸ σόν.
τέλος δὲ κάμψαιμ' ὥσπερ ἠρξάμην βίου.

ΘΕΡΑΠΩΝ

ἄναξ, θεοὺς γὰρ δεσπότας καλεῖν χρεών,
ἆρ' ἄν τί μου δέξαιο βουλεύσαντος εὖ;
Ιπ.   καὶ κάρτα γ'· ἦ γὰρ οὐ σοφοὶ φαινοίμεθ' ἄν.   90
Θε.   οἶσθ' οὖν βροτοῖσιν ὃς καθέστηκεν νόμος;
Ιπ.   οὐκ οἶδα· τοῦ δὲ καί μ' ἀνιστορεῖς πέρι;
Θε.   μισεῖν τὸ σεμνὸν καὶ τὸ μὴ πᾶσιν φίλον.
Ιπ.   ὀρθῶς γε· τίς δ'οὐ σεμνὸς ἀχθεινὸς βροτῶν;
Θε.   ἐν δ' εὐπροσηγόροισίν ἐστί τις χάρις;   95
Ιπ.   πλείστη γε, καὶ κέρδος γε σὺν μόχθῳ βραχεῖ.
Θε.   ἦ κἀν θεοῖσι ταὐτὸν ἐλπίζεις τόδε;

Ιπ.   εἴπερ γε θνητοί θεῶν νόμοισι χρώμεθα.

Θε.   πῶς οὖν σὺ σεμνὴν δαίμον' οὐ προσεννέπεις;

Ιπ.   τίν'; εὐλαβοῦ δὲ μή τί σου σφαλῇ στόμα.   100

Θε.   τήνδ' ἢ πύλαισι σαῖς ἐφέστηκεν πέλας.

Ιπ.   πρόσωθεν αὐτὴν ἁγνὸς ὢν ἀσπάζομαι.

Θε.   σεμνή γε μέντοι κἀπίσημος ἐν βροτοῖς.   103

Ιπ.   οὐδείς μ' ἀρέσκει νυκτὶ θαυμαστὸς θεῶν.   106

Θε.   τιμαῖσιν, ὦ παῖ, δαιμόνων χρῆσθαι χρεών.   107

Ιπ.   ἄλλοισιν ἄλλος θεῶν κἀνθρώπων μέλει.   104

Θε.   εὐδαιμονοίης, νοῦν ἔχων ὅσον σε δεῖ.   105

Ιπ.   χωρεῖτ', ὀπαδοί, καὶ παρελθόντες δόμους   108
          σίτων μέλεσθε· τερπνὸν ἐκ κυναγίας
          τράπεζα πλήρης· καὶ καταψήχειν χρεὼν   110
          ἵππους, ὅπως ἂν ἅρμασι ζεύξας ὕπο
          βορᾶς κορεσθεὶς γυμνάσω τὰ πρόσφορα.
          τὴν σὴν δὲ Κύπριν πόλλ' ἐγὼ χαίρειν λέγω.

Θε.   ἡμεῖς δέ, τοὺς νέους γὰρ οὐ μιμητέον
          φρονοῦντας οὕτως, ὡς πρέπει δούλοις λέγειν   115
          προσευχόμεσθα τοῖσι σοῖς ἀγάλμασιν,
          δέσποινα Κύπρι· χρὴ δὲ συγγνώμην ἔχειν.
          εἴ τίς σ' ὑφ' ἥβης σπλάγχνον ἔντονον φέρων
          μάταια βάζει, μὴ δόκει τούτου κλυεῖν·
          σοφωτέρους γὰρ χρὴ βροτῶν εἶναι θεούς.   120

ΧΟΡΟΣ

          Ὠκεανοῦ τις ὕδωρ στάζουσα πέτρα λέγεται,   [στρ. α
          βαπτὰν κάλπισι πα-
             γὰν ῥυτὰν προιεῖσα κρημνῶν.
          τόθι μοί τις ἦν φίλα   125
          πορφύρεα φάρεα
          ποταμίᾳ δρόσῳ
          τέγγουσα, θερμᾶς δ' ἐπὶ νῶτα πέτρας
          εὐαλίου κατέβαλλ'· ὅθεν μοι
          πρώτα φάτις ἦλθε δεσποίνας,   130

          τειρομέναν νοσερᾷ κοίτᾳ δέμας ἐντὸς ἔχειν [ἀντ. α
          οἴκων, λεπτὰ δὲ φά-
             ρη ξανθὰν κεφαλὰν σκιάζειν·
          τριτάταν δέ νιν κλύω   135
          τάνδ' ἀβρωσίᾳ

στόματος ἁμέραν
Δάματρος ἀκτᾶς δέμας ἁγνὸν ἴσχειν,
κρυπτῷ πάθει θανάτου θέλουσαν
κέλσαι ποτὶ τέρμα δύστανον.　　　　　　　　140

†σὺ γὰρ† ἔνθεος, ὦ κούρα,　　　　　　　[στρ. β
εἴτ᾽ ἐκ Πανὸς εἴθ᾽ Ἑκάτας
ἢ σεμνῶν Κορυβάντων φοι-
　　τᾶς ἢ ματρὸς ὀρείας;
†σὺ δ᾽† ἀμφὶ τὰν πολύθη-　　　　　　　145
　　ρον Δίκτυνναν ἀμπλακίαις
ἀνίερος ἀθύτων πελάνων τρύχῃ;
φοιτᾷ γὰρ καὶ διὰ Λίμ-
　　νας χέρσον θ᾽ ὕπερ πελάγους
δίναις ἐν νοτίαις ἅλμας.　　　　　　　150

ἢ πόσιν, τὸν Ἐρεχθειδᾶν　　　　　　　[ἀντ. β
ἀρχαγόν, τὸν εὐπατρίδαν
ποιμαίνει τις ἐν οἴκοις κρυπ-
　　τᾷ κοίτᾳ λεχέων σῶν;
ἢ ναυβάτας τις ἔπλευ-　　　　　　　155
　　σεν Κρήτας ἔξορμος ἀνὴρ
λιμένα τὸν εὐξεινότατον ναύταις
φήμαν πέμπων βασιλεί-
　　ᾳ, λύπᾳ δ᾽ ὕπερ παθέων
εὐναία δέδεται ψυχά;　　　　　　　160

φιλεῖ δὲ τᾷ δυστρόπῳ γυναικῶν　　　[ἐπῳδ.
ἁρμονίᾳ κακὰ
δύστανος ἀμηχανία συνοικεῖν
ὠδίνων τε καὶ ἀφροσύνας.
δι᾽ ἐμᾶς ᾖξέν ποτε νηδύος ἅδ᾽　　　　165
αὔρα· τὰν δ᾽ εὔλοχον οὐρανίαν
τόξων μεδέουσαν ἀΰτευν
Ἄρτεμιν, καί μοι πολυζήλωτος αἰεὶ
σὺν θεοῖσι φοιτᾷ.

– – – ἀλλ᾽ ἥδε τροφὸς γεραιὰ πρὸ θυρῶν　　170
τήνδε κομίζουσ᾽ ἔξω μελάθρων.
[στυγνὸν δ᾽ ὀφρύων νέφος αὐξάνεται.]

τί ποτ᾽ ἐστὶ μαθεῖν ἔραται ψυχή,
τί δεδήληται
δέμας ἀλλόχροον βασιλείας.   175

ΤΡΟΦΟΣ

ὦ κακὰ θνητῶν στυγεραί τε νόσοι·
τί σ᾽ ἐγὼ δράσω, τί δὲ μὴ δράσω;
τόδε σοι φέγγος, λαμπρὸς ὅδ᾽ αἰθήρ·
ἔξω δὲ δόμων ἤδη νοσερᾶς
δέμνια κοίτης.   180
δεῦρο γὰρ ἐλθεῖν πᾶν ἔπος ἦν σοι,
τάχα δ᾽ ἐς θαλάμους σπεύσεις τὸ πάλιν.
ταχὺ γὰρ σφάλλῃ κοὐδενὶ χαίρεις,
οὐδέ σ᾽ ἀρέσκει τὸ παρόν, τὸ δ᾽ ἀπὸν
φίλτερον ἤγῃ.   185
κρεῖσσον δὲ νοσεῖν ἢ θεραπεύειν·
τὸ μέν ἐστιν ἁπλοῦν, τῷ δὲ συνάπτει
λύπη τε φρενῶν χερσίν τε πόνος.
πᾶς δ᾽ ὀδυνηρὸς βίος ἀνθρώπων
κοὐκ ἔστι πόνων ἀνάπαυσις.   190
ἀλλ᾽ ὅτι τοῦ ζῆν φίλτερον ἄλλο
σκότος ἀμπίσχων κρύπτει νεφέλαις.
δυσέρωτες δὴ φαινόμεθ᾽ ὄντες
τοῦδ᾽ ὅτι τοῦτο στίλβει κατὰ γῆν
δι᾽ ἀπειροσύνην ἄλλου βιότου   195
κοὐκ ἀπόδειξιν τῶν ὑπὸ γαίας,
μύθοις δ᾽ ἄλλως φερόμεσθα.

ΦΑΙΔΡΑ

αἴρετέ μου δέμας, ὀρθοῦτε κάρα·
λέλυμαι μελέων σύνδεσμα φίλων.
λάβετ᾽ εὐπήχεις χεῖρας, πρόπολοι.   200
βαρύ μοι κεφαλῆς ἐπίκρανον ἔχειν·
ἄφελ᾽, ἀμπέτασον βόστρυχον ὤμοις.
Τρ.   θάρσει, τέκνον, καὶ μὴ χαλεπῶς
μετάβαλλε δέμας·
ῥᾷον δὲ νόσον μετά θ᾽ ἡσυχίας   205
καὶ γενναίου λήματος οἴσεις.
μοχθεῖν δὲ βροτοῖσιν ἀνάγκη.

Φα. αἰαῖ·
πῶς ἂν δροσερᾶς ἀπὸ κρηνῖδος
καθαρῶν ὑδάτων πῶμ' ἀρυσαίμαν
ὑπό τ' αἰγείροις ἔν τε κομήτῃ 210
λειμῶνι κλιθεῖσ' ἀναπαυσαίμαν;
Τρ. ὦ παῖ, τί θροεῖς;
οὐ μὴ παρ' ὄχλῳ τάδε γηρύσῃ,
μανίας ἔποχον ῥίπτουσα λόγον;
Φα. πέμπετέ μ' εἰς ὄρος· εἶμι πρὸς ὕλαν 215
καὶ παρὰ πεύκας, ἵνα θηροφόνοι
στείβουσι κύνες
βαλιαῖς ἐλάφοις ἐγχριμπτόμεναι.
πρὸς θεῶν· ἔραμαι κυσὶ θωΰξαι
καὶ παρὰ χαίταν ξανθὰν ῥῖψαι 220
Θεσσαλὸν ὅρπακ',
ἐπίλογχον ἔχουσ' ἐν χειρὶ βέλος.
Τρ. τί ποτ', ὦ τέκνον, τάδε κηραίνεις;
τί κυνηγεσίων καί σοι μελέτη;
τί δὲ κρηναίων νασμῶν ἔρασαι; 225
πάρα γὰρ δροσερὰ πύργοις συνεχὴς
κλειτύς, ὅθεν σοι πῶμα γένοιτ' ἄν.
Φα. δέσποιν' ἁλίας Ἄρτεμι Λίμνας
καὶ γυμνασίων τῶν ἱπποκρότων,
εἴθε γενοίμαν ἐν σοῖς δαπέδοις 230
πώλους Ἐνετὰς δαμαλιζομένα.
Τρ. τί τόδ' αὖ παράφρων ἔρριψας ἔπος;
νῦν δὴ μὲν ὄρος βᾶσ' ἐπὶ θήρας
πόθον ἐστέλλου, νῦν δ' αὖ ψαμάθοις
ἐπ' ἀκυμάντοις πώλων ἔρασαι. 235
τάδε μαντείας ἄξια πολλῆς,
ὅστις σε θεῶν ἀνασειράζει
καὶ παρακόπτει φρένας, ὦ παῖ.
Φα. δύστηνος ἐγώ, τί ποτ' εἰργασάμην;
ποῖ παρεπλάγχθην γνώμης ἀγαθῆς; 240
ἐμάνην, ἔπεσον δαίμονος ἄτῃ.
φεῦ φεῦ, τλήμων.
μαῖα, πάλιν μου κρύψον κεφαλήν,
αἰδούμεθα γὰρ τὰ λελεγμένα μοι.
κρύπτε· κατ' ὄσσων δάκρυ μοι βαίνει 245

καὶ ἐπ'αἰσχύνην ὄμμα τέτραπται.
τὸ γὰρ ὀρθοῦσθαι γνώμην ὀδυνᾷ,
τὸ δὲ μαινόμενον κακόν· ἀλλὰ κρατεῖ
μὴ γιγνώσκοντ' ἀπολέσθαι.

Τρ.   κρύπτω· τὸ δ' ἐμὸν πότε δὴ θάνατος   250
σῶμα καλύψει;
πολλὰ διδάσκει μ' ὁ πολὺς βίοτος·
χρῆν γὰρ μετρίας εἰς ἀλλήλους
φιλίας θνητοὺς ἀνακίρνασθαι
καὶ μὴ πρὸς ἄκρον μυελὸν ψυχῆς,   255
εὔλυτα δ' εἶναι στέργηθρα φρενῶν
ἀπό τ' ὤσασθαι καὶ ξυντεῖναι·
τὸ δ' ὑπὲρ δισσῶν μίαν ὠδίνειν
ψυχὴν χαλεπὸν βάρος, ὡς κἀγὼ
τῆσδ' ὑπεραλγῶ.   260
βιότου δ' ἀτρεκεῖς ἐπιτηδεύσεις
φασὶ σφάλλειν πλέον ἢ τέρπειν
τῇ θ' ὑγιείᾳ μᾶλλον πολεμεῖν.
οὕτω τὸ λίαν ἧσσον ἐπαινῶ
τοῦ μηδὲν ἄγαν·   265
καὶ ξυμφήσουσι σοφοί μοι.

Χο.   γύναι γεραιά, βασιλίδος πιστὴ τροφέ,
Φαίδρας ὁρῶμεν τάσδε δυστήνους τύχας,
ἄσημα δ' ἡμῖν ἥτις ἐστὶν ἡ νόσος·
σοῦ δ' ἂν πυθέσθαι καὶ κλυεῖν βουλοίμεθ' ἄν.   270

Τρ.   οὐκ οἶδ', ἐλέγχουσ'· οὐ γὰρ ἐννέπειν θέλει.
Χο.   οὐδ' ἥτις ἀρχὴ τῶνδε πημάτων ἔφυ;
Τρ.   ἐς ταὐτὸν ἥκεις· πάντα γὰρ σιγᾷ τάδε.
Χο.   ὡς ἀσθενεῖ τε καὶ κατέξανται δέμας.
Τρ.   πῶς δ' οὔ, τριταίαν γ' οὖσ' ἄσιτος ἡμέραν;   275
Χο.   πότερον ὑπ' ἄτης ἢ θανεῖν πειρωμένη;
Τρ.   †θανεῖν† ἀσιτεῖ δ' εἰς ἀπόστασιν βίου.
Χο.   θαυμαστὸν εἶπας, εἰ τάδ' ἐξαρκεῖ πόσει.
Τρ.   κρύπτει γὰρ ἥδε πῆμα κοὔ φησιν νοσεῖν.
Χο.   ὁ δ' ἐς πρόσωπον οὐ τεκμαίρεται βλέπων;   280
Τρ.   ἔκδημος ὢν γὰρ τῆσδε τυγχάνει χθονός.
Χο.   σὺ δ' οὐκ ἀνάγκην προσφέρεις πειρωμένη
νόσον πυθέσθαι τῆσδε καὶ πλάνον φρενῶν;
Τρ.   ἐς πάντ' ἀφῖγμαι κοὐδὲν εἴργασμαι πλέον.

οὐ μὴν ἀνήσω γ᾽ οὐδὲ νῦν προθυμίας, 285
ὡς ἂν παροῦσα καὶ σύ μοι ξυμμαρτυρῇς
οἷα πέφυκα δυστυχοῦσι δεσπόταις.
ἄγ᾽, ὦ φίλη παῖ, τῶν πάροιθε μὲν λόγων
λαθώμεθ᾽ ἄμφω, καὶ σύ θ᾽ ἡδίων γενοῦ
στυγνὴν ὀφρῦν λύσασα καὶ γνώμης ὁδόν, 290
ἐγώ θ᾽ ὅπῃ σοι μὴ καλῶς τόθ᾽ εἱπόμην
μεθεῖσ᾽ ἐπ᾽ ἄλλον εἶμι βελτίω λόγον.
κεἰ μὲν νοσεῖς τι τῶν ἀπορρήτων κακῶν,
γυναῖκες αἵδε συγκαθιστάναι νόσον·
εἰ δ᾽ ἔκφορός σοι συμφορὰ πρὸς ἄρσενας, 295
λέγ᾽, ὡς ἰατροῖς πρᾶγμα μηνυθῇ τόδε.
εἶέν· τί σιγᾷς; οὐκ ἐχρῆν σιγᾶν, τέκνον,
ἀλλ᾽ ἤ μ᾽ ἐλέγχειν, εἴ τι μὴ καλῶς λέγω,
ἢ τοῖσιν εὖ λεχθεῖσι συγχωρεῖν λόγοις.
φθέγξαι τι, δεῦρ᾽ ἄθρησον. ὦ τάλαιν᾽ ἐγώ, 300
γυναῖκες, ἄλλως τούσδε μοχθοῦμεν πόνους,
ἴσον δ᾽ ἄπεσμεν τῷ πρίν· οὔτε γὰρ τότε
λόγοις ἐτέγγεθ᾽ ἥδε νῦν τ᾽ οὐ πείθεται.
ἀλλ᾽ ἴσθι μέντοι—πρὸς τάδ᾽ αὐθαδεστέρα
γίγνου θαλάσσης—εἰ θανῇ, προδοῦσα σοὺς 305
παῖδας, πατρῴων μὴ μεθέξοντας δόμων,
μὰ τὴν ἄνασσαν ἱππίαν Ἀμαζόνα,
ἣ σοῖς τέκνοισι δεσπότην ἐγείνατο,
νόθον φρονοῦντα γνήσι᾽, οἶσθα νιν καλῶς,
Ἱππόλυτον . . . 310
        Φα. οἴμοι.
              Τρ. θιγγάνει σέθεν τόδε;
Φα. ἀπώλεσάς με, μαῖα, καί σε πρὸς θεῶν
τοῦδ᾽ ἀνδρὸς αὖθις λίσσομαι σιγᾶν πέρι.
Τρ. ὁρᾷς; φρονεῖς μὲν εὖ, φρονοῦσα δ᾽ οὐ θέλεις
παῖδάς τ᾽ ὀνῆσαι καὶ σὸν ἐκσῶσαι βίον.
Φα. φιλῶ τέκν᾽· ἄλλῃ δ᾽ ἐν τύχῃ χειμάζομαι. 315
Τρ. ἁγνὰς μέν, ὦ παῖ, χεῖρας αἵματος φορεῖς;
Φα. χεῖρες μὲν ἁγναί, φρὴν δ᾽ ἔχει μίασμά τι.
Τρ. μῶν ἐξ ἐπακτοῦ πημονῆς ἐχθρῶν τινος;
Φα. φίλος μ᾽ ἀπόλλυσ᾽ οὐχ ἑκοῦσαν οὐχ ἑκών.
Τρ. Θησεύς τιν᾽ ἡμάρτηκεν ἐς σ᾽ ἁμαρτίαν; 320

Φα.   μὴ δρῶσ᾽ ἔγωγ᾽ ἐκεῖνον ὀφθείην κακῶς.
Τρ.   τί γὰρ τὸ δεινὸν τοῦθ᾽ ὅ σ᾽ ἐξαίρει θανεῖν;
Φα.   ἔα μ᾽ ἁμαρτεῖν· οὐ γὰρ ἐς σ᾽ ἁμαρτάνω.
Τρ.   οὐ δῆθ᾽ ἑκοῦσά γ᾽, ἐν δὲ σοὶ λελείψομαι.
Φα.   τί δρᾷς; βιάζῃ, χειρὸς ἐξαρτωμένη;   325
Τρ.   καὶ σῶν γε γονάτων, κοὐ μεθήσομαί ποτε.
Φα.   κάκ᾽, ὦ τάλαινα, σοὶ τάδ᾽, εἰ πεύσῃ, κακά.
Τρ.   μεῖζον γὰρ ἤ σου μὴ τυχεῖν τί μοι κακόν;
Φα.   ὀλῇ· τὸ μέντοι πρᾶγμ᾽ ἐμοὶ τιμὴν φέρει.
Τρ.   κἄπειτα κρύπτεις, χρήσθ᾽ ἱκνουμένης ἐμοῦ;   330
Φα.   ἐκ τῶν γὰρ αἰσχρῶν ἐσθλὰ μηχανώμεθα.
Τρ.   οὔκουν λέγουσα τιμιωτέρα φανῇ;
Φα.   ἄπελθε πρὸς θεῶν δεξιάν τ᾽ἐμὴν μέθες.
Τρ.   οὐ δῆτ᾽, ἐπεί μοι δῶρον οὐ δίδως ὃ χρῆν.
Φα.   δώσω· σέβας γὰρ χειρὸς αἰδοῦμαι τὸ σόν.   335
Τρ.   σιγῷμ᾽ ἂν ἤδη· σὸς γὰρ οὑντεῦθεν λόγος.
Φα.   ὦ τλῆμον, οἷον, μῆτερ, ἠράσθης ἔρον.
Τρ.   ὃν ἔσχε ταύρου, τέκνον; ἢ τί φῂς τόδε;
Φα.   σύ τ᾽, ὦ τάλαιν᾽ ὅμαιμε, Διονύσου δάμαρ.
Τρ.   τέκνον, τί πάσχεις; συγγόνους κακορροθεῖς;   340
Φα.   τρίτη δ᾽ ἐγὼ δύστηνος ὡς ἀπόλλυμαι.
Τρ.   ἔκ τοι πέπληγμαι· ποῖ προβήσεται λόγος;
Φα.   ἐκεῖθεν ἡμεῖς, οὐ νεωστί, δυστυχεῖς.
Τρ.   οὐδέν τι μᾶλλον οἶδ᾽ ἃ βούλομαι κλυεῖν.
Φα.   φεῦ·
        πῶς ἂν σύ μοι λέξειας ἁμὲ χρὴ λέγειν;   345
Τρ.   οὐ μάντις εἰμὶ τἀφανῆ γνῶναι σαφῶς.
Φα.   τί τοῦθ᾽ ὃ δὴ λέγουσιν ἀνθρώπους ἐρᾶν;
Τρ.   ἥδιστον, ὦ παῖ, ταὐτὸν ἀλγεινόν θ᾽ ἅμα.
Φα.   ἡμεῖς ἂν εἶμεν θατέρῳ κεχρημένοι.
Τρ.   τί φῄς; ἐρᾷς, ὦ τέκνον; ἀνθρώπων τίνος;   350
Φα.   ὅστις ποθ᾽ οὗτός ἐσθ᾽, ὁ τῆς Ἀμαζόνος . . .
Τρ.   Ἱππόλυτον αὐδᾷς;
                     Φα. σοῦ τάδ᾽, οὐκ ἐμοῦ κλύεις.
Τρ.   οἴμοι, τί λέξεις, τέκνον; ὥς μ᾽ ἀπώλεσας.
        γυναῖκες, οὐκ ἀνασχέτ᾽· οὐκ ἀνέξομαι
        ζῶσ᾽, ἐχθρὸν ἦμαρ, ἐχθρὸν εἰσορῶ φάος.   355
        ῥίψω μεθήσω σῶμ᾽, ἀπαλλαχθήσομαι
        βίου θανοῦσα· χαίρετ᾽, οὐκέτ᾽ εἴμ᾽ἐγώ.

οἱ σώφρονες γάρ, οὐχ ἑκόντες ἀλλ᾽ ὅμως,
κακῶν ἐρῶσι. Κύπρις οὐκ ἄρ᾽ ἦν θεός,
ἀλλ᾽ εἴ τι μεῖζον ἄλλο γίγνεται θεοῦ,   360
ἣ τήνδε κἀμὲ καὶ δόμους ἀπώλεσεν.

Xo.   ἄιες ὤ, ἔκλυες ὤ,   [στρ.
ἀνήκουστα τᾶς
τυράννου πάθεα μέλεα θρεομένας;
ὀλοίμαν ἔγωγε πρὶν σᾶν, φίλα,
κατανύσαι φρενῶν. ἰὼ μοι, φεῦ φεῦ·   365
ὦ τάλαινα τῶνδ᾽ ἀλγέων·
ὦ πόνοι τρέφοντες βροτούς.
ὄλωλας, ἐξέφηνας ἐς φάος κακά.
τίς σε παναμέριος ὅδε χρόνος μένει;
τελευτάσεταί τι καινὸν δμοις·   370
ἄσημα δ᾽ οὐκέτ᾽ ἐστὶν οἷ φθίνει τύχα
Κύπριδος, ὦ τάλαινα παῖ Κρησία.

Φα.   Τροζήνιαι γυναῖκες, αἳ τόδ᾽ ἔσχατον
οἰκεῖτε χώρας Πελοπίας προνώπιον,
ἤδη ποτ᾽ ἄλλως νυκτὸς ἐν μακρῷ χρόνῳ   375
θνητῶν ἐφρόντισ᾽ ᾗ διέφθαρται βίος.
καί μοι δοκοῦσιν οὐ κατὰ γνώμης φύσιν
πράσσειν κάκιον· ἔστι γὰρ τό γ᾽ εὖ φρονεῖν
πολλοῖσιν· ἀλλὰ τῇδ᾽ ἀθρητέον τόδε·
τὰ χρήστ᾽ ἐπιστάμεσθα καὶ γιγνώσκομεν,   380
οὐκ ἐκπονοῦμεν δ᾽, οἱ μὲν ἀργίας ὕπο,
οἱ δ᾽ ἡδονὴν προθέντες ἀντὶ τοῦ καλοῦ
ἄλλην τιν᾽. εἰσὶ δ᾽ ἡδοναὶ πολλαὶ βίου,
μακραί τε λέσχαι καὶ σχολή, τερπνὸν κακόν,
αἰδώς τε· δισσαὶ δ᾽ εἰσίν, ἡ μὲν οὐ κακή,   385
ἡ δ᾽ ἄχθος οἴκων· εἰ δ᾽ ὁ καιρὸς ἦν σαφής,
οὐκ ἂν δύ᾽ ἤστην ταῦτ᾽ ἔχοντε γράμματα.
ταῦτ᾽ οὖν ἐπειδὴ τυγχάνω φρονοῦσ᾽ ἐγώ,
οὐκ ἔσθ᾽ ὁποίῳ φαρμάκῳ διαφθερεῖν
ἔμελλον, ὥστε τοὔμπαλιν πεσεῖν φρενῶν.   390
λέξω δὲ καί σοι τῆς ἐμῆς γνώμης ὁδόν,
ἐπεί μ᾽ ἔρως ἔτρωσεν, ἐσκόπουν ὅπως
κάλλιστ᾽ ἐνέγκαιμ᾽ αὐτόν. ἠρξάμην μὲν οὖν
ἐκ τοῦδε, σιγᾶν τήνδε καὶ κρύπτειν νόσον·

γλώσσῃ γὰρ οὐδὲν πιστόν, ἢ θυραῖα μὲν   395
φρονήματ᾽ ἀνδρῶν νουθετεῖν ἐπίσταται,
αὐτὴ δ᾽ ὑφ᾽ αὐτῆς πλεῖστα κέκτηται κακά.
τὸ δεύτερον δὲ τὴν ἄνοιαν εὖ φέρειν
τῷ σωφρονεῖν νικῶσα προυνοησάμην.
τρίτον δ᾽, ἐπειδὴ τοισίδ᾽ οὐκ ἀξήνυτον   400
Κύπριν κρατῆσαι, κατθανεῖν ἔδοξέ μοι,
κράτιστον (οὐδεὶς ἀντερεῖ) βουλευμάτων.
ἐμοὶ γὰρ εἴη μήτε λανθάνειν καλὰ
μήτ᾽ αἰσχρὰ δρώσῃ μάρτυρας πολλοὺς ἔχειν.
τὸ δ᾽ ἔργον ἤδη τὴν νόσον τε δυσκλεᾶ,   405
γυνή τε πρὸς τοῖσδ᾽ οὖσ᾽ ἐγίγνωσκον καλῶς,
μίσημα πᾶσιν· ὡς ὄλοιτο παγκάκως
ἥτις πρὸς ἄνδρας ἤρξατ᾽ αἰσχύνειν λέχη
πρώτη θυραίους. ἐκ δὲ γενναίων δόμων
τόδ᾽ ἦρξε θηλείαισι γίγνεσθαι κακόν·   410
ὅταν γὰρ αἰσχρὰ τοῖσιν ἐσθλοῖσιν δοκῇ,
ἦ κάρτα δόξει τοῖς κακοῖς γ᾽ εἶναι καλά.
μισῶ δὲ καὶ τὰς σώφρονας μὲν ἐν λόγοις,
λάθρᾳ δὲ τόλμας οὐ καλὰς κεκτημένας·
αἳ πῶς ποτ᾽, ὦ δέσποινα ποτνία Κύπρι,   415
βλέπουσιν ἐς πρόσωπα τῶν ξυνευνετῶν
οὐδὲ σκότον φρίσσουσι τὸν ξυνεργάτην
τέραμνά τ᾽ οἴκων μή ποτε φθογγὴν ἀφῇ;
ἡμᾶς γὰρ αὐτὸ τοῦτ᾽ ἀποκτείνει φίλαι,
ὡς μήποτ᾽ ἄνδρα τὸν ἐμὸν αἰσχύνασ᾽ ἁλῶ,   420
μὴ παῖδας οὓς ἔτικτον· ἀλλ᾽ ἐλεύθεροι
παρρησίᾳ θάλλοντες οἰκοῖεν πόλιν
κλεινῶν Ἀθηνῶν, μητρὸς οὕνεκ᾽ εὐκλεεῖς.
δουλοῖ γὰρ ἄνδρα, κἂν θρασύσπλαγχνός τις ᾖ,
ὅταν ξυνειδῇ μητρὸς ἢ πατρὸς κακά.   425
μόνον δὲ τοῦτό φασ᾽ ἁμιλλᾶσθαι βίῳ,
γνώμην δικαίαν κἀγαθὴν ὅτῳ παρῇ·
κακοὺς δὲ θνητῶν ἐξέφην᾽, ὅταν τύχῃ,
προθεὶς κάτοπτρον ὥστε παρθένῳ νέᾳ
χρόνος· παρ᾽ οἷσι μήποτ᾽ ὀφθείην ἐγώ.   430
Χο.   φεῦ φεῦ, τὸ σῶφρον ὡς ἁπανταχοῦ καλὸν
        καὶ δόξαν ἐσθλὴν ἐν βροτοῖς καρπίζεται.
Τρ.   δέσποιν᾽, ἐμοί τοι συμφορὰ μὲν ἀρτίως

ἡ σὴ παρέσχε δεινὸν ἐξαίφνης φόβον·
νῦν δ᾽ ἐννοοῦμαι φαῦλος οὖσα, κἂν βροτοῖς   435
αἱ δεύτεραί πως φροντίδες σοφώτεραι.
οὐ γὰρ περισσὸν οὐδὲν οὐδ᾽ ἔξω λόγου
πέπονθας· ὀργαὶ δ᾽ ἐς σ᾽ ἀπέσκηψαν θεᾶς.
ἐρᾷς (τί τοῦτο θαῦμα;) σὺν πολλοῖς βροτῶν·
κἄπειτ᾽ ἔρωτος οὕνεκα ψυχὴν ὀλεῖς;   440
οὔ τἄρα λύει τοῖς ἐρῶσι τῶν πέλας
ὅσοι τε μέλλουσ᾽, εἰ θανεῖν αὐτοὺς χρεών.
Κύπρις γὰρ οὐ φορητὸν ἢν πολλὴ ῥυῇ,
ἣ τὸν μὲν εἴκονθ᾽ ἡσυχῇ μετέρχεται,
ὃν δ᾽ ἂν περρισὸν καὶ φρονοῦνθ᾽ εὕρῃ μέγα,   445
τοῦτον λαβοῦσα πῶς δοκεῖς καθύβρισεν.
φοιτᾷ δ᾽ ἀν᾽ αἰθέρ᾽, ἔστι δ᾽ ἐν θαλασσίῳ
κλύδωνι Κύπρις, πάντα δ᾽ ἐκ ταύτης ἔφυ·
ἥδ᾽ ἐστὶν ἡ σπείρουσα καὶ διδοῦσ᾽ ἔρον,
οὗ πάντες ἐσμὲν οἱ κατὰ χθόν᾽ ἔκγονοι.   450
ὅσοι μὲν οὖν γραφάς τε τῶν παλαιτέρων
ἔχουσιν αὐτοί τ᾽ εἰσὶν ἐν μούσαις ἀεί,
ἴσασι μὲν Ζεὺς ὥς ποτ᾽ ἠράσθη γάμων
Σεμέλης, ἴσασι δ᾽ ὡς ἀνήρπασέν ποτε
ἡ καλλιφεγγὴς Κέφαλον ἐς θεοὺς Ἕως   455
ἔρωτος οὕνεκ᾽· ἀλλ᾽ ὅμως ἐν οὐρανῷ
ναίουσι κοὐ φεύγουσιν ἐκποδὼν θεούς,
στέργουσι δ᾽, οἶμαι, ξυμφορᾷ νικώμενοι.
σὺ δ᾽ οὐκ ἀνέξῃ; χρῆν σ᾽ ἐπὶ ῥητοῖς ἄρα
πατέρα φυτεύειν ἢ ᾽πὶ δεσπόταις θεοῖς   460
ἄλλοισιν, εἰ μὴ τούσδε γε στέρξεις νόμους.
πόσους δοκεῖς δὴ κάρτ᾽ ἔχοντας εὖ φρενῶν
νοσοῦνθ᾽ ὁρῶντας λέκτρα μὴ δοκεῖν ὁρᾶν;
πόσους δὲ παισὶ πατέρας ἡμαρτηκόσιν
συνεκκομίζειν Κύπριν; ἐν σοφοῖσι γὰρ   465
τόδ᾽ ἐστὶ θνητῶν, λανθάνειν τὰ μὴ καλά.
οὐδ᾽ ἐκπονεῖν τοι χρὴ βίον λίαν βροτούς·
οὐδὲ στέγην γὰρ ᾗ κατηρεφεῖς δόμοι
καλῶς ἀκριβώσαις ἄν· ἐς δὲ τὴν τύχην
πεσοῦσ᾽ ὅσην σύ, πῶς ἂν ἐκνεῦσαι δοκεῖς;   470
ἀλλ᾽ εἰ τὰ πλείω χρηστὰ τῶν κακῶν ἔχεις,
ἄνθρωπος οὖσα κάρτα γ᾽ εὖ πράξειας ἄν.

    ἀλλ᾽, ὦ φίλη παῖ, λῆγε μὲν κακῶν φρενῶν,
    λῆξον δ᾽ ὑβρίζουσ᾽, οὐ γὰρ ἄλλο πλὴν ὕβρις
    τάδ᾽ ἐστί, κρείσσω δαιμόνων εἶναι θέλειν,   475
    τόλμα δ᾽ ἐρῶσα· θεὸς ἐβουλήθη τάδε·
    νοσοῦσα δ᾽ εὖ πως τὴν νόσον καταστρέφου.
    εἰσὶν δ᾽ ἐπῳδαὶ καὶ λόγοι θελκτήριοι·
    φανήσεταί τι τῆσδε φάρμακον νόσου.
    ἦ τἄρ᾽ ἂν ὀψέ γ᾽ ἄνδρες ἐξεύροιεν ἄν,   480
    εἰ μὴ γυναῖκες μηχανὰς εὑρήσομεν.
Χο. Φαίδρα, λέγει μὲν ἥδε χρησιμώτερα
    πρὸς τὴν παροῦσαν ξυμφοράν, αἰνῶ δὲ σέ.
    ὁ δ᾽ αἶνος οὗτος δυσχερέσρερος λόγων
    τῶν τῆσδε καί σοι μᾶλλον ἀλγίων κλυεῖν.   485
Φα. τοῦτ᾽ ἔσθ᾽ ὃ θνητῶν εὖ πόλεις οἰκουμένας
    δόμους τ᾽ ἀπόλλυσ᾽, οἱ καλοὶ λίαν λόγοι·
    οὐ γάρ τι τοῖσιν ὠσὶ τερπνὰ χρὴ λέγειν
    ἀλλ᾽ ἐξ ὅτου τις εὐκλεὴς γενήσεται.
Τρ. τί σεμνομυθεῖς; οὐ λόγων εὐσχημόνων   490
    δεῖ σ᾽ ἀλλὰ τἀνδρός. ὡς τάχος διιστέον,
    τὸν εὐθὺν ἐξειπόντας ἀμφὶ σοῦ λόγον.
    εἰ μὲν γὰρ ἦν σοι μὴ 'πὶ συμφοραῖς βίος
    τοιαῖσδε, σώφρων δ᾽ οὖσ᾽ ἐτύγχανες γυνή,
    οὐκ ἄν ποτ᾽ εὐνῆς οὕνεχ᾽ ἡδονῆς τε σῆς   495
    προῆγον ἄν σε δεῦρο· νῦν δ᾽ ἀγὼν μέγας
    σῶσαι βίον σόν, κοὐκ ἐπίφθονον τόδε.
Φα. ὦ δεινὰ λέξασ᾽, οὐχὶ συγκλήσεις στόμα
    καὶ μὴ μεθήσεις αὖθις αἰσχίστους λόγους;
Τρ. αἴσχρ᾽, ἀλλ᾽ ἀμείνω τῶν καλῶν τάδ᾽ ἐστί σοι·   500
    κρεῖσσον δὲ τοὔργον, εἴπερ ἐκσώσει γέ σε,
    ἢ τοὔνομ᾽, ᾧ σὺ κατθανῇ γαυρουμένη.
Φα. ἃ μή σε πρὸς θεῶν, εὖ λέγεις γὰρ αἰσχρὰ δέ,
    πέρα προβῇς τῶνδ᾽· ὡς ὑπείργασμαι μὲν εὖ
    ψυχὴν ἔρωτι, τᾀσχρὰ δ᾽ ἢν λέγῃς καλῶς   505
    ἐς τοῦθ᾽ ὃ φεύγω νῦν ἀναλωθήσομαι.
Τρ. εἴ τοι δοκεῖ σοι ... χρῆν μὲν οὔ σ᾽ ἁμαρτάνειν,
    εἰ δ᾽ οὖν, πιθοῦ μοι· δευτέρα γὰρ ἡ χάρις.
    ἔστιν κατ᾽ οἴκους φίλτρα μοι θελκτήρια
    ἔρωτος, ἦλθε δ᾽ ἄρτι μοι γνώμης ἔσω,   510
    ἅ σ᾽ οὔτ᾽ ἐπ᾽ αἰσχροῖς οὔτ᾽ ἐπὶ βλάβῃ φρενῶν

παύσει νόσου τῆσδ᾽, ἢν σὺ μὴ γένῃ κακή.
[δεῖ δ᾽ ἐξ ἐκείνου δή τι τοῦ ποθουμένου
σημεῖον, πλόκον τιν᾽ ἢ πέπλων ἄπο,
λαβεῖν ἢ συνάψαι τ᾽ἐκ δυοῖν μίαν χάριν.] 515

Φα.   πότερα δὲ χριστὸν ἢ ποτὸν τὸ φάρμακον;
Τρ.   οὐκ οἶδ᾽· ὄνασθαι, μὴ μαθεῖν βούλου τέκνον.
Φα.   δέδοιχ᾽ ὅπως μοι μὴ λίαν φανῇς σοφή.
Τρ.   πάντ᾽ ἂν φοβηθεῖσ᾽ ἴσθι· δειμαίνεις δὲ τί;
Φα.   μή μοί τι Θησέως τῶνδε μηνύσῃς τόκῳ. 520
Τρ.   ἔασον, ὦ παῖ· ταῦτ᾽ ἐγὼ θήσω καλῶς.

μόνον σύ μοι, δέσποινα ποτνία Κύπρι,
συνεργὸς εἴης. τἄλλα δ᾽ οἷ᾽ ἐγὼ φρονῶ
τοῖς ἔνδον ἡμῖν ἀρκέσει λέξαι φίλοις.

ΧΟΡΟΣ

Ἔρως, Ἔρως, ὁ κατ᾽ ὀμμάτων   [στρ. α 525
στάζων πόθον, εἰσάγων γλυκεῖαν
ψυχᾷ χάριν οὓς ἐπιστρατεύσῃ,
μή μοί ποτε σὺν κακῷ φανείης
μηδ᾽ ἄρρυθμος ἔλθοις.
οὔτε γὰρ πυρὸς οὔτ᾽ ἄστρων ὑπέρτερον βέλος 530
οἷον τὸ τᾶς Ἀφροδίτας ἵησιν ἐκ χερῶν
Ἔρως ὁ Διὸς παῖς.

ἄλλως ἄλλως παρά τ᾽ Ἀλφεῷ   [ἀντ. α 535
Φοίβου τ᾽ ἐπὶ Πυθίοις τεράμνοις
βούταν φόνον Ἑλλὰς ⟨αἶ᾽⟩ ἀέξει,
Ἔρωτα δέ, τὸν τύραννον ἀνδρῶν,
τὸν τᾶς Ἀφροδίτας
φιλτάτων θαλάμων κλῃδοῦχον, οὐ σεβίζομεν, 540
πέρθοντα καὶ διὰ πάσας ἱέντα συμφορᾶς
θνατοὺς ὅταν ἔλθῃ.

τὰν μὲν Οἰχαλίᾳ   [στρ. β 545
πῶλον ἄζυγα λέκτρων,
ἄνανδρον τὸ πρὶν καὶ ἄνυμφον, οἴκων
ζεύξασ᾽ ἀπ᾽ Εὐρυτίων
δρομάδα ναΐδ᾽ ὅπως τε βάκ- 550
    χαν σὺν αἵματι, σὺν καπνῷ,

φονίοισι νυμφείοις
Ἀλκμήνας τόκῳ Κύπρις ἐξέδωκεν· ὦ
τλάμων ὑμεναίων.

ὦ Θήβας ἱερὸν   [ἀντ. β 555
τεῖχος, ὦ στόμα Δίρκας,
συνείποιτ' ἂν ἁ Κύπρις οἷον ἕρπει.
βροντᾷ γὰρ ἀμφιπύρῳ
τοκάδα τὰν διγόνοιο Βακ-   560
χου νυμφευσαμένα πότμῳ
φονίῳ κατηύνασεν.
δεινὰ γὰρ τὰ πάντ' ἐπιπνεῖ, μέλισσα δ' οἷ-
α τις πεπόταται.

Φα.   σιγήσατ', ὦ γυναῖκες· ἐξειργάσμεθα.   565
Χο.   τί δ' ἐστί, Φαίδρα, δεινὸν ἐν δόμοισί σοι;
Φα.   ἐπίσχετ', αὐδὴν τῶν ἔσωθεν ἐκμάθω.
Χο.   σιγῶ· τὸ μέντοι φροίμιον κακὸν τόδε.
Φα.   ἰώ μοι, αἰαῖ·
         ὦ δυστάλαινα τῶν ἐμῶν παθημάτων.   570
Χο.   τίνα θροεῖς αὐδάν; τίνα βοᾷς λόγον;
         ἔνεπε, τίς φοβεῖ σε φήμα, γύναι,
         φρένας ἐπίσσυτος;
Φα.   ἀπωλόμεσθα· ταῖσδ' ἐπιστᾶσαι πύλαις   575
         ἀκούσαθ' οἷος κέλαδος ἐν δόμοις πίτνει.
Χο.   σὺ παρὰ κλῇθρα, σοὶ μέλει πομπίμα
         φάτις δωμάτων·
         ἔνεπε δ' ἔνεπέ μοι, τί ποτ' ἔβα κακόν;   580
Φα.   ὁ τῆς φιλίππου παῖς Ἀμαζόνος βοᾷ
         Ἱππόλυτος, αὐδῶν δεινὰ πρόσπολον κακά.
Χο.   ἰὰν μὲν κλύω, σαφὲς δ' οὐκ ἔχω·   585
         γεγώνει δ' οἷα διὰ πύλας ἔμολεν
         ἔμολέ σοι βοά.
Φα.   καὶ μὴν σαφῶς γε τὴν κακῶν προμνήστριαν,
         τὴν δεσπότου προδοῦσαν ἐξαυδᾷ λέχος.   590
Χο.   ὤμοι ἐγὼ κακῶν· προδέδοσαι φίλα.
         τί σοι μήσομαι;
         τὰ κρύπτ' ἐκπέφηνε, διὰ δ' ὄλλυσαι,
         αἰαῖ ἒ ἔ, πρόδοτος ἐκ φίλων.   595

Φα. ἀπώλεσέν μ’ εἰποῦσα συμφορὰς ἐμάς,
     φίλως καλῶς δ’ οὐ τήνδ’ ἰωμένη νόσον.
Χο. πῶς οὖν; τί δράσεις, ὦ παθοῦσ’ ἀμήχανα;
Φα. οὐκ οἶδα πλὴν ἕν, κατθανεῖν ὅσον τάχος,
     τῶν νῦν παρόντων πημάτων ἄκος μόνον.   600
Ιπ. ὦ γαῖα μῆτερ ἡλίου τ’ ἀναπτυχαί,
     οἵων λόγων ἄρρητον εἰσήκουσ’ ὄπα.
Τρ. σίγησον, ὦ παῖ, πρὶν τιν’ αἰσθέσθαι βοῆς.
Ιπ. οὐκ ἔστ’ ἀκούσας δειν’ ὅπως σιγήσομαι.
Τρ. ναί, πρός σε τῆσδε δεξιᾶς εὐωλένου.   605
Ιπ. οὐ μὴ προσοίσεις χεῖρα μηδ’ ἅψῃ πέπλων;
Τρ. ὦ πρός σε γονάτων, μηδαμῶς μ’ ἐξεργάσῃ.
Ιπ. τί δ’, εἴπερ, ὡς φῇς, μηδὲν εἴρηκας κακόν;
Τρ. ὁ μῦθος, ὦ παῖ, κοινὸς οὐδαμῶς ὅδε.
Ιπ. τά τοι κάλ’ ἐν πολλοῖσι κάλλιον λέγειν.   610
Τρ. ὦ τέκνον, ὅρκους μηδαμῶς ἀτιμάσῃς.
Ιπ. ἡ γλῶσσ’ ὀμώμοχ’, ἡ δὲ φρὴν ἀνώμοτος.
Τρ. ὦ παῖ, τί δράσεις; σοὺς φίλους διεργάσῃ;
Ιπ. ἀνέπτυσ’· οὐδεὶς ἄδικός ἐστί μοι φίλος.
Τρ. σύγγνωθ’· ἁμαρτεῖν εἰκὸς ἀνθρώπους, τέκνον.   615
Ιπ. ὦ Ζεῦ, τί δὴ κίβδηλον ἀνθρώποις κακὸν
     γυναῖκας ἐς φῶς ἡλίου κατῴκισας;
     εἰ γὰρ βρότειον ἤθελες σπεῖραι γένος,
     οὐκ ἐκ γυναικῶν χρῆν παρασχέσθαι τόδε,
     ἀλλ’ ἀντιθέντας σοῖσιν ἐν ναοῖς βροτοὺς   620
     ἢ χαλκὸν ἢ σίδηρον ἢ χρυσοῦ βάρος
     παίδων πρίασθαι σπέρμα του τιμήματος,
     τῆς ἀξίας ἕκαστον, ἐν δὲ δώμασιν
     ναίειν ἐλευθέροισι θηλειῶν ἄτερ.
     [νῦν δ’ ἐς δόμους μὲν πρῶτον ἄξεσθαι κακὸν   625
     μέλλοντες ὄλβον δωμάτων ἐκτίνομεν.]
     τούτῳ δὲ δῆλον ὡς γυνὴ κακὸν μέγα·
     προσθεὶς γὰρ ὁ σπείρας τε καὶ θρέψας πατὴρ
     φερνὰς ἀπῴκισ’, ὡς ἀπαλλαχθῇ κακοῦ.
     ὁ δ’ αὖ λαβὼν ἀτηρὸν ἐς δόμους φυτὸν   630
     γέγηθε κόσμον προστιθεὶς ἀγάλματι
     καλὸν κακίστῳ καὶ πέπλοισιν ἐκπονεῖ
     δύστηνος, ὄλβον δωμάτων ὑπεξελών.
     [ἔχει δ’ ἀνάγκην· ὥστε κηδεύσας καλῶς

γαμβροῖσι χαίρων σῴζεται πικρὸν λέχος,   635
ἢ χρηστὰ λέκτρα πενθεροὺς δ' ἀνωφελεῖς
λαβὼν πιέζει τἀγαθῷ τὸ δυστυχές.]
ῥᾷστον δ' ὅτῳ τὸ μηδέν· ἀλλ' ἀνωφελὴς
εὐηθίᾳ κατ' οἶκον ἵδρυται γυνή.
σοφὴν δὲ μισῶ· μὴ γὰρ ἔν γ' ἐμοῖς δόμοις   640
εἴη φρονοῦσα πλείον' ἢ γυναῖκα χρή.
τὸ γὰρ κακοῦργον μᾶλλον ἐντίκτει Κύπρις
ἐν ταῖς σοφαῖσιν· ἡ δ' ἀμήχανος γυνὴ
γνώμῃ βραχείᾳ μωρίαν ἀφῃρέθη.
χρῆν δ' ἐς γυναῖκα πρόσπολον μὲν οὐ περᾶν,   645
ἄφθογγα δ' αὐταῖς συγκατοικίζειν δάκη
θηρῶν, ἵν' εἶχον μήτε προσφωνεῖν τινα
μήτ' ἐξ ἐκείνων φθέγμα δέξασθαι πάλιν.
νῦν δ' †αἱ μὲν ἔνδον δρῶσιν αἱ κακαὶ† κακὰ
βουλεύματ', ἔξω δ' ἐκφέρουσι πρόσπολοι.   650
ὡς καὶ σύ γ' ἡμῖν πατρός, ὦ κακὸν κάρα,
λέκτρων ἀθίκτων ἦλθες ἐς συναλλαγάς·
ἁγὼ ῥυτοῖς νασμοῖσιν ἐξομόρξομαι
ἐς ὦτα κλύζων. πῶς ἂν οὖν εἴην κακός,
ὃς οὐδ' ἀκούσας τοιάδ' ἁγνεύειν δοκῶ;   655
εὖ δ' ἴσθι, τοὐμόν σ' εὐσεβὲς σῴζει, γύναι·
εἰ μὴ γὰρ ὅρκοις θεῶν ἄφαρκτος ᾑρέθην,
οὐκ ἄν ποτ' ἔσχον μὴ οὐ τάδ' ἐξειπεῖν πατρί.
νῦν δ' ἐκ δόμων μέν, ἔστ' ἂν ἐκδημῇ χθονὸς
Θησεύς, ἄπειμι, σῖγα δ' ἕξομεν στόμα·   660
θεάσομαι δὲ σὺν πατρὸς μολὼν ποδὶ
πῶς νιν προσόψῃ καὶ σὺ καὶ δέσποινα σή.
[τῆς σῆς δὲ τόλμης εἴσομαι γεγευμένος.]
ὄλοισθε. μισῶν δ' οὔποτ' ἐμπλησθήσομαι
γυναῖκας, οὐδ' εἴ φησί τίς μ' ἀεὶ λέγειν·   665
ἀεὶ γὰρ οὖν πώς εἰσι κἀκεῖναι κακαί.
ἢ νύν τις αὐτὰς σωφρονεῖν διδαξάτω
ἢ κἄμ' ἐάτω ταῖσδ' ἐπεμβαίνειν ἀεί.

Φα.   τάλανες ὦ κακοτυχεῖς   [ἀντ.
           γυναικῶν πότμοι·
           τίν' ἢ νῦν τέχναν ἔχομεν ἢ λόγον   670
           σφαλεῖσαι κάθαμμα λύειν †λόγου†;

ἐτύχομεν δίκας· ἰὼ γᾶ καὶ φῶς.
πᾷ ποτ᾽ ἐξαλύξω τύχας;
πῶς δὲ πῆμα κρύψω, φίλαι;
τίς ἂν θεῶν ἀρωγὸς ἢ τίς ἂν βροτῶν   675
πάρεδρος ἢ ξυνεργὸς ἀδίκων ἔργων
φανείη; τὸ γὰρ παρ᾽ ἡμῖν πάθος
πέραν δυσεκπέρατον ἔρχεται βίου.
κακοτυχεστάτα γυναικῶν ἐγώ.

Χο.   φεῦ φεῦ, πέπρακται, κοὐ κατώρθωνται τέχναι,   680
        δέσποινα, τῆς σῆς προσπόλου, κακῶς δ᾽ ἔχει.
Φα.   ὦ παγκακίστη καὶ φίλων διαφθορεῦ,
        οἷ᾽ εἰργάσω με. Ζεύς σε γεννήτωρ ἐμὸς
        πρόρριζον ἐκτρίψειεν οὐτάσας πυρί.
        οὐκ εἶπον,—οὐ σῆς προυνοησάμην φρενός;—   685
        σιγᾶν ἐφ᾽ οἷσι νῦν ἐγὼ κακύνομαι;
        σὺ δ᾽ οὐκ ἀνέσχου· τοιγὰρ οὐκέτ᾽ εὐκλεεῖς
        θανούμεθ᾽. ἀλλὰ δεῖ με δὴ καινῶν λόγων·
        οὗτος γὰρ ὀργῇ συντεθηγμένος φρένας
        ἐρεῖ καθ᾽ ἡμῶν πατρὶ σὰς ἁμαρτίας,   690
        ἐρεῖ δὲ Πιτθεῖ τῷ γέροντι συμφοράς,
        πλήσει τε πᾶσαν γαῖαν αἰσχίστων λόγων.
        ὄλοιο καὶ σὺ χὤστις ἄκοντας φίλους
        πρόθυμός ἐστι μὴ καλῶς εὐεργετεῖν.
Τρ.   δέσποιν᾽, ἔχεις μὲν τἀμὰ μέμψασθαι κακά,   695
        τὸ γὰρ δάκνον σου τὴν διάγνωσιν κρατεῖ·
        ἔχω δὲ κἀγὼ πρὸς τάδ᾽, εἰ δέξῃ, λέγειν.
        ἔθρεψά σ᾽ εὔνους τ᾽ εἰμί· τῆς νόσου δέ σοι
        ζητοῦσα φάρμαχ᾽ ηὗρον οὐχ ἁβουλόμην.
        εἰ δ᾽ εὖ ἔπραξα, κάρτ᾽ ἂν ἐν σοφοῖσιν ἦ·   700
        πρὸς τὰς τύχας γὰρ τὰς φρένας κεκτήμεθα.
Φα.   ἦ γὰρ δίκαια ταῦτα κἀξαρκοῦντά μοι,
        τρώσασαν ἡμᾶς εἶτα συγχωρεῖν λόγοις;
Τρ.   μακρηγοροῦμεν· οὐκ ἐσωφρόνουν ἐγώ.
        ἀλλ᾽ ἔστι κἀκ τῶνδ᾽ ὥστε σωθῆναι, τέκνον.   705
Φα.   παῦσαι λέγουσα· καὶ τὰ πρὶν γὰρ οὐ καλῶς
        παρήνεσάς μοι κἀπεχείρησας κακά.
        ἀλλ᾽ ἐκποδὼν ἄπελθε καὶ σαυτῆς πέρι
        φρόντιζ᾽· ἐγὼ γὰρ τἀμὰ θήσομαι καλῶς.

	ὑμεῖς δέ, παῖδες εὐγενεῖς Τροζήνιαι,	710
	τοσόνδε μοι παράσχετ᾽ ἐξαιτουμένη,	
	σιγῇ καλύπτειν ἀνθάδ᾽ εἰσηκούσατε.	
Χο.	ὄμνυμι σεμνὴν Ἄρτεμιν, Διὸς κόρην,	
	μηδὲν κακῶν σῶν ἐς φάος δείξειν ποτέ.	
Φα.	καλῶς ἐλέξαθ᾽· ἐν δὲ †προτρέπουσ᾽ ἐγὼ	715
	εὕρημα† δή τι τῆσδε συμφορᾶς ἔχω	
	ὥστ᾽ εὐκλεᾶ μὲν παισὶ προσθεῖναι βίον	
	αὐτή τ᾽ ὄνασθαι πρὸς τὰ νῦν πεπτωκότα.	
	οὐ γάρ ποτ᾽ αἰσχυνῶ γε Κρησίους δόμους	
	οὐδ᾽ ἐς πρόσωπον Θησέως ἀφίξομαι	720
	αἰσχροῖς ἐπ᾽ ἔργοις οὕνεκα ψυχῆς μιᾶς.	
Χο.	μέλλεις δὲ δὴ τί δρᾶν ἀνήκεστον κακόν;	
Φα.	θανεῖν· ὅπως δέ, τοῦτ᾽ ἐγὼ βουλεύσομαι.	
Χο.	εὔφημος ἴσθι. **Φα.** καὶ σύ γ᾽ εὖ με νουθέτει.	
	ἐγὼ δὲ Κύπριν, ἥπερ ἐξόλλυσί με,	725
	ψυχῆς ἀπαλλαχθεῖσα τῇδ᾽ ἐν ἡμέρᾳ	
	τέρψω· πικροῦ δ᾽ ἔρωτος ἡσσηθήσομαι.	
	ἀτὰρ κακόν γε χἀτέρῳ γενήσομαι	
	θανοῦσ᾽, ἵν᾽ εἰδῇ μὴ ᾽πὶ τοῖς ἐμοῖς κακοῖς	
	ὑψηλὸς εἶναι· τῆς νόσου δὲ τῆσδέ μοι	730
	κοινῇ μετασχὼν σωφρονεῖν μαθήσεται.	

Χο.	ἠλιβάτοις ὑπὸ κευθμῶσι γενοίμαν,	[στρ. α
	ἵνα με πτεροῦσσαν ὄρνιν	
	θεὸς ἐν ποταναῖς	
	ἀγέλαις θείη·	
	ἀρθείην δ᾽ ἐπὶ πόντιον	735
	κῦμα τᾶς Ἀδριηνᾶς	
	ἀκτᾶς Ἠριδανοῦ θ᾽ ὕδωρ,	
	ἔνθα πορφύρεον σταλάσ-	
	σουσ᾽ ἐς οἶδμα [πατρὸς] τάλαιναι	
	κόραι Φαέθοντος οἴκτῳ δακρύων	740
	τὰς ἠλεκτροφαεῖς αὐγάς.	

Χο.	Ἑσπερίδων δ᾽ ἐπὶ μηλόσπορον ἀκτὰν	[ἀντ. α
	ἀνύσαιμι τᾶν ἀοιδῶν,	
	ἵν᾽ ὁ πορφυρέας πον-	
	τομέδων λίμνας	

ναύταις οὐκέθ ὁδὸν νέμει,   745
σεμνὸν τέρμονα κυρῶν
οὐρανοῦ, τὸν Ἄτλας ἔχει,
κρῆναί τ᾽ ἀμβρόσιαι χέον-
    ται Ζηνὸς [μελάθρων] παρὰ κοίταις,
ἵν᾽ ὀλβιόδωρος αὔξει ζαθέα   750
χθὼν εὐδαιμονίαν θεοῖς.

ὦ λευκόπτερε Κρησία   [στρ. β
    πορθμίς, ἃ διὰ πόντιον
    κῦμ᾽ ἁλίκτυπον ἅλμας
ἐπόρευσας ἐμὰν ἄνασσαν ὀλβίων ἀπ᾽ οἴκων   755
κακονυμφοτάταν ὄνασιν.
ἦ γὰρ ἀπ᾽ ἀμφοτέρων †ἦ† Κρησίας ⟨τ᾽⟩ ἐκ γᾶς
    δυσόρνις
ἔπτατο κλεινὰς Ἀθήνας Μουνίχου τ᾽ ἀκ-   760
    ταῖσιν ἐκδήσαντο πλεκτὰς πεισμάτων ἀρ-
    χὰς ἐπ᾽ ἀπείρου τε γᾶς ἔβασαν.

ἀνθ᾽ ὧν οὐχ ὁσίων ἐρώ-   [ἀντ. β
    των δεινᾷ φρένας Ἀφροδί-   765
    τας νόσῳ κατεκλάσθη·
χαλεπᾷ δ᾽ ὑπέραντλος οὖσα συμφορᾷ τεράμνων
ἄπο νυμφιδίων κρεμαστὸν
ἅψεται ἀμφὶ βρόχον λευκᾷ καθαρμόζουσα δειρᾷ,   770
δαίμονα στυγνὸν καταιδεσθεῖσα τάν τ᾽ εὔ-
    δοξον ἀνθαιρουμένα φήμαν ἀπαλλάσ-
    σουσά τ᾽ ἀλγεινὸν φρενῶν ἔρωτα.   775

ΤΡΟΦΟΣ (ἔσωθεν)
    ἰοὺ ἰού·
    βοηδρομεῖτε πάντες οἱ πέλας δόμων·
    ἐν ἀγχόναις δέσποινα, Θησέως δάμαρ.
Χο.   φεῦ φεῦ, πέπρακται· βασιλὶς οὐκέτ᾽ ἔστι δὴ
    γυνή, κρεμαστοῖς ἐν βρόχοις ἠρτημένη.
Τρ.   οὐ σπεύσετ᾽; οὐκ οἴσει τις ἀμφιδέξιον   780
    σίδηρον, ᾧ τόδ᾽ ἅμμα λύσομεν δέρης;
Χο.   φίλαι, τί δρῶμεν; ἦ δοκεῖ περᾶν δόμους
    λῦσαί τ᾽ ἄνασσαν ἐξ ἐπισπαστῶν βρόχων;
— — τί δ᾽; οὐ πάρεισι πρόσπολοι νεανίαι;

	τὸ πολλὰ πράσσειν οὐκ ἐν ἀσφαλεῖ βίου.	785
Τρ.	ὀρθώσατ᾽ ἐκτείναντες ἄθλιον νέκυν·	
	πικρὸν τόδ᾽ οἰκούρημα δεσπόταις ἐμοῖς.	
Χο.	ὄλωλεν ἡ δύστηνος, ὡς κλύω, γυνή·	
	ἤδη γὰρ ὡς νεκρόν νιν ἐκτείνουσι δή.	

ΘΗΣΕΥΣ

	γυναῖκες, ἴστε τίς ποτ᾽ ἐν δόμοις βοὴ	790
	†ἠχὼ βαρεῖα προσπόλων† ἀφίκετο;	
	οὐ γὰρ τί μ᾽ ὡς θεωρὸν ἀξιοῖ δόμος	
	πύλας ἀνοίξας εὐφρόνως προσεννέπειν.	
	μῶν Πιτθέως τι γῆρας εἴργασται νέον;	
	πρόσω μὲν ἤδη βίοτος, ἀλλ᾽ ὅμως ἔτ᾽ ἂν	795
	λυπηρὸς ἡμῖν τούσδ᾽ ἂν ἐκλίποι δόμους.	
Χο.	οὐκ ἐς γέροντας ἥδε σοι τείνει τύχη,	
	Θησεῦ· νέοι θανόντες ἀλγύνουσί σε.	
Θη.	οἴμοι, τέκνων μοι μή τι συλᾶται βίος;	
Χο.	ζῶσιν, θανούσης μητρὸς ὡς ἄλγιστά σοι.	800
Θη.	τί φής; ὄλωλεν ἄλοχος; ἐκ τίνος τύχης;	
Χο.	βρόχον κρεμαστὸν ἀγχόνης ἀνήψατο.	
Θη.	λύπῃ παχνωθεῖσ᾽ ἢ ἀπὸ συμφορᾶς τίνος;	
Χο.	τοσοῦτον ἴσμεν· ἄρτι γὰρ κἀγὼ δόμους,	
	Θησεῦ, πάρειμι σῶν κακῶν πενθήτρια.	805
Θη.	αἰαῖ, τί δῆτα τοῖσδ᾽ ἀνέστεμμαι κάρα	
	πλεκτοῖσι φύλλοις, δυστυχὴς θεωρὸς ὤν;	
	χαλᾶτε κλῇθρα, πρόσπολοι, πυλωμάτων,	
	[ἐκλύσαθ᾽ ἁρμούς, ὡς ἴδω δυσδαίμονα]	809
	ἐκλύεθ᾽ ἁρμούς, ὡς ἴδω πικρὰν θέαν	825
	γυναικός, ἥ με κατθανοῦσ᾽ ἀπώλεσεν.	810

Χο.	ἰὼ ἰὼ τάλαινα μελέων κακῶν·	
	ἔπαθες, εἰργάσω	
	τοσοῦτον ὥστε τούσδε συγχέαι δόμους,	
	αἰαῖ τόλμας,	
	βιαίως θανοῦσ᾽ ἀνοσίῳ τε συμ-	
	φορᾷ σᾶς χερὸς πάλαισμα μελέας.	815
	τίς ἄρα σάν, τάλαιν᾽, ἀμαυροῖ ζόαν;	

| Θη. | ὤμοι ἐγὼ πόνων· ἔπαθον, ὦ τάλας, | [στρ. |
| | τὰ μάκιστ᾽ ἐμῶν κακῶν. ὦ τύχα, | |

ὥς μοι βαρεῖα καὶ δόμοις ἐπεστάθης,
κηλὶς ἄφραστος ἐξ ἀλαστόρων τινός·   820
κατακονὰ μὲν οὖν, ἀβίοτος βίος·
κακῶν δ᾽, ὦ τάλας, πέλαγος εἰσορῶ
τοσοῦτον ὥστε μήποτ᾽ἐκνεῦσαι πάλιν
μηδ᾽ ἐκπερᾶσαι κῦμα τῆσδε συμφορᾶς.   824
τίνι λόγῳ, τάλας, τίνι τύχαν σέθεν   826
βαρύποτμον, γύναι, προσαυδῶν τύχω;
ὄρνις γὰρ ὥς τις ἐκ χερῶν ἄφαντος εἶ,
πήδημ᾽ ἐς Ἅιδου κραιπνὸν ὁρμήσασά μοι.
αἰαῖ αἰαῖ, μέλεα μέλεα τάδε πάθη.   830
πρόσωθεν δέ ποθεν ἀνακομίζομαι
τύχαν δαιμόνων ἀμπλακίαισι τῶν
        πάροιθέν τινος.

Χο.   οὐ σοὶ τάδ᾽, ὦναξ, ἦλθε δὴ μόνῳ κακά,
πολλῶν μετ᾽ ἄλλων δ᾽ ὤλεσας κεδνὸν λέχος.   835

Θη.   τὸ κατὰ γῆς θέλω, τὸ κατὰ γῆς κνέφας   [ἀντ.
μετοικεῖν σκότῳ θανών, ὦ τλάμων,
τῆς σῆς στερηθεὶς φιλτάτης ὁμιλίας·
ἀπώλεσας γὰρ μᾶλλον ἢ κατέφθισο.
†τίνος κλύω† πόθεν θανάσιμος τύχα,   840
γύναι, σάν, τάλαιν᾽, ἔβα, καρδίαν;
εἴποι τις ἂν τὸ πραχθέν, ἢ μάτην ὄχλον
στέγει τύραννον δῶμα προσπόλων ἐμῶν;
ὤμοι μοι ⟨   ⟩ σέθεν,
μέλεος, οἷον εἶδον ἄλγος δόμων,   845
οὐ τλητὸν οὐδὲ ῥητόν. ἀλλ᾽ ἀπωλόμην·
ἔρημος οἶκος, καὶ τέκν᾽ ὀρφανεύεται.
⟨αἰαῖ αἰαῖ,⟩ ἔλιπες ἔλιπες, ὦ φίλα
γυναικῶν ἀρίστα θ᾽ ὁπόσας ὁρᾷ
φέγγος θ᾽ ἁλίοιο καὶ νυκτὸς ἀ-   850
στερωπὸν σέλας.

Χο.   ὦ τάλας, ὅσον κακὸν ἔχει δόμος·
δάκρυσί μου βλέφαρα καταχυθέντα τέγ-
        γεται σᾷ τύχᾳ.
τὸ δ᾽ ἐπὶ τῷδε πῆμα φρίσσω πάλαι.   855
Θη.   ἔα ἔα·
τί δή ποθ᾽ ἥδε δέλτος ἐκ φίλης χερὸς

ἠρτημένη; θέλει τι σημῆναι νέον;
ἀλλ' ἦ λέχους μοι καὶ τέκνων ἐπιστολὰς
ἔγραψεν ἡ δύστηνος, ἐξαιτουμένη;
θάρσει, τάλαινα· λέκτρα γὰρ τὰ Θησέως   860
οὐκ ἔστι δῶμά θ' ἥτις εἴσεισιν γυνή.
καὶ μὴν τύποι γε σφενδόνης χρυσηλάτου
τῆς οὐκέτ' οὔσης οἴδε προσσαίνουσί με.
φέρ' ἐξελίξας περιβολὰς σφραγισμάτων
ἴδω τί λέξαι δέλτος ἥδε μοι θέλει.   865
Χο.   φεῦ φεῦ· τόδ' αὖ νεοχμὸν ἐκδοχαῖς
       ἐπεισφρεῖ θεὸς κακόν. †ἐμοὶ [μὲν οὖν
                                ἀβίοτος βίου]
       τύχα πρὸς τὸ κρανθὲν εἴη τυχεῖν·†
       ὀλομένους γάρ, οὐκέτ' ὄντας, λέγω,
       φεῦ φεῦ, τῶν ἐμῶν τυράννων δόμους.   870
       [ὦ δαῖμον, εἴ πως ἔστι, μὴ σφήλῃς δόμους,
       αἰτουμένης δὲ κλῦθί μου· πρὸς γάρ τινος
       οἰωνὸν ὥστε μάντις εἰσορῶ κακόν].
Θη.   οἴμοι, τόδ' οἷον ἄλλο πρὸς κακῷ κακόν,
       οὐ τλητὸν οὐδὲ λεκτόν· ὦ τάλας ἐγώ.   875
Χο.   τί χρῆμα; λέξον, εἴ τί μοι λόγου μέτα.
Θη.   βοᾷ βοᾷ δέλτος ἄλαστα· πᾷ φύγω
       βάρος κακῶν; ἀπὸ γὰρ ὀλόμενος οἴχομαι,
       οἷον οἷον εἶδον [ἐν] γραφαῖς μέλος
       φθεγγόμενον τλάμων.   880
Χο.   αἰαῖ, κακῶν ἀρχηγὸν ἐκφαίνεις λόγον.
Θη.   τόδε μὲν οὐκέτι στόματος ἐν πύλαις
       καθέξω δυσεκπέρατον ὀλοὸν
       κακόν· ἰὼ πόλις.
       Ἱππόλυτος εὐνῆς τῆς ἐμῆς ἔτλη θιγεῖν   885
       βίᾳ, τὸ σεμνὸν Ζηνὸς ὄμμ' ἀτιμάσας.
       ἀλλ', ὦ πάτερ Πόσειδον, ἃς ἐμοί ποτε
       ἀρὰς ὑπέσχου τρεῖς, μιᾷ κατέργασαι
       τούτων ἐμὸν παῖδ', ἡμέραν δὲ μὴ φύγοι
       τήνδ', εἴπερ ἡμῖν ὤπασας σαφεῖς ἀράς.   890
Χο.   ἄναξ, ἀπεύχου ταῦτα πρὸς θεῶν πάλιν,
       γνώσῃ γὰρ αὖθις ἀμπλακών· ἐμοὶ πιθοῦ.
Θη.   οὐκ ἔστι· καὶ πρός γ' ἐξελῶ σφε τῆσδε γῆς·
       δυοῖν δὲ μοίραιν θατέρᾳ πεπλήξεται·

ἢ γὰρ Ποσειδῶν αὐτὸν εἰς Ἅιδου δόμους 895
θανόντα πέμψει τὰς ἐμὰς ἀρὰς σέβων
ἢ τῆσδε χώρας ἐκπεσὼν ἀλώμενος
ξένην ἐπ᾽ αἶαν λυπρὸν ἀντλήσει βίον.

Χο. καὶ μὴν ὅδ᾽ αὐτὸς παῖς σὸς ἐς καιρὸν πάρα
Ἱππόλυτος· ὀργῆς δ᾽ ἐξανεὶς κακῆς, ἄναξ 900
Θησεῦ, τὸ λῷστον σοῖσι βούλευσαι δόμοις.

Ιπ. κραυγῆς ἀκούσας σῆς ἀφικόμην, πάτερ,
σπουδῇ· τὸ μέντοι πρᾶγμ᾽ ὅτῳ στένεις ἔπι
οὐκ οἶδα, βουλοίμην δ᾽ ἂν ἐκ σέθεν κλυεῖν.
ἔα, τί χρῆμα; σὴν δάμαρθ᾽ ὁρῶ, πάτερ, 905
νεκρόν· μεγίστου θαύματος, τόδ᾽ ἄξιον·
ἣν ἀρτίως ἔλειπον, ἣ φάος τόδε
οὔπω χρόνος παλαιὸς εἰσεδέρκετο.
τί χρῆμα πάσχει; τῷ τρόπῳ διόλλυται;
πάτερ, πυθέσθαι βούλομαι σέθεν πάρα. 910
σιγᾷς; σιωπῆς δ᾽ οὐδὲν ἔργον ἐν κακοῖς·
[ἡ γὰρ ποθοῦσα πάντα καρδία κλυεῖν
κἂν τοῖς κακοῖσι λίχνος οὖσ᾽ ἁλίσκεται.]
οὐ μὴν φίλους γε, κἄτι μᾶλλον ἢ φίλους,
κρύπτειν δίκαιον σάς, πάτερ, δυσπραξίας. 915

Θη. ὦ πόλλ᾽ ἁμαρτάνοντες ἄνθρωποι μάτην,
τί δὴ τέχνας μὲν μυρίας διδάσκετε
καὶ πάντα μηχανᾶσθε κἀξευρίσκετε,
ἓν δ᾽ οὐκ ἐπίστασθ᾽ οὐδ᾽ ἐθηράσασθέ πω,
φρονεῖν διδάσκειν οἷσιν οὐκ ἔνεστι νοῦς; 920

Ιπ. δεινὸν σοφιστὴν εἶπας, ὅστις εὖ φρονεῖν
τοὺς μὴ φρονοῦντας δυνατός ἐστ᾽ ἀναγκάσαι.
ἀλλ᾽ οὐ γὰρ ἐν δέοντι λεπτουργεῖς, πάτερ,
δέδοικα μή σου γλῶσσ᾽ ὑπερβάλλῃ κακοῖς.

Θη. φεῦ, χρῆν βροτοῖσι τῶν φίλων τεκμήριον 925
σαφές τι κεῖσθαι καὶ διάγνωσιν φρενῶν,
ὅστις τ᾽ ἀληθής ἐστιν ὅς τε μὴ φίλος,
δισσάς τε φωνὰς πάντας ἀνθρώπους ἔχειν,
τὴν μὲν δικαίαν τὴν δ᾽ ὅπως ἐτύγχανεν,
ὡς ἡ φρονοῦσα τἄδικ᾽ ἐξηλέγχετο 930
πρὸς τῆς δικαίας, κοὐκ ἂν ἠπατώμεθα.

Ιπ. ἀλλ᾽ ἦ τις ἐς σὸν οὖς με διαβαλὼν ἔχει

φίλων, νοσοῦμεν δ᾽ οὐδὲν ὄντες αἴτιοι;
ἔκ τοι πέπληγμαι· σοὶ γὰρ ἐκπλήσσουσί με
λόγοι, παραλλάσσοντες ἔξεδροι φρενῶν.   935

Θη.   φεῦ τῆς βροτείας—ποῖ προβήσεται;—φρενός.
τί τέρμα τόλμης καὶ θράσους γενήσεται;
εἰ γὰρ κατ᾽ ἀνδρὸς βίοτον ἐξογκώσεται,
ὁ δ᾽ ὕστερος τοῦ πρόσθεν εἰς ὑπερβολὴν
πανοῦργος ἔσται, θεοῖσι προσβαλεῖν χθονὶ   940
ἄλλην δεήσει γαῖαν ἢ χωρήσεται
τοὺς μὴ δικαίους καὶ κακοὺς πεφυκότας.
σκέψασθε δ᾽ ᾽ἐς τόνδ᾽, ὅστις ἐξ ἐμοῦ γεγὼς
ᾔσχυνε τἀμὰ λέκτρα κἀξελέγχεται
πρὸς τῆς θανούσης ἐμφανῶς κάκιστος ὤν.   945
δεῖξον δ᾽, ἐπειδή γ᾽ ἐς μίασμ᾽ ἐλήλυθα,
τὸ σὸν πρόσωπον δεῦρ᾽ ἐναντίον πατρί.
σὺ δὴ θεοῖσιν ὡς περρισὸς ὢν ἀνὴρ
ξύνει; σὺ σώφρων καὶ κακῶν ἀκήρατος;
οὐκ ἂν πιθοίμην τοῖσι σοῖς κόμποις ἐγὼ   950
θεοῖσι προσθεὶς ἀμαθίαν φρονεῖν κακῶς.
ἤδη νυν αὔχει καὶ δι᾽ ἀψύχου βορᾶς
†σίτοις† καπήλευ᾽, Ὀρφέα τ᾽ ἄνακτ᾽ ἔχων
βάκχευε πολλῶν γραμμάτων τιμῶν καπνούς·
ἐπεί γ᾽ ἐλήφθης. τοὺς δὲ τοιούτους ἐγὼ   955
φεύγειν προφωνῶ πᾶσι· θηρεύουσι γὰρ
σεμνοῖς λόγοισιν, αἰσχρὰ μηχανώμενοι.
τέθνηκεν ἥδε· τοῦτό σ᾽ ἐκσώσειν δοκεῖς;
ἐν τῷδ᾽ ἁλίσκῃ πλεῖστον, ὦ κάκιστε σύ·
ποῖοι γὰρ ὅρκοι κρείσσονες, τίνες λόγοι   960
τῆσδ᾽ ἂν γένοιντ᾽ ἄν, ὥστε σ᾽ αἰτίαν φυγεῖν;
μισεῖν σε φήσεις τήνδε καὶ τὸ δὴ νόθον
τοῖς γνησίοισι πολέμιον πεφυκέναι;
κακὴν ἄρ᾽ αὐτὴν ἔμπορον βίου λέγεις,
εἰ δυσμενείᾳ σῇ τὰ φίλτατ᾽ ὤλεσεν.   965
ἀλλ᾽ ὡς τὸ μῶρον ἀνδράσιν μὲν οὐκ ἔνι,
γυναιξὶ δ᾽ ἐμπέφυκεν; οἶδ᾽ ἐγὼ νέους
οὐδὲν γυναικῶν ὄντας ἀσφαλεστέρους,
ὅταν ταράξῃ Κύπρις ἡβῶσαν φρένα·
τὸ δ᾽ ἄρσεν αὐτοὺς ὠφελεῖ προσκείμενον.   970
νῦν οὖν—τί ταῦτα σοῖς ἁμιλλῶμαι λόγοις

νεκροῦ παρόντος μάρτυρος σαφεστάτου;—
ἔξερρε γαίας τῆσδ᾽ ὅσον τάχος φυγάς,
καὶ μήτ᾽ Ἀθήνας τὰς θεοδμήτους μόλῃς
μήτ᾽ εἰς ὅρους γῆς ἧς ἐμὸν κρατεῖ δόρυ. 975
εἰ γὰρ παθών γέ σου τάδ᾽ ἡσσηθήσομαι,
οὐ μαρτυρήσει μ᾽ Ἴσθμιος Σίνις ποτὲ
κτανεῖν ἑαυτὸν ἀλλὰ κομπάζειν μάτην,
οὐδ᾽ αἱ θαλάσσῃ σύννομοι Σκιρωνίδες
φήσουσι πέτραι τοῖς κακοῖς μ᾽ εἶναι βαρύν. 980

Χο. οὐκ οἶδ᾽ ὅπως εἴποιμ᾽ ἂν εὐτυχεῖν τινα
θνητῶν· τὰ γὰρ δὴ πρῶτ᾽ ἀνέστραπται πάλιν.

Ιπ. πάτερ, μένος μὲν ξύντασίς τε σῶν φρενῶν
δεινή· τὸ μέντοι πρᾶγμ᾽, ἔχον καλοὺς λόγους,
εἴ τις διαπτύξειεν οὐ καλὸν τόδε. 985
ἐγὼ δ᾽ ἄκομψος εἰς ὄχλον δοῦναι λόγον,
ἐς ἥλικας δὲ κὠλίγους σοφώτερος·
ἔχει δὲ μοῖραν καὶ τόδ᾽· οἱ γὰρ ἐν σοφοῖς
φαῦλοι παρ᾽ ὄχλῳ μουσικώτεροι λέγειν.
ὅμως δ᾽ ἀνάγκη, ξυμφορᾶς ἀφιγμένης, 990
γλῶσσάν μ᾽ ἀφεῖναι. πρῶτα δ᾽ ἄρξομαι λέγειν
ὅθεν μ᾽ ὑπῆλθες πρῶτον ὡς διαφθερῶν
οὐκ ἀντιλέξοντ᾽. εἰσορᾷς φάος τόδε
καὶ γαῖαν· ἐν τοῖσδ᾽ οὐκ ἔνεστ᾽ ἀνὴρ ἐμοῦ,
οὐδ᾽ ἢν σὺ μὴ φῇς, σωφρονέστερος γεγώς. 995
ἐπίσταμαι γὰρ πρῶτα μὲν θεοὺς σέβειν
φίλοις τε χρῆσθαι μὴ ἀδικεῖν πειρωμένοις
ἀλλ᾽ οἷσιν αἰδὼς μήτ᾽ ἐπαγγέλειν κακὰ
μήτ᾽ ἀνθυπουργεῖν αἰσχρὰ τοῖσι χρωμένοις,
οὐκ ἐγγελαστὴς τῶν ὁμιλούντων, πάτερ, 1000
ἀλλ᾽ αὐτὸς οὐ παροῦσι κἀγγὺς ὢν φίλοις.
ἑνὸς δ᾽ ἄθικτος, ᾧ με νῦν ἔχειν δοκεῖς·
λέχους γὰρ ἐς τόδ᾽ ἡμέρας ἁγνὸν δέμας.
οὐκ οἶδα πρᾶξιν τήνδε πλὴν λόγῳ κλύων
γραφῇ τε λεύσσων· οὐδὲ ταῦτα γὰρ σκοπεῖν 1005
πρόθυμός εἰμι, παρθένον ψυχὴν ἔχων.
†καὶ δὴ† τὸ σῶφρον τοὐμὸν οὐ πείθει σ᾽ ἴσως·
δεῖ δή σε δεῖξαι τῷ τρόπῳ διεφθάρην.
πότερα τὸ τῆσδε σῶμ᾽ ἐκαλλιστεύετο
πασῶν γυναικῶν; ἢ σὸν οἰκήσειν δόμον 1010

ἔγκληρον εὐνὴν προσλαβὼν ἐπήλπισα;
μάταιος ἄρ᾽ ἦν, οὐδαμοῦ μὲν οὖν φρενῶν.
ἀλλ᾽ ὡς τυραννεῖν ἡδύ; τοῖσι σώφροσιν
ἥκιστά γ᾽ †εἰ μὴ† τὰς φρένας διέφθορεν
θνητῶν ὅσοισιν ἁνδάνει μοναρχία.   1015
ἐγὼ δ᾽ ἀγῶνας μὲν κρατεῖν Ἑλληνικοὺς
πρῶτος θέλοιμ᾽ ἄν, ἐν πόλει δὲ δεύτερος
σὺν τοῖς ἀρίστοις εὐτυχεῖν ἀεὶ φίλοις·
πράσσειν τε γὰρ πάρεστι, κίνδυνός τ᾽ ἀπὼν
κρείσσω δίδωσι τῆς τυραννίδος χάριν.   1020
ἓν οὐ λέλεκται τῶν ἐμῶν, τὰ δ᾽ ἄλλ᾽ ἔχεις·
εἰ μὲν γὰρ ἦν μοι μάρτυς οἷός εἰμ᾽ ἐγὼ
καὶ τῆσδ᾽ ὁρώσης φέγγος ἠγωνιζόμην,
ἔργοις ἂν εἶδες τοὺς κακοὺς διεξιών·
νῦν δ᾽ ὅρκιόν σοι Ζῆνα καὶ πέδον χθονὸς   1025
ὄμνυμι τῶν σῶν μήποθ᾽ ἄψασθαι γάμων
μηδ᾽ ἂν θελῆσαι μηδ᾽ ἂν ἔννοιαν λαβεῖν.
ἦ τἄρ᾽ ὀλοίμην ἀκλεὴς ἀνώνυμος
[ἄπολις ἄοικος, φυγὰς ἀλητεύων χθόνα,]
καὶ μήτε πόντος μήτε γῆ δέξαιτό μου   1030
σάρκας θανόντος, εἰ κακὸς πέφυκ᾽ ἀνήρ.
τί δ᾽ ἥδε δειμαίνουσ᾽ ἀπώλεσεν βίον
οὐκ οἶδ᾽, ἐμοὶ γὰρ οὐ θέμις πέρα λέγειν.
ἐσωφρόνησε δ᾽ οὐκ ἔχουσα σωφρονεῖν,
ἡμεῖς δ᾽ ἔχοντες οὐ καλῶς ἐχρώμεθα.   1035
Χο.   ἀρκοῦσαν εἶπας αἰτίας ἀποστροφὴν
ὅρκους παρασχών, πίστιν οὐ σμικράν, θεῶν.
Θη.   ἆρ᾽ οὐκ ἐπῳδὸς καὶ γόης πέφυχ᾽ ὅδε,
ὃς τὴν ἐμὴν πέποιθεν εὐοργησίᾳ
ψυχὴν κρατήσειν, τὸν τεκόντ᾽ ἀτιμάσας;   1040
Ἱπ.   καὶ σοῦ γε κάρτα ταῦτα θαυμάζω, πάτερ·
εἰ γὰρ σὺ μὲν παῖς ἦσθ᾽, ἐγὼ δὲ σὸς πατήρ,
ἔκτεινά τοί σ᾽ ἂν κοὐ φυγαῖς ἐζημίουν,
εἴπερ γυναικὸς ἠξίους ἐμῆς θιγεῖν.
Θη.   ὡς ἄξιον τόδ᾽ εἶπας· οὐχ οὕτω θανῇ·   1045
[ὥσπερ σὺ σαυτῷ τόνδε προύθηκας νόμον·]
ταχὺς γὰρ Ἅιδης ῥᾷστος ἀνδρὶ δυστυχεῖ·
ἀλλ᾽ ἐκ πατρῴας φυγὰς ἀλητεύων χθονὸς
ξένην ἐπ᾽ αἶαν λυπρὸν ἀντλήσεις βίον.

[μισθὸς γὰρ οὗτός ἐστιν ἀνδρὶ δυσσεβεῖ.] 1050

Ιπ. οἴμοι, τί δράσεις; οὐδὲ μηνυτὴν χρόνον
δέξῃ καθ᾽ ἡμῶν, ἀλλά μ᾽ἐξελᾷς χθονός;

Θη. πέραν γε Πόντου καὶ τόπων Ἀτλαντικῶν,
εἴ πως δυναίμην, ὡς σὸν ἐχθαίρω κάρα.

Ιπ. οὐδ᾽ ὅρκον οὐδὲ πίστιν οὐδὲ μάντεων 1055
φήμας ἐλέγξας ἄκριτον ἐκβαλεῖς με γῆς;

Θη. ἡ δέλτος ἥδε κλῆρον οὐ δεδεγμένη
κατηγορεῖ σου πιστά· τοὺς δ᾽ὑπὲρ κάρα
φοιτῶντας ὄρνις πόλλ᾽ ἐγὼ χαίρειν λέγω.

Ιπ. ὦ θεοί, τί δῆτα τοὐμὸν οὐ λύω στόμα, 1060
ὅστις γ᾽ ὑφ᾽ ὑμῶν, οὓς σέβω, διόλλυμαι;
οὐ δῆτα· πάντως οὐ πίθοιμ᾽ ἂν οὕς με δεῖ,
μάτην δ᾽ ἂν ὅρκους συγχέαιμ᾽ οὓς ὤμοσα.

Θη. οἴμοι, τὸ σεμνὸν ὥς μ᾽ ἀποκτεινεῖ τὸ σόν.
οὐκ εἶ πατρῴας ἐκτὸς ὡς τάχιστα γῆς; 1065

Ιπ. ποῖ δῆθ᾽ ὁ τλήμων τρέψομαι; τίνος ξένων
δόμους ἔσειμι, τῇδ᾽ ἐπ᾽ αἰτίᾳ φυγών;

Θη. ὅστις γυναικῶν λυμεῶνας ἥδεται
ξένους κομίζων καὶ ξυνοικούρους κακῶν.

Ιπ. αἰαῖ, πρὸς ἧπαρ· δακρύων ἐγγὺς τόδε, 1070
εἰ δὴ κακός γε φαίνομαι δοκῶ τε σοί.

Θη. τότε στενάζειν καὶ προγιγνώσκειν σ᾽ ἐχρῆν
ὅτ᾽ ἐς πατρῴαν ἄλοχον ὑβρίζειν ἔτλης.

Ιπ. ὦ δώματ᾽, εἴθε φθέγμα γηρύσαισθέ μοι
καὶ μαρτυρήσαιτ᾽ εἰ κακὸς πέφυκ᾽ ἀνήρ. 1075

Θη. ἐς τοὺς ἀφώνους μάρτυρας φεύγεις σοφῶς·
τὸ δ᾽ ἔργον, οὐ λέγον, σε μηνύει κακόν.

Ιπ. φεῦ·
εἴθ᾽ ἦν ἐμαυτὸν προσβλέπειν ἐναντίον
στάνθ᾽, ὡς ἐδάκρυσ᾽ οἷα πάσχομεν κακά.

Θη. πολλῷ γε μᾶλλον σαυτὸν ἤσκησας σέβειν 1080
ἢ τοὺς τεκόντας ὅσια δρᾶν δίκαιος ὤν.

Ιπ. ὦ δυστάλαινα μῆτερ, ὦ πικραὶ γοναί·
μηδείς ποτ᾽ εἴη τῶν ἐμῶν φίλων νόθος.

Θη. οὐχ ἕλξετ᾽ αὐτόν, δμῶες; οὐκ ἀκούετε
πάλαι ξενοῦσθαι τόνδε προυννέποντά με; 1085

Ιπ. κλαίων τις αὐτῶν ἄρ᾽ ἐμοῦ γε θίξεται·
σὺ δ᾽ αὐτός, εἴ σοι θυμός, ἐξώθει χθονός.

Θη. δράσω τάδ᾽, εἰ μὴ τοῖς ἐμοῖς πείσῃ λόγοις·
οὐ γάρ τις οἶκτος σῆς μ᾽ ὑπέρχεται φυγῆς.

Ιπ. ἄραρεν, ὡς ἔοικεν· ὦ τάλας ἐγώ, 1090
ὡς οἶδα μὲν ταῦτ᾽, οἶδα δ᾽ οὐχ ὅπως φράσω.
ὦ φιλτάτη μοι δαιμόνων Λητοῦς κόρη,
σύνθακε, συγκύναγε, φευξούμεσθα δὴ
κλεινὰς Ἀθήνας. ἀλλὰ χαιρέτω πόλις
καὶ γαῖ᾽ Ἐρεχθέως· ὦ πέδον Τροζήνιον, 1095
ὡς ἐγκαθηβᾶν πόλλ᾽ ἔχεις εὐδάιμονα,
χαῖρ᾽· ὕστατον γάρ σ᾽ εἰσορῶν προσφθέγγομαι.
ἴτ᾽, ὦ νέοι μοι τῆσδε γῆς ὁμήλικες,
προσείπαθ᾽ ἡμᾶς καὶ προπέμψατε χθονός·
ὡς οὔποτ᾽ ἄλλον ἄνδρα σωφρονέστερον 1100
ὄψεσθε, κεἰ μὴ ταῦτ᾽ ἐμῷ δοκεῖ πατρί.

Χο. ἦ μέγα μοι τὰ θεῶν μελεδήμαθ᾽, ὅταν φρένας [στρ. α
ἔλθῃ
λύπας παραιρεῖ· ξύνεσιν δέ τις ἐλπίδι κεύθων 1105
λείπεται ἔν τε τύχαις θνατῶν καὶ ἐν ἔργμασι λευσ-
σων·
ἄλλα γὰρ ἄλλοθεν ἀμείβεται, μετὰ δ᾽ ἵσταται
ἀνδράσιν αἰὼν
πολυπλάνητος αἰεί. 1110

εἴθε μοι εὐξαμένᾳ θεόθεν τάδε μοῖρα παράσχοι, [ἀντ. α
τύχαν μετ᾽ ὄλβου καὶ ἀκήρατον ἄλγεσι θυμόν·
δόξα δὲ μήτ᾽ ἀτρεκὴς μήτ᾽ αὖ παράσημος ἐνείη, 1115
ῥᾴδια δ᾽ ἤθεα τὸν αὔριον μεταβαλλομένα
χρόνον αἰεὶ
βίον συνευτυχοίην.

οὐκέτι γὰρ καθαρὰν φρέν᾽ ἔχω, παρὰ δ᾽ ἐλπίδ᾽ [στρ. β
ἃ λεύσσω· 1120
ἐπεὶ τὸν Ἑλλανίας φανερώτατον ἀστέρ᾽ †ἀθήνας† 1123
εἴδομεν εἴδομεν ἐκ πατρὸς ὀργᾶς
ἄλλαν ἐπ᾽ αἶαν ἱέμενον. 1125
ὦ ψάμαθοι πολιήτιδος ἀκτᾶς,
ὦ δρυμὸς ὄρεος ὅθι κυνῶν
ὠκυπόδων [ἐπέβας θεᾶς] μέτα θῆρας ἔναιρεν
Δίκτυνναν ἀμφὶ σεμνάν. 1130

οὐκέτι συζυγίαν πώλων Ἐνετᾶν ἐπιβάσῃ   [ἀντ. β
τὸν ἀμφὶ Λίμνας τρόχον κατέχων ποδὶ γυμνάδος
                                        ἵππου·
μοῦσα δ᾽ ἄυπνος ὑπ᾽ ἄντυγι χορδᾶν   1135
λήξει πατρῷον ἀνὰ δόμον·
ἀστέφανοι δὲ κόρας ἀνάπαυλαι
Λατοῦς βαθεῖαν ἀνὰ χλόαν·
νυμφιδία δ᾽ ἀπόλωλε φυγᾷ σᾷ   1140
λέκτρων ἅμιλλα κούραις.

ἐγὼ δὲ σᾷ δυστυχίᾳ   ἐπῳδ.
δάκρυσιν διοίσω
πότμον ἄποτμον· ὦ τάλαινα μᾶτερ,
ἔτεκες ἀνόνατα· φεῦ,   1145
μανίω θεοῖσιν.
ἰὼ ἰώ·
συζύγιαι Χάριτες, τί τὸν τάλαν᾽ ἐκ πατρίας γᾶς
οὐδὲν ἄτας αἴτιον
πέμπετε τῶνδ᾽ ἀπ᾽ οἴκων;   1150
— — — καὶ μὴν ὀπαδὸν Ἱππολύτου τόνδ᾽ εἰσορῶ
σπουδῇ σκυθρωπὸν πρὸς δόμους ὁρμώμενον.

ΑΓΓΕΛΟΣ
                 ποῖ γῆς ἄνακτα τῆσδε Θησέα μολὼν
                 εὕροιμ᾽ ἄν, ὦ γυναῖκες; εἴπερ ἴστε μοι
                 σημήνατ᾽· ἆρα τῶνδε δωμάτων ἔσω;   1155
Χο.   ὅδ᾽ αὐτὸς ἔξω δωμάτων πορεύεται.
Αγ.   Θησεῦ, μερίμνης ἄξιον φέρω λόγον
                 σοὶ καὶ πολίταις οἵ τ᾽ Ἀθηναίων πόλιν
                 ναίουσι καὶ γῆς τέρμονας Τροζηνίας.
Θη.   τί δ᾽ ἔστι; μῶν τις συμφορὰ νεωτέρα   1160
                 δισσὰς κατείληφ᾽ ἀστυγείτονας πόλεις;
Αγ.   Ἱππόλυτος οὐκέτ᾽ ἔστιν, ὡς εἰπεῖν ἔπος·
                 δέδορκε μέντοι φῶς ἐπὶ σμικρᾶς ῥοπῆς.
Θη.   πρὸς τοῦ; δι᾽ ἔχθρας μῶν τις ἦν ἀφιγμένος
                 ὅτου κατήσχυν᾽ ἄλοχον ὡς πατρὸς βίᾳ;   1165
Αγ.   οἰκεῖος αὐτὸν ὤλεσ᾽ ἁρμάτων ὄχος
                 ἀραί τε τοῦ σοῦ στόματος, ἃς σὺ σῷ πατρὶ
                 πόντου κρέοντι παιδὸς ἠράσω πέρι.

Θη.   ὦ θεοὶ Πόσειδόν θ'· ὡς ἄρ' ἦσθ'ἐμὸς πατὴρ
        ὀρθῶς, ἀκούσας τῶν ἐμῶν κατευγμάτων.   1170
        πῶς καὶ διώλετ'; εἰπέ, τῷ τρόπῳ Δίκης
        ἔπαισεν αὐτὸν ῥόπτρον αἰσχύναντά με;
Αγ.   ἡμεῖς μὲν ἀκτῆς κυμοδέγμονος πέλας
        ψήκτραισιν ἵππων ἐκτενίζομεν τρίχας
        κλαίοντες· ἦλθε γάρ τις ἄγγελος λέγων   1175
        ὡς οὐκέτ' ἐν γῇ τῇδ' ἀναστρέψοι πόδα
        Ἱππόλυτος, ἐκ σοῦ τλήμονας φυγὰς ἔχων.
        ὁ δ' ἦλθε ταὐτὸν δακρύων ἔχων μέλος
        ἡμῖν ἐπ' ἀκτάς, μυρία δ' ὀπισθόπους
        φίλων ἅμ' ἔστειχ' ἡλίκων ⟨θ'⟩ ὁμήγυρις.   1180
        χρόνῳ δὲ δή ποτ' εἶπ' ἀπαλλαχθεὶς γόων·
        Τί ταῦτ' ἀλύω; πειστέον πατρὸς λόγοις.
        ἐντύναθ' ἵππους ἅρμασι ζυγηφόρους,
        δμῶες· πόλις γὰρ οὐκέτ' ἔστιν ἥδε μοι.
        τοὐνθένδε μέντοι πᾶς ἀνήρ ἠπείγετο,   1185
        καὶ θᾶσσον ἢ λέγοι τις ἐξηρτυμένας
        πώλους παρ' αὐτὸν δεσπότην ἐστήσαμεν.
        μάρπτει δὲ χερσὶν ἡνίας ἀπ' ἄντυγος,
        αὐταῖς ἐν ἀρβύλαισιν ἁρμόσας πόδας.
        καὶ πρῶτα μὲν θεοῖς εἶπ' ἀναπτύξας χέρας·   1190
        Ζεῦ, μηκέτ' εἴην, εἰ κακὸς πέφυκ' ἀνήρ·
        αἴσθοιτο δ' ἡμᾶς ὡς ἀτιμάζει πατὴρ
        ἤτοι θανόντας ἢ φάος δεδορκότας.
        κἀν τῷδ' ἐπῆγε κέντρον ἐς χεῖρας λαβὼν
        πώλοις ἁμαρτῇ· πρόσπολοι δ' ὑφ' ἅρματος   1195
        πέλας χαλινῶν εἱπόμεσθα δεσπότῃ
        τὴν εὐθὺς Ἄργους κἀπιδαυρίας ὁδόν.
        ἐπεὶ δ' ἔρημον χῶρον εἰσεβάλλομεν,
        ἀκτή τις ἔστι τοὐπέκεινα τῆσδε γῆς
        πρὸς πόντον ἤδη κειμένη Σαρωνικόν.   1200
        ἔνθεν τις ἠχὼ χθόνιος, ὡς βροντὴ Διός,
        βαρὺν βρόμον μεθῆκε, φρικώδη κλυεῖν·
        ὀρθὸν δὲ κρᾶτ' ἔστησαν οὖς τ' ἐς οὐρανὸν
        ἵπποι, παρ' ἡμῖν δ' ἦν φόβος νεανικὸς
        πόθεν ποτ' εἴη φθόγγος. ἐς δ' ἁλιρρόθους   1205
        ἀκτὰς ἀποβλέψαντες ἱερὸν εἴδομεν
        κῦμ' οὐρανῷ στηρίζον, ὥστ' ἀφῃρέθη

Σκίρωνος ἀκτὰς ὄμμα τοὐμὸν εἰσορᾶν,
ἔκρυπτε δ᾽ Ἰσθμὸν καὶ πέτραν Ἀσκληπιοῦ.
κἄπειτ᾽ ἀνοιδῆσάν τε καὶ πέριξ ἀφρὸν 1210
πολὺν καχλάζον ποντίῳ φυσήματι
χωρεῖ πρὸς ἀκτὰς οὗ τέθριππος ἦν ὄχος.
αὐτῷ δὲ σὺν κλύδωνι καὶ τρικυμίᾳ
κῦμ᾽ ἐξέθηκε ταῦρον, ἄγριον τέρας·
οὗ πᾶσα μὲν χθὼν φθέγματος πληρουμένη 1215
φρικῶδες ἀντεφθέγγετ᾽, εἰσορῶσι δὲ
κρεῖσσον θέαμα δεργμάτων ἐφαίνετο.
εὐθὺς δὲ πώλοις δεινὸς ἐμπίπτει φόβος·
καὶ δεσπότης μὲν ἱππικοῖσιν ἤθεσιν
πολὺς ξυνοικῶν ἥρπασ᾽ ἡνίας χεροῖν, 1220
ἕλκει δέ, κώπην ὥστε ναυβάτης ἀνήρ,
ἱμᾶσιν ἐς τοὔπισθεν ἀρτήσας δέμας·
αἱ δ᾽ ἐνδακοῦσαι στόμια πυριγενῆ γνάθοις
βίᾳ φέρουσιν, οὔτε ναυκλήρου χερὸς
οὔθ᾽ ἱπποδέσμων οὔτε κολλητῶν ὄχων 1225
μεταστρέφουσαι. κεἰ μὲν ἐς τὰ μαλθακὰ
γαίας ἔχων οἴακας εὐθύνοι δρόμον,
προυφαίνετ᾽ ἐς τὸ πρόσθεν, ὥστ᾽ ἀναστρέφειν,
ταῦρος, φόβῳ τέτρωρον ἐκμαίνων ὄχον·
εἰ δ᾽ ἐς πέτρας φέροιντο μαργῶσαι φρένας, 1230
σιγῇ πελάζων ἄντυγι ξυνείπετο,
ἐς τοῦθ᾽ ἕως ἔσφηλε κἀνεχαίτισεν
ἁψῖδα πέτρῳ προσβαλὼν ὀχήματος.
σύμφυρτα δ᾽ ἦν ἅπαντα· σύριγγές τ᾽ ἄνω
τροχῶν ἐπήδων ἀξόνων τ᾽ ἐνήλατα, 1235
αὐτὸς δ᾽ ὁ τλήμων ἡνίαισιν ἐμπλακεὶς
δεσμὸν δυσεξέλικτον ἕλκεται δεθείς,
σποδούμενος μὲν πρὸς πέτραις φίλον κάρα
θραύων τε σάρκας, δεινὰ δ᾽ ἐξαυδῶν κλυεῖν·
Στῆτ᾽, ὦ φάτναισι ταῖς ἐμαῖς τεθραμμέναι, 1240
μή μ᾽ ἐξαλείψητ᾽· ὦ πατρὸς τάλαιν᾽ ἀρά·
τίς ἄνδρ᾽ ἄριστον βούλεται σῶσαι παρών;
πολλοὶ δὲ βουληθέντες ὑστέρῳ ποδὶ
ἐλειπόμεσθα. χὠ μὲν ἐκ δεσμῶν λυθεὶς
τμητῶν ἱμάντων οὐ κάτοιδ᾽ ὅτῳ τρόπῳ 1245
πίπτει, βραχὺν δὴ βίοτον ἐμπνέων ἔτι·

ἵπποι δ' ἔκρυφθεν καὶ τὸ δύστηνον τέρας
ταύρου λεπαίας οὐ κάτοιδ' ὅποι χθονός.
δοῦλος μὲν οὖν ἔγωγε σῶν δόμων, ἄναξ,
ἀτὰρ τοσοῦτόν γ' οὐ δυνήσομαί ποτε,   1250
τὸν σὸν πιθέσθαι παῖδ' ὅπως ἐστὶν κακός,
οὐδ' εἰ γυναικῶν πᾶν κρεμασθείη γένος
καὶ τὴν ἐν Ἴδῃ γραμμάτων πλήσειέ τις
πεύκην· ἐπεί νιν ἐσθλὸν ὄντ' ἐπίσταμαι.
Χο.   αἰαῖ· κέκρανται συμφορὰ νέων κακῶν,   1255
οὐδ' ἔστι μοίρας τοῦ χρεών τ' ἀπαλλαγή.
Θη.   μίσει μὲν ἀνδρὸς τοῦ πεπονθότος τάδε
λόγοισιν ἥσθην τοῖσδε· νῦν δ' αἰδούμενος
θεούς τ' ἐκεῖνόν θ', οὕνεκ' ἐστὶν ἐξ ἐμοῦ,
οὔθ' ἥδομαι τοῖσδ' οὔτ' ἐπάχθομαι κακοῖς.   1260
Αγ.   πῶς οὖν; κομίζειν, ἢ τί χρὴ τὸν ἄθλιον
δράσαντας ἡμᾶς σῇ χαρίζεσθαι φρενί;
φρόντιζ'· ἐμοῖς δὲ χρώμενος βουλεύμασιν
οὐκ ὠμὸς ἐς σὸν παῖδα δυστυχοῦντ' ἔσῃ.
Θη.   κομίζετ' αὐτόν, ὡς ἰδὼν ἐν ὄμμασιν   1265
τὸν τἄμ' ἀπαρνηθέντα μὴ χρᾶναι λέχη
λόγοις τ' ἐλέγξω δαιμόνων τε συμφοραῖς.
Χο.   σὺ τὰν θεῶν ἄκαμπτον φρένα καὶ βροτῶν
ἄγεις, Κύπρι, σὺν δ' ὁ ποι-
κιλόπτερος ἀμφιβαλὼν   1270
ὠκυτάτῳ πτερῷ·
ποτᾶται δὲ γαῖαν εὐάχητόν θ'
ἁλμυρὸν ἐπὶ πόντον,
θέλγει δ' Ἔρως ᾧ μαινομένᾳ κραδίᾳ
πτανὸς ἐφορμάσῃ χρυσοφαής 〈   〉   1275
φύσιν ὀρεσκόων σκύμνων πελαγίων θ'
ὅσα τε γᾶ τρέφει
τά τ' αἰθόμενος ἅλιος δέρκεται
ἄνδρας τε· συμπάντων βασιληΐδα τι-   1280
μάν, Κύπρι, τῶνδε μόνα κρατύνεις.

ΑΡΤΕΜΙΣ
σὲ τὸν εὐπατρίδην Αἰγέως κέλομαι
παῖδ' ἐπακοῦσαι·
Λητοῦς δὲ κόρη σ' Ἄρτεμις αὐδῶ.   1285

Θησεῦ, τί τάλας τοῖσδε συνήδῃ,
παῖδ᾽ οὐχ ὁσίως σὸν ἀποκτείνας
ψευδέσι μύθοις ἀλόχου πεισθεὶς
ἀφανῆ; φανερὰν δ᾽ ἔσχεθες ἄτην.
πῶς οὐχ ὑπὸ γῆς τάρταρα κρύπτεις   1290
δέμας αἰσχυνθείς,
ἢ πτηνὸς ἄνω μεταβὰς †βίοτον†
πήματος ἔξω πόδα τοῦδ᾽ ἀνέχεις;
ὡς ἔν γ᾽ ἀγαθοῖς ἀνδράσιν οὔ σοι
κτητὸν βιότου μέρος ἐστίν.   1295
ἄκουε, Θησεῦ, σῶν κακῶν κατάστασιν.
καίτοι προκόψω γ᾽ οὐδέν, ἀλγυνῶ δέ σε·
ἀλλ᾽ ἐς τόδ᾽ ἦλθον, παιδὸς ἐκδεῖξαι φρένα
τοῦ σοῦ δικαίαν, ὡς ὑπ᾽ εὐκλείας θάνῃ,
καὶ σῆς γυναικὸς οἶστρον ἢ τρόπον τινὰ   1300
γενναιότητα. τῆς γὰρ ἐχθίστης θεῶν
ἡμῖν ὅσαισι παρθένειος ἡδονὴ
δηχθεῖσα κέντροις παιδὸς ἠράσθη σέθεν·
γνώμῃ δὲ νικᾶν τὴν Κύπριν πειρωμένη
τροφοῦ διώλετ᾽ οὐχ ἑκοῦσα μηχαναῖς,   1305
ἢ σῷ δι᾽ ὅρκων παιδὶ σημαίνει νόσον.
ὁ δ᾽, ὥσπερ οὖν δίκαιον, οὐκ ἐφέσπετο
λόγοισιν, οὐδ᾽ αὖ πρὸς σέθεν κακούμενος
ὅρκων ἀφεῖλε πίστιν, εὐσεβὴς γεγώς·
ἡ δ᾽ εἰς ἔλεγχον μὴ πέσῃ φοβουμένη   1310
ψευδεῖς γραφὰς ἔγραψε καὶ διώλεσεν
δόλοισι σὸν παῖδ᾽, ἀλλ᾽ ὅμως ἔπεισέ σε.

Θη. οἴμοι.
Αρ. δάκνει σε, Θησεῦ, μῦθος; ἀλλ᾽ ἔχ᾽ ἥσυχος,
τοὐνθένδ᾽ ἀκούσας ὡς ἂν οἰμώξῃς πλέον.
ἆρ᾽ οἶσθα πατρὸς τρεῖς ἀρὰς ἔχων σαφεῖς;   1315
ὧν τὴν μίαν παρεῖλες, ὦ κάκιστε σύ,
ἐς παῖδα τὸν σόν, ἐξὸν εἰς ἐχθρῶν τινα.
πατὴρ μὲν οὖν σοι πόντιος φρονῶν καλῶς
ἔδωχ᾽ ὅσονπερ χρῆν, ἐπείπερ ᾔνεσεν·
σὺ δ᾽ ἔν τ᾽ ἐκείνῳ κἀν ἐμοὶ φαίνῃ κακός,   1320
ὃς οὔτε πίστιν οὔτε μάντεων ὄπα
ἔμεινας, οὐκ ἤλεγξας, οὐ χρόνῳ μακρῷ
σκέψιν παρέσχες, ἀλλὰ θᾶσσον ἤ σ᾽ ἐχρῆν

ἀρὰς ἐφῆκας παιδὶ καὶ κατέκτανες.

Θη. δέσποιν᾽, ὀλοίμην. 1325

Αρ. δείν᾽ ἔπραξας, ἀλλ᾽ ὅμως
ἔτ᾽ ἔστι καί σοι τῶνδε συγγνώμης τυχεῖν·
Κύπρις γὰρ ἤθελ᾽ ὥστε γίγνεσθαι τάδε,
πληροῦσα θυμόν. θεοῖσι δ᾽ ὧδ᾽ ἔχει νόμος·
οὐδεὶς ἀπαντᾶν βούλεται προθυμίᾳ 1330
τῇ τοῦ θέλοντος, ἀλλ᾽ ἀφιστάμεσθ᾽ ἀεί.
ἐπεί, σάφ᾽ ἴσθι, Ζῆνα μὴ φοβουμένη
οὐκ ἄν ποτ᾽ ἦλθον ἐς τόδ᾽ αἰσχύνης ἐγὼ
ὥστ᾽ ἄνδρα πάντων φίλτατον βροτῶν ἐμοὶ
θανεῖν ἐᾶσαι. τὴν δὲ σὴν ἁμαρτίαν 1335
τὸ μὴ εἰδέναι μὲν πρῶτον ἐκλύει κάκης·
ἔπειτα δ᾽ ἡ θανοῦσ᾽ ἀνήλωσεν γυνὴ
λόγων ἐλέγχους, ὥστε σὴν πεῖσαι φρένα.
μάλιστα μέν νυν σοὶ τάδ᾽ ἔρρωγεν κακά,
λύπη δὲ κἀμοί· τοὺς γὰρ εὐσεβεῖς θεοὶ 1340
θνήσκοντας οὐ χαίρουσι· τούς γε μὴν κακοὺς
αὐτοῖς τέκνοισι καὶ δόμοις ἐξόλλυμεν.

Χο. καὶ μὴν ὁ τάλας ὅδε δὴ στείχει,
σάρκας νεαρὰς ξανθόν τε κάρα
διαλυμανθείς. ὦ πόνος οἴκων,
οἷον ἐκράνθη δίδυμον μελάθροις 1345
πένθος θεόθεν καταληπτόν.

Ιπ. αἰαῖ αἰαῖ·
δύστηνος ἐγώ, πατρὸς ἐξ ἀδίκου
χρησμοῖς ἀδίκοις διελυμάνθην. 1350
ἀπόλωλα τάλας, οἴμοι μοι.
διά μου κεφαλῆς ᾄσσουσ᾽ ὀδύναι
κατά τ᾽ ἐγκέφαλον πηδᾷ σφάκελος·
σχές, ἀπειρηκὸς σῶμ᾽ ἀναπαύσω.
ἒ ἔ· 1355
ὦ στυγνὸν ὄχημ᾽ ἵππειον, ἐμῆς
βόσκημα χερός,
διά μ᾽ ἔφθειρας, κατὰ δ᾽ ἔκτεινας.
φεῦ φεῦ· πρὸς θεῶν, ἀτρέμα, δμῶες.
χροὸς ἑλκώδους ἅπτεσθε χεροῖν. 1360
τίς ἐφέστηκεν δεξιὰ πλευροῖς;

πρόσφορά μ᾽ αἴρετε, σύντονα δ᾽ ἕλκετε
τὸν κακοδαίμονα καὶ κατάρατον
πατρὸς ἀμπλακίαις. Ζεῦ Ζεῦ, τάδ᾽ ὁρᾷς;
ὅδ᾽ ὁ σεμνὸς ἐγὼ καὶ θεοσέπτωρ,   1365
ὅδ᾽ ὁ σωφροσύνῃ πάντας ὑπερσχών,
προὖπτον ἐς Ἅιδην στείχω, κατ᾽ ἄκρας
ὀλέσας βίοτον, μόχθους δ᾽ ἄλλως
τῆς εὐσεβίας
εἰς ἀνθρώπους ἐπόνησα.   1370

αἰαῖ αἰαῖ·
καὶ νῦν ὀδύνα μ᾽ ὀδύνα βαίνει·
μέθετέ με τάλανα,
καί μοι θάνατος παιὰν ἔλθοι.
†προσαπόλλυτέ μ᾽ ὄλλυτε τὸν δυσδαί-   1375
        μονα·† ἀμφιτόμου λόγχας ἔραμαι,
διαμοιρᾶσαι κατά τ᾽ εὐνᾶσαι
τὸν ἐμὸν βίοτον.
ὦ πατρὸς ἐμοῦ δύστανος ἀρά·
μιαιφόνον τι σύγγονον
παλαιῶν προγεννη-   1380
        τόρων ἐξορίζεται
κακὸν οὐδὲ μένει,
ἔμολέ τ᾽ ἐπ᾽ ἐμέ—τί ποτε, τὸν οὐ-
        δὲν ὄντ᾽ ἐπαίτιον κακῶν;
ἰώ μοί μοι.
τί φῶ; πῶς ἀπαλλά-   1385
        ξω βιοτὰν ἐμὰν
τοῦδ᾽ ἀνάλγητον πάθους;
εἴθε με κοιμάσειε τὸν
δυσδαίμον᾽ Ἅιδα μέλαι-
        να νύκτερός τ᾽ ἀνάγκα.

Αρ.   ὦ τλῆμον, οἵᾳ συμφορᾷ συνεζύγης·
        τὸ δ᾽ εὐγενές σε τῶν φρενῶν ἀπώλεσεν.   1390
Ιπ.   ἔα·
        ὦ θεῖον ὀσμῆς πνεῦμα· καὶ γὰρ ἐν κακοῖς
        ὢν ᾐσθόμην σου κἀνεκουφίσθην δέμας.
        ἔστ᾽ ἐν τόποισι τοισίδ᾽ Ἄρτεμις θεά.

Αρ.	ὦ τλῆμον, ἔστι, σοί γε φιλτάτη θεῶν.	
Ιπ.	ὁρᾷς με, δέσποιν᾽, ὡς ἔχω, τὸν ἄθλιον;	1395
Αρ.	ὁρῶ· κατ᾽ ὄσσων δ᾽οὐ θέμις βαλεῖν δάκρυ.	
Ιπ.	οὐκ ἔστι σοι κυναγὸς οὐδ᾽ ὑπηρέτης.	
Αρ.	οὐ δῆτ᾽· ἀτάρ μοι προσφιλής γ᾽ ἀπόλλυσαι.	
Ιπ.	οὐδ᾽ ἱππονώμας οὐδ᾽ ἀγαλμάτων φύλαξ.	
Αρ.	Κύπρις γὰρ ἡ πανοῦργος ὧδ᾽ ἐμήσατο.	1400
Ιπ.	οἴμοι· φρονῶ δὴ δαίμον᾽ ἥ μ᾽ ἀπώλεσεν.	
Αρ.	τιμῆς ἐμέμφθη, σωφρονοῦντι δ᾽ ἤχθετο.	
Ιπ.	τρεῖς ὄντας ἡμᾶς ὤλεσ᾽, ᾔσθημαι, μία.	
Αρ.	πατέρα γε καὶ σὲ καὶ τρίτην ξυνάορον.	
Ιπ.	ᾤμωξα τοίνυν καὶ πατρὸς δυσπραξίας.	1405
Αρ.	ἐξηπατήθη δαίμονος βουλεύμασιν.	
Ιπ.	ὦ δυστάλας σὺ τῆσδε συμφορᾶς, πάτερ.	
Θη.	ὄλωλα, τέκνον, οὐδέ μοι χάρις βίου.	
Ιπ.	στένω σε μᾶλλον ἢ ᾽μὲ τῆς ἁμαρτίας.	
Θη.	εἰ γὰρ γενοίμην, τέκνον, ἀντὶ σοῦ νεκρός.	1410
Ιπ.	ὦ δῶρα πατρὸς σοῦ Ποσειδῶνος πικρά.	
Θη.	ὡς μήποτ᾽ ἐλθεῖν ὤφελ᾽ ἐς τοὐμὸν στόμα.	
Ιπ.	τί δ᾽; ἔκτανές τἄν μ᾽, ὡς τότ᾽ ἦσθ᾽ ὠργισμένος.	
Θη.	δόξης γὰρ ἦμεν πρὸς θεῶν ἐσφαλμένοι.	
Ιπ.	φεῦ·	
	εἴθ᾽ ἦν ἀραῖον δαίμοσιν βροτῶν γένος.	1415
Αρ.	ἔασον· οὐ γὰρ οὐδὲ γῆς ὑπὸ ζόφον	
	θεᾶς ἄτιμοι Κύπριδος ἐκ προθυμίας	
	ὀργαὶ κατασκήψουσιν ἐς τὸ σὸν δέμας,	
	σῆς εὐσεβείας κἀγαθῆς φρενὸς χάριν.	
	ἐγὼ γὰρ αὐτῆς ἄλλον ἐξ ἐμῆς χερὸς	1420
	ὃς ἂν μάλιστα φίλτατος κυρῇ βροτῶν	
	τόξοις ἀφύκτοις τοῖσδε τιμωρήσομαι.	
	σοὶ δ᾽, ὦ ταλαίπωρ᾽, ἀντὶ τῶνδε τῶν κακῶν	
	τιμὰς μεγίστας ἐν πόλει Τροζηνίᾳ	
	δώσω· κόραι γὰρ ἄζυγες γάμων πάρος	1425
	κόμας κεροῦνταί σοι, δι᾽ αἰῶνος μακροῦ	
	πένθη μέγιστα δακρύων καρπουμένῳ·	
	ἀεὶ δὲ μουσοποιὸς ἐς σὲ παρθένων	
	ἔσται μέριμνα, κοὐκ ἀνώνυμος πεσὼν	
	ἔρως ὁ Φαίδρας ἐς σὲ σιγηθήσεται.	1430

σὺ δ᾽, ὦ γεραιοῦ τέκνον Αἰγέως, λαβὲ
σὸν παῖδ᾽ ἐν ἀγκάλαισι καὶ προσέλκυσαι·
ἄκων γὰρ ὤλεσάς νιν· ἀνθρώποισι δὲ
θεῶν διδόντων εἰκὸς ἐξαμαρτάνειν.
καὶ σοὶ παραινῶ πατέρα μὴ στυγεῖν σέθεν,   1435
Ἱππόλυτ᾽· ἔχεις γὰρ μοῖραν ᾗ διεφθάρης.
καὶ χαῖρ᾽· ἐμοὶ γὰρ οὐ θέμις φθιτοὺς ὁρᾶν
οὐδ᾽ ὄμμα χραίνειν θανασίμοισιν ἐκπνοαῖς·
ὁρῶ δέ σ᾽ ἤδη τοῦδε πλησίον κακοῦ.

Ιπ.   χαίρουσα καὶ σὺ στεῖχε, παρθέν᾽ ὀλβία·   1440
μακρὰν δὲ λείπεις ῥᾳδίως ὁμιλίαν.
λύω δὲ νεῖκος πατρὶ χρῃζούσης σέθεν·
καὶ γὰρ πάροιθε σοῖς ἐπειθόμην λόγοις.
αἰαῖ, κατ᾽ ὄσσων κιγχάνει μ᾽ ἤδη σκότος·
λαβοῦ, πάτερ, μου καὶ κατόρθωσον δέμας.   1445

Θη.   οἴμοι, τέκνον, τί δρᾷς με τὸν δυσδαίμονα;
Ιπ.   ὄλωλα καὶ δὴ νερτέρων ὁρῶ πύλας.
Θη.   ἦ τὴν ἐμὴν ἄναγνον ἐκλιπὼν χέρα;
Ιπ.   οὐ δῆτ᾽, ἐπεί σε τοῦδ᾽ ἐλευθερῶ φόνου.
Θη.   τί φής; ἀφίης αἵματος μ᾽ ἐλεύθερον;   1450
Ιπ.   τὴν τοξόδαμνον Ἄρτεμιν μαρτύρομαι.
Θη.   ὦ φίλταθ᾽, ὡς γενναῖος ἐκφαίνῃ πατρί.
Ιπ.   ὦ χαῖρε †καὶ σύ†, χαῖρε πολλά μοι, πάτερ.
Θη.   οἴμοι φρενὸς σῆς εὐσεβοῦς τε κἀγαθῆς.
Ιπ.   τοιῶνδε παίδων γνησίων εὔχου τυχεῖν.   1455
Θη.   μή νυν προδῷς με, τέκνον, ἀλλὰ καρτέρει.
Ιπ.   κεκαρτέρηται τἄμ᾽· ὄλωλα γάρ, πάτερ.
κρύψον δέ μου πρόσωπον ὡς τάχος πέπλοις,
Θη.   †ὦ κλείν᾽ Ἀθῆναι Παλλάδος θ᾽ ὁρίσματα,†
οἵου στερήσεσθ᾽ ἀνδρός. ὦ τλήμων ἐγώ,   1460
ὡς πολλά, Κύπρι, σῶν κακῶν μεμνήσομαι.

Χο.   κοινὸν τόδ᾽ ἄχος πᾶσι πολίταις
ἦλθεν ἀέλπτως.
πολλῶν δακρύων ἔσται πίτυλος·
τῶν γὰρ μεγάλων ἀξιοπενθεῖς   1465
φῆμαι μᾶλλον κατέχουσιν.

Selected Bibliography

Alexiou, D. 2020. "Phaedra and Hippolytus: The Intertextual Journey of the Mytheme in 21st Century's Drama Plays." *CHS Research Bulletin* 8. http://nrs.harvard.edu/ urn-3:hlnc.essay:AlexiouD.Phaedra_and_Hippolytu.2020.

Allen, J. T., and G. Italie. 1954. *A Concordance to Euripides.* Berkeley: University of California Press; London: Cambridge University Press.

Bailey, C., E. A. Barber, C. M. Bowra, J. D. Denniston, and D. L. Page (eds.). 1936. *Greek Poetry and Life: Essays Presented to Gilbert Murray on His Seventieth Birthday.* Oxford: Clarendon.

Barrett, W. S. 1964. *Euripides: Hippolytos.* Oxford: Oxford University Press.

Battezatto, L. 2014. "Meter and Rhythm." In *Encyclopedia of Greek Tragedy,* edited by H. M. Roisman, vol. 2, 822–39. Chichester: Wiley-Blackwell.

Beer, J. 2004. *Sophocles and the Tragedy of Athenian Democracy.* Westport, CT: Praeger.

Bers, V. 2014. "Audiences at the Greek Tragic Plays." In *Encyclopedia of Greek Tragedy,* edited by H. M. Roisman, vol. 1, 173–8. Chichester: Wiley-Blackwell.

Bosher, K. 2014. "Ancient Greek Theaters." In *Encyclopedia of Greek Tragedy,* edited by H. M. Roisman, vol. 1, 101–9. Chichester: Wiley-Blackwell.

Casali, S. 1995. "Strategies of Tension (Ovid *Heroides* 4)." *PCPS* 41: 1–15.

Clay, D. 1982. "Unspeakable Words in Greek Tragedy." *AJP* 103, no. 3: 277–98.

Cropp, M., K. H. Lee, and D. Sansone (eds.). 1999–2000. *Euripides and Tragic Theatre in the Late Fifth Century.* Illinois Classical Studies 24–25. Champaign, IL: Stipes.

Csapo, E., and W. J. Slater. 1995. *The Context of Ancient Drama.* Ann Arbor: University of Michigan Press.

Damen, M. 1989. "Actor and Character in Greek Tragedy." *Theatre Journal* 41, no. 3: 316–40.

Denniston, J. D. 1991 (1950). *The Greek Particles.* 2nd ed. Revised by K. J. Dover. London: Duckworth.

Devine, A. M., and L. D. Stephens. 1980. "Rules for Resolutions: The Zielinskian Canon." *TAPhA* 110: 63–79.

Diggle, J. 1984. *Euripidis Fabulae,* vol. 1. Oxford: Oxford University Press.

Dodds, E. R. 1925. "The ΑΙΔΩΣ of Phaedra and the Meaning of the *Hippolytus.*" *CR* 39: 102–4.

Easterling, P. E. 2014. "Hypothesis." In *Encyclopedia of Greek Tragedy,* edited by H. M. Roisman, vol. 2, 706–10. Chichester: Wiley-Blackwell.

Easterling, P., and E. Hall (eds.). 2002. *Greek and Roman Actors.* Cambridge: Cambridge University Press.

Ferguson, J. 1984. *Euripides: Hippolytus.* Bristol: Bristol Classical Press.

Finglass, P. J. 2020. "The Textual Tradition of Euripides' Dramas." In *Brill's Companion to Euripides,* edited by A. Markantonatos, vol. 1, 29–48. Leiden: Brill.

Fitton, J.-W. 1967. Review of W. S. Barrett, *Euripides' Hippolytus. Pegasus* 8: 17–43.

Fitzgerald, G. J. 1973. "Misconception, Hypocrisy, and the Structure of Euripides' *Hippolytus.*" *Ramus* 2: 20–40.

Foley, H. P. 2012. *Reimagining Greek Tragedy on the American Stage.* Berkeley: University of California Press.

Furley, W. D. 1996. "Phaedra's Pleasurable *Aidos* (Eur. *Hipp.* 380–7)." *CQ* 46: 84–90.

Gibert, J. C. 1997. "Euripides' *Hippolytus* Plays: Which Came First?" *CQ* 47: 85–97.

Goodwin, W. W. 2001 (1875). *Syntax of the Moods and Tenses of the Greek Verb.* Bristol: Bristol Classical Press.

———. 2004 (1894). *Greek Grammar.* Bristol: Bristol Classical Press.

Grube, G. M. A. 1941. *The Drama of Euripides.* London: Methuen.

Hall, E. 2002. "The Singing Actors of Antiquity." In *Greek and Roman Actors,* edited by P. Easterling and E. Hall, 3–38. Cambridge: Cambridge University Press.

Halleran, M. R. (ed. and trans.). 1995. *Euripides: Hippolytus.* Warminster: Aris & Phillips.

Hamilton, R. 1982. *Euripides' Hippolytus.* Bryn Mawr, PA: Bryn Mawr Commentaries.

Harrison, G. W. M. (ed.). 2000. *Seneca in Performance.* London: Duckworth/Classical Press of Wales.

Harry, J. E. 1904. *Euripides, Hippolytus; Edited with Introduction, Notes, and Critical Appendix.* Boston: Ginn.

Hose, M. 2008. *Euripides: Der Dichter der Leidenschaften.* Munich: Beck.

Kamen, D. 2013. *Status in Classical Athens.* Princeton, NJ: Princeton University Press.

Kileen, J. F. 1996. "Euripides 'Hippolytus' 1440f." *Hermes* 124: 111–13.

Knox, B. M. W. 1986 (1952). "The Hippolytus of Euripides." In Knox, *Word and Action: Essays on the Ancient Theater,* 205–30. Baltimore: Johns Hopkins University Press.

Kovacs, D. 1980. "Shame, Pleasure, and Honor in Phaedra's Great Speech (Euripides, *Hippolytus* 375–387)." *AJP* 101, no. 3: 287–303.

———. 1995. *Euripides: Children of Heracles, Hippolytus, Andromache, Hecuba.* Cambridge, MA: Harvard University Press.

Larkin, M. T. 1971. *Language in the Philosophy of Aristotle.* The Hague: Mouton.

Lawall, G., and S. Lawall. 1986. *Euripides, Hippolytus: A Companion with Translation*. Bristol: Bristol Classical Press.

Levett, B. 2014. *"Deus ex Machina."* In *Encyclopedia of Greek Tragedy*, edited by H. M. Roisman, vol. 1, 277–9. Chichester: Wiley-Blackwell.

Liapis, V. 2012. *A Commentary on the "Rhesus" Attributed to Euripides*. New York: Oxford University Press.

Liddell, H. G., R. Scott, and H. S. Jones (rev.). 1996. *A Greek-English Lexicon*. 9th ed. with rev. supplement. Oxford: Clarendon.

Llewellyn-Jones, L. 2003. *Aphrodite's Tortoise: The Veiled Woman of Ancient Greece*. Swansea: Classical Press of Wales.

———. 2014. "Costume (and Shoes)." In *Encyclopedia of Greek Tragedy*, edited by H. M. Roisman, vol. 1, 252–4. Chichester: Wiley-Blackwell.

Luschnig, C. A. E. 2014. "Props." In *Encyclopedia of Greek Tragedy*, edited by H. M. Roisman, vol. 1, 1015–22. Chichester: Wiley-Blackwell.

Maas, P. 1962. *Greek Metre*. Translated by H. Lloyd-Jones. Oxford: Clarendon.

Markantonatos, A. (ed.). 2020. *Brill's Companion to Euripides*. 2 vols. Leiden: Brill.

Mckee, T. L. 2017. "A Rich Reward in Tears: Hippolytus and Phaedra in Drama, Dance, Opera and Film." PhD thesis, Open University. https://oro.open.ac.uk/48796/1/Thesis.pdf.

Meineck, P. 2011. "The Neuroscience of the Tragic Mask." *Arion* 19, no. 1: 113–58.

———. 2014. "Theater Architecture." In *Encyclopedia of Greek Tragedy*, edited by H. M. Roisman, vol. 3, 1386–8. Chichester: Wiley-Blackwell.

Mills, S. 2002. *Euripides: Hippolytus*. London: Duckworth.

Moorhouse, A. C. 1982. *The Syntax of Sophocles*. Leiden: Brill.

Moretti, J.-C. 1999–2000. "The Theater of the Sanctuary of Dionysus Eleuthereus in Late Fifth-Century Athens." In *Euripides and Tragic Theatre in the Late Fifth Century*, edited by M. Cropp, K. H. Lee, and D. Sansone, 377–98. Illinois Classical Studies 24–25. Champaign, IL: Stipes.

Osterud, S. 1970. "Who Sings the Monody 669–79 in Euripides' *Hippolytus?*" *GRBS* 11, no. 4: 307–20.

Owen, A. S. 1936. "The Date of the *Electra* of Sophocles." In *Greek Poetry and Life: Essays Presented to Gilbert Murray on His Seventieth Birthday*, edited by C. Bailey, E. A. Barber, C. M. Bowra, J. D. Denniston, and D. L. Page, 145–57. Oxford: Clarendon.

Parker, L. P. E. 2001. "Where Is Phaedra?" *Greece & Rome* 48: 45–52.

Patterson, C. B. 1990. "Those Athenian Bastards." *Classical Antiquity* 9: 40–73.

Pavlovskis, Z. 1977. "The Voice of the Actor in Greek Tragedy." *CW* 71, no. 2: 113–23.

Pickard-Cambridge, A. 1973. *The Dramatic Festivals of Athens*. 2nd ed. Revised by J. Gould and D. M. Lewis. Oxford: Clarendon.

Raven, D. S. 1962. *Greek Metre: An Introduction*. London: Faber and Faber.

Reckford, K. J. 1974. "Phaedra and Pasiphae: The Pull Backward." *TAPhA* 104: 307–28.

Roisman, H. M. 1985. "Hesiod's *Atē* Again." *Scripta Classica Israelica* 8–9: 11–15.

———. 1999. *Nothing Is As It Seems: The Tragedy of the Implicit in Euripides' Hippolytus*. Lanham, MD: Rowman & Littlefield.

———. 2000a. "Meter and Meaning." *New England Classical Journal* 27: 182–99.

———. 2000b. "A New Look at Seneca's *Phaedra*." In *Seneca in Performance*, edited by G. W. M. Harrison, 73–86. London: Duckworth/Classical Press of Wales.

———, ed. 2014. *Encyclopedia of Greek Tragedy*. 3 vols. Chichester: Wiley-Blackwell.

———. 2018. "The Rhesus—A Prosatyric Play." *Hermes* 146: 432–46. For abstract see https://www.ingentaconnect.com/contentone/fsv/hermes/2015/00000143/00000001/art00001.

———. 2020. *Sophocles' Electra*. Oxford Greek and Latin College Commentaries. Oxford: Oxford University Press.

———. 2021. *Tragic Heroines in Ancient Greek Drama*. London: Bloomsbury Academic.

———. 2022. *Euripides: Andromache*. London: Bloomsbury Academic.

———. Forthcoming (a). "Character and Characterization." In *Looking at Greek Drama*, edited by D. Stuttard. London: Bloomsbury Academic.

———. Forthcoming (b). "Tragedy and Rhetoric." In *Companion to Ancient Rhetoric*, edited by S. Papaioannou and A. Serafim. Berlin: de Gruyter.

———. Forthcoming (c). "Reflections and Mirror Images in *Hippolytus*." In *Looking at Euripides' Hippolytus*, edited by D. Stuttard. London: Bloomsbury Academic.

Silk, M. S. (ed.). 1996. *Tragedy and the Tragic: Greek Theatre and Beyond*. Oxford: Clarendon.

Smyth, H. W. 1984 (1956). *Greek Grammar*. Revised by G. M. Messing. Cambridge, MA: Harvard University Press.

Sommerstein, A. H. 2010. *The Tangled Ways of Zeus: And Other Studies in and around Greek Tragedy*. Oxford: Oxford University Press.

Stockert, W. 1994a. *Euripides: Hippolytus*. Stutgardiae et Lipsiae: in aedibus B. G. Teubneri.

———. 1994b. "Zum Text des Euripidischen *Hippolytos*." *Prometheus* 20: 211–33.

Taplin, O. 1985. *Greek Tragedy in Action*. Reprint with revisions. Berkeley: University of California Press; London: Routledge.

———. 1996. "Comedy and the Tragic." In *Tragedy and the Tragic: Greek Theatre and Beyond*, edited by M. S. Silk, 188–202. Oxford: Clarendon.

Tierney, M. 1937/1938. "The 'Hippolytus' of Euripides." *Proceedings of the Royal Irish Academy: Archaeology, Culture, History, Literature* 44: 59–74.

Torrance, I. 2019. *Euripides*. London: Tauris.

Valtadorou, A.-S. 2018. "Hippolytus' Neglect of *Eros*: A Dialogue between Euripides' Drama and Sarah Kane's *Phaedra's Love*." *New Voices in Classical Reception Studies* 12: 68–87.

Walton, J. M. 1987. *Living Greek Theatre: A Handbook of Classical Performance and Modern Production*. Westport, CT: Greenwood.

Wilamowitz-Moellendorff, U. von. 1891. *Euripides: Hippolytos*. Berlin: Weidmann.

————. 1907. *Griechische Tragödien*, vol. 1. Berlin: Weidmann.

————. 1963 [1875]. *Analecta Euripidea*. Hildesheim: Olms.

Wiles, D. 1997. *Tragedy in Athens: Performance Space and Theatrical Meaning*. Cambridge: Cambridge University Press.

Willink, C. W. 1968. "Some Problems of Text and Interpretation in the *Hippolytus*." *CQ* 18: 11–43.

Winnington-Ingram, R. P. 1960. "Hippolytus: A Study in Causation." In *Entretiens sur l'antiquité classique: Euripide*, vol. 6, 169–97. Geneva: Fondation Hardt.

INDEX